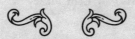

AS ANGUS WALKED FORWARD, PEOPLE FELL AWAY

His stern dark eyes searched the dance floor, and then he saw Bonnie. She slowly moved forward to greet him. There was a hush as they walked towards each other, Bonnie so fair and so guileless, and Angus so full of wild darkness. When they met in the middle of the Great Hall, Angus put his arms around her. "I have come to take you away," he said.

Bonnie smiled. "I know." Her clear young voice rang out without hesitation.

Bonnie and Angus walked out of the Great Hall, past Lord and Lady Bartholomew, past the MacGregors, and out into the night.

Also by Erin Pizzey

The Snow Leopard of Shanghai
The Consul General's Daughter
First Lady
The Watershed

Published by
HarperPaperbacks

Erin Pizzey

In The Shadow Of The Castle

HarperPaperbacks
A Division of HarperCollinsPublishers

HarperPaperbacks *A Division of* HarperCollins*Publishers*
10 East 53rd Street, New York, N.Y. 10022

Copyright © 1984 by Erin Pizzey
All rights reserved. No part of this book may be used or reproduced in any manner whatsoever without written permission of the publisher, except in the case of brief quotations embodied in critical articles and reviews. For information address HarperCollins*Publishers*,
10 East 53rd Street, New York, N.Y. 10022.

A hardcover edition of this book was published in Great Britain in 1984 by Hamish Hamilton Ltd.
A paperback edition of this book was published in Great Britain in 1985 by Corgi Books. This edition is published by arrangement with Corgi Books.

Cover photo by Herman Estevez

First HarperPaperbacks printing: December 1992

Printed in the United States of America

HarperPaperbacks and colophon are trademarks of HarperCollins*Publishers*

10 9 8 7 6 5 4 3 2

This book is dedicated to Linsey,
who died for love many years ago

ACKNOWLEDGMENTS

I would like to thank Claire Smith for her help with the synopsis of this novel, my sister Kate Grierson who continued to pay our mortgage, Mr. Gutteridge at the Midland Bank who kindly continued to offer us overdraft facilities, Pauline Rodriguez at the Bank of Santa Fe who was unfailingly helpful in our time of need, Marcella Gonzales at New Mexico Federal Savings and Loan who helped us buy our lovely house, Michael and Joseph Boyle at Computerland for all their help with the printing and preparation of the manuscript, Mr. Whyte and the staff of Culloden House Hotel for introducing us to the romance of the Highlands, Peter and Marjorie Maas for reading the manuscript and making many useful comments, and my husband Jeff Shapiro whose dedicated and sensitive editing made this book possible.

Finally, I give my thanks to my house editor Christopher Sinclair-Stevenson whose suggestions were invaluable.

The sins of the father shall be visited upon their children even unto the third and fourth generations.
—Exodus

PART ONE

Both Sides of the Tracks

Chapter 1

Nothing ever happens in Merrill, Pennsylvania, except that, one day in 1945, James and Laura Fraser sought refuge there from James's mother.

Augustine Fraser was a true Boston matriarch. She sat in her palatial home, the Great House at Lexington, and ruled the family's many acres with an iron hand. Her life was devoted to keeping alive the history of the Frasers, who had fled from Scotland after the "Clearances."

Fortunately for Augustine, her grandmother Evangeline had run the family business with great foresight. When the Fraser shipping empire showed signs of decline, she moved into the railroad business. Finally the Fraser family ceased to trade at all, and they lived on the returns from prudent investments and sound stocks. From a very early age, however, Augustine was aware that, wealthy as the family might be, they were not counted among the first families of Boston.

Throughout her childhood, she was well tutored with other young girls of Catholic descent. She attended dances where she observed that such families as the Shattocks, the Appletons, and the Saltonstalls danced exclusively with each other. Those elegant and confident young girls made Augustine uncomfortably aware that her family had once been Highland cave-dwellers, eking out a meagre existence after the horrors of Culloden.

Augustine's mother, a Maclean by birth, was eager that her daughter should be accepted into Boston society. Between them they compiled a list from the Boston Social Register, and it was agreed that one day Augustine would marry a name from that list. The problem was that those families tended to intermarry, leaving very little room for outsiders. Augustine would not be deterred.

She was a striking woman, very tall, with the family crest of blonde hair and those magical eyes which she inherited from her grandfather Malcolm. Unlike many of the women in the family, who tended to be delicate and feminine, Augustine looked as though she had been born to steer a large ship across turbulent waters.

She was an only child. Her adoring father, Duncan Fraser, worked all morning juggling with money. At three o'clock every afternoon he went to his club. The evenings were then given over to his young daughter. First they would enter the orchid house, where Augustine would imagine lions and tigers lying in wait for them. Many of the beautiful open-faced flowers exuded a dangerous menacing power. She usually asked to be carried through the domed glass house to see the camellias whose pink and white fleshy flowers delighted her. Then they wandered on through the tropical house, an exact replica of the Palm House at Kew. Duncan was famous for his ability to grow a huge variety of tropical trees. Here he had let loose several families of marmosets and added colour to the lush green background with flocks of multi-coloured butterflies.

Once out of the greenhouses, Duncan and Augustine would inspect the great lawn that rolled for two acres interrupted only by flower-beds filled with roses. Bordering the lawn were dense rhododendron bushes. Beyond the densest of them all, through an arch, lay the kitchen gardens. For all his wealth, Duncan remained at heart a Scottish peasant. Deep in his bones lay the folk memory of those starving years of his forefathers. The sight of the carrots, marching in proud rows until they were halted by an army of potatoes, gave him a sense of innocent, but intense pride. Often, standing by the herb garden inhaling the evening smell of moist crumbling earth mingled with rosemary, tarragon, and thyme, he would thank God for his church, his money and, above all, for his little girl.

Sheila, his wife, was a good woman, but his daughter took priority in his life. To him she was not just a child; she was a miracle. Swinging her onto his shoulder, he would return to the Great House. Singing cheerfully, the two of them would locate Augustine's English nanny who then would whisk her away in time for supper. Most nights, Duncan would entertain business friends with their wives. Augustine would make it her business to slip out of the nursery and head for the drawing-room. Her nanny had long given up making any attempt to recapture her charge. She knew that Duncan would only wave her away while Augustine would throw her an insolent smile from the safety of Duncan's lap.

For the first six years of her life, Augustine listened to the men talking business. When she was too old to sit on her father's knee, she pulled up a chair by his side. By the time she turned sixteen, she would join in the conversation and astound her elders by the breadth of her erudition.

By now her mother had very little control over her headstrong daughter. Anything Augustine asked for was promptly supplied by her father. For her birthday he gave her a horse and carriage of her own along with a driver and footman. Sheila protested that Augustine was too young to ride unchaperoned, but Duncan laughed and said that no one would dare touch the daughter of Duncan Fraser.

The only battle that Sheila ever won occurred when she

insisted that Augustine attend a finishing school. "I hear," she said nervously one night at the dinner table, "that Mary Windsor is to open a school for young ladies in Boston."

Duncan looked up. "Indeed? And what is the purpose of the school?"

"To marry young girls off to disgusting rich old men," Augustine interjected.

"Really, child," Sheila snapped. "Don't listen to her, dear. The purpose of the school is to give a girl like Augustine a broad education in the liberal arts. She can learn other languages and she can study music." She frowned at Augustine. "You must admit, you have spent more time riding horses than you have practising your embroidery."

Augustine reflected that her father would obviously be taken with the idea. He made every effort to wear the right clothes and to polish his manners until they were impeccable, but underneath the veneer of social grace he still felt very vulnerable. The Bostonians were aloof and hostile to anyone but their own. Duncan was a proud man. In his travels, he had discovered that New York asked how much money you had, Pennsylvania asked who you *are*, but Boston only wanted to know who you *were*. The Frasers were nobodies in Boston. Even if the weight of their gold could fill the house of a Lowell, Duncan would never be invited to sit at the table of a Lowell. This fact irked him.

He looked now at his beautiful daughter, and he knew he wanted her to marry into a family that would put her in the forefront of Boston society. Augustine knew her father's thoughts. She looked at him. "I'll go to the school if it'll help me find a husband." She laughed. "I'll find one to suit us, Papa. He'll be a sickly fellow, and after I've had a son I'll terrorize my husband into an early grave. Then I'll be free to come home." This, in fact, was exactly what she did.

* * *

On the sixteenth of February, 1925, at 9:30 p.m., James Henry Forbes was born. Augustine felt enormously relieved upon giving birth. She had attended the Windsor School from which she graduated when she turned twenty. After a year of moving in the proper circles of Boston, she met and married Andrew Forbes. Although anxious to have a son right away, she found herself unable to conceive for ten years. She sometimes questioned her own fertility, but more often she chastised her husband for not being potent enough to impregnate her. She occupied her time largely by engrossing herself in the study of her own family history, and by attending regular meetings at the Boston League of Scottish Women. She was, after all, still a Fraser. At last, she discovered she was pregnant. Andrew, too, was relieved by the birth of his son, for now, he hoped, his wife finally would respect him.

She was thirty-one. When she held her newborn son, she felt the first stirrings of love. She had only known these feelings for her father. The boy had inherited her blue eyes, and he had a thick swatch of blond hair. Her husband stood nervously beside her. "He doesn't look a bit like you," Augustine remarked coldly. "He's one of us. A Fraser."

Andrew flushed. His wife's attitude towards him had not changed in the least. "Sometimes I think you only married me for my name," he said angrily.

Augustine smiled into his petulant, spoiled face. "I am a good wife to you. I run your house well. What more do you want?"

Andrew shrugged. "A woman who could love me. It's not much to ask."

Augustine laughed. "Don't be silly. You get all the loving you need from your lady-friends. Do I complain? Do I faint, or check your pockets like other women do? No. I let you get on with your life, and you let me get on with mine."

Life for Augustine, now that she had James, changed considerably. She was an excellent mother, and doted on her little boy. Andrew became very jealous of her relationship with her son. He was a weak and a selfish man, but Augustine did not regret the marriage. She had very little time for anyone else but her father.

It had been after terrible scenes with his family that Andrew had offered to marry her. "Net curtain Scottish," his mother had called Augustine. "I don't care. She's beautiful and I want to marry her," Andrew had insisted.

Augustine had been the most exciting débutante of her season. Andrew was entranced by her, and he remained insistent against his family's disapproval. Finally, the Forbes family relented. Andrew was, after all, the youngest son and therefore never destined to head the family. Augustine and Andrew married, though there was never any love lost between the Forbes women and the Frasers. Augustine relished her new position.

Mr. and Mrs. Andrew Forbes now lived on Commonwealth Avenue in Boston's Back Bay. During the day, Augustine would spend time with her baby, and then she would visit with friends. During the evening, she would attend the theatre or give lavish dinner parties for her friends.

By the time young James was ten, he was aware that his parents could not stay in the same room without fighting. He had to admit, on behalf of his father, that his mother was becoming more and more domineering. Andrew would retaliate with waspish comments. James loved his mother very much, and felt little more than pity for his weak father. The only man who could silence Augustine, James knew, was her father.

The boy grew up in a house full of tension, until the day his father came home from work with a troubled cough. The doctors diagnosed tuberculosis, and Andrew was shipped off to an expensive sanatorium in Switzerland. There he died, much to Augustine's relief. Being married had bored her. Sex was best left to the dogs. Now, after years of waiting, her childhood fantasy could become a reality. She immediately sold the house on Commonwealth Avenue and returned with her son to her father's home in Lexington.

When her mother died, Augustine was fifty years old. Duncan, now nearing ninety, treated his nineteen-year-old grandson more like a son. He had great plans for James to become a lawyer. James had attended a small boys' school which he had hated. To satisfy his mother's ambitions and his grandfather's dreams, James applied to Harvard upon graduating from his academy.

The news that James had been accepted filled Duncan Fraser with great joy. A few hours later he died quietly in his sleep as he dreamed of his grandson and the recognition he would achieve as one of Boston's great lawyers. Duncan's death left a deep emptiness in Augustine's heart. She had never imagined it possible to live in the world without her father standing firmly at its centre. Now, she realized, James was all she had left. He became her single-minded concern in life.

James succeeded without much effort at Harvard. He was popular in many circles on the Harvard campus. Augustine used her influence to ensure that James was not drafted into the armed forces. America could send its other sons to fight the Germans and the Japanese, she thought, but I have only one son.

Chapter 2

Because of the upheavals of the Second World War, servants were hard to find, otherwise Augustine would not have chosen to take Laura O'Rourke into her house as a parlour maid. There was something in Laura's face that made Augustine want to shrink from her. But, Augustine reasoned, she is clean, and good maids are hard to find. She looked at the young girl standing quietly in front of her and asked, "Where are you from?"

"My mother lives in Merrill. That's a small town in Pennsylvania, and there aren't many jobs down there. I've been staying with my aunt in Boston until I find a job here." Laura tried to smile engagingly. Old biddy, she thought silently. Rich old bag. "I'll work hard, ma'am. I'm used to looking after a family. I'm the eldest child, and my father died in a terrible accident."

"Oh, I am sorry, dear," Augustine said.

"He was a fine man," Laura said virtuously. "We miss him very much, and my mother has to bring up all ten of us on a washerwoman's pay."

Augustine, seeing the tears in the child's eyes, relented. "Well, I'll give you a try. Could you bring your things and start on Friday?"

"Indeed I will. Thank you, ma'am. Thank you." Laura was genuinely pleased. She had won the first round of her private game. She skipped down the front stairs of the Great House and on down the drive. One day, she thought, this will all be mine.

Laura's father was a thick fat hulk of a coal man. When Laura was born in the middle of a freezing winter in 1928, her father's first words to his wife were, "Another goddamn girl. I don't want no more girls." He seized the child from the midwife's arms and stumbled down the narrow hall to the kitchen. The midwife was too frightened to protest. She also knew that such reactions were very common. Baby girls were a luxury for the rich. Little boys, on the other hand, could earn their keep from an early age. Men like Mick O'Rourke knew that a girl would only cost him money and deplete the funds which he kept to buy himself whisky. "You, you old bitch," he said to his wife. "You're no good to me while you're laid up on your back, so I'm off to my sister's where a man can at least get a decent meal." He stood looking at the two women, swaying from side to side. "See you clean her up properly," he said to the midwife. "And you, have my dinner on the table the day after tomorrow." His wife nodded weakly. He grabbed his hat, and the little house shook when he slammed the door.

The two women looked at each other. "I'm sorry, Jenny," the midwife said.

"Quick. Get the baby," Jenny was frantic.

The midwife rushed into the kitchen. She looked around the bleak little room which was furnished only with a scrubbed pine table, the old cooking range, and a rusty sink. She heard a faint cry coming from the pail under the sink. Lifting the lid, she saw the baby, her tiny form still covered in blood. "I have her!" the midwife shouted to Jenny. "Poor little thing," she crooned softly to the baby. "It might be better that you had never been born." While the midwife bathed the child with water heated on the range, she reflected that had she not believed in God's good grace, she should well have left the baby where it was. That Mick is a fearsome man, she thought. I wonder how the little one will survive. Once she had thoroughly cleaned the baby, the midwife took her back to an anxious Jenny. "What will you call her?" the midwife asked.

Jenny smiled at the child. "I'll call her Laura. It's such a pretty name. And maybe she'll have better luck than I did."

Her work done, the midwife packed her bag of instruments. "I'll be back to see you tomorrow," she said. "Are you sure you'll be all right?"

"Yes, I'll be fine. The children will be home from school in a minute. I'll get Dennis and Patrick to tend the fires, and Mary and Pauline will get supper ready."

"I'll say good-bye then."

Jenny watched her go with sadness. Most of the women around her were married to the same sort of man as her Mick. Each night, Lindberg Street filled with the sounds of shouting and screaming. The next day one of the women would be seen with two black eyes and several missing teeth.

Laura, oblivious to all this, sucked blissfully at her mother's breast.

Jenny had truly loved Mick when she first saw him at the local dance hall. He had thick black curly hair and a wide smile which he used as soon as he caught sight of the little red-head staring at him from across the room. "Seen a ghost?" he asked as he swung her into his arms for a dance. Jenny was speechless. This was more than she had ever imagined. She always had dreamed of the day when a handsome young man would ask her to dance. As the dream progressed, she would then marry him, they would have two children, and they would live happily ever after. Here she was now, at her first dance ever, and the first part of her dream was coming true already. "I've never seen you here," Mick said, his mouth close to her ear.

"This is my first time," she said shyly. "I'm not very good at dancing."

Jenny's sister watched her enviously from the other side of the room. "She'll be married before you know it," her sister said to a friend.

"Not to Mick, I hope," the friend replied. "He has a temper on him like no one I know. I hear he drinks as well. It's because he's Irish, you know. Listen, you should tell your sister to watch out."

As Jenny walked home with her sister, stars danced beside her. "I'm in love," she told her mother as they walked through the screen door of her house. "I'm going to marry him," she told her crippled father, as she bent over to kiss the old man good night. And marry him she did, oblivious to the pleas of her family and friends who warned her of his temperament.

Even the local policeman, a man who had known Mick O'Rourke since his childhood, stopped by the house when he heard the news. "The boy and his family are no good," he warned Jenny.

Jenny shook her bright red hair and said firmly, "If I love him, he'll change. What is it they say? 'The love of a good woman can change any man.'"

"Jenny," the policeman said, "I've seen more cases of men beating up their wives than any other crime in my area. If you marry this man, you'll be lucky if you live to regret it."

Jenny remembered the policeman's kind, well-meaning face and his words of warning all those years ago. Now she was thirty. She had been married to Mick for thirteen years, all of them terrible. From the moment the couple left the small wedding party given by her parents, Mick changed. Her wedding night was a disaster. He lunged and plunged until she screamed for mercy. Her screams only seemed to excite him more. Eventually he fell asleep and she prayed to God for deliverance. She was pregnant from that night, and almost every year after. Mick demanded sex whenever he felt like it. As the children were born and grew up in the tiny shack of a house, they could hear their father grunting away in the room next door until he was satisfied.

Mary had been born first, followed by Pauline, Patrick, and

Dennis. In between their births, Jenny had miscarried three times. Once Mick had kicked her so many times in the stomach that she quickly miscarried the baby that would have been another son. Finally there came Laura. Jenny held the newborn baby very close while she wondered what Mick would say when he came home.

"So you rescued the little rat." Mick was in a good mood. His sister had fussed over him and had given him a couple of dollars for the racetrack. He picked up Laura by the back of her neck as one would pick up a puppy. Only a few hours old, she had the sense to hang quietly. "Well, you can live," he said to Laura as he threw her back to her mother. "Where's dinner?"

"Here it is. Your favourite." She pushed a mound of pork and beans towards him. Undoing his belt and his fly-buttons, Mick let his stomach spill out loosely. He stubbed out his short cigar on the kitchen table and threw the butt on the floor. Jenny put Laura in her orange-crate of a crib and returned to tend to her husband.

Laura always knew she was different. She would look at her hands and feet, and think, These are the hands and feet of a lady. "Laura," her mother would say, "stop dreaming." Laura would lift her pretty face to her mother, whom she so closely resembled, and smile a private smile.

Mick hated Laura. He terrorized the other children until Patrick and Dennis both became as violent as he was. The two older girls were pale shadows that flitted from room to room behind their mother. For Laura, however, Mick held a special hatred, for he could see in her eyes how much she despised him. He also knew that he could not break her spirit. There was a secret space inside Laura that he could never invade. She would lie and she would steal. She was as devious as her father, but even when he first raped her in the little woodshed next to the house she didn't scream. Afterwards, in a bed shared with her sisters, Laura cried quietly to herself. Mick, who had enjoyed the experience, was still quite shaken by the fact that she had refused to show any fear. She's tough, he thought, but I swear I'll break her.

When Laura was seven, her mother died of an ectopic pregnancy. Mary, the oldest daughter, was ordered by her father to run the family. Laura, he demanded, was to share his bed. The rest of the children didn't comment. There was no point. Incest was common on the streets and was simply never discussed. Often a father would use the young girls until they menstruated, and then he would choose a younger one. Mary and Pauline were grateful that he left them alone.

By the time Laura was eleven, Mick drank enough to become impotent. If Laura could not make him erect, Mick would fly into a rage and beat her. Struggling under his great bulk, she would take him in her mouth, or she would let him tie her to the bed and whip her with one of the long pliable canes he kept in the closet. After her first period, he only penetrated her anally. As he pushed his way into her, she plotted to get away. She knew she would have to leave in secret for a place where he could never find her

Laura decided, when she was fifteen, that the only way she could make enough money to get away was by offering oral sex to the men who frequented the public lavatory in Merrill. This way, she would not run the risk of pregnancy or disease. A friend of hers, whose mother was a prostitute, told her that she could earn fifty cents a time. A hundred men, Laura thought, will get me enough money to go to Boston, and it will keep me until I find a job.

The first few times she was nervous, but the bushes were thick by the public lavatory. Many of the men were drunk and maudlin, and often they would give her a dollar if she promised to be there again. She risked a beating from her father if she was not in his bed in time, but she knew Mick to be a man of habit. He was never home before eleven at night, so she was safe. Her brothers and sisters thought she was seeing a boy every night, but they kept their mouths shut.

By the time she reached her sixteenth birthday, she had amassed one hundred and fifty dollars. A fortune, she said to herself. Now to find a rich family with sons. Laura had had everything planned for years.

That she chose to apply to Augustine for a job was a matter of fate. Augustine's photograph had been on the front page of a Boston newspaper. Laura arrived at the bus station in Boston, deposited her bags in a coin-operated locker, and promptly bought herself a newspaper to look for a job. There she saw Augustine's picture. "Mrs. Forbes, the most generous patron of the arts in Boston, and her son James attended last night the. . . ." Laura read no further. She found the number of the Forbes residence in the telephone book, and she telephoned the housekeeper.

"Yes, we are looking for a parlour maid," the housekeeper said. Laura put the 'phone down and smiled her secret smile. So it's going to be James Forbes, she thought.

Chapter 3

Laura moved into the Great House on Friday. She knew she had lied her way into the job, but nothing would stand in her way. With her first week's pay, she bought herself a satin nightdress and fantasized about her meeting with James. There were pictures of him all over the house. A blond giant, she thought. How lucky to have picked by chance such a handsome man. Her little room under the eaves of the attic had a curiously sloping roof. Laura spent her free time repainting and decorating the rather bare room. Dark brown, she said when she first saw it. Dark brown with cream satin sheets. After several weeks, she achieved her ambition. The small room had taken on an atmosphere of warm sensuality.

The rest of the staff did not know what to make of this girl. Parlour maids usually chose a footman or a chauffeur or perhaps even a gardener to escort them. Laura, however, gave no indication that she was interested in any of these. She seemed to view her colleagues with great indifference. "What does she want?" a puzzled footman asked the butler.

The butler shook his head. "I've no idea, but I can tell you now she's trouble."

Laura went about her business. She loathed Augustine, but she did not resent her job. Here in the gracious setting of one of the most beautiful houses in the city, she could learn all she needed to know about the rich. Augustine was at the helm of Boston society. She gave the best parties, and Laura closely observed the conversation and manners of Boston's leading women as she served them.

Stealthily Laura worked her way into Augustine's life. Gradually Augustine found herself talking to the quiet demure parlour maid. "Laura," she would say, "I have Henry Cabot and his wife coming for lunch. Could you see that Mrs. Cabot is shown the garden while I do business with Mr. Cabot?"

"Yes, ma'am. I would be delighted. May I take her to the greenhouses myself? The gardeners are too rough for a lady's company."

Augustine smiled. "That's very good of you, Laura. Thank you." Laura smiled.

During lunch Mrs. Cabot said to Augustine, "Your pretty little parlour maid is a treasure, dear. I am inclined to steal her from you. How rare to find someone of that class so knowledgeable about plants."

Laura lurked by the green baize door, listening to the two women. She was well pleased with herself. The time she had spent in the private library reading about tropical plants had paid off. She looked down at her hands. They too were responding to her care. Now that she no longer had to skivvy for her father, she was able to remodel herself completely. Gone was the harassed child from Merrill, Pennsylvania. Now she was a graceful woman.

Later that night she looked at herself in a mirror which she had installed on the wall at the far end of her bedroom. She took off her parlour maid's uniform, leaving only her little white pleated cap on her head. Good, she thought. Even four weeks of good food showed. Five feet tall with her red hair up under the cap, she looked like a miniature of the statue of Venus which stood in the hall. She raised her arms to loosen her hair. The thick red strands cascaded down her back. She turned sideways and viewed the vibrant hair that reached almost to her ivory white buttocks. She moaned with pleasure. Slowly and sensuously she began to pinch herself. She could see her skin flush and bruise as she pinched the flesh harder and harder. In an ecstasy of pain she sought even more pleasure. She reached for her hairbrush. Hitting herself in a frenzy, she finally fell exhausted into a deep sleep. She woke up the next morning feeling completely refreshed. She lay on her pillow, content. Now she knew what she had been missing. Pain.

Laura first saw James from her bedroom window. The whole house had been in an uproar for a week. James was coming home from Harvard for his summer break. The man of the house was returning. Augustine held separate audiences with each member of her staff. The gardeners were instructed to pick the finest bougainvillaea and hibiscus for James's bedroom. The chauffeur was to see that James's 1934 Hispano Suiza sports-car was polished like an apple. The butler would inspect the cellar and see that the Château Lafite '27 was brought up ready for decanting. The footmen were alerted to be on their best behaviour. Finally, James's personal valet was to see that all the master's clothes were in order. "All that fuss for just one man," Laura said to herself as she watched him enter the house. He looked tiny so far away.

At lunch she peeked into the dining-room. He was talking animatedly to his mother. Mmm, Laura mused. Looks virginal to me. She went back to the great hall, and as she walked past the rows of statues, she tweaked the flaccid penis of a Greek athlete. I'll change all that, she thought.

"Who's the new little parlour maid?" James asked his mother a week later.

"Oh, that's Laura. Very intelligent little thing."

"Hmm. I saw her in town yesterday. She's a cut above the usual maid we have. I must say she knows how to dress."

"Yes," Augustine agreed, "but there's something odd about her that I just can't put my finger on."

James laughed. "Woman's intuition, eh?"

"Something like that." Augustine frowned. "I don't know much about her, but she seems to have had a hard life. Poor thing."

Later that day a telegram came for Laura. James happened to be in the main hall when she opened it. "Bad news, is it?" he asked kindly.

"Yes," she trembled, and fell into a dead faint in his arms. She had scrunched the telegram into the palm of her hand, so he had no way of knowing what it said. He carried her into the drawing-room, marvelling at how light she was.

Laura lay in his arms with her eyes tightly shut, revelling in her situation. The telegram was from her sister Mary, whom she had notified of her new address as soon as she had moved in. Her father was dead, the telegram said. He had been run over by a bus. Serves the bastard right, she thought, as James deposited her apparently lifeless form gently on a large Chesterfield. She peeked at him through her lashes. All that concern on his face, she thought, he's going to be a pushover. Slowly she opened her eyes. She allowed tears to well up and to run down her cheeks. James held her hand.

"What's happened?" asked one of the footmen who were now gathered by the door trying to get a glimpse.

"Leave her alone," ordered James as he quickly dismissed them. "Is it your family?" he asked Laura.

She nodded, and then she whispered, "My mother . . . She's dead, and I wasn't there to hold her." She burst into loud sobs.

James put his arms around her. "I'm so sorry," he said. "Have you any other family? Do you want to see them? You'll want to go to the funeral?"

Laura shook her head. "I don't have any brothers or sisters. Just my mom and me." She was crying in earnest now. "She's already been buried. The neighbours had trouble finding where I was." She sniffed. "But I mustn't burden you with all this. I must get back to my chores now. I'm all right." She looked into James's blue eyes. "Thank you, sir, for being so kind."

James looked embarrassed. "That's all right. Don't mention it. I'm so sorry your mother died. I can't imagine what I'd do if anything happened to mine. She is the love of my life."

Not for long she won't be, Laura thought. "She's a wonderful woman," Laura said.

"Here. Take my handkerchief and wipe your face," James offered, reaching into his pocket. Laura took the cloth and slowly left the room. She stood in the doorway and looked at him over her shoulder. The sunlight caught the red in her hair. Her white apron curtained her breasts, and her black skirt strained in its effort to girdle her buttocks. God she's sexy, James thought. He was shocked that he should entertain such a notion when she had so recently been in tears.

"I'm an orphan now," she said forlornly. "I feel so alone."

"You're not alone," James said. "You have us." He smiled at her. "Take the day off. Or the rest of the week if you want."

She smiled back at him. "Thank you, sir. I'll take the day, but Mrs. Forbes is having a big dinner party tomorrow, and she likes me to serve."

"All right. But get some rest." James was impressed. She really is a devoted little thing, he thought. Not many like that nowadays.

"You know," he remarked to his mother that evening at dinner, "Laura fainted this morning. She got a telegram saying that her mother died. She has no other family, poor thing."

"That's odd. I thought she told me she had lots of brothers and sisters." Augustine frowned. "I suppose I must be wrong. I must be mixing her up with one of the other parlour maids. Never mind."

Up in her bedroom, Laura was exultant. "Who's clever?" she crowed to herself as she looked into the big mirror on the wall. "Who's going to own this house? Who's going to tell Augustine to fuck off?" She lay in the middle of her satin-sheeted bed. Her hair spread out like a fan on the huge plump pillows. She imagined James hitting her savagely with a whip.

Over the weeks she watched James constantly. She soon realized that he was a fairly unassuming kind young man. Nick, his best friend from Harvard, came to visit. "Wow! That parlour maid is gorgeous. Have you had her yet?" Nick asked.

James looked at Nick. "Don't be silly. You know I'm not like that." He shook his head. "Really, Nick, you're incorrigible."

"Well, if you don't want her, mind if I try?" Nick said with a raised eyebrow.

"I suppose not, but one shouldn't really. Not with servants."

"Oh, James. You're such an idiot. Of course one does it with the servants. Else how on earth do men get their share without paying for it?"

"But what happens if she gets pregnant?"

"That, old man, is every man's fear. But no problem is insurmountable. You just blame it on the chauffeur, send her off to serve in another house with your highest recommendations, and replace her with a new nubile goddess."

James really hadn't considered the possibility of having sex with Laura, though she had figured in his dreams a lot. Suddenly he very much didn't want Nick to have her.

Laura was highly amused when she was propositioned by Nick. Very useful, she thought, while she gracefully brushed him off. When Nick returned to his parents' home in New York, she approached James very shyly. "I don't want to speak ill of your friend, sir." She lowered her lashes and her voice sank to a whisper. "It's just that I . . . um . . . I really should tell you. . . ."

James had to bend close to hear her. What white skin she had, he thought. He looked at the faint pale-blue veins at her temples, and then his gaze fell to the swell of her breasts. He felt an almost uncontrollable urge to touch them.

"Mr. Johnson propositioned me," she said. "I thought you should know. I mean, I'm not like that at all, but he may try one of the other maids, and none of them are virgins, you know." She looked at him wide-eyed. "And you know what Mrs. Forbes would say."

James nodded. He knew indeed what his mother would say. He shuddered at the thought. "Thank you for telling me, Laura. I'll see it never happens again." He felt furious with Nick.

"Thank you, sir." Laura gave him a wide warm smile.

"And one thing more. Please, sir, I'm trying to improve myself. Would you recommend a good book for me to buy?"

"Oh no, don't spend your hard-earned money on books. We've got hundreds. I'll make you a reading list, and you can use our library."

Laura clapped her hands. "Oh, that is kind, sir. I'd love that. I'm afraid I missed most of my education because I had to look after my poor mother."

"Never mind. You can catch up now. Let's see. I think you should start with *Anna Karenina* by a Russian named Leo Tolstoi. It's all about a beautiful woman who dies for love."

"That does sound wonderful," said Laura, and she returned happily to her work as James planned to educate this lovely young creature.

"By the way, mother," James said to Augustine as their limousine neared Boston, "I told Laura that she could use the library. She wants to brush up on her education."

Augustine nodded. "No harm in that, I suppose. . . . I know what it is. What it is that bothers me about her, I mean. It's her eyes. They're like hard-boiled eggs."

"Do you really think so?" James was surprised. "I thought they were quite gentle really."

"No, that's what I can't work out." Augustine tapped the glass partition of the silver Rolls Royce as the car drove through Copley Square. "Peter," she called out, "take us to Bonwit's and wait outside for us. You know, James," she said, returning her attention to her son, "she's such a quiet little girl, but those eyes . . ." She shook her head.

The same eyes stared back at Laura as she stood in front of the big mirror in her room. She was painting herself with lipstick. She had drawn huge circles around her nipples, her mouth, and her stomach. She had painted her eyelashes until they were thick and clotted with mascara. She had tried to read the first few pages of *Anna Karenina*, but she found the Russian names impossible, and there were so many of them that they made her head spin. The room was hot and stuffy. She could smell her own musky scent mixed with the odour of sweat. She turned the radio on. A clarinet broke the silence with the hoarse rasp of Harlem jazz. Then a double bass came in, followed by a trumpet. The beat quickened and Laura began to dance. Wilder and wilder grew the music. Laura abandoned herself completely to the beat. Finally panting, she fell down on the bed. Putting on her dressing-gown, she picked up her soap and her loofah. She slipped up the narrow corridor and into the maids' bathroom. Then she ran a steaming hot bath, and scrubbed herself with the loofah until she bled.

James was studying in the library when Laura came in with her book. "Very sad. Very moving," she said, having quickly read the last few chapters.

James looked up. "Isn't it though? I loved that novel. It was so romantic."

"Would you think I was forward if I asked you if I could read quietly at the back of the library. Monday is my day off, and my room is too hot at this time of day. I promise I won't disturb you."

"Certainly. I'll choose another book for you. Try Heming-way. *For Whom the Bell Tolls*. You'll find that it's a much faster read than the Tolstoi."

God, it looks thick, Laura thought. "Oh thank you, sir." She took the book from him, brushing his fingers with hers. He looked startled for a moment. He turned back to his books as she settled at the far end of the library.

He found he was very aware of her presence. He could smell her perfume where their hands had inadvertently touched. He sniffed his fingers—a curious smell, a mixture of perfume and a musky, slightly foxy smell. He felt himself suddenly very aroused. He mentally shook his head. Stop it, he commanded himself, but he could not rid himself of the feeling. Laura sat quietly reading the novel. Between them the room was charged with sexual excitement and tension.

By now Laura knew all of James's habits. She made it her business to read in the library on her days off. James found he missed her presence the one day she was unable to go to the library because she had flu. "Ma'am," she said one morning to Augustine, "would you mind if I had a swim in the evening. I know the staff have their pool hours, but the doctor says I will have a severe back problem if I don't swim before going to bed."

"Of course, Laura. As long as we do not have guests, I don't see why not. Just check the engagement diary to see that Mr. Forbes is not having a pool-side party."

"Thank you, ma'am." Dropping her customary curtsey, Laura retired to her room.

That evening she was floating on her back at the corner of the pool when she saw James come in dressed in his white towelling robe. He threw off his robe and dived in. Within seconds she lay in his arms. He was in no hurry to let her go. He swam with her to where he could stand, and then he carried her into the shallow end. She was wearing a black ruched halter-necked bathing suit. Her breasts, squeezed by the halter-neck, bulged invitingly forward. She lay limply in his arms, her hair thick and dripping over his skin. He gazed down at her, hypnotized by the slightly parted lips. Suddenly he bent his head and hungrily kissed her. She made a show of resistance, then she responded. He gently forced her lips open, and his tongue touched hers. He had fumbled with many of the girls who invaded the university from time to time, and he had made love to a few. But he had never felt such an overwhelming lust for any woman.

He finally had to stop for air. Laura looked at him. She

looked like a small hurt child. "I'm sorry," he said. "I shouldn't have done that."

She shook her head. "Don't apologize, sir. We just forgot ourselves. That's all." She put her hand over her mouth. "We won't speak of it again."

James looked relieved. "All right. Thank you," he said, depositing her on the marble ledge of the pool. "Thank you." He stayed in the water, waiting for his excitement to subside. Laura strolled to where she had dropped her bathrobe. His hungry eyes followed the roll of her buttocks.

Hmm, she thought. That'll give him something to think about.

The following Monday she slipped into the library wearing a very tight pencil skirt and red polo-necked sweater. A large white belt cinched her tiny waist. She went towards her place at the back of the library. James was conscious of the rasp of her nylons and the click of her shoes as she walked up the polished floor. The air was electric between them. He couldn't study. He shifted about restlessly in his chair. Since he had kissed her, he had been unable to concentrate on anything at all. This must be love, he thought, confused by the powerful emotion he was feeling. One can't love a servant, he reasoned with himself, but she's such a sweet vulnerable little thing. He remembered her warm wet body against his chest. I do love her, he said to himself. In a week's time, he would be going back to Harvard. He suddenly knew he would miss her very much indeed.

Later that night he got drunk by himself in the drawing-room; his mother was in town at the ballet. James tried to rid himself of an irresistible urge to tell Laura that he loved her. By midnight, he gave in. Lurching like a sailor in a storm, he climbed to the top of the house. Laura had the room next to the pigeon loft. He knew which was hers because he had seen her often at her window. All the other servants lived on lower floors of the house; there was no one to see him, though he would have been too drunk to notice even if there had been. "Laura." He knocked at her door. "Laura." She lay waiting, wide awake. "Laura, it's me. James. I want to talk to you." He rattled the door-knob. "Please, Laura. It's important." She moved slowly to the door. "Laura . . ." he said again, but there she was, standing very quietly in front of him at the door to her warm brown room.

She was wearing a pale blue satin night-dress. He could see her nipples under the thin material. "I just wanted to tell you. . . ." He took her in his arms and carried her to the bed. She lay watching him while he tore off his clothes. She allowed him to take off her night-dress and to gaze at her perfect body. He ran his hand through her pubic hair and over her round breasts. He turned her over and examined her back and her buttocks. Her skin felt warm and smooth. She had no hair under her arms, he noticed. This made him feel curiously protective.

Finally he stroked the inside of her legs until she obediently parted them. For James this moment was the most intensely sexual moment of his life. Laura clenched the muscles of her vagina as tightly as she could, and made obligatory sounds of pain. "I won't hurt you, darling. Just relax." James tried his utmost to overcome the need to plunge himself into her sweet-smelling body. Suddenly he could hold himself no longer, and he sank into wave upon wave of ecstasy.

When he was finished, he fell immediately into a deep and drunken sleep. Laura lay beside him triumphant. When she woke him at six the next morning he was horrified. How could he have treated her like that? He quickly started to apologize. She put a finger on his lips. "This will be our secret," she said. "A girl can't be a virgin forever, and you're a marvellous lover." She kissed him lightly on the lips. He was erect again. They made love in the early grey dawn. James was more satisfied than he had ever imagined possible; Laura was immeasurably bored. I'll have to play it straight until we're married, she told herself.

All through that day James veered between joy and terror. What if she got pregnant? He asked her as soon as he visited her room that night. "Don't worry," she said. "A girl can only get pregnant at a certain time of the month, and I'm past it now. We're safe for the next six days."

James drew a sigh of relief. "Thank God for that," he said.

Over the next six days they made love each night until he was exhausted. James had never imagined that sex could be this exciting. Laura was totally uninhibited and quite shameless. "You learn very fast," he said after one particularly energetic bout. In between love-making, he lay beside her and told her everything: how awful life had been when his father was alive and his mother constantly quarrelling with him, how responsible he felt for his mother and the house. Laura encouraged him to pour out all his fears and his worries. James had never felt so comfortable with a woman before. Laura listened avidly. She mentally filed away everything he said for possible use later on.

On the last night before he went back to Harvard, he cried in her arms and said he loved her. She hugged him. "I love you too, James, but it's our secret. No one must know."

The next day, as the chauffeur pulled away from the house, James looked out of the car window and up to her bedroom window. She was waiting to wave to him. He was already missing her. "I won't be able to write to you," he had explained, "because my mother would recognize the handwriting. I can't telephone because the servants know my voice. But what I'll do is get my friend Sam Chudnofsky to phone and ask for you. Then Sam can hand the phone to me and I can talk to you myself. Okay?"

She had nodded. Good, she had thought, that's one witness if he ever tried to deny anything.

* * *

James made Sam phone so regularly that the servants teased Laura about having a boyfriend. "Sam Chudnofsky is on the phone again," the footman would say. "Tell him the servants are not allowed phone calls during working hours," the footman scolded.

Laura enjoyed repeating the reprimand down the phone to James. He laughed. "How are you?" he asked.

"Fine. We're having. . . . I mean, your mother is having twelve people to dinner tonight." Stupid fool, she chastised herself. I nearly slipped up. Indeed she had been dreaming of the day when the house would belong to her and James, and Augustine would have been moved into the guest house behind the pool. The only fly in the ointment, she knew, was that she was not yet pregnant. Well, she consoled herself, there is always the next time.

James began to come back for frequent weekends. He found being away from Laura unbearable. It was as if a rope were tied to his heart, and the other end, he imagined, tied to Laura. The rope tugged at him painfully. He now knew what the phrase "heartbroken" really meant. If being away from her meant this much pain, then he could not live without her. Their romance would have to be a secret, though. He knew his mother would never tolerate a relationship between her son and a servant. As it was, he lived in fear of what his mother might do if she ever found out. Her wrath, he knew, could be devastating.

"You're spending a lot of time at home," Augustine said to him on his seventh visit.

"I know," he said. "The thrill and novelty of college life are wearing a little thin. I must say, a lot of it is very juvenile."

"Any girlfriends yet?" Laura heard Augustine ask. Laura was serving lunch. It delighted her to see James flushing at the question.

"No one in particular," he said, catching Laura's eye. "Not anyone you'd like to meet, anyway."

Augustine wiped her mouth with her linen napkin. "Thank you, Laura. You may go."

"Yes, ma'am." Laura left the room.

Augustine watched her go, and then said, "I don't know what's got into that girl. She walks around looking like a cat that's swallowed a canary. She's getting quite rude. The chef has been complaining a lot about her lately."

"Why have you upset the chef?" James asked Laura when they were in bed together that night.

"He's a bossy old man, and besides," she raised her eyebrows, "he tries to feel my bottom."

"Oh, does he? And I always thought he wasn't interested in women."

"Come on." Laura threw herself on top of him. "Let's play licking." At least, she thought as she nipped him gently with her teeth, this is less boring than bouncing up and down.

Much to her relief, she found just before Christmas that her period was three weeks late. She kept the news to herself until she was three months overdue. Then, on her day off, she went to a doctor in town and had her pregnancy officially confirmed. She thought long and hard about how best to break the news. She lay in bed at night planning scenes. She imagined the look of horror when she told Augustine that she was carrying the future son and heir of the Forbes family in her belly. She saw herself dressed in white, getting married in a huge Catholic cathedral in Boston. She had acquired a catechism and a missal which she left lying around her room. She had convinced James that she was a Catholic. They often talked about God and other religious subjects which bored her dreadfully. James, like his mother, was a very devout Catholic. Now, Laura imagined, all three of them could go to church on Sundays together. She lay and she plotted.

The old bag will have to hurry the wedding before I begin to show, she reasoned. In her mind's eye, she could see the

diamonds on her fingers. She could feel the luxurious uphol-
stery of the cars. She could scent the smell of success already
hers. She patted her stomach. Just like taking candy from a
kid, she thought, like falling off a log. She drifted off to sleep
with a smile on her face.

James was home for his Easter break. By now he was totally
addicted to Laura. It was only when he was with her that he
felt alive. Her moods could switch from wild excitement to
utter despair. She would make love to him with total abandon
or lie sobbing in his arms. Sometimes she would sulk, other
times she seemed to glow with a joy that could have lit the
world. Never did he find her dull or boring. Electricity flowed
from her body. In fact, she seemed connected in some strange
way to some vast supply of energy. Avidly he would take her
in his arms in order to slake a fierce thirst. Always he would
lie replete, only to find himself needing her again.

His mother, obsessed as she was with the history of Scotland and also with her spreading business empire, was emotionally remote. But Laura provided a fire in his life, and he
knew that without her the rest of the world seemed like a heap
of ashes.

One morning as he prepared to leave her room, she stumbled to the door with her hand across her mouth. "What's the
matter?" he asked anxiously.

"I just feel a little sick. Nothing to worry about." Laura had
rehearsed this moment for many weeks. After she had returned from the bathroom, she looked pale and drawn.
"James," she said, pulling him down on the bed, "I have
something to tell you."

James was alarmed by the urgency in her voice. She was
trembling. "Come on, Laura. Nothing can be that bad.
What's the matter?" He put his arms about her and buried his
face in her hair.

"I think I'm pregnant."

James heard the word "pregnant." It reverberated in his head. It had a crystal-clear hard ring to the first syllable. "Pregnant?" he said. "Did you say you were pregnant?"

She nodded. "I've missed three periods, and I can feel movement. Here. Put your hand on my stomach." She lay back on the bed and lifted her nightdress. James looked at the slight swell of her belly rising from the tangle of pubic hair. He noted that her full breasts seemed engorged, and that thick blue veins had risen by her nipples which had turned from bright pink to a shade of brown.

He gingerly put his hand on her stomach. He felt a churning and a shifting under his hand. He looked at her. She nodded, "That's your son, James."

"I believe you, but shouldn't you go to a doctor?"

She bit her lip. "I'm afraid of doctors."

"I'll take you," he said protectively. "Dr. Jones is a good doctor. He's known me all my life. I trust him."

Laura began to cry. "I didn't mean for this to happen," she sobbed. "I really didn't." She looked at James. "Don't worry, though. I'll go away from here. I can go back to Merrill. And I'll take care of the baby. I really don't want to be a burden to you."

James looked at her and shook his head. "No, Laura. I would never let you go. I love you too much, and now our baby. We must get married for all our sakes." In a way, James was relieved. The decision to tell his mother would be easier now that Laura was pregnant. She wouldn't be able to stay angry for long, particularly with the prospect of her first grandson. After she recovers from the shock, James thought, she'll get used to the idea.

On Laura's day off, James and Laura met outside the State House and walked over to Dr. Jones's surgery on Mt. Vernon Street. Laura seemed dreadfully nervous. "Don't worry," James encouraged her. "You're in good hands, and we must do everything we can to see that our baby is a fine healthy fellow." They walked down the cobblestoned street, past the cherry trees in blossom, and up the stairs to the brick house in which Dr. Jones tended to his select group of patients. He gave her a little push into Dr. Jones's surgery. "Go on," said James. "He's waiting for you. I'll be sitting right here in the waiting-room if you need me."

Once inside the surgery, Laura glared at the doctor. "I know I'm three months pregnant, but James is worried about me. You don't need to examine me. I just need you to give me some iron pills."

The doctor was taken aback. He had been the Forbeses' family doctor for many years. When James had made the appointment in his own name, the doctor had assumed that he would be seeing James. "I see," he said nervously. "Mrs. . . . ah . . . Miss . . .'"

"Miss O'Rourke." Laura's voice was sharp. "The answer is yes. I'm carrying James's child. There is nothing to be done about it. We are to be married as soon as possible." She looked at the doctor. "I don't expect you to approve, or anybody else, for that matter. But he loves me. That's what counts."

The old man looked at her across his large mahogany desk. "And do you love him?" he asked softly. Laura didn't bother to answer. She slammed out of the office into the waiting-room. Dr. Jones sat in silence for several minutes. Then he picked up the phone. To hell with professional ethics, he thought. I owe this call to Augustine.

By the time James got home Augustine had regained her composure. She ordered the housekeeper to tell Laura that she wanted to see her as soon as she came in. By six o'clock in the evening, Laura had returned on her own to Lexington and had just entered the kitchen when the housekeeper waylaid her. "Mrs. Forbes wants to see you," she said. "She's in a terrible rage about something." The housekeeper looked knowingly at Laura. Gossip around the house had been saying for some time now that Laura was entertaining the young master. She's a deep one, that girl, thought the housekeeper, as she smiled blandly at Laura. I wouldn't put it past her. "Run along now," she said. "Mrs. Forbes is in the drawing-room."

Laura felt as though a fire was consuming her brain. She felt a sudden flow of energy. She walked quietly along the corridor and knocked on the drawing-room door. A cold evening rain beat against the window-panes. Augustine sat by the fireplace in a winged armchair. From the door Laura could not see her face. The room was silent. The yellow chrysanthemums gave a burst of colour in their yellow porcelain bowl on the grand piano. Laura stood silent. "I believe you have something to tell me." Augustine's voice was thin and high.

Laura took a deep breath. God, that damned doctor, she thought. Well, here goes. "Yes." Laura walked across the huge room. She looked at the Chinese symbols on the thick pile carpet. "Yes," she said again. "I'm pregnant."

"I see." Augustine rose from her chair. She towered over Laura. For a moment Laura thought that Augustine might hit her. "May I ask if you have any plans for the child?"

Laura raised her chin. *"We* have plans," she said. "James has asked me to marry him."

Augustine looked aghast. "James, marry you? Never," she said vehemently. "Never. I won't allow it."

"Do you want your grandson to be born a bastard?" Laura asked impudently.

Augustine was shaking with anger. "Don't you dare threaten me. As far as I'm concerned, you can leave right now. I don't care what happens to you or your offspring. I don't want my son mixed up with some rotten little hussy like you."

Laura grinned. "If I were you, I wouldn't risk losing him by firing me. He'll go with me. You'll see." Despite her apparent confidence, Laura was shaken underneath. *The old witch really isn't taking the news too well,* she thought. *Oh well, James will make her see sense.*

"I want you out of this house as soon as you've packed your things."

Laura nodded. "Yes, Mrs. Forbes." She left the room.

Augustine sent for James. When he arrived, she didn't mince her words. "I had a call from Dr. Jones. He told me that you have made Laura pregnant. I've told the little slut to leave this house immediately."

James was horrified. "You can't do that to her, mother. I'm just as much to blame. You can't turn her out into the rain like that. She has nowhere to go tonight. Anyway," he said, "if she goes, I go. Do you understand?"

Augustine stared at him. "James, she is just a parlour maid."

James shook his head. "Not to me, she isn't. She is going to be my wife."

Augustine turned away. "How could you do this to me, James? After all these years." James tried to put his arms around her. She shrugged him off. "No. Don't touch me. You disgust me. How *could* you?"

James sighed deeply. "I know this is not what you wanted for me, mother, but I do love her. I hate being without her. I can't explain, but when I'm not with her I'm not alive."

"I always knew there was something evil about her." Augustine remembered her first interview with Laura. "I should have trusted my instincts about that little tramp. Why did I let that piece of trash set foot in our house?"

"Please, mother. Don't talk about her like that."

Augustine stood and stared at her son. "James, she is leaving this house tonight. I can't stop you going with her, but if you do. . . ." She shook her head remembering Laura's warning. "The only way you can ever return is without her."

"Then you'll never see me again. Goodbye, mother." James left the room and went straight to Laura's bedroom. He looked at her sitting, a forlorn little heap, on her bed. "Darling," he said, "let's get packed, and I'll book a room for us in a hotel for the night. Tomorrow I can get a special licence, and we can be married by the end of the week."

Laura looked up at him. "Do we have to leave this house?"

"Yes. Mother is adamant, but don't worry. It will be just for a while until she gets over the shock." James sounded far more confident than he felt. He had only a small allowance to live on from the legacy his grandfather had left him. He would have to leave Harvard and get a job. There would be enough money for them to live without any luxuries. That he didn't mind. The thought of leaving the Great House, however, saddened him. He looked out of the window at the trees dripping with rain. He knew he would miss the grounds and the greenhouses. Never mind, he thought. I'll have Laura and she'll have me. He smiled at Laura. "Well," he said, "at least we have my Hispano Suiza, and we can always sell it for a good price. Come on. I'm going to pack my things now. I'll meet you here as soon as I've finished."

Diamond tie-pin, gold cufflinks, pearl cufflinks. . . . James was systematically sorting out his stud-box. Thank God, he thought, for my godmother's birthday presents every year. He looked around his bedroom and frowned. I'll miss this room, he thought. He went over to the cupboard where his clothes hung in neat rows. Don't think I'll be needing my tailcoat any more. He sorted out a practical collection of everyday clothing. What I can't take now, I can have sent to me. . . . He filled two suitcases and, after looking around the room for the last time, he went to collect Laura.

"Hey," he said to her. "Come on, cheer up. Really. Mother will come around, and we'll be back." Laura, however, had a horrid suspicion that Augustine would never change her mind. Laura knew that Augustine was just as powerful as she. "I'll go say goodbye to mother," James said. "You go to the car."

James walked down to the drawing-room. The fire was out, and Augustine sat staring at the wall. "We're leaving now, mother," James said awkwardly. "I'm sorry it has to be this way. But I couldn't see my future wife and child abandoned. Laura needs me. My child needs me. You must understand."

"I don't." Augustine's voice was cold. "I don't understand at all. Yesterday my world was safe and orderly. My son was at Harvard. . . ." she shook her head. "And today all is chaos. Where did I go wrong?"

"You didn't go wrong." James looked at her. She suddenly looked years older. "No, you didn't go wrong. It's just that I fell in love with Laura. I'm sorry she's pregnant, but I would have married her anyway once I had passed my law exams and could earn a living. You do see that, don't you? Lots of girls get married because they're pregnant these days."

"Not in our family, they don't." Augustine's mouth was a thin line. "And to a servant."

"Mother, you are such a snob. Laura is a good sweet girl, and she's a good Catholic."

"Neither of you is a good Catholic. You've been living in sin."

James sighed. "Times are different now. Anyway, are you sure you want us to go?"

Augustine nodded. "If you insist on being with that woman, there is no place for you here."

"All right." James could see that she would not be moved. "We'll go. When we have an address I'll send for the rest of my things. I'll go to the bank tomorrow. . . ." But Augustine was no longer listening to his words. She was staring blankly again at the wall.

Thank God that's over, thought James as he climbed into

the big car. "Okay. Let's go to the Copley Plaza. We might as well have a last comfortable night."

As they drove from Lexington to Boston, Laura tried to sound cheerful. She had never considered that Augustine would even dream of abandoning her only son. She looked sideways at James. He was concentrating on driving. To be with Laura was his only ambition in life. He was smiling as he drove. "Just think," he said, "we'll be married in a few days."

Laura suddenly caught a glimpse of endless boredom. His gentle honest face suddenly made her want to scream. If only she could wake up and end this nightmare. The baby moved in her stomach. She held her peace. "That'll be lovely," she said.

Chapter 4

The next day James took Laura to see his bank manager. Mr. Llewelyn was not delighted with the news of James's impending marriage. James, however, had the hundred dollars a month left to him by his grandfather at his disposal, and there was nothing Llewelyn could do about that.

Laura soon learned the hard facts of Boston social mores. The whole city, formerly James's playground, suddenly slammed the door in the faces of both James and Laura. By mid-afternoon, James was shaking his head in disbelief. He had asked his Boston friends to help, but every one provided a quick excuse. "Terribly sorry," his Harvard room-mate said, "but my mother won't have you in the house. You know what good friends my mother and your mother have always been."

James put down the receiver of the pay-phone. He stood in the hall next to the men's room at the restaurant in the Hotel Vendôme. They had had to leave the Copley Plaza. A second night there would have exhausted their funds. Where will we sleep tonight? James wondered. He walked slowly back to the table. James sat down and took a small sip of his tea. "Well," he said sadly to Laura, "not even Tom will take us in."

Laura looked at him. Poor weak fool, she thought. He's lost his play-pen, and he doesn't know what to do. There's no mommy to cry to. But, she comforted herself, we can manage until the baby is born. Then Augustine will have to let us move back in. "Darling," she said at last, "I have an idea. Let's go back to Merrill. At least I know people there who won't turn us away. And, when the baby is born, your mother will give in and we can come back. Boston is much too expensive for us to survive on a hundred dollars a month."

James pushed aside the teapot and put his hand over hers. "All right," he said. "Let's pretend we're having an adventure together." He grinned at her. "I love you, Laura. Come on. We better hit the road."

The journey to Merrill was long and boring. Laura slept most of the way. James drove until midnight, and then he pulled the car into a roadside motel in New Jersey. The next morning they left early. "We should be there by lunchtime," James said cheerfully.

"Don't expect too much," Laura said, suddenly nervous. Her plan to get married immediately in Boston had fallen through. She felt very vulnerable; she had no wedding ring to bind James closely to her.

"Don't worry, Laura. I'd be happy with you in a rabbit hutch," James said. Laura smiled. The effort of being continually nice to him was becoming a strain. "You know," James continued, "I think I'm going to change my name to Fraser. That way we can be completely anonymous." Laura nodded. Being anonymous had definitely not been part of her plan.

The sun was glaring as they drove into Merrill. Its brightness did nothing to disguise the drabness of the streets and the shabbiness of the small clapboard houses. Laura felt like crying. She could feel the mean wretched way of life enfolding her once again. Her nostrils flared at the sour smell of the poor pushing past each other on the dirty street. James smiled down at her. "This must be the poor section of town. God, it's awful."

"It's where I was born," Laura snapped. "Not everyone lives in mansions, you know."

"I'm sorry, darling. I really didn't mean to hurt you. Let's find a comfortable hotel, and then we can think about renting a house tomorrow. It won't be for long. We'll be back at the Great House just as soon as the baby is born. Mother would never turn her back on an heir to all that she owns."

"What if it's a girl?" Laura asked.

James sighed. "I don't know, Laura. I don't think mother cares very much for girls. I really can't say."

"Anyway," Laura frowned, "it *is* a boy. I can tell by the way he kicks. You carry boys in the front and girls in the back."

James put his hand on her stomach. "Wow," he said, his eyes shining. "He really can kick."

The Post House hotel stood in the centre of Merrill. James was a bit dismayed when he realized that it was the only hotel in the small town. Laura laughed. "I used to dream about staying here when I was a child. It seemed like the height of luxury. Now," she said, glancing at the small and stuffy hotel bedroom, "it looks awful."

James and Laura spent the next day looking for a house to rent. Anything on offer was so dilapidated that James shook his head. "I couldn't bear to see you live like that," he said firmly to Laura as they sat for the second night in their hotel room. "Here's what we'll do. We can sell my car to buy a house. My allowance should be enough for us to eat and to pay our bills. Then, when we go back to Lexington, I can buy a new car. What do you think?"

Laura nodded. "But before we do anything," she said, "even before we buy a house, we must get married. Lots of people know me in town, and I would hate for anyone to think I was living with you without a wedding ring on my finger."

"Of course." James was immediately contrite. "I feel we're already married. But you're right."

The days flashed by. Four weeks later, Laura, the new Mrs. Fraser, stood in the middle of her own house. She and James had been married quietly in the office of the local Justice of the Peace. James had sold his Hispano Suiza for a good price to the used car lot which catered to the residents of the wealthier side of town. With the proceeds, James and Laura bought a house in the part of Merrill which lay between the comfortable homes of the well-off and the bleak shacks of the poor. Well, it's not much, Laura said to herself, but at least I'm a respectable married woman. The baby stirred inside her. Its head had been pushing down for the last few days, and Laura could feel contractions gripping her back.

James was totally attentive. He had decided that he would stay home with Laura until the baby was born. If mother won't have us back, he reasoned privately so as not to upset Laura by the mention of such a possibility, then I'll get a job.

Number 20 Gothenburg Street was a cut above the sleazy area of Merrill. The little two-storey frame house was neatly painted. A wide porch hugged the house, and the rooms inside were square and spacious. "I really like this place," James would say to Laura in the evenings. Laura, lying heavily in a rocking chair on the porch, would grunt as if in agreement. Shit-hole, she would say to herself.

Laura did not leave the house at all during the last weeks of her pregnancy. James went alone into town to buy the food, and he marvelled at the choices he was forced to make.

"I didn't know there were so many different brands of butter," he said, excited as a child. That's because your servants always used to do the shopping, Laura thought. "You stay put, Laura," James said brightly. "I'll cook supper."

Gradually James took over the cleaning and the cooking altogether. It's only because she's so pregnant and needs her rest, he thought, as he picked up yet another pile of Laura's clothes. He was busy all day in the house. When he wasn't cooking or cleaning, he was in the garden. "This is something I do know about," he said happily. "I always used to help the gardeners. Just look at that night-scented stock. Isn't it beautiful?"

It was evening as they sat on their front porch in the silence of a Merrill suburb night. Neat square lawns marched up the street. The fire hydrants were all painted a cheerful yellow. Birds sang in the big beech and chestnut trees. Cats lazily stretched and yawned, getting ready for a good night's hunting. The dogs licked themselves, wondering when they would be fed. James sighed. "I'm really happy, Laura. You know, I could live like this forever."

Laura shifted her great belly. "Well, I couldn't. I'd die of boredom."

James smiled. "It won't be long now, my love. Let me help you. You look tired. Here." He pulled her out of the rocking chair and held her close to him. "I do miss making love." He ran his fingers through her lank hair. "Come on. Let me wash it for you. I noticed you're having trouble keeping it clean. It must be difficult when you're so pregnant."

Laura shrugged. "I can't be bothered," she said.

Lying in bed that night, James remembered Laura in the early days, when she was a happy laughing girl with shining red hair and a sweet musky smell. Now, he had to admit, she was sullen and bad-tempered. He put his arm across her sleeping form. She moved away sharply. Gone were the nights when they lay in each other's arms.

Lately Laura had been drinking wine at dinner. Most evenings she was too befuddled even to remember how she got to bed. "The midwife said red wine was good for the blood when you are pregnant," she would counter when James tried to remonstrate. The truth that Laura could never tell James was that she drank wine to keep in practice for the fine life she was sure she would lead when they returned to Boston. The wine she drank now was Californian, not French like the fine vintages she used to pour into Augustine's crystal glass, but it was wine nonetheless. The other women of Merrill could drink their beer and their whisky; Laura would hold fast to her wine. James watched her stumble into bed every night. Never mind, he thought, she'll change after the baby is born.

At six o'clock p.m., on the seventh of July, 1945, Laura gave birth to a baby in Merrill General Hospital. The only time Laura screamed was when the doctor told her that her baby was a girl. "Take her away! I don't want her!" she yelled.

The doctor wrapped the baby in a hospital blanket and said to the attending nurse, "Mrs. Fraser is upset. Take the baby to the father and then put her in the nursery. Tell Mr. Fraser I'll see him in my office."

The nurse cuddled the baby on her breast. She's gorgeous, the nurse thought. "You have a baby girl, Mr. Fraser," she said. When the nurse put the baby into James's arms, he stared at the baby's face.

Suddenly he felt as though a huge circle had turned inside him. He was now joined into one whole by the birth of the part of himself which so far had been untouched and out of reach. It was the part that rejoiced in the smell of polish, that delighted in the accurate rising of an apple pie, that relished the times when he stopped in the garden to look at the delicate pink of a flower petal. He was now whole. His female form lay in his arms. Tears poured down his cheeks. An ancient Scottish word came to his lips from the well that lay inside him.

"My bonnie girl," he said. "My beautiful girl," and he kissed her on the forehead.

"I have to take her to the nursery now," the nurse said kindly. "The doctor asked me to tell you to see him in his office."

"Bonnie," James said firmly. "She'll be called 'Bonnie.'"

"That's a beautiful name." The nurse smiled at his intensity. "Bonnie it is," she said. She picked up the baby from James's arms and bustled down the corridor. James rose in a reverie and walked slowly to the doctor's office.

The doctor was tired. "I just wanted to say that your wife is a remarkable woman." He paused and sighed. "She seemed to positively enjoy the pain of delivery. I must say, I haven't seen anything quite like it before. But then, this is my first year in the maternity wards."

James nodded. "I have noticed that Laura doesn't seem to feel much pain. She once jammed her fingers in the car door, and she just laughed." He frowned. "But she had a rough time as a child, and I expect she was used to hiding any feeling she had."

"Maybe," the doctor said as he leaned forward and put his elbows on his desk. "But I do want to warn you that she may well suffer post-natal depression. That means she will be depressed and cry a lot. Do you have someone to be with her?"

"I'll be there," James said. "Don't worry. We will probably be going back to Boston." Suddenly James didn't care if he went back or not.

After leaving the doctor's office, James went into Laura's room to share with her the joy of this recent miracle. Laura was already asleep. James leaned over her and kissed her softly on the forehead. "Thank you," he whispered to her. "I'll visit you tomorrow after you've had a good night's rest." He tiptoed out of the room and switched off the light. All he needed now to complete his happiness was his mother's approval of his child.

* * *

"Mother." James was nervous. "Mother, you have a little grand-daughter." There was a silence and then the phone slammed down. James stood in the narrow hospital corridor looking at the telephone receiver in his hand. He felt a terrible hurt in his heart. The magical gift which he had just held so closely in his arms was already rejected. He shook his head with discouragement. Suddenly exhausted, he went home.

In the Great House, Augustine was crying. She'll look just like that tramp Laura, she thought. Now if it had been a boy and had looked like a Fraser . . . that might have been different. She sighed and raised herself up from her armchair. Slowly she walked across the drawing-room. She stopped by the window and stared out. The die was cast. "No going back," she told herself. "No child of that tramp will ever darken these doors." Augustine lowered her head in pain. She knew that James never again would walk into the great hall and take her in his arms. "Out of the depths I have cried unto thee, O Lord," she whispered.

The day Bonnie was due to come home, James filled the house with flowers. If Bonnie wasn't good enough for Augustine and for the Great House, James resolved, then at least she would set her huge blue eyes on colourful banks of flowers that would shine like jewels.

After preparing the house, James went to the rich end of Merrill to buy Laura a sumptuous nightdress. Walking among the elegant shaded streets, he felt no envy, no wish to live among the prosperous or to share their wealth. He realized that he was perfectly happy in his square white house set in the trim rows of other houses. He liked the easy familiarity of his neighbours. He enjoyed leaning across his picket fence in the backyard to return a ball to his neighbour's son.

Laura would have nothing to do with the neighbours. "Trash," she called them. James made friends with a man up the street. When Laura allowed him to, he would go fishing for trout with his friend in the Allegheny River. Today, however, was a special day. His wife and his daughter were coming home. James felt himself utterly blessed to be alive. He returned to his neighbourhood, put the last touches to the food he had prepared for the homecoming, put the bottle of champagne he had bought for the occasion into the icebox, and took the bus to the hospital.

Laura was not in a good mood. "Here," she said, dumping the baby into his arms. "The damned thing hasn't stopped crying since this morning. You take her." The baby looked up at her father and immediately stopped crying. Her tiny mouth attempted to assemble itself into a smile. Little gurgling sounds of joy dribbled down her chin. James gazed at her enraptured. Laura slammed down the lid on her suitcase. "Don't drool over her. You've already spoiled her rotten. Come on. Give me a hand."

They left the hospital and James hailed a cab to take them back to the house. They climbed into the back seat and Laura said casually, "Anyway, I'm not calling her Bonnie. I'm calling her Augustine."

James felt a flash of panic. He had lied during Laura's days in the hospital. He had not dared to tell her about his conversation with his mother. He was worried that the doctor's prediction might come true if Laura thought they would never live in the Great House again. During his days alone, he slowly began to recognize that his love for her was far greater than was hers for him. Emotionally direct as he was, he now began to recognize that the Laura he thought he knew was very rarely present in his wife. Even in the hospital she had made very little effort to talk to him. She brightened only when the nurses or the doctors were about. To them she appeared cheerful and full of fun. But James felt that she somehow blamed him for the fact that the baby was a girl. "That's an awfully long name," he said at last.

"Well, she looks just like your mother. And it's a sure bet your mother will like that."

James knew he had better tell the truth. "Actually, Laura, I did tell my mother the day Bonnie was born. She put the phone down on me. There's no going back."

Laura's eyes went blank. She drummed her fists on her knees. She wanted to scream, but she would not let go in front of the cab-driver. James tried to cover her hands in his, but she threw him off. The baby, sensing the tension in the taxi, began to cry.

"Hey," the cab-driver turned and beamed at them, "she's hungry. I can tell," he said with great pride, "I've got seven at home myself. Good pair of lungs on that kid. Just listen to her holler." Laura and James sat in silence for the remainder of the trip home. Only the cab-driver chuckled occasionally to himself as he listened to Bonnie's cries. "Here you go," he finally said, "Number twenty Gothenburg." He helped Laura out of his cab and put her suitcase on the pavement. "Good luck to you both," he said and, pausing for a moment, he lifted the white lace shawl with his huge cracked fingers, yellow with nicotine. His big Irish face crimsoned, and his eyes filled with sentimental tears. "She's pretty as an angel," he said. "Look at her hair. Fit for the Virgin Mary. You look after her now," he said sternly as he turned to Laura, "or the fairies will be taking her away. They like the pretty ones."

"Mind your own business," said Laura. She pulled the baby away and put the shawl back over the baby's head. "Go on. Get lost, and take your filthy hands off my child."

"Laura. . . ." James was aghast. Laura pushed the baby into James's hands, turned on her heel, and walked up the path to the porch, leaving James to follow with his daughter and the suitcase.

The driver shook his head. Poor dumb jerk, he thought. He doesn't know what he's got there. The driver got into his cab and thanked God for his fat smiling wife.

Once inside, Laura let go. "Why won't that fucking bitch of a mother of yours take us back?" she raved.

James stood holding the baby who began to cry when she heard Laura screaming. "I'm sorry, Laura. I really am."

"Sorry's not good enough. What good is sorry if I'm stuck in a dump like this with you for the rest of my life?"

James looked up. "There's nothing I can do, Laura. But I promise you I'll make you as happy as I possibly can."

"Happy?" Laura snorted. "You . . . make me happy? You couldn't make a pregnant cow happy. You're not a man. You're a worm. You don't even know how to make me happy in bed, let alone anywhere else. I hate you! I hate you!" Laura began to throw all the vases full of bright flowers one by one onto the floor.

James stood in the dining-room and listened to the sounds of the smashing glass. Suddenly a world that had seemed to him full of colour turned grey. The red petals that scattered in confusion at his feet reassembled themselves into a small trickle of blood that seemed to lead to his heart. He felt drained and empty.

Laura had stormed up to the bedroom in her rampage through the house. She now came down the stairs with her new nightdress in shreds. "That is the last time you enter my bedroom," she said. "From now on your place is in the guest room. You'll have to find somebody else to put up with your prick. I'm not going to any more. I'll make my own arrangements now."

James shook his head. "No, Laura. I'd never be unfaithful to you. A vow is a vow. Anyway we can discuss this later. The baby is hungry. She needs to be fed."

"Then you'd better damned well feed her yourself."

"But you're breast-feeding her, aren't you?"

"Not any more." Laura looked down at her breasts. "It's a disgusting business. All of it."

"What are we going to give her?"

"I don't know. You'd better go to the drug store and figure that one out for yourself."

James looked at her. "But Bonnie is your daughter. A helpless baby. Would you let her go hungry?"

"I don't give a shit about her. She is the reason we can't go back to the Great House. She is the reason I can't sit at the head of the table and ring the servants' bell so some poor little girl like me can come running in to do what I want. It's all her fucking fault. If she had been a boy, things would have been different. If I'd known that you'd phoned your mother, I'd have thrown her into a trash can. She doesn't deserve to live."

"All right, all right." James could see she was working herself up again. "I'll take the baby with me and go to the drug store. Mrs. Schwartz is very helpful." He left quickly.

Mrs. Schwartz was very sympathetic. "Poor little one. Here. I'll make you a bottle now." She bustled behind the glass screen. James sat on a chair and waited.

He looked down at Bonnie who lay in his lap whimpering from hunger. Poor little tyke, he thought. "Never mind," he said softly to her. "Your mother is just going through a depression. She'll get over it. I'll look after you for now." He thought of his gold studs and diamond tie-pins. I can sell those and stay home for a while, he thought.

Mrs. Schwartz came around the counter with a warm bottle of milk. "My little bubela," she said in that voice special to fat wrinkled grandmothers. "My little kindelach. Here." She put the bottle into James's hand. "You learn how to feed your little girl. Your poor wife must be upset if she has no breast-milk. You can show her." James sat on the chair, awkwardly pressing the nipple of the bottle against Bonnie's lips. At first the baby wrinkled her face with disgust at the feel of the rubber teat, but once she had tasted the milk she looked pleased and settled down to suck contentedly. "Look at the little shayna!" cried Mrs. Schwartz. "Boychik," she said, gently hitting James on the back of his head, "you're going to be a heck of a father. Now I will tell you how to make the bottles."

James returned home with six bottles, washing instructions, and three tins of baby powder. "Come back if you need any help" were Mrs. Schwartz's parting words.

Laura was drunk. The empty bottle of champagne lay on the floor. "Go to bed," James said. "I'll see to the baby."

"Bed?" she yelled. "Bed with you. . . . It's all you think about, you dirty son of a bitch." She lurched forward.

"You must be very tired. I'll sleep in the spare room with the baby. You have a good night's sleep. Things will look better in the morning."

But things never looked better for Laura. After two weeks of crying and complaining, one day she disappeared. James was desperate. After twenty-four hours he went to the police. That evening a policeman stopped by the house to say that Laura had been located at the home of her sister Mary. "And," he continued with great embarrassment, "she says she'll come home when she feels like it."

Although James was relieved to know that she had come to no harm, he was surprised to hear she had any relatives. When she finally did come home two days later, he questioned her about her family. She tossed her head in the air and said, "They were dead as far as I was concerned. I wasn't ever going to see them again, but now that I'm stuck in this goddamn dump, I might as well have some fun."

"What's that bruise on your leg?" James asked with concern.

"Oh, that," Laura laughed. "A guy in the bar tried to pick me up, and then there was a fight and my brother Patrick needed a hand, so I got kicked."

James looked bewildered. There was a smile on Laura's face that he hadn't seen before. "Doesn't it hurt?"

"Now it does," Laura admitted, "but at the time it was exciting. I didn't feel a thing."

James looked sadly at Laura. "I've been thinking, you know. I can't give you the things you need, or the excitement. I don't want to force you to live with me. Would you like a separation? I could live here with Bonnie, and you are welcome to visit her any time you want."

Laura looked at him. "No thank you. I'll live here as long as I have my freedom to come and go. After all, she's my daughter too. I wouldn't desert her. That would be a matter of shame to me, and it would be all over town in no time. I'm going to be a respectable married woman, not like my sisters and their side-kicks." She grinned. "Mary is a prostitute right now. As for Patrick," she shook her head, "he's just got out of prison for knifing a man. No, James. You won't get rid of me that easy. Even this is better than the street I grew up in. No, I'll stay."

James shrugged. A weariness cloaked his heart. He so much wanted to love her and to care for her. She still had the power to hold his attention. Even now, when she was happy and smiling, his heart ached for her.

Laura started to slop around the house during the daytime. Then, come nightfall, she would remove the rows of tightly clamped curlers from her hair, stamp out yet another cigarette, and put on a tight skirt and an even tighter jersey, and totter into the night on the spike-heeled black shoes. Once he had settled the baby, James would sit by the kitchen stove and read. Soon he would have to get a job.

Chapter 5

Bonnie's first memories were very jumbled. She recalled a warm yellow light bathing her face through the dappled green leaves of the chestnut tree on the lawn. She remembered the white sides of her pram and the smiling face of her father, who would lift her out and carry her to the porch where he would sit with her bottle in his hand and feed her, and sing nursery rhymes to her. Superimposed on these lovely relaxed moments was her mother's face, always fierce and angry. She soon flinched when her mother picked her up. Laura's arms were stiff and unfeeling. Laura rarely had anything to do with Bonnie.

For the first few years of the child's life, Laura used the house to sleep in unless she was out with her men-friends. Often she came back drunk, and she would clumsily pull off her clothes to display her bruises. "Look at that," she would say with pride. "Why can't you be a man and fuck me so hard I bleed?"

James would push her out of the room. "Don't talk like that in front of the child."

Bonnie's most vivid memory of her mother was the first day she saw Laura with two black eyes. "Mommy had an accident," James told her. "She fell down."

Bonnie looked at her mother's pretty face, and she felt a great sorrow. "Mommy hurt," she said. She went over to her mother to pat Laura's knee with her chubby hand.

"You're making the child soft, James," said Laura.

James had by now learned to ignore Laura. He had a full-time job as a gardener at a big house on the other side of town. His employers were kind to him. They recognized his breeding, but asked no questions regarding his situation.

They also allowed him to take Bonnie to work. There, when the weather was good, he worked in the sunshine with Bonnie alongside him. When the weather was bad, they worked in the greenhouses.

By the time Bonnie was three years old, Laura began to find her useful to fetch and carry things. If Bonnie didn't carry out her mother's orders fast enough, Laura would slap her sharply. One day, when James returned home from his shopping, he saw deep bruises on the child's leg. He had suspected that Laura was hitting his daughter, but she would do it so quickly and so secretly that he never could be sure. Now, seeing the marks on his child, he was filled with a blinding rage. He found himself holding Laura by the throat. "Don't you dare ever lay a finger on her again," he said, "or I'll throw you out of here for ever."

Laura was badly shaken. At first she had been excited by the passion in the man, but then she realized that the passion was reserved for his daughter, not for her. Laura had no intention of leaving the house. Between his income as head gardener and the money he still received from the allowance in Boston, they could live quite comfortably. James had even bought a little car. Laura resolved to make it her business to show at least some affection for Bonnie.

James was surprised and pleased by the change in Laura. So far he had relied on Mrs. Schwartz to help him bring up Bonnie, but suddenly Laura seemed to take more of an interest in the child. He would come home tired after a day's work, and Laura would take Bonnie from him and bathe her and play with her. Laura quite enjoyed her new role. She liked making up stories and playing tickling games. For her part, Bonnie grew to love her charming, apparently affectionate mother. By the time she was old enough for school, she would obediently fetch anything that Laura wanted, make cups of coffee for her mother, and generally wait on her hand and foot as she had watched her father do.

* * *

Laura also decided that she would reclaim her place in James's heart and in his bed. She resolved that they should begin to entertain and to mix with the neighbours. After all, she told herself, Augustine must die some time, and then James would be due to inherit quite a large sum from his father's will. Even if the old cow did disinherit him. Also, having once glimpsed the dimensions of James's rage, Laura found trying to recapture that moment with his hands about her throat sexually titillating. She began a long-term plan to seduce James back into her arms.

"James," she said one day, "I've been to see Dr. Jennings. He says he would like to see you tomorrow after work."

"What about?" James asked.

"Well, it's me, actually. You see, I haven't really been myself since Bonnie was born, have I?"

"No. You certainly haven't." James was wary now. He was used to Laura's sudden changes of behaviour. This smiling shy woman was a Laura he hadn't recognized in the past few years. "All right. If you really want me to go," he said, "I will."

"Thank you," she said, and for a moment James felt an old familiar tug at his heart.

Dr. Jennings was quite abrupt with James. "Your wife has had a very bad nervous breakdown. She has come to my surgery quite regularly, and I've noticed how terribly distraught she has been. I must say, Mr. Fraser, you seem to have been remarkably blind to her suffering."

James shifted his feet uncomfortably. "Well, she's changed so much, almost beyond recognition. I thought she didn't love me any more." James paused.

The doctor's face was cold. "She was suffering from a psychosis. You did not recognize her as being clinically ill. You only chose to take her behaviour personally."

"But she rejected her own child."

"That's quite normal. Young women unprepared for motherhood often reject the first child for a while." By now Dr. Jennings was softening. He could see the hurt and the concern in James's face. "I'm sure you really love your wife, and I know you'll do all you can to help her. She is such a delightful woman, and she truly loves you and the child."

James looked at the doctor. His voice caught in his throat. "Really, Dr. Jennings? Did she say that? She said she loved me?"

Dr. Jennings was a kindly man. Seeing James's distress, he left his desk and put his hand on his shoulder. "Now, young man, you go back to that wonderful wife of yours. My advice to you is to take her in your arms and say you're sorry."

"Oh, I will. How could I have been so cruel and stupid? All I want is to have my Laura back. Thank you, Dr. Jennings."

The old man beamed at him. "You're a very lucky young man," he said, showing James out of his surgery.

Laura received James's humble apologies with a wry smile of amusement on her face which she kept pressed against his chest. He had come bounding into the house with a huge bunch of flowers and a bottle of her favourite wine. They spent the evening making vows to wipe out the past and to begin their lives together again.

Bonnie was now at school, and for a while all went well. James moved back into Laura's bedroom, and Laura even tolerated his efforts at making love to her. She stopped drinking, and she cut herself off from her family. She managed to keep the house reasonably clean. When Bonnie came home from school every day she was expected to clean the floors and to do all the dirty work in the house. There was an unspoken agreement between Bonnie and her mother that Bonnie would not mention these chores to her father.

James, for his part, was happy. He still loved his job, and

by now he very rarely thought of Augustine in the Great House. His mother's rejection of the two people whom he most loved in the world was enough to distance him from his former life. Only one small nagging doubt lingered in his heart: an uneasiness would creep over him when he made love to Laura. He felt he could never truly reach her. She appeared to be physically satisfied, but emotionally she seemed absent.

Just occasionally, in the throes of passion, Laura demanded that he hit her. The mere thought of hurting someone he so loved made him go limp. Laura would apologize immediately and return to arousing him gently. James would put the incident out of his mind. Their life continued at an even and peaceful pace. To all the neighbours, they appeared a loving and united couple with a stunningly beautiful daughter.

By the time Bonnie was eight years old, Laura was sick and tired of playing happy marriages. She had thrown herself into the role of perfect wife and mother for nearly four years. She was very, very bored. One day, she opened the backdoor to the coal-man. Bonnie was away at school. James was at work, and the coal-man was grinning at her. She had never seen him before. He was new to the job. "What's there to grin about?" Laura said sharply to the misshapen little man with the sack of coal on his back.

"Nothing you'd like to hear about," he said.

"Put the coal in the shed, and come back for the money," said Laura as she continued to busy herself in the kitchen. She couldn't get the look in the coal-man's eyes out of her mind. They were pale blue with a yellow ring in the centre. They looked like goat's eyes. They were cold and cruel and, she realized with a familiar surge of lust, exciting. She could hear the thump of the coal hitting the wooden floor of the shed. The coal-man whistled to himself.

He stood outside the kitchen door when he had finished.

Laura let him in. He waited, still grinning, in the middle of the kitchen in his filthy boots and his stained greasy leather waistcoat. One of his shoulders was higher than the other, and there were food stains all down his shirt. He smelled strongly of sweat, coal, and tobacco. Laura's nostrils flared. As he came towards her she made an attempt to push him off, but his huge loose lips were on her mouth. He bent her back on the kitchen table, tearing at her clothes. Within minutes he was lunging fiercely at her. She felt the old glorious ecstasy of pain. For the first time in four years, she was totally satisfied.

Finished, he said, "Let's have a cup of coffee." Dishevelled and panting, Laura nodded her head. "What's a fine lusty woman like you doing living in a fancy place like this?" he asked.

Laura looked at him. "I come from the other side of the tracks. But this life is more comfortable at least."

He shook his head. "Might be more comfortable, but you ain't living."

"I know," Laura nodded.

"Well, my name's Charlie. I'm new in town. And you're Mrs. . . .?"

Laura smiled. "I'm Laura." She paused. "We could do this every week, you know. Nobody will find out."

Charlie grinned. "You'd be surprised how many dames around here are like you. I have my hands full," and he leered at her, "just trying to keep them all happy."

Laura nodded. "Everybody thinks it all happens on the wrong side of the tracks. But I know it goes on all over. Underneath, we're all the same really." A sudden vision of Augustine with her missal and her prayers rose into Laura's mind. "Well, almost all of us, I suppose," she said.

Charlie frowned. "Not my mother. She was a saint, God rest her soul. Well," he said, downing his cup of coffee, "I gotta go now. See you next week. I've got work to do." Again, he flashed his lopsided, broken-toothed smile.

Laura went up to her bedroom when he had gone. She changed her clothes, lay on the bed, and smiled. "I knew something would turn up," she chuckled. She fell into a deep dreamless sleep.

Every week Charlie would stop by with the coal. Soon he realized that Laura was only satisfied if he hurt her. She was insatiable. He was afraid of really satisfying her because she told him that if he bruised her too much her husband would notice. On a few occasions they totally forgot themselves. "What on earth have you done to your back?" James said one night as he and Laura were getting ready for bed. "There's a deep scratch right across your shoulders."

"Oh that!" Laura said. "I was picking berries at the end of the backyard, and I slipped under the barbed wire. It caught me."

"Poor darling." James pulled her to him. He picked her up and put her on the bed. Slowly he made love to her. Feeling her respond, he groaned with pleasure. "I love you, Laura," he said. "I love you."

After several months James noticed that Laura was unusually happy, almost euphoric. He was delighted to have her dancing around the house singing to herself, but he felt a vague misgiving. Was this the beginning of the old Laura returning? No, he assured himself. It's just that she's finally settled into this happy life. James felt infinitely blessed.

In the February before Bonnie's ninth birthday, James was busy digging into the crisp winter earth. Suddenly his shovel hit something hard. He pushed his hand into the soil to remove what he assumed to be a stone. A sharp pain shot up his arm as he felt the broken bottle. He wrapped his bleeding hand in a cloth which he always kept in his pocket, and knocked at the back door to ask for a bandage. His employer, seeing that the cut would not stop bleeding, insisted that James see a doctor at once.

Dr. Jennings stitched the gash. "It's a deep one," he said. "If you want this cut to heal at all, you had better give your hand a good rest. I suggest you stay at home for the rest of the week."

Following the doctor's instructions, James returned to his house. He walked through the front door and into the kitchen, only to see his wife on all fours with Charlie grunting on top of her. They were too absorbed to see him standing there, but James could see the ecstasy on Laura's face only too clearly. He knew that he could never bring himself to abuse her like that. A sickening chill wrapped itself around him. He felt overwhelmingly revolted. Turning on his heel, he left the room and went upstairs. He quickly began to pack his belongings.

Laura heard his footsteps above. "Oh, my God!" she said, heaving Charlie off her. Charlie fell on his back like a huge beetle. He writhed on the floor. "Get up, you idiot," Laura hissed. "James is here." Charlie was up and out of the door like a flash. Laura straightened her clothes and went upstairs to the bedroom. "What are you doing, James?" she said.

"Packing. I'm taking Bonnie and I'm leaving."

Laura took a deep breath. Her voice went absolutely cold. "You can go ahead and leave, but just you try to take my daughter. I'll tell the police that you've kidnapped her, and they'll stop you before you get ten miles from here. You couldn't take her away from me if you tried."

James looked at her. "The police can stop me if they want. All I have to do is tell the judge what I've seen."

Laura smiled. "And what did you see, James?"

"You," he said. "You with that filthy animal."

"No." Laura shook her head confidently. "You were imagining it. You think any judge would believe your word against mine? Who would believe that a sweet young thing like me would have anything to do with the coal-man? After all, I am very well respected here. By everyone. I could call up an army of witnesses in my defence. Especially Dr. Jennings. He thinks the sun shines out of my asshole." She gave an unpleasant laugh. "Besides, I told Dr. Jennings that you've been seeing other women. He feels sorry for me. So, how do you think that would look to a judge? Who do you think they'd let keep Bonnie? A sweet little mother, or a third-rate gardener who cheats on his wife?"

"I'm not the one who cheats."

"Would the court see it that way? I'm nobody's fool, James. You wouldn't have a hope in hell against me. Bonnie stays with me."

James knew he was defeated. "Look, Laura," he said. "You never loved me. You never even wanted me. All you wanted was my money. You'll never get that. I can't live in the same house as you any more." He stared at her. "I can't believe I've been such a fool for so long. Looking at you now, I can see you properly for the first time since I met you. You are a disgusting human being."

Laura's face hardened. "You're a fine one to talk. You and your rich pampered friends. Serves you right. For the first time in your life you see what a woman really wants, and it disgusts you. I'm not the problem; you are. Anyway, I've been planning to tell you to go for a long time now. I'm bored. I've been bored to tears for all the years I've known you. Life isn't Sunday school, you know. Now, get your rich little ass out of my house and keep the hell out of my life."

"I'm going to wait to say good-bye to Bonnie." James looked over Laura's head as if she did not exist. "I'll send you money for Bonnie, and when she leaves I'll still send you some money for yourself because I promised to take care of you. You can keep the car. You can sell it if you need to." He cleared his throat. "Once I leave this house you will never see me again. But I want you to promise, if you're capable of such a thing, that you will keep your men out of this house and away from Bonnie."

Laura looked at him. "Okay," she said. "I promise."

"Of course I've learned not to trust you,' James said, "so I'll hire a private detective to watch the house at all times. And, if he ever reports to me that men are going in and out of this house, I will cut off the money and take Bonnie from you. I will not let my little girl be hurt by you or your filthy men. Do you understand?"

Laura nodded. She knew that, so long as she looked after Bonnie, James would support her. She could always find men and use her sister's place. "I understand," she said.

"I'll wait on the porch for Bonnie."

James sat in the rocking chair, contemplating the shattered remains of his life. Around him stood the bare trees. Merrill was in the grip of a cold winter. Hoar-frost glistened and sparkled on the grass. Lamps had been lit and shone yellow through the windows of the houses along the street. Plumes of smoke rose from the chimneys. For James, everything lay disintegrated at his feet. He could see his beloved daughter coming down the street towards him. Seeing him on the porch, she began to run towards him, her long blonde hair flying behind her, her cheeks red with the cold. She flung herself into his arms. "Daddy," she said, looking at his suitcase, "where are you going?"

"Away, darling." There were tears in his eyes. "I'm going away because your mother will be happier without me. I'm no good to her. But you will be all right. Bonnie," he took her by the shoulders, "I want you to work hard at school. Get into a good college, and get a career. I love you so much, but I can't stay here. All that would happen is that your mother and I would destroy each other, and you would suffer. I couldn't bear to see that happen to you. This way she can lead her own life, and I will have to make a life for myself."

Bonnie stood, quietly crying, while he spoke. She didn't

know what to say. "But I can't live without you," she sobbed.
"I can't."

They were both crying now. "This is the best thing I can
do for you, Bonnie. My leaving, there'll be peace in the house
for you. Someday you'll know what I mean." Picking her up,
he hugged her fiercely. He put her down and walked onto the
little gravel path. Bonnie heard his shoes scrunch as he went.
She heard the white picket-gate squeak as he opened it. The
last she ever saw of her father was his resolute back as he
walked down the street carrying his suitcase. Bonnie stood
immobile. For the rest of her life, she was to look for a man
with whom she could share the same warmth and passion that
she had shared with her father.

Laura had watched the two of them through the sitting-
room window. She called to her daughter. "Bonnie, come
here, child. You'll catch cold standing out there. Come in."
Bonnie turned, entered the house, and started to walk silently
up the stairs. "Don't you want to know why your father left?"
Laura asked.

Bonnie shook her head. "We didn't love him enough. If we
did, he would have stayed." With that awful thought, she
burst into tears and ran to her bedroom.

 Chapter 6

For Bonnie, living alone with Laura became a nightmare.
The huge gaping wound left by her father's absence refused
to heal. Laura didn't bother to hide her drinking or her
contempt for her daughter. "Fucking little cunt," Laura
would hiss at her in a drunken rage. "You clean this place real
good." And she would lash out at the child.

Bonnie was too ashamed of her mother's dishevelled condition to bring her friends home. Her only consolation was Mitzi, her friend from school. Mitzi lived on Bailey Street. She came from a warm Jewish family. "If you don't got family, you don't got nothing," Mitzi's energetic mother would say, clasping Bonnie to her bosom. "Come, mein shayna kint. Have a bissela kugel." Pinching Bonnie's cheek, she would usher her into her warm steaming kitchen where Mitzi's grandmother would be forever baking. Those moments kept Bonnie sane.

The private detective whom James had hired to watch the house was also the person to deliver the money. Through him Laura endeavoured to find out where her husband was. She would try to seduce him if necessary in order to get information about James. The man refused all her invitations. All he would say was that Mr. Fraser sent the money regularly. Laura kept to the promise she had made to James for fear of losing her income. She still had many men-friends, but she kept them away from the house. On the frequent nights when Laura was out, Bonnie would sit by herself, fearfully waiting for the sound of her mother's stumbling footsteps and then the crash of the door flying open. Laura would lurch into the kitchen. Sometimes she would hang over the sink and vomit. Other times she would harangue Bonnie, berating her for not being a son. She would accuse Bonnie of ruining her, Laura's life. Bonnie would generally remain silent. She knew by now that arguing with her mother was useless and only made her violent.

Bonnie resolved that she would work hard at school and then get away. Periodically she felt confused by her feelings of love for her mother. She would lie in bed and remember the good times when the three of them were happy. She remembered her mother playing with her and telling her stories. Now, she could see how much the alcohol had ravaged Laura's face. When she was out with a particularly violent man, she would come home bruised and sometimes bleeding. Her nose had been broken on several occasions. Its bridge was thickened now, and her face had lost its innocence.

One night Laura came home with her mouth swollen and two front teeth missing. Bonnie shook her head. "I don't know why you have to do this to yourself, mom."

"You don't know shit." Long ago Laura had given up her airs and graces and her attempts at fine language. "Your fucking father left me with you to look after. What d'ya expect me to do? Teach Sunday school?"

Bonnie lived in two worlds. At school she was a model student. With Mitzi, at her house on Bailey Street, she was a charming well-mannered young girl. Mrs. Abramowitz would shake her head. "She'll make some shegetz a beautiful bride. Such a shame," she would say to Mitzi while eyeing her son Aaron, "if only she weren't a shicksa."

Mitzi would laugh at her mother. "Don't worry about Aaron. He would never marry a shicksa. They can't cook. Where would he be without some yiddisha maydalach to keep his matzah balls warm?"

Mitzi's mother and grandmother would roll with laughter. "Where does she get such a thought?" the grandmother would ask. "My Mitzi, you shouldn't say such things," she would say, her face red with laughter.

Leaving Bailey Street, Bonnie would walk a few blocks to her other world. She usually arrived at her own house to find Laura out. Bonnie would put her school-books down on the kitchen table and clear up the mess. She does it on purpose, Bonnie would think. There were heaps of clothes to launder, stacks of dirty dishes to wash, and ashtrays piled high with cigarette ends. When she had put everything in order, Bonnie would sit down and begin her homework.

By the time she was fifteen, Bonnie was already taller than her mother. She did not know it, but she looked just like her grandmother Augustine. She was timid and withdrawn, but if necessary she could stand up for herself. Laura would frequently hit Bonnie, but deliberately in a way that the marks would not show for the detective to see. The hitting stopped one day, however, when Bonnie said to her mother, "If you ever lay a hand on me again, I'll leave this house."

Laura was taken aback by the strength in her daughter's voice. "Where would you go with no money?"

"I can go to Mitzi's house, and then I would leave school and get a job."

Laura burst into tears. "Who would look after me? I'll be all alone. First your father left me, and now you're threatening to go. What will become of me?"

Bonnie felt instantly guilty. "I won't leave you, mom. But you have to stop hitting me. I don't deserve it, you know."

"I'm sorry, darling. Really, I am," Laura said, blowing her nose. "Come on. Let's have a drink."

Bonnie shook her head. "No, mom. I'm not ever going to drink. Look what it does to you."

Laura considered getting angry. No point, she decided. Instead, she went to the kitchen and picked up a bottle of whisky.

Bonnie's academic record was such that she graduated from high school *magna cum laude*. Her classmates were mostly eighteen; she was a year younger. She planned to get a summer job and then go to the local university. It won't be long before I can leave Merrill, Bonnie told herself. Once I finish college, I'll be free to start my life.

When Augustine saw the hand-writing on the envelope she tore open the letter in a fever of impatience. It was postmarked Hong Kong.

"Dear mother," the letter began. "I am giving this letter to the Catholic priest who is visiting me to send to you. The doctors tell me I have very little time left. No doubt by the time you get this I may be dead. I have contracted cancer. Apparently the type I have is rapid and most often fatal. However, I do not write to worry you with my illness. I write to say how sorry I am that I did not listen to you.

"You were right and I was wrong. Laura proved to be everything you said she was. Through my blind obstinacy, I lost not only my mother but also my beloved daughter Bonnie. Please, mother, for my sake, go and see the child. She will need your help now that I am no longer able to send money. I have been in the merchant navy all these years. I cannot die peacefully without knowing that someone cares for my daughter. I beg of you to go and see her.

"I am tired now and anxious for this letter to reach you. Once again, although it is far too late to make any difference to our lives, I want you to know that I love you and that I have always loved you.

"Your son, James"

Augustine went to the telephone and put a call in to the hospital in Hong Kong. As she waited agitatedly, they located the doctor who had been treating James. "I'm afraid your son died last night," a distant voice said. "He died very peacefully. He opened his eyes just before he died, he smiled at the nurse, and he said, 'Bonnie.' We all cared for him very much, especially the nurses. Was Bonnie his wife?"

"No." Augustine was crying. "Bonnie is his daughter." She pulled herself together. "She's my granddaughter."

"I'm so sorry about your son's death," the doctor continued. "He talked of you often, especially in the last few days. Shall I help you arrange to have his body sent home?"

Augustine sighed. "Well, I suppose it really is his wife's decision . . . but then again," she said, "please have his body placed in a mahogany casket, and I will send one of my staff on the plane today to return with it. His place is here with me." Augustine put down the receiver; she knew she had no choice but to fulfil her son's last wish. She would go to Merrill to see her granddaughter.

Augustine went to see Laura that very day. "I have deliberately chosen to visit you while Bonnie is at work," she said, staring in disgust at Laura's broken nose and missing teeth. Because Augustine had warned Laura that she was coming, Laura was at least sober and the house tidy. But it was still gloomy and the paint peeled from the front porch. Augustine continued, "James's body will arrive the day after tomorrow. I have arranged for the funeral to take place in the Great House chapel. I want Bonnie to stay with me for a while. James asked me to look after her."

Laura looked down at her feet. "How will I live without any money? I've devoted my life to my girl. I have no qualifications . . ."

"I am coming to that." Augustine drew herself up. "I am prepared to make you a generous allowance, provided that you make no effort to contact Bonnie. If she wants to see you, I am sure she will. But I want you to leave her alone. Is that understood? Of course there is the possibility that she may not want to stay with me and would prefer to return to you, but I rather think not," she said, looking at the threadbare carpets and the holes in the cushions.

"All right," Laura nodded. "She needs someone behind her. She's a very smart girl. I won't stand in her way."

Augustine prepared to leave. "She is to be on tomorrow's three o'clock flight to Boston. She will be met at the airport."

Laura nodded. "She'll be ready."

"And you will not attend the funeral," said Augustine. It was not a question; it was an order. Again Laura nodded. Never did like them anyway, she thought, as she saw Augustine to the door. "My accountant will telephone you in the morning," said Augustine.

"Yes, ma'am." Laura just caught herself before she

dropped a curtsey. Fucking old bitch, she mouthed at the car as it pulled away from the kerb.

"Well, well," Laura beamed at herself in the hall mirror. "At last we are moving up in the world." She waltzed up the hall and into the kitchen. "Maybe after all these years things are finally going to go right for me." She put the kettle on the stove, lit a cigarette, and began to plot. She was interrupted by Bonnie's arrival.

"Hi, mom," said Bonnie as she walked into the kitchen. "What are you doing there? You're miles away."

Laura blinked. "Guess what, darling? Your grandma has been to see me. Sit down." She patted the chair beside her. "I have something to tell you. I'm afraid your father died a few days ago."

Bonnie's eyes filled with tears. "Oh, mom, I'll never see him again. I'd always hoped I could find him."

Laura wasn't listening. "Your grandmother wants me to put you on the plane and she will meet you at Boston airport. Your father's funeral will be in the family chapel. Your grandmother wants you to stay with her afterwards for as long as you like."

Bonnie looked dismayed. "Without you? Aren't you going to the funeral?"

Laura lowered her eyes. "Your grandmother and me, we never got on too well. After all, I was one of her servants. No, Bonnie, you have to go by yourself. I'll help you pack. This is your chance to get into a good college, not like the one here. You're bright, you know, and you're pretty. You should be married to a rich young man in no time."

"I don't want to marry anyone, mom." Bonnie recognized her mother's indifference to the subject of James's death. She had learned by now to keep conversations confined to what Laura wanted to talk about. Bonnie would have to save her grief for later. "I just want to get straight A's and find a good career. I might go into social work or maybe psychology."

Laura allowed a tear to slide down her face. "I'll miss you, darling."

Bonnie impulsively threw her arms around her mother. "Oh, mom. I'll miss you. But I'll be back often to see you. What will you do for money now that dad won't be sending any?"

Laura smiled a small tight martyred smile. "I'll manage. I might get a little job."

"If grandma gives me an allowance, I'll send it all to you. I promise."

"Thank you, darling," and Laura hesitated. "I know I've been difficult in the past, Bonnie." Her voice shook. "But it was only because I missed your father. I've never married again, have I?" Bonnie nodded. Laura took her daughter by the hand. "I promise from now on I'll stop drinking, and I'll stay away from men. I want you to be proud of me."

Bonnie smiled. "That would be marvellous, mom." The two of them ascended the stairs together. They packed Bonnie's few clothes into an old battered suitcase. The next day Laura and Bonnie caught the bus to the airport. A first class ticket was waiting for Bonnie at the check-in counter.

"Is that all your luggage?" the counter-clerk asked, looking at the small shabby suitcase lying forlorn on the conveyor-belt alongside the rich leather cases of other passengers.

"I'm afraid so," Bonnie blushed.

"Get on with your work," Laura snapped angrily at the clerk. "And don't make personal remarks, you schmuck." Laura's face was flushed.

"Mother, you promised," said Bonnie.

Laura grinned. "I know. That's the last time." She squeezed her daughter's hand. "Being good doesn't come easy."

Bonnie kissed her mother good-bye and went through the PASSENGERS ONLY doorway. As Bonnie turned to wave, she felt a surge of guilt, an urge to run back to the small figure in the distance. But she heard her father's clear words saying: "Go to a good college and get a career." The voice was so loud and so distinct that Bonnie looked around. Everybody was busy boarding the plane. She nodded her head. Okay, dad. That's what I'll do.

Chapter 7

Bonnie had never been on a plane before. The seats seemed huge and luxurious; the stewardesses endlessly attentive to this shabbily dressed young girl. On her arrival at Logan Airport in Boston, she was ushered into the VIP lounge. A tall elderly woman rose to her feet with the help of a stick. She held out her hand. "You must be Bonnie," she said, looking into the eyes which she knew were her son's. The old lady shook her head. "If only I'd known," she said. "You are a Fraser through and through."

Bonnie looked up at her grandmother. "Why, I look just like you. Don't I?" Bonnie smiled. "I always wondered what you looked like. Dad never talked much about his past life."

"I know." Augustine put her arm around Bonnie's shoulder. "I have been a stubborn old woman. But," she gave Bonnie a slight squeeze, "I am going to make up for that. I promise."

On the drive back to Lexington, Bonnie told her grandmother about the dreadful day when her father walked out of her life. "I always felt I was somehow to blame," she said.

"No," her grandmother corrected her. "You were not to blame at all. Marriage could never have worked between the two of them."

Bonnie sighed. "I do hope mom will be all right without me. I look after her, you know."

"That's good of you." Augustine's heart, which for so many years seemed made of stone, cracked slightly. This simple child of seventeen sitting beside her in the Rolls Royce reminded her so much of her son. The same shining eyes and the broad forehead. . . . Apart from the physical beauty, Bonnie had the simple direct qualities that so many of the Frasers seemed to inherit from their forefathers, as if the modern generation still retained some of the innocence of the moors and the mountains of Scotland.

The Rolls Royce drew up in front of the Great House. Bonnie was speechless. "You mean, this is where my father was born?" she said at last. "He actually lived here?" Augustine nodded. "Gosh, he must have loved mom very much to have given up all of this for her."

Augustine looked at Bonnie. "Yes. He did. James was a man of honour, and," she laughed, "we Frasers tend to give our hearts only once in our lives." She shook her head. "Mine I gave to my father. Maybe it's just as well that your father left when he did so you still have a heart to give to some man who will truly love you."

Bonnie shook her head vehemently. "No, Grandma. I don't want to get married. I promised dad I'd get a career."

"We can talk about all that later," said Augustine, as the chauffeur held the car door open. "But first you must meet the servants."

Augustine introduced Bonnie to a small gaggle of footmen, maids, and finally the housekeeper and the head butler. Bonnie was bewildered. The senior housekeeper, who had been a contemporary of Laura's, took Bonnie by the hand. "Don't worry, Miss Bonnie. I knew your mother. We were parlour maids together. You come to me if you have any questions, and I'll do my best to answer them." Mrs. O'Neal was plump and homely, but her fierce devotion to Augustine had accelerated her promotion through the ranks. Now she ruled the Great House with an iron hand.

Passing down the line of servants, they finally came to a young girl of Bonnie's age. "This is Morag," said Augustine. "She is to be your personal maid."

Bonnie looked at Augustine. "I don't need a personal maid."

Augustine looked at her granddaughter. "You have a lot to learn, Bonnie," she said sharply. "Don't question my decisions." With that, Augustine swept off into the far reaches of the house.

"I'll show you to your room," Morag offered. "Here. I'll get one of the footmen to take your bag." Bonnie felt mortified as a liveried servant carried her scuffed suitcase up the palatial stairs.

Once inside the bedroom, Bonnie stood in the middle of the room thinking that all this was probably just a happy dream that would be over in a minute and that she would wake up in her own bleak little bedroom with the big brown water stain in the right-hand corner. "I'll unpack for you," said Morag.

"Oh I can't let you do that," Bonnie exclaimed. "Please don't. Honestly. I can do it myself."

Morag shook her head. "This is my job, Miss Bonnie. Madam made me promise I'd look after you. She knows you'll be lonely at first. I can help teach you everything you have to know. It took me months to learn how to lay a formal table for dinner." She grinned mischievously. "Now you'll have to learn how to eat it all with the right knives and forks."

Bonnie looked at her. "I've never seen such a grand house. There isn't one like it in Merrill." She shook her head. "I'm glad that I have someone my own age in the house." She smiled at Morag. "At least we can talk to each other. I've never had money. My mother was a maid here."

Morag had already been primed by stories in the servants'

quarters. She looked at Bonnie sympathetically. "My folks don't have a dime, but we were a happy family." She paused. "People here really do love your grandmother. She's good to us all."

By the time Bonnie's few belongings were put away in the cavernous drawers of the old bow-fronted chest of drawers it was time for Bonnie to get ready for dinner with her grandmother. "I'll run your bath and then leave you alone," said Morag.

Bonnie's bathroom had been modernized, and its furnishings matched those in her bedroom. Bonnie lay in the pink bath and stared at the pink lavatory across the room. The curtains, matching the curtains in her bedroom, were made of thick white chintz. Scattered all over the curtains were small swags of pink flowers which seemed to tumble off onto the chairs, the carpet, and the four-poster bed. The effect of these flowers strewn about everywhere was like lying in the middle of a summer garden. On the bedside table stood a tall vase of yellow tea roses. Her bed was made of solid, roundly carved mahogany. The canopy of the bed reached to the ceiling. Bonnie was enchanted.

After the bath, she put on her only formal dress, a simple grey dress with a Peter Pan collar. The bodice was tight, and the skirt pleated. Her penny loafers were old, but she had polished them until they shone. Morag found Bonnie lying on the bed gazing at the ceiling. "I don't believe this is happening to me," she said.

"You'll get used to it, but it will take weeks to find your way around. There are more than a hundred rooms in this house."

"Really?" Bonnie was fascinated. "Wow," was all she could say as Morag led her back down the huge spiral staircase to the main dining-room.

"Don't worry," said Morag. "You're not eating in this room tonight. This is the dining-room we use when your grandmother entertains."

Bonnie could not imagine swallowing a bit of food in this marble and gold-pillared dining-room. "I'd choke with fright," she said to Morag.

"No, you wouldn't. You'll get used to it. Of course, it will be full for your father's funeral."

Bonnie nodded. "Everything has happened so fast I haven't had time to think about him."

The two young women were, by now, at the library door. Augustine was sitting by the empty grate. She wore a pale blue silk dress. For the first time, Bonnie noticed the diamonds on Augustine's slim fingers. The jewels caught the light from the heavy crystal chandeliers which hung from the high ceiling. "I have never seen so many books in my life," said Bonnie. "Not even in our public library." Bonnie looked at the rows upon rows of books all bound in leather. Each title was tooled in gold, and at the bottom of each spine there was stamped the Fraser crest.

"Yes," said Augustine. "We have a fine library. Malcolm Fraser, your ancestor, first began the collection, and I added to it as did my father and his father before him. Come now. Join me, and let's make plans." Bonnie told her attentive grandmother all about her wish to attend a good university. "I must admit," Augustine said when Bonnie had stopped talking for a moment, "I know it's far too late to apply to the Ivy Leagues . . . but your mother said you graduated high school a year early, and *magna cum laude?*"

Bonnie nodded. "I vowed to dad before he left that I would work hard, and I never break my vows."

Augustine nodded. "No, a vow is a vow before God. Tell me, Bonnie. Do you attend mass?"

Bonnie hung her head. "No. After dad left, I didn't have much time for God. Mom kind of went to pieces, and I felt terribly betrayed. Before, dad and I used to go every Sunday."

Augustine looked at her. "God is forgiving. You will meet Father Gregory in our chapel here in the grounds. He will say a requiem mass for your father. Maybe you will find it in your heart to come back to the Church."

They talked all through their dinner as if they had known each other for years. Augustine told Bonnie about the arrangements for the funeral, and said that she would look into universities for Bonnie. As Augustine kissed her granddaughter good-night, she said, "We must take you into town tomorrow and buy you some new clothes."

Bonnie fell asleep thinking of her father. Augustine knelt stiffly by her own bed. "Dear God," she prayed. "I thank you for my granddaughter. I pray that I can care for her and keep her from harm." Then she prayed for the soul of her son, for her friends, for her servants, for the house, and finally for herself. Though deeply saddened by the knowledge of her son's death, she was at the same time comforted by the presence of her granddaughter. "The Lord giveth," she whispered, "and the Lord taketh away. Blessed is the name of the Lord." Augustine quickly fell into a deep sleep.

The chapel at the Great House was famous for its stained glass windows. The soaring arches and the high altar were modelled on those in the cathedral at Chartres. Malcolm Fraser, moved by the worship of God frozen in architecture, had commissioned its construction after a visit to France.

Bonnie was at first bemused by the multitude of mourners who filed into the richly carved mahogany pews of the chapel. Augustine, dressed in black with a simple strand of pearls around her neck, hid her sorrow under a black lace veil. Bonnie took her place beside her grandmother, her pale blonde hair covered by a small black hat. Once her eyes had become accustomed to the soft light of the huge wax candles on the altar, she saw the red glow of the mahogany casket lying in state to one side. Suddenly, the few hectic days since she learned of her father's death became meaningless. She was left with the naked pain of her loss. For a moment she feared she would faint. Augustine saw her sway slightly, and she gently took her hand. "Not in front of the servants," Augustine said, indicating a row of retainers to their left. Bonnie nodded and felt the colour come back into her cheeks.

The requiem mass was a long and solemn occasion. The male choir responded to the chanting of the priests. The young boys' voices rose higher and higher. In a particularly pure burst of song, the voice of a soloist rose quivering in the air and seemed to spiral around a wisp of incense smoke. Bonnie felt them continuing upwards and joining briefly in a moment of communion. It was then that she truly accepted that her father was dead.

As the congregation knelt in prayer, Augustine leaned heavily upon her stick as she lowered herself stiffly to her knees. Kneeling beside her granddaughter, Augustine prayed for the soul of her son and for Bonnie's happiness.

Many of the Boston Episcopalians would not attend the service itself, but were present when the family vault was opened and James laid to rest. After everyone had filed past Augustine offering their condolences, the huge dining-room of the Great House became quickly filled with the cream of Boston society, busily exchanging their news and gossip. Bonnie stood by her grandmother, overawed. "I've never seen so many people in one room," she said.

Augustine smiled. "Your father was much loved as a young man. All those Boston matrons were in hot pursuit when he was old enough to marry."

Bonnie flinched. "But he married my mom."

Augustine nodded. "And what a blessing that turned out to be. Didn't it?" She put her hand on Bonnie's shoulder. "Now I have you."

Bonnie remembered with a jolt that she had forgotten completely to contact her mother since she had come to Boston. "Can I slip away and phone mom?" she asked.

"Of course, my dear," said Augustine.

Bonnie negotiated her way past the Rembrandts hanging on the dining-room walls, through the hall filled with other Dutch masters, and finally found her way back to her bedroom. She sat on the bed for a few moments, thinking of all that had happened to her since she left Merrill.

"I was wondering when you would call." Laura's voice was aggrieved. "I've been sitting by the phone waiting."

"I'm sorry, mom. I've been so busy. Grandma took me into Boston for new clothes, and this place is huge." Bonnie went on to tell her mother about the funeral. "I feel dad's at peace," she said, "and I'm glad he's buried here with his family."

Laura held her tongue. Augustine's accountant had negotiated a contract with Laura that gave her twenty-five thousand dollars each year, provided that she stayed out of her daughter's life except for the occasions when Bonnie wanted to contact her. "It all sounds very beautiful, darling," Laura said diplomatically. Her voice sounded warm and loving. "Actually, I went to church today, and I asked the priest to say a mass for James."

"Did you, mom? That's marvellous. Father Gregory here says you know him. He remembers you very well."

"I'll bet he does," Laura laughed. "I always hoped he'd marry us in a Boston cathedral."

"Poor mom," Bonnie said, feeling Laura's isolation.

"Don't worry about me, Bonnie. I'm all right. I've given up drinking and I am having the house re. . . . I mean I'm redecorating the house myself. It gives me something to do. By the way, your friend Mitzi phoned."

"Did she? I must give her a call. I've got so much to tell her."

After Bonnie had finished talking to her mother, she returned to the noise and bustle of the funeral gathering. In Merrill, Laura put down the phone and turned cheerfully to the painters who were decorating her house. "That was my daughter," she said with a smile. "A wonderful girl. Here. Let me get you some more coffee."

"Who are those dowdy-looking women over there in the corner?" Bonnie asked Augustine.

Augustine smiled. The fresh innocence of the child enchanted her. "Those are the 'low-heelers.' They are women from the first families of Boston. If you look across from them, you can see all the well-dressed women of fashion, but those dowdy ladies, as you put it, have most of the money in the room."

Bonnie shook her head. "I obviously have a lot to learn."

Augustine smiled and put her arm around Bonnie. Together they moved into the throng. Bonnie stood alone listening to the clipped Boston accents around her while Augustine talked amiably to her guests. Morag, serving behind the great tables, saw that Bonnie looked lost. She slipped through the crowd until she was at Bonnie's side. "Are you all right?" she asked, tapping her on the shoulder.

"I suppose so," Bonnie sighed. "It's all very confusing. I don't know whether to be happy or sad."

Morag smiled. "Be happy. Your father would have been very proud and pleased to see you here." With that comforting thought, Bonnie turned to a group of women standing near her and joined in their conversation.

A week later, Bonnie had appointments for interviews at several of the leading universities and colleges nearby. Out of all of them, she fell in love with Pembroke college in Providence, Rhode Island. Augustine was a little surprised by her preference. She had hoped that Bonnie would set her heart on Smith or Wellesley, but Bonnie's determination convinced Augustine to follow her granddaughter's instincts. "All right, child," she said. "If you have decided to apply to Pembroke, then I will respect your decision. I must warn you, though, not to be disappointed if you are rejected. You are applying unusually late. I know many schools would overlook this irregularity if I were to promise a large donation, but Pembroke is an institution of great integrity. It would be pointless for me to try to get you in by means of influence."

Bonnie nodded. "I wouldn't want to be accepted that way. I would want to know that, if I do get in, it's because they want me."

In due course, Bonnie heard from the Pembroke admissions department that they had considered her late application and that, because of her excellent record at Merrill High and because of the impression she had made at her interview, she was accepted to begin her studies in September. Bonnie was ecstatic. "I must go and stay with mom before I start college," she said to Augustine as her grandmother hugged her with delight.

All the way back to Merrill, Bonnie was dreading seeing her mother again. Although Laura always sounded both sober and content on the phone, Bonnie still felt that her mother could not be trusted. Away from Laura, Bonnie was able to feel compassion and even love for her mother, but faced now with the prospect of seeing the reality of Laura again Bonnie felt a painful confusion of emotions. When she spotted Laura standing by the passenger terminal, however, she was pleasantly surprised and enormously relieved. Laura wore a pleated brown skirt, a neat white blouse, and brown high-heeled shoes. "You look marvellous," Bonnie said as she kissed her. "Oh, and you've had your teeth fixed."

Laura laughed. "I told you I'd turned over a new leaf, didn't I?"

"You did, but I'm afraid I didn't know whether to believe you or not."

"Come on," said Laura, picking up Bonnie's expensive leather suitcase, "just wait 'til you see the house."

Bonnie was amazed by what she saw when the cab pulled

up in front of number twenty Gothenburg Street. The fence and the house had been repainted. Once inside, she ran to her old bedroom. Everything looked clean and new. Even the water stain on the wall was gone. "Where did you get the money to do all this?" she asked.

Laura shrugged. "I have a little part-time job, and I have plenty of time on my hands to paint and to garden."

"Oh yes," said Bonnie. "I promised you I'd save my allowance. Well, I've saved it over the summer, and I have a cheque for you in the suitcase."

"That's kind of you," said Laura as she kissed Bonnie on the forehead. "I'll use the money to pay the heating bill this winter. I've been worried how I would get the money together."

"Well, you don't have to worry any more. Oh, mom, I'm so glad to see you looking happy and settled."

Laura looked at her daughter and laughed uneasily. "Yes, my life has changed. I have gone back to the Church. Father John is a very spiritual man, very inspiring. I go to mass every morning now, twice on Sundays."

Bonnie was impressed. That night as she lay in her freshly painted room, Bonnie thanked God for his attention to her mother. Laura lay in her own bed, thinking about Father John. Those piercing black eyes, his long slender fingers, the cruel curve of his mouth. . . . delicious, Laura thought with a shudder.

Everyone in Mitzi's family was delighted to see Bonnie again. "Bubela!" Mrs. Abramowitz cried out as she opened the front door, her plump arms outstretched waiting to squeeze Bonnie. She pressed a kiss against Bonnie's cheek. When all the preliminary hugging and kissing was over, Bonnie was led to the kitchen table where she sat with Mitzi, Mrs. Abramowitz, and Mitzi's grandmother to have a cup of tea and to catch up on all their news. Aaron was away working at a summer camp in Maine. Mitzi had stayed home to help her mother around the house. When the four women had finished their tea, Mitzi led Bonnie up to her bedroom so that they could talk more privately. "Mom is quite different now," Bonnie told her friend. "We can sit and talk and really have a good time."

Mitzi was pleased. "Sometimes it takes a real shock like your dad dying to make a person stop and think. I'm glad for you." While Mitzi spoke, Bonnie noticed a twinkle in her friend's eye that she had not seen before.

"What's happened to you, Mitzi? You look like you're about to burst into flower."

"I thought you'd never ask," Mitzi said, and then she blushed. "I'm getting engaged."

"Getting engaged?" Bonnie was incredulous. "But you haven't even begun college."

"I don't want to go to college," Mitzi confessed. "I just want to get married and have babies."

"Oh, Mitzi . . . You have to do something with your life first. What about all our plans to travel to Europe together?"

Mitzi grinned. "I'll be pregnant by then with any luck. Anyway, you'll like him. He's a good Jewish boychik, and a dentist, yet."

Bonnie laughed. "Well, I suppose I'll forgive him then for marrying you, but I won't forgive him for stealing my travelling companion." The two girls talked the rest of the afternoon away, with Bonnie describing her plans for college, and Mitzi imagining the house she would look after with her future husband.

Two weeks later, Bonnie flew back to Boston on a Friday. "Don't worry about me," Laura had said at the airport. "I'll be all right." She kissed her daughter good-bye. "My life's quite full now. I'll go to confession tonight, and I'm very busy with the Church, you know." She smiled at Bonnie. "I'm even thinking of having my nose fixed. I reckon I've looked like a prizefighter long enough." This time as Bonnie waved to her mother she saw a woman who appeared confident and in control of her life. She really has changed, Bonnie reflected. A feeling of contentment swept through her as the plane rose high above the clouds. She settled back to the book Augustine had given her all about the castles of Scotland and the history of the Fraser family.

Thousands of feet below, Laura was making her way to the local Catholic church. Her personal reformation had not required much effort. When she had attended mass for her dead husband, she realized with surprise just how satisfying it could be to sublimate her sexual needs from the physical to the spiritual. Father John standing at the altar in prayer suddenly took on a great significance. Laura, for once, disciplined herself to read the accounts of the lives of the saints. She read with particular interest about those saints who flagellated themselves to the glory of God. Laura immediately recognized this as the required path of her devotion. She bought herself a riding crop, and every night she would lash her back until it bled. Week after week, she would kneel at the confessional. "Bless me, Father, for I have sinned."

Father John had quickly learned to recognize her voice, and to dread her revelations. "How have you sinned, my child?" the priest was bound to ask.

Laura could hear him shuffling uncomfortably in the enclosed confessional booth. With her lips pressed close to the grille that separated her from him, she would begin. "Last night I had a dream that I was mounted by a dog. A huge German shepherd. We had intercourse, and then a group of men in masks with chains in their hands entered my room . . ."

Father John sighed. He listened to her litany, and when she was spent he would forgive her sins and instruct her to say ten Hail Marys, three Our Fathers, and grant her absolution. Dutifully Laura would leave the confessional and kneel in a nearby pew to say her prayers. Feeling totally rejuvenated, she would make her way home each Friday night, have a bite to eat, and fall into bed. It was the one night of the week when she deemed additional penance to be unnecessary.

Chapter 8

Brown University, which incorporated Pembroke, was everything Bonnie hoped for. Her dormitory stood in the centre of the horseshoe of buildings on the campus, and her room looked out over the tall trees and black iron lamp-posts of the lovely Pembroke green. Bonnie quickly felt at home in college life. She attended concerts in Sayles Hall. She listened to lectures by professors who stood framed by the organ pipes in Alumnae Hall. She studied in the peaceful quiet of the John Carter Brown Library. As she sat in one of the leather armchairs with a fine oriental carpet at her feet and tapestries behind her on the walls, she remembered with a smile the library at the Great House. Her work finished, she walked through the arch at Faunce House, floating in a sea of students. In the silence of the library, and in the clamour of Faunce House, Bonnie felt equally at peace.

The other girls in her dormitory were friendly, and soon Bonnie was involved in many of the college societies and clubs. She studied hard and did well. Augustine would descend for various occasions, and Laura came to Providence to visit her daughter towards the end of the spring term. Even Laura had to admit that Bonnie was well-liked by her fellow students and respected by her professors.

Throughout her entire career at college, Bonnie, although

popular and never lonely, avoided serious involvements with any of the Brown men. Many of them asked her out to football games, to parties, and to movies at the local theatre. Bonnie did indeed go out on the occasional date and to the odd party, but she found it impossible to pay serious thought to any of her beaux. They seemed very nice and very sincere, but Bonnie held in her heart a vision of manhood in the shape of her father. None of the men around her came close to resembling that vision. Word soon got around not only that she was brainy but also that she was frigid.

These rumours didn't much bother Bonnie, even when they were spitefully repeated to her by a girl in her dorm. Bonnie listened calmly and said nothing. Later, she confided in her roommate Clara. "I don't care what anyone says," Bonnie told her. "I've got too much to do in my life to waste my time being worried by that sort of adolescent gossip. Anyway, the last thing I'm interested in right now is getting tied down to some pimply youth."

Clara laughed. They were both sitting in their dormitory room. It was a Saturday night. All the other girls on their hall had been hysterically getting dressed and made-up. Their dates, meanwhile, lounged around on the porch outside the dormitory, waiting restlessly as the sun set over Providence.

"Why is it that girls feel it's the end of the world if they don't have a date on a Saturday night?"

Suddenly Clara looked serious. "It's easy for you to say that, Bonnie. You're beautiful, and you can take your pick of men when you want to. But for girls like me, who aren't much to look at and don't have a rich family behind them, this is probably the one and only chance we have to meet men who will marry us. If I don't find someone by the time I graduate, my chances of ever finding anyone are pretty slim." She sighed. "Peter's dropped me because I wouldn't sleep with him. God, my mother didn't have that problem when she went to school. But I can't risk getting pregnant. Anyway, I don't want to sleep with him. And it would be dumb of me to sleep with him just because I'm afraid that if I don't he'd find someone else who will. Where's the romance in that? Nowhere, that's where. So now here I sit: dateless on a Saturday night, quickly becoming an old maid."

"Oh, Clara," Bonnie laughed.

"Go on. Laugh. It won't be so funny when I'm seventy and still no date has shown up."

Bonnie sat by her window. Looking down, she could see the last two suitors on the porch still waiting impatiently. "No, Clara, it's just that I can't take any of this seriously," she said. "I mean, here are all these girls, working their tails off. But, for most of them, all it would take would be an offer of marriage from one of those guys down there, and they'd drop everything to get married. Doesn't make any sense. Take my best-friend Mitzi from back in Merrill. She's just written to say that she's pregnant. Can you imagine? She's my age and she's pregnant. And we spent all those years planning our trip to Europe together. Well, she's not going to do much travelling now."

"What's wrong with wanting babies?" Clara asked.

Bonnie shook her head. "Nothing's wrong. It's just all so dishonest. Look at Molly. Straight A's, goes out with Jonathan Choate, gets herself pregnant on purpose, refuses to have an abortion, his family doesn't want a scandal, so he marries her, and there they are, living off campus in some little apartment. Now she spends her time throwing up all day, and he's off seeing Tina with the terrifying tits. It just doesn't seem right."

Clara joined Bonnie by the window. "Where will it all end, I ask myself?" Clara said in a most tragic voice with the back of her hand pressed against her forehead. "Where will it all end?"

"Come on," said Bonnie, to break the ensuing silence. "Let's go down to Thayer Street and get a meatball sub. I'm starved."

* * *

After her first year at college, Bonnie spent her summer working at a children's home in Boston. "I know I don't need the money, Grandma, but I can't stay home all day and do nothing. I have to feel I'm doing something for myself. My friends are all happy spending their time chasing men."

Augustine smiled. "That is quite normal at your age, dear."

"I know, but none of the men I meet can hold a candle to dad."

Augustine was sitting in the drawing-room in her favourite chair. Bonnie sat beside her in the old rocker. Augustine had been reading her Bible. "You know," said Augustine, "maybe it's a curse, for the Fraser men seem to be a special breed of men." She looked up at the portrait of Duncan her own father. "Now *there* was a man."

Bonnie got to her feet and walked around the huge room looking at the paintings of the Fraser men. She stopped in front of a very battered old canvas in the far corner. "Who's that? I haven't noticed this picture before."

"That," Augustine said, "was James Fraser. He was one of the two survivors of the massacre at Drummossie Castle two hundred years ago. He was Malcolm Fraser's father. Malcolm had always intended to send for him when he made his fortune, but the old man died before Malcolm could send him money. A member of the Fraser clan back in Scotland sent that portrait years later."

Bonnie stood looking at her ancestor. "He looks very like dad, doesn't he?"

Augustine nodded. "Yes. In fact, that's who your father was named after. And you look exactly like Malcolm's wife Evangeline."

Bonnie suddenly felt as if time and her history had opened a door behind her. All the portraits on the walls were welded into who Bonnie Fraser was, is, and will be. "Grandma, doesn't life sort of repeat itself again and again?"

Augustine thought for a moment. "I don't think *life* does; I think *people* make the same mistakes again and again." Her face was bitter. "If I'd loved my father less and my husband more, maybe your father would not have felt the need to desert us all."

Bonnie put her hand on the old woman's shoulder. "Don't think like that. . . . You'll see: I'll have a great career, and then just before it's too late I'll marry a marvellous man, have six great-grandchildren for you, and we'll all live happily ever after."

During her second year at Pembroke, Bonnie declared her major in psychology. She still took courses in English literature, and she decided to take piano lessons. From time to time she would hear from her mother, but gradually they drifted apart. For most of her sophomore year, Bonnie kept her head in her books. One day she saw her old friend, Michael Edwards, in the distance. Mike was a pre-law major. His path very rarely crossed Bonnie's but when it did the two talked of Merrill and of their mutual friend Mitzi. Mitzi, Mike reported to Bonnie, was now a contented wife and mother with a small boy and a baby on the way.

"Not for me," Bonnie said. Mike only stood and looked at her with great longing. "Listen, Mike," she said, "I have to run. I've got a piano lesson and I'm about to be late. Nice seeing you." Bonnie gathered her books and dashed across the blue-green grass, her hair streaming out behind her. Mike sighed as he watched her go. What a waste of a beautiful girl, he thought. She's married to her books.

As the end of Bonnie's senior year approached, Augustine asked her granddaughter what she would like for a graduation present. "A trip to Europe," Bonnie answered without hesitation.

Augustine smiled. "You know, I've always regretted that I

never left Boston, but with all this to take care of I really never had the time. So you will have to be my eyes and ears as you travel."

Bonnie's face lit up. "I'll go to Scotland and look for Frasers."

"There are plenty of Frasers, my dear," Augustine laughed, "but you'll need introductions. One of your ancestors, Malcolm's daughter, married an Englishman. Let me see," she said as she walked slowly to the writing desk. "Ah. Here it is." She took out a Fraser genealogy which she herself had compiled. "Now," said Augustine while Bonnie stared at the complicated diagrams, "there's Malcolm's daughter . . . she married Philip Bartholomew. He inherited a title from his father. Their descendant is Simon Bartholomew. He married Margaret . . . and now . . ." she flipped the pages, "now Simon and Margaret Bartholomew live in Suffolk, not far from Colchester. I shall write to them and ask them to receive you. I believe they have a girl of your age."

"Thank you, Grandma." Bonnie was delighted. Although she had many girl-friends at Brown, she had never found anyone she felt closer to than she did to Mitzi. The thought of meeting a cousin of her own age was an interesting prospect.

In June 1967, Bonnie graduated from university at the age of twenty-one. Both Laura and Augustine attended the commencement ceremony to watch Bonnie receive her degree. As Bonnie's name was called, Augustine watched her granddaughter walk to the podium. She could see the intelligence and warmth in Bonnie's face, yet she also saw a naïveté which she found worrying. She has so much more to learn, thought Augustine. For all Bonnie's academic ability, Augustine knew, she had used her studies as a refuge from the turmoil of a quickly changing world. America was embroiled in an age of crisis. Its traditional attitudes to love, marriage, war, and peace were all in total upheaval. Old ideals were quickly being broken, while new ideals were appearing in such great numbers that no one knew quite what to think. Universities in particular were the crucible of the Sixties where brave plans for the future were tested and refined. Yet Bonnie remained largely oblivious to the experiments in politics and sexuality which surrounded her in the university. Her world was her books. Never mind, Augustine reassured herself as she watched Bonnie, the travel will do her good. She'll be exposed to a whole world of possibility.

Bonnie sat through the ceremony in a confusion of elation and sadness to be leaving the college that had done so much to educate her. In the audience, Augustine treated Laura with icy politeness. Laura, demurely dressed, deferred to the older woman. After the ceremony was over, Laura quickly congratulated Bonnie, kissed her daughter, and left. Bonnie asked Augustine to wait while she said her good-byes.

Other girls hugged and kissed each other, promising to keep in touch, but Bonnie quietly wandered alone through the campus, saying good-bye to the buildings themselves. She smiled at the John Carter Brown Library which had been her sanctuary. She waved to the ivy that clung to the walls of Faunce House. She walked to the Pembroke Campus and sat quietly on a stone bench in the calm of the green.

Finally she visited her favourite teacher, Professor Kalowski. He sat in his office in the Psychology Department. The old man, who had studied in Vienna when Freud and Jung were in their prime, took Bonnie's face in his hands. "My child, take good care of yourself. You have a brilliant future ahead of you. Don't throw yourself away on some worthless man."

"I won't," she smiled. "I haven't yet, and I won't ever. I must go, Professor. My grandmother is waiting for me."

He nodded. "Go with God's blessing. And I am always here if you need me." She knows so little about men, he thought. What will happen the first time she falls in love? He shook his head.

Bonnie walked back to meet Augustine at the dean's office where Augustine was having a quiet word with the dean and his wife. In appreciation of Bonnie's four happy years at the university, Augustine had offered scholarships for three girls whose parents were unable to pay the fees. This had been Bonnie's idea, as she was well aware that only by chance had she been able to go to Brown. "Goodbye, Bonnie," the dean said at last. He had noticed the quiet soft-spoken student during her first year and had always taken a special interest in her. He had appreciated the fact that she had not flaunted her wealth in the way some students did. "We hope to see you again at the reunions," he said kindly to her as Bonnie and Augustine prepared to leave.

Bonnie smiled. "I'll be coming back when I'm ninety," she said.

For the entire drive back to Lexington, Bonnie discussed with her grandmother her plans for Europe. She was going to stay with the Bartholomews in their London home, and then go with them up to Scotland to visit relations. "Perfect," Bonnie said. "Absolutely perfect."

Augustine smiled. "After you've said goodbye to your mother, we will go shopping. I must ask Lady Bartholomew what she suggests you wear."

Bonnie made a face. "I've heard that the English lords and ladies dress like gardeners. That suits me fine."

"Nonsense, my child. I won't have my granddaughter looking like a tramp."

"Okay, you can dress me like a proper lady," Bonnie said, kissing her grandmother on the cheek, "but that doesn't mean I'll ever marry some wizened old English lord."

"It's a deal," Augustine laughed. The car turned into the driveway of the Great House. Bonnie danced out of the car and into the house.

* * *

Laura was in a good mood when Bonnie arrived in Merrill to say goodbye. She had made a most satisfying confession that had left Father John reeling with shock. "Mrs. Fraser," he said yet again, "don't you think you should seek help for your uncontrollable thoughts and urges?"

"No, Father. No one can help except God. You, as my priest, are my intercessor. You have God's ear and, through prayer and fasting, I will eventually cleanse myself of this dreadful affliction."

Father John shook his head. After four years of her weekly confessions, the priest dreaded Friday. Her low voice trembling with emotion, she would pour out one degrading dream after another. Father John found it almost impossible to believe that this sweet, angelic-looking little woman could be possessed by such impure demons. His confusion over what to do about her was compounded by the fact that Laura was such a help in the church. She was the pillar of the Little League of Mary. She arranged the flowers on the pulpit, and recently she had offered to embroider new vestments for the priest. Father John found himself confounded by the two aspects of Laura he saw: the saint in the midst of his parishioners, and the urgent sinner on the other side of the grille.

"I met this man last week," she confessed. "I was up a dark alley. He had a bottle in his hand. He raped me and then. . . ."

"Did you report it to the police?" the priest interrupted. He did not want to hear any more.

Laura smiled. She loved the moment he cut her off. She felt powerful. Father John gave her absolution, and she left the church after slipping twenty-five dollars in the offering box. Her twenty-five dollars made a great difference to Father John's life. His was a mean living in a poor Irish neighbourhood. His mother had intended that her only son should go to Rome, not remain stuck in his home town of Merrill. "I'll ask the Bishop what to do about Mrs. Fraser," he told himself. "This sort of thing must happen to other priests."

Laura was pleased to see Bonnie. Bonnie thought her mother looked considerably thinner than when she had last seen her. Laura also looked haggard. Despite the success of the recent operation on her nose, her face had a petulant air. "You look tired, mom," Bonnie said as she put her suitcase down in the hall.

"I've been working hard for the church fête."

For the four days of Bonnie's visit, Laura talked of nothing but Father John. "He wants to meet you, so I've promised to take you to mass tomorrow," said Laura.

Bonnie was eager to see a man who could turn her mother into such a dedicated member of his church. When she did meet him after mass, she was puzzled. On the surface, he seemed such a worldly priest. I suppose I am used to Father Gregory who is so mild and so gentle, she reasoned. Father John had long thin hands that were clammy, and an over-hanging forehead with deep-set eyes. He made Bonnie nervous. "He looks quite fierce, doesn't he?" she said to her mother on their way home.

"He does indeed. You should hear him saying the stations of the cross," Laura said.

Bonnie had noticed that the walls in Father John's church were covered by huge murals depicting all forms of human suffering. The paintings showed Christ being whipped. The canvases themselves seemed to drip with blood. "That sort of Catholicism puts me off," she said to her mother at supper. "Sometimes I feel all that talk of the nails and the blood must be bad for young children. The church I went to with dad on the other side of town wasn't a bit like that. Why don't you go there?"

"I have dedicated my life to Father John and his church, that's why."

"Oh. I see. Well, as long as you're happy."

"I am." Laura looked at Bonnie. "I've never been happier in my life."

When Laura saw her daughter off at the airport, she was relieved to see her go. Her obsession with the priest was such that she didn't like anyone to disturb her thoughts. Once Bonnie was on the plane, Laura raced home. That evening, as on most evenings, she embroidered vestments, and then, having lashed herself severely for her faults of the day, she fell asleep dreaming of Father John with a cane in his hand.

Augustine was too frail to see Bonnie off at Logan airport on her flight to Europe. She was now seventy-three, and her legs were giving her trouble. She sat with Bonnie in her drawing-room, checking that all arrangements were in order. "I've written a letter of introduction for you to the manager of the Midland Bank in Knightsbridge. I've had a large sum deposited for you there. If you find you need more, just tell me. You should also have with you the letter introducing you to a solicitor's firm over there, just in case you find you need any legal assistance."

Bonnie checked in her purse. "Yes," she said. "The letters are all right here."

"Good. And be sure to open an account for yourself at Harrods when you're in London. I understand they have everything you could ever want. So you don't have to worry about running out of anything." Bonnie laughed. Augustine heard a tinge of uneasiness behind Bonnie's laugh. "Bonnie," she said. "Is there anything that's worrying you?"

"Oh Grandma, it's just that I'm nervous about making a bad impression on our family over there. And not just them. What will people think of me over there? What if I do everything all wrong?"

"Bonnie," Augustine said kindly, "there is something you must understand. The English think themselves socially superior to everyone else in the world. They are particularly rude about Americans. They consider Americans loud and vulgar and bossy. But you, Bonnie, have nothing to be ashamed of. You are a Fraser, and the Frasers were a noble house of Scotland long before the English had any manners at all. In fact, we do not consider the Royal Family to be as old or as important as we are."

Bonnie was amazed. "Really?"

"Oh yes," Augustine continued. "They are fairly new in the order of things. But you'd probably upset a lot of people if you mentioned that fact, so keep it to yourself. Just bear it in mind. And, if you find you are being patronized by anyone, just remember who you are."

"I will remember, Grandma. Thank you." Bonnie leaned down to her grandmother in the armchair and hugged her. Augustine pressed her lips tightly against Bonnie's cheek. "I'll be back at Christmas," said Bonnie, and she turned to walk out of the door. "Goodbye," said Augustine, "and may God keep you safe."

Bonnie stopped and turned to face her grandmother. "I love you, Grandma," she said.

Augustine sat very quietly as her eyes filled with tears. "Since the day my son walked out that door, I never thought I would hear those words spoken to me ever again." A tear rolled down her cheek. "I love you too, Bonnie." She wiped her eye and smiled. "You'd better go now, or you'll make an old woman cry."

Bonnie smiled. "Goodbye, Grandma."

Bonnie turned in her seat to look back at the Great House as the Rolls Royce pulled out of the drive to take her to the airport. Her eye rose from the grand steps in front of the house, up the magnificent façade, and came to rest at a little window on the uppermost storey of the building. It was from that window that Laura O'Rourke had watched the arrival of James Forbes twenty-two long years before.

PART TWO

Roses, Roses, All the Way

Chapter 9

Hoskins, the chauffeur, had nothing to say as he drove Bonnie from the airport to the Bartholomews' London house. Privately, he was tired of chauffeuring rich pampered young ladies about in the Volvo. He also resented the fact that he no longer had his fleet of beautiful cars, the Rollses and the Bentleys. The old order had broken down. Along with the new austerity, many of the staff had been laid off. Hoskins was expected to help with the hoovering of the Bartholomews' numerous Persian rugs. Still, he comforted himself, Lord Bartholomew still needs me, and while I have my health I have my living.

The car drew up outside Lord Bartholomew's elegant Hamilton Terrace house, quite obviously built at a time when quality not quantity was the hall-mark. Johnson, the butler, ushered Bonnie into the house.

"Welcome, Miss Fraser. We have been expecting you. We hope you had a good journey." Johnson, as Bonnie was to discover, always referred to himself in the plural. He felt that, as head of the household below stairs, he spoke for himself and for Lord Bartholomew.

"Yes. Thank you." Bonnie was amazed. Though she had

been both very rich and very poor, she had never seen both conditions exist in the same house. The paintings in the square hall were no doubt of Bartholomew ancestors, sumptuously dressed and dripping with jewels. The large Persian carpets on the floor had obviously seen better days. There were several struts missing in the bannister which wound up the spiral staircase. Bonnie's attention was suddenly distracted by several exuberant dogs which came bounding into the hall ahead of a young woman. One of the dogs, a Great Dane, reared up and slobbered a greeting all over her face.

"Get down, Morgan, you fool! Heel!"

Bonnie wiped her face. "He's certainly friendly." She looked warily at the dog who seemed the size of a small horse.

"Oh, he's a marvellous animal. Kills everything that isn't human, and he hates the dustmen. I'm Teresa. Named after the saint, you know," she laughed.

While Teresa babbled on, Bonnie inspected her new cousin. Teresa was two inches taller than Bonnie. She had huge hands and feet, and legs that looked like tree trunks. But she had lovely thick black hair, smiling green eyes, and a small red mouth. She reminded Bonnie of a Renoir painting that hung in the Boston Museum of Fine Arts.

"Mummy always hopes I'll refuse an offer of rape and choose to die like my namesake," Teresa said. "Chance'd be a fine thing. Anyway," she paused for breath, "you must be our cousin Bonnie."

Bonnie nodded. She was having trouble with Teresa's clipped staccato voice, but she liked her immediately.

"Thank God," Teresa said cheerfully, leading her to the drawing-room, "you're not one of those snub-nosed buck-toothed American girls that seem to have been pushed out by a sausage machine."

Bonnie laughed, a little shocked by her cousin's uninhibited opinions. "Is that how you think of Americans over here?"

"Oh yes. When we think of Americans at all we think they

have three national characteristics: they all wear bri-nylon, they all have at least two cameras slung around their necks, and they all chew gum."

Bonnie blushed. "I chew gum," she confessed.

"What do Americans think of us?" Teresa asked over her shoulder.

Bonnie hesitated. "Well. . . ."

"Come on. You can tell me."

Bonnie frowned. "I suppose we mostly think of you as cold and not very clean because you don't take showers."

"Oh well, that's not too bad. You're right. English people think that too much hot water leads to bad habits." She threw herself into a large sofa, and lay with her legs over the arm. "Mummy would kill me if she saw me like this, but after all those years in a nunnery I feel I've only just begun to live."

Bonnie sat decorously on the other sofa. "A nunnery?"

"Oh yes. Mummy's a very devout Catholic, and she wanted at least one daughter to be a nun, and of course a son to become a priest. I've let her down, you know." She swung her feet to the ground. "We're the same age, and I've only been out of the convent four months. I feel as though I've lost those four years of my life. It isn't that I don't love God. It's just that I used to drive the other novices mad with my noisy feet, and," she looked at Bonnie, "I never stop talking."

Bonnie smiled at her cousin. "That's okay with me. I've been locked away as well. Not like you, but really concentrating on getting a B.A. in psychology, and then when I go back I'm going to get my Masters so that I can be a social worker."

"No men in your life?" Teresa asked.

"No. Not really. I never met anyone that really fascinated me. Do you know what I mean?" Bonnie was surprised to hear herself talking so candidly. "I mean all the men I met just seemed like boys to me."

Teresa nodded. "Well, I just made do. You'll meet Henry. He's my latest. His father is a director of Shell. They have pots of money, but mummy says they're not one of us. Poor old thing. She can't cope with what's happening in the world today. The swinging Sixties caught her unawares."

"How lovely to see you at last."

Bonnie turned round and saw Lady Bartholomew advancing across the shabby carpet. She was a tall thin woman in a plain navy blue suit over a white pleated shirt. *She* should have been the nun, Bonnie thought. She rose to her feet. "How do you do, Lady Bartholomew."

"Do call me Margaret." Lady Bartholomew smiled. "After all, we are family, aren't we? And how is your dear grandmother?"

"Grandma is very well. She sends you her regards, and I have a small package for you."

Suddenly Lady Bartholomew noticed her large cheerful daughter strewn across her formal sofa. "Teresa," she said, "if I've told you once I've told you a thousand times. You may not live in this house as if it were a stable. Ladies do not sprawl with their legs apart. Please sit up and keep your knees together."

"Oh, mummy." Teresa pulled at her minuscule skirt. "Times have changed. You know all this 'ladies' stuff is out."

Lady Bartholomew drew herself up. "Teresa," she said icily, "nothing ever really changes. Only on the surface. Remember, I was born in the flapper era. Everyone expected to dance on the tables at the Ritz all their lives. But wars soon put a stop to that. Now, everyone predicts a social revolution. There will never be a social revolution in England because, come what may, the working classes know their place. Men like Hoskins and Johnson would give their lives for us, and we will always take care of them."

Teresa made a face. "It's not the servants or the great British working classes. It's all those ridiculously high standards you keep on about. Daddy's just as bad. Don't you see? It's not like that any more." Bonnie, meanwhile, continued to stand not knowing what to do with herself as the two women argued.

"It is precisely our standards," Lady Bartholomew continued, "that made Britain the centre of a great empire, and because there are some of us who will never relax those standards the country will come to its senses again in the next few years. You'll see." She turned to Bonnie. "I'm sorry, my dear. I normally don't allow conversation about religion or politics. We believe such subjects are a matter of personal opinion and private concern."

"You forgot to mention sex," Teresa snorted.

Lady Bartholomew shot her daughter a furious look. "Teresa, show Bonnie her room and then get changed for dinner."

"Come on, Bonnie." Teresa heaved herself to her feet. "Let's go upstairs. See you later, mother dear." Teresa bounded towards the door. Bonnie followed her. The dogs erupted into action. "Whew," Teresa panted as she burst into Bonnie's bedroom. "God, I'd hate to be a rabbit with that lot after me." Morgan the Great Dane deposited himself on the vast oak bed. Bonnie looked around the room. Well, she thought, I suppose it *is* old . . . "The bathroom's down the passage," said Teresa, scooping up a couple of Jack Russell terriers. "I'll be back to collect you at seven thirty."

Bonnie's stomach gave a twinge of disappointment. She had been warned about European eating habits. She was used to eating dinner at six. Never mind, she comforted herself. I'm looking forward to good old-fashioned English cooking, roast beef and Yorkshire pudding.

Her first look in the bathroom convinced Bonnie that she would rather wait until the next morning to bathe. The bathtub was a Victorian monstrosity, crouching white and sinister against the wall. Unattractive green tiles marched around the room. The floor was laid with thick green linoleum. Despite the room's unattractiveness, however, Bonnie was so tired and tense after her long flight that she decided to opt after all for a hot steaming bath. She leaned gingerly over the tub and turned one of the tarnished brass taps. Nothing happened. She stood back, puzzled. She walked over to the basin and tried the hot tap. Suddenly there was a rattle and a clank and a tremendous juddering of the pipes that lay exposed along the walls of the bathroom. After a convulsive explosion, a small trickle of water ran from the tap into the bath. The basin tap leaked in sympathy. Bonnie abandoned the bath and settled for a quick wash in the basin. She left the bathroom hurriedly. The bath-tub seemed poised on its huge clawed feet ready to rear up and attack her.

Back in her bedroom, she put on a long pink dress that tied at the waist. She took out a small diamond necklace from her suitcase, and then plaited her hair into a tight roll at the back of the neck. "Ready yet?" said Teresa as she crashed through the door. She had made an attempt to dress for dinner. She wore a large amount of multi-coloured material that billowed unevenly about her feet. "Come on. Daddy gets stroppy if we're late for sherry."

Bonnie followed Teresa out of the door. Morgan, who had been lying on the bed as if dead, decided not to let Bonnie out of his sight. He raised himself and marched down the stairs at her heels.

"I have invited all the family for dinner to meet you," Margaret said as she crossed the hall to the drawing-room with the two girls in tow.

Only Lord Bartholomew was in the drawing-room. He stared at Bonnie as if he had seen a ghost. "My goodness, Margaret," he said. "Doesn't she look like Malcolm's girl."

Margaret laughed. "You'll have to get used to Simon," she said to Bonnie. "He talks as if the Fraser family never dies."

Simon Bartholomew was rarely interested in young gels, as he called them. His daughter's friends were loud and silly and they usually wore too much scent. The only women that really interested Simon were his boat *Lady Luck*, moored in Chichester harbour, and his wife. The latter was a damn fine horsewoman and a good shot. A man couldn't ask for more. But, he thought, staring at Bonnie as she walked towards him, *what a beautiful filly*. She moved like a boat with the wind behind her, and her eyes reminded him of the calm of the ocean on a hot sunny day. "Good evening," he said. "Welcome to our family."

"Good heavens," Teresa broke into a giggle. "You've quite bowled daddy over. I've never heard him be nice to anyone except the dogs."

Simon stiffened, clearly regretting that he had allowed himself to become sentimental. Sentiment was for servants, his public school had taught him. Clearing his throat, he rebuked his daughter. "Four years in a nunnery have done little to improve your manners. See that Bonnie has a glass of sherry."

Teresa flushed. Her father preferred to rule his family as he felt a Catholic patriarch should. Teresa was the only child to rebel against his iron grip. Ignoring her, Simon Bartholomew turned to greet his daughter Pauline who had arrived with Francis, the ghastly man she lived with. "What sort of a fellow would wear sandals to dinner?" he muttered inaudibly as he dutifully kissed his daughter. He made a mental note to ask his wife to notify Pauline that her man was not welcome at dinner with his toes showing. After all, he reminded himself, I did relax the rules on dress, the men no longer had to wear dinner jackets.

Francis shook his father-out-of-law's hand with mock geniality. The truth was that he was terrified of the old man. Simon looked every inch a Fraser. He stood six foot four in his socks. He was blond and built like a buttress on Tower Bridge. Sitting all day in his chambers dealing with complicated international contracts, combined with too much port at the Athenaeum, had ensured a massive paunch and face resembling a map of the world.

Mary came next. Oh God, Simon thought, the Marxist midget, dandruff and all. He hoped Mary would have taken her mother's quiet warning and refrain from saying pinko things during dinner. After kissing Mary he pointedly refused to shake the midget's hand. He had never, in the two years that his daughter had been living with this man, ever brought himself to say his name: Cyril. Cyril was a Jew name.

There had been one of them at Simon's school. He remembered the smarmy little fellow, and how they would debag him to see his Johnny, as Simon's nanny used to call it, shorn of its foreskin. Nasty little sneak. The boy had whined to his father, who had endowed the school with enormous sums of money. Being a Catholic school, St. Gregory's was not as rich as Eton or Harrow, and the Fathers had succumbed and let the Jew boy in—provided, of course, that he changed his religion. A maharajah's son was one thing, but a Jew boy, never. After all, those wogs could at least handle a cricket bat; a Jew did nothing with his time but count money.

All this Simon thought as he looked at Cyril. Cyril cringed under the old man's ferocious gaze.

Cyril turned to Bonnie and began to question her about the American President.

"I'm afraid I don't know anything about politics," Bonnie said.

Mary, standing next to Cyril, snorted. "Don't worry. Most people in this country don't know the name of the Prime Minister, let alone care. One day all that will change. The people will rise up and attack the bourgeoisie."

Bonnie interrupted her. "Aren't we the bourgeoisie? I mean, you and me?"

Mary was quite flushed by this time. She laughed. "You don't have to be one of them," and she gestured at her father. "You can be one of us." But, before she could begin to recruit Bonnie for the cause, she was interrupted by the noisy arrival of her four brothers.

Bonnie was astonished. Physically they were magnificent specimens, all tall, all blond, and all thick-set. But the effect they had on the room was as if the human equivalent of four Morgans had been let loose. They all talked at the tops of their voices, and they seemed to charge about without any sense of direction. Margaret tried in vain to calm "the boys," as she called them, even though they were all in their thirties. Suddenly Matthew, the eldest, who was clearly his mother's favourite, the priest of the family, caught sight of Bonnie standing quietly by the fireplace. "Here she is, Luke," Matthew said. Followed by his three brothers, he hurried over.

Margaret introduced them. "After three girls I despaired of sons, so I promised St. Jude I would name any boys I had after the apostles. He blessed me with four. This is Matthew, and that's Mark, and the last two are, hardly surprisingly, Luke and John. And then," Margaret said, shooting Teresa a sideways glance, "seven years later we were blessed with Teresa."

John smiled at Bonnie. "Now that I've seen you, and you're not tartan American, I'm going to bag you for the Argyll party on Friday."

Bonnie calculated that she had four days in which to settle down and find her way around. "I'd love to go," she said. She never really enjoyed parties, but John looked so wistfully at her. Besides, Teresa had promised to be there too.

"Dinner is served." Johnson stood by the door. Lord Bartholomew offered his wife his arm. Matthew took Bonnie's elbow. "We're next," he said, and they all filed into the dining-room. Bonnie looked at the grandfather clock in the corner. Half-past eight, she thought. I'll die of starvation and they'll have to bury me before I even get to this Argyll party.

Dinner did nothing to change her mind. There were only two courses. The first was a pink flannel that lay menacingly on her plate. Next to it sat a grey heap of mashed potatoes and a mountain of watery green sprouts.

"I hope you like our famous Wiltshire gammon," Margaret called down the table. "Cook's speciality. I'm afraid it's leftovers tonight. We had it hot last night, but fortunately cook is an excellent saver. I must say," she addressed her husband, "I do think the brussel sprouts are a little soggy, but they don't always reheat well."

Bonnie hacked away at the flaccid piece of meat. The brussel sprouts disintegrated into soggy green puddles before she could even put them into her mouth. The mashed potatoes concealed lumps of concrete that threatened to choke her. In desperation she tried to talk to Lord Bartholomew. "What a lovely taste your wine has," she said.

Simon Bartholomew was pleased. The gel was obviously intelligent. Gels don't normally notice things like that.

A slight scuffle accompanied the arrival of Ann. She slid into her seat under her father's stern gaze. "Late again," he shouted. "I will not have you turning up at any old time."

Ann looked down at her plate. "I had a whole bus-load of Germans disappear on me. I'm sorry, daddy."

"A whole bus-load of Germans disappear? And a good thing too, I say. Why didn't you leave them wherever they were? Probably in some filthy pornographic shop looking at lewd pictures of naked women."

Matthew cleared his throat nervously.

Simon looked at Bonnie. "The gel understands perfectly well. The country is slowly sinking into the waves under a tide of tourists that cheat our shops and despoil our daughters." He shot a filthy look at Cyril. "If it's not tourists, it's aliens, foreigners."

Margaret lifted her hand at the other end of the table. "Let's talk about next weekend's shooting, shall we?" she said. "The Percies are so pleased we are all going down for the weekend."

"I'm not going." Mary looked defiantly at her father. "I don't want to see mutilated birds stuffed into shooting bags.

I think it is all disgusting." She looked at Bonnie. "Have you ever been on a shooting party?"

Bonnie shook her head. She knew that many of Augustine's friends scoured the New England countryside looking for things to kill, but it was not a pastime that Augustine would encourage. Although Augustine had no time for most animals, she loved her birds and her horses, and she would never harm a living thing if she could avoid it.

"Never mind," said Teresa, seeing the look of panic in Bonnie's face. She grinned. "I stay in the house and put my feet up. You can keep me company." Bonnie was immediately grateful.

Bonnie was served something that looked rather like vomit. "Have you never had apple custard before?" Margaret asked.

Bonnie shook her head. The apple sauce was very green, and the custard was very yellow and lumpy. The whole family fell upon the disgusting mixture with cries of joy. Only Cyril, used to his mother's kosher cooking, threw Bonnie a sympathetic look.

"I'm afraid I've eaten so much, I have no room for dessert," Bonnie said.

"You mean 'pudding,' " Teresa corrected her. "Don't worry, we have apple custard all the time, so you'll have plenty more chances to try it."

"Oh," said Bonnie faintly.

Lord Bartholomew had finished. He pushed back his chair. "I'm off to the library," he announced.

The rest of the family waited for coffee. Bonnie felt dreadfully tired. "Do you mind?" she asked Pauline who sat across from her. "I'm suddenly feeling jet-lagged."

Pauline nodded. "Do go up. Can you find your way?"

"Yes. Anyway," Bonnie laughed, "I think Morgan will act as my escort."

* * *

Upstairs in her cold bedroom, with its lukewarm iron radiator and rough blankets, Bonnie lay half asleep. I feel like Alice in Wonderland, she thought, just after she took the medicine. Everything is so small. She fell asleep dreaming of Lord Bartholomew as the mad hatter.

Chapter 10

Bonnie's first full day in England began with a downpour that lashed at her window pane. Lying in bed, listening to the rain, depressed her especially as she had imagined upon waking that she was in her own flower-strewn room in Lexington. Standing at the window, Bonnie remembered the Bartholomew family dinner from the night before. She assumed the Bartholomews were a typical aristocratic English family. If so, then they seemed far more open and outgoing than she had been led to believe the English could be. She had heard much about the English reserve, but this family positively bubbled with enthusiasm and, as for directness, they verged on rudeness. All in all, she thought, I like them.

There was a thunderous knock on the door, and there stood Teresa. Morgan rose to his feet and stretched. "Not dressed yet? That's all right. Go back to bed if you want to." Teresa was dressed in a kilt and a navy blue sweater that made her eyes look an even deeper green.

"I'm okay," Bonnie smiled.

"Where would you like to go today?"

"Well, grandma suggested I open an account at Harrods. Maybe we should do that?"

"Marvellous!" Teresa nodded enthusiastically. "We could

hang out in the men's department and see if we can pick up some choice specimens." She threw herself into the shabby armchair by the window.

Bonnie was surprised. "Teresa, you don't spend your life chasing men, do you?"

Teresa nodded. "Before I became a nun, I would never admit that I did, but now I'm twenty-three. I'm fed up with other girls' weddings. I want a wedding, a house, and a man of my own. I'm tired of living with daddy's temper and mummy's bad opinion of me. Anyway, there are only so many eligible Catholic bachelors in town, and most of them are being snapped up. Except one man, Angus MacPherson. No one can catch him."

"Really?" Bonnie was interested.

"Yes." Teresa looked at Bonnie. "Angus has broken more hearts than I have china plates." She shook her head. "But I don't know. He's beautiful to look at, but . . ." She laughed. "I don't know why I'm telling you all this. I suppose because at some point you will meet him. He took me out to dinner once, and do you know what? He didn't even ask me to sleep with him. I was furious. There I was offering him my virginity at eighteen. I even got fitted with a diaphragm. Just for him." She threw back her head and laughed. She had the whitest teeth Bonnie had ever seen. "God, Bonnie. I don't even remember what we ate or drank. He just mesmerized me. He has that effect on all women as far as I can see. Anyway, I'll let you get dressed, and then we'll go shopping."

After Bonnie had endured a quick shudderingly cold bath, she chose a short pleated yellow skirt with a matching yellow poplin blouse. She tied her hair up on top of her head and put her sensible herringbone tweed coat over her arm. Morgan followed her downstairs. Johnson ushered her into the dining-room.

In the light of day, the room was cold and gloomy. The dark oak-panelled walls closed in on her. But her sense of claustrophobia vanished when Teresa came bounding in and joined her at the long Elizabethan refectory table. "I was too tired to ask last night," said Bonnie, "but where do all your brothers and sisters live?"

"Well, the boys live in one of mummy's houses in Cheyne Walk. That's down by the river. And my three sisters have a flat each in a house in Oakley Street, just off the King's Road in Chelsea. Have you ever heard of Chelsea?"

Bonnie nodded. "Oh yes. I saw an article in *Time* magazine. It sounds great."

"I'll take you there after we've been to Harrods. What do you want for breakfast?"

Bonnie shrugged her shoulders. "Just toast and coffee."

"Okay." Teresa rang a bell. "Toast and coffee for Miss Fraser. I'll have my usual breakfast."

"Yes, Miss Bartholomew," said the very plain little maid with red raw hands. Bonnie thought wistfully of Morag. Though Morag was a servant, Bonnie knew that service would only be a fleeting part of Morag's life. She had often talked to Bonnie about how she would continue evening classes until she had sufficient grades to qualify for college. Looking at the Bartholomew maid, however, Bonnie knew that she would always be a servant in someone's house. There was an air of hopelessness about her.

"Penny for your thoughts," Teresa broke the silence.

"Well, I was wondering if just anyone can be Prime Minister here. In America a shoe-shine boy knows he can get to be President if he wants to."

Teresa frowned. "Yes, I suppose anyone *can* be the Prime Minister, but there's a big difference between England and America. Here, you are born into a family. That makes you what you are. No amount of money can get you accepted if you're not born into the right family. It has changed a bit in recent years. But only at the bottom levels. I mean, we are one of the oldest Catholic families in the country. I can't just marry anybody. He's got to be landed gentry. I certainly couldn't marry Henry. He's not one of us. Mummy and daddy use their titles, but long ago dropped all the 'honourable' stuff. In fact it's really not done to use the word in front of one's name. At the bottom of the heap among the country families, you do get people marrying into the professional middle classes. But I know mummy wouldn't allow me to marry out of our circle." She frowned. "It must be very different in America."

Bonnie shook her head. "Not in Boston, it isn't. We have what we call wasps, White Anglo-Saxon Protestants, some of whom consider themselves the original Boston settlers. God, they really are unbearable snobs, and they own most of the property and the money in the city. But everyone else feels they are as extinct as dodos."

Teresa made a face. "They're certainly not extinct here. Everyone thinks all the decisions are made in Parliament, but that's not true. All the major decisions that involve this country are made by daddy and his friends."

Bonnie looked shocked. "Gee. That isn't very democratic."

"No," Teresa agreed, "but it's always been like that. I'm not making this up, you know. I hear daddy and his cronies from the Foreign Office talking in the library."

Their conversation was interrupted by the maid carrying in a huge tray, which she set down on the sideboard. "We'll help ourselves," Teresa told her. "You can go. You must have plenty to do."

"She looks so unhappy," Bonnie said.

Teresa nodded. "Her mother's living with a man who drinks and beats her. At least Peggy is safe living in our house."

Bonnie shuddered. She pictured her mother's bruised face. "How awful," she said.

"Well, that sort of man can't communicate very well so they use their fists. It's a way of showing they care, or so Mary says, and she's a social worker. She ought to know, I suppose."

Bonnie shook her head. "I don't believe that idea about it being a sign of love. Maybe if you can't express yourself you do lash out, but you can't hit the person you love."

Teresa wasn't really listening. She was at the sideboard piling food on to her plate. She returned to the table and sat down. "There, Bonnie, is a good English breakfast." On her plate lay a piece of fried bread, two eggs, bacon, and fried tomatoes. "Let's talk about something else," Teresa said matter-of-factly. "What are you going to wear to the Argyll party on Friday night?"

Bonnie thought for a moment. "Well, I have a favourite black dress that grandma won't let me wear because she says I'm too young to wear black, but I snuck it into my suitcase anyway."

"Sounds great," said Teresa, as she tucked into her breakfast. She wiped the plate with a crust of toast and gave it to Morgan. "I know, I know. You Americans, all vitamins and hygiene, but I'm afraid we love our animals even more than we love children. I sometimes think that if daddy had a choice between me and his favourite hunter, he'd choose the bloody horse. By the way, do you hunt?"

Bonnie shook her head. "No, I don't. You see, I've only lived with grandma for four years. Before that I lived with my mother and we were very poor, so I don't do anything a properly brought up girl should do. I do ride, but I can't play bridge or tennis or anything like that. I don't actually want to shoot. I hate the idea of killing things."

"Oh, that's right. I remember you said that last night. I know what you mean, though. One does actually learn how to be a lady from the moment you're put into your Silver Cross pram. Tell you what, though, I'm not considered 'nice' by other mothers. I'm too loud and I have opinions. Even in these more enlightened days, you're not supposed to think if you want to get married. Do you sleep around?"

Bonnie blushed. "No, I don't." She again thought of Laura with shame. "I know girls who do, but it doesn't seem to make them happy, unless they manage to get pregnant and get the guy to marry them. Even then I don't know how happy they really are."

Teresa rose from her chair. "Well, I do. You have to now, or nobody takes you out. With everybody having sex everywhere, you either do it or stay at home and wait for Prince Charming. I'm not waiting. At least this way, if I end up an old maid, I'll have a trunkful of memories." She grinned at Bonnie. "Anyway, John will make a pass at you. I can tell."

"Your brother John?"

"Yes, him."

"But we're cousins."

"Not first cousins, you aren't."

"I prefer to wait for my Prince Charming."

"It'll be a long wait. There aren't many of them about. Come on." Teresa was collecting her coat in the hall. "Let's dash."

Teresa's driving left a lot to be desired. Her little dented Mini shot through the traffic like a demented bluebottle. Bonnie was appalled. "Teresa!" she yelled as they hurtled down Park Lane towards Knightsbridge. "Slow down!"

"I can't. This is the one time I can really be myself. Get out of the way, you bastard!" she leaned out of her window and shrieked at an impeccably dressed gentleman with a black bowler hat on his head. "Do you know the best way to pick up men?" Bonnie shook her head. "I'll show you. Watch this."

Teresa raced along the road, choosing a victim. After a few minutes, she spotted a silver Lotus Elan being driven by a young man with a cheerful friendly face. "Got him," said

Teresa. "Hold on tight. Here goes." Teresa stamped on the accelerator, shot out of the traffic, raced up beside her victim, and then neatly overtook him. Once directly in front of him, she slammed on her brakes. The young man, with a horrified look on his face, braked hard. It was too late, and his beautiful car hit the back of the little Mini. Teresa sat in the car looking very pleased with herself.

The young man got out. "I say," he said, "you did cut in, you know."

Teresa gave him her wide pink smile. "I know, but we were being chased by a car full of awful-looking thugs, so I had to get away. I'm terribly sorry. Have we damaged your car?"

"No, just a dent on the fender, but I think I've dented your Mini. Let's have a look." Teresa got out of the car, and they both inspected the damage. Bonnie, mortified with embarrassment, stayed where she was. She could hear the shouts and insults from all the cars held up behind them. At last Teresa sauntered back to the Mini. She got into the car. "Goodbye, then." She waved to the young man. "His name is Timothy, he went to Winchester, he's a Catholic, and he's going to the Argylls' party." She looked so pleased with herself that Bonnie had to laugh. "That's better." Teresa looked at Bonnie. "It's nice to see you let go. You know, you're so serious about everything. Life's full of fun, really."

Bonnie smiled. "I suppose it is."

Bonnie filled in a form in the accounts department, and then Teresa dragged her off to the food hall, to see the displays of fish on the long white marble counters. Their final visit was to the men's department. A brisk walk through was sufficient for Teresa to pronounce the place officially dead. "Nothing there at all worth picking up. Just a man who was at Sherborne."

"How do you know?" Bonnie asked.

"His tie. But only clergymen's sons and farmers go to Sherborne. It doesn't rate at all."

"Boy, your class system is really rigid, isn't it?"

"Yes," Teresa nodded. "It is. Come on. I'll take you down the King's Road, and buy you lunch in your first English pub."

The pub was very crowded. Teresa seemed to know everyone. She introduced Bonnie to various groups of people, and then pushed her way to the bar. "Two half-pints and two pork-pies," she ordered.

"Pork-pies?" Bonnie said.

"You'll love them. They're very English."

Bonnie watched the barman pull a white-handled lever. A dark brown liquid filled the glass. He stopped just as the white foam crested the rim. "There," he said smiling at Bonnie. "This your first beer?"

Bonnie shook her head. "We have beer in Boston, but it's not flat like that."

"This is good old English bitter. Best in the world. 'Ere. Try it." He put the glass into Bonnie's hand.

She smelled the rich thick smell of the hops, then took a tentative sip. The liquid was heavy and bitter at first, but then she could taste the sweetness of the malt. She nodded. "I really like that," she said.

The barman smiled proudly. 'Ave it on the 'ouse," he said. They found a table in the corner. "Jennifer!" Teresa gave a high-pitched scream. "Where have you been, darling?" Bonnie winced as the two girls exchanged greetings at the tops of their voices. Where is this great British reserve? she wondered. "Darling, this is my cousin Bonnie Fraser. She's from Boston."

"Oh really?" Jennifer was a thin tense girl. She wore a Chanel suit, and Bonnie thought she looked anorexic. Her brown eyes rested anxiously on Bonnie's face. "I have cousins there. Do you know Douglas Cabot?"

Bonnie shook her head. "No, I'm afraid I don't."

"Well, do you know Amy Saltonstall?"

Bonnie shook her head again. "No, I . . ."

Teresa butted in. "You must understand, Bonnie, that England is a very small island. We all know each other here. There are only two per cent of us who all go to the same schools, and our families own ninety per cent of all the money in England."

Bonnie was amazed. "Who told you that?"

"Cyril, of course. He's always going on about it as if it were some sort of sin, or something."

Jennifer looked down at her hands. Bonnie saw the engagement ring, "When I marry Andrew," Jennifer explained, "we'll join up a vast part of Wales. Mummy is very proud of that fact." She looked haunted.

"Do you want to marry Andrew?" Teresa asked.

Jennifer flushed. "Not really." She dropped her voice. "You see, we have the land and the castle, but his family also have lots of money. So in a way I have to marry him so that daddy can keep the estate up."

Bonnie felt an immediate sympathy for the girl. "Gee, I'd hate to have to marry for money," she said.

Jennifer was about to answer when Andrew, who had been drinking at the bar with his friends, caught sight of Bonnie. "Well, hello there," he bellowed. "Jenny, do introduce me to this gorgeous girl."

Bonnie looked at him. He really does look like a pig, she thought. He had a very white face with pink fleshy cheeks. His hair was blond and bristly. He stuck out his pudgy hand and squeezed Bonnie's hand hard. "Hello, old girl. We haven't met before. My name's Andrew Wynn."

Bonnie shuddered.

Teresa prodded Andrew in the stomach. "Still the same old beer-gut, Porky?" she laughed.

"Still the same old tree-trunks, Sausage?" he retorted.

Jennifer intervened. "Come on, you two. No fighting." Andrew grabbed Jennifer's arm and pulled her into the scrum at the bar. "Bring Bonnie to the wedding," Jennifer called out over her shoulder to Teresa.

Teresa looked pleased. "I'm glad she's invited you. It'll be the wedding of the season."

"How could you bear to watch her marry someone she doesn't love?"

"Bonnie, there you go again," Teresa said with some impatience. "Most girls don't marry for love. They marry for money, or to have babies, or because their parents want them to. Honestly, if anyone with the right background asked me to marry him, I'd say yes like a shot. Even if he was four-foot nine and smelt like Cyril. Mary can't marry Cyril because he's a Jew, and daddy would disinherit her. Anyway, if you're going to wait for love, you'll probably be an old maid."

"It all sounds so miserable."

It was still only October, but a winter chill could already be felt in the air. As Bonnie sat with John under a huge marquee in the Argylls' garden, she longed for a fur coat. An appalling dinner had been served and cleared away, and Bonnie was sipping champagne. These days, she allowed herself a little wine, though she was always careful to stay away from anything stronger. Awful memories of her mother were never far from her mind. She noticed that several of the men at the party and a few of the women were extremely drunk.

John, sensing her unease, fended off other invitations to her to dance. "She's not dancing with anybody else except me," he said firmly to a queue of admirers. Teresa had found Timothy, the young man with the dented fender. Timothy seemed thoroughly alarmed at being so firmly bagged by her as she became progressively more demanding and more drunk. "Come on. Get up and dance," she ordered. Bonnie wished that Teresa didn't have to bully quite so much. No wonder she has such trouble with men, Bonnie thought.

She suddenly realized that Teresa was so used to her fierce

dominating father that any other man she met she treated like a servant. "Teresa," Bonnie called out. "Give the poor man a break. You've danced him off his feet."

"All right, all right," Teresa conceded. "That only leaves me with you, my dear brother. Come on, Johnny."

John didn't dare argue. He looked at Tim. "Take care of Bonnie for me," he said.

"I will," Tim said. He looked enormously relieved. He pulled his chair up next to Bonnie. "She belongs in a rugger team, not on a dance floor," he said, mopping his forehead with a handkerchief.

"She's actually a lovely girl." Bonnie's face lit up. "Really, if you get to know her. She's not at all as tough as she makes out."

Timothy made a face. "I really don't like girls who boss a chap about. I don't know why a girl like Teresa gives a man such a hard time."

Bonnie looked at his pleasant face and thought, Well, I do. There were a lot of faces like Tim's in the crowd. Nice, well-bred, excellent manners, but dull. Many of the girls were just as vacuous. From what she had seen of England so far, she felt that the middle classes were as bland and as uninteresting as the milk pudding they had grown up on.

The evening was coming to an end. "Shall we go, Bonnie?" John said quickly, as he returned with Teresa. He helped her to her feet. The streets were empty as John drove quietly along the Embankment. Unlike the rest of his family he had not sold his expensive car when they were no longer fashionable. He owned an Alfa Romeo. The thick leather seats and the beautiful woodwork delighted Bonnie. Despite her years of poverty, Bonnie had an immediate appreciation of the sensuous, luxurious quality of well-crafted objects. She lay back and watched the wide grey river slide by. Outlined in lights, the bridges seemed to hang gracefully in the cool night air. The trees, stripped of their leaves, sighed in the slight wind.

"I have to admit," she said to John, "London really can be beautiful."

John smiled at her. "Yes. I love London, and soon I'll take you out and show you the town. But tonight I must get you back to bed. We'll be leaving for the country tomorrow at about eleven. Most of the family are going down in Mary's shooting brake. I'll take Teresa down and I was hoping to take you, if you'd like to join us."

Bonnie smiled. "If you promise not to fight with your sister, I will."

John laughed. He turned on the radio. "How about a little music? What do you like?"

"Oh, can you find something classical? I'm starved for music." Teresa had a radio in her car, but she listened only to pop tunes.

As the soothing second movement of the Brahms violin concerto played softly, Bonnie relaxed. Very soon they were at the door of the Bartholomew house. "Good night Bonnie," John said as he stood beside her on the doorstep. He pulled her gently to him and pressed his firm cool lips to hers.

"Good night, John," she said.

He's a really nice man, she thought as she got ready for bed. She remembered the warm clean smell of him. Morgan, who had been lying outside her room waiting for her, thumped his tail enthusiastically. She said her prayers and almost immediately fell asleep.

Chapter 11

It was three o'clock the next afternoon when John's car cruised through Colchester and on into Manningtree. "My, the land is so flat," Bonnie said as she looked out at the rich chocolate-coloured earth.

"In the winter the winds blow all the way from Russia," John told her. "Look." He pointed to a large cock pheasant which took to the air with a clatter of wings.

"What a gorgeous sight," Bonnie exclaimed. "Look at the blues and greens of its neck. Are those the birds you're going to kill tomorrow?"

"Yes. We shoot them during the season, which starts in October, and then we leave them alone for another year."

"I don't understand why you need to kill animals at all. You have all the food you want."

"I've thought about that a lot just recently," John said very seriously. "But I've come to a conclusion that will probably sound stupid to you."

"Try me."

"Well, it's like this. Life, when I was young, was a series of schools, then jobs, and now I'm a lawyer. I live in suits, a bowler hat, and a rolled umbrella. In the evening, we all go out dancing or to the theatre or to the cinema. It's all terribly regimented. So when I'm out in the fields with a gun in my hands, I forget about my civilized life, and I feel I am a man again, pitting myself against a hostile environment, getting food for the table to feed my family. I know it all sounds a bit silly, but does that make any sense?"

"Maybe, I don't know. But I have to admit, I do see how difficult it must be for you to feel male in a city like London, trapped in an office, shut away from everyday life. I suppose, for me, I can always know that I'm a woman, because at least I can have a child. Of course, in the old days, the Boston merchants took their sons with them when they sailed to the East, and the farms were run by the whole family. Maybe you wouldn't feel so redundant if you ran a farm."

"No, I thought about that. Our farm is run by the farm manager. There's no real farming left in this part of the country, except for some big estates or a few small-holders who farm for themselves. Actually, it's a science now. I must say, daddy refused to have battery calves, not because he's particularly soft-hearted, but because he calls that sort of farming 'new-fangled.' Anyway, you can see the farm for yourself now. If you look across the fields there, you can see the weather-vane on the hay barn."

"Oh, isn't it lovely." Bonnie suddenly saw a piece of English history rolled out before her. The long road ran between the ploughed fields. Crows nested in the bare trees. The Elizabethan manor house stood back from the road, and to its right were the farm buildings. The barns were piled high with hay. The cows stood in line waiting to be called into the shed for milking. Bonnie got out of the car and walked through the wrought-iron gates into a courtyard. "Goodness," she said to John. "I had expected a huge building."

John smiled. "No. Elizabethan farmhouses have tiny rooms and small windows. Glass was very expensive back in those days. Look at the front door. Imagine how much smaller men were then. I always have to bend my head to get into the house."

"Wait for me!" screamed Teresa who had just woken up.

Mrs. Stuart, the housekeeper, came out of the house rubbing her hands on her pinafore. "How very nice to see you," she greeted John and Teresa. She took Bonnie's hand in hers. "You must be tired, dear. I've made a pot of tea, and it's nearly four o'clock. Let's go into the kitchen."

Bonnie realized that she had not even been inside the kitchen at Hamilton Terrace. She looked at Teresa.

Teresa smiled. "Life is much less formal in the country, ever since daddy decided the socialists might shoot him as an exploiting capitalist. He got rid of almost all the servants and just kept a few. Do you remember, Winnie," she said to Mrs. Stuart, "when we had butlers and parlour maids down here? God, was it stiff!"

"Actually," John butted in, "it's not that our lot are just scared of getting shot; they've been moving all their cash out of the country as fast as they can. Daddy and his cronies think that within the next thirty years the whole economy will collapse, both here and in Europe. Everywhere will go socialist, and all their land and property will be confiscated."

Bonnie looked impressed. "Really? As bad as that?"

"Well, there'll be an attempt at a heavy right-wing leadership, but no one believes it'll work."

Teresa rolled her eyes. "You've been listening to Cyril, haven't you?"

They began to walk to the kitchen. The corridor was long and narrow, with grey flag-stones on the floor. Solid wooden doors opened off various rooms. At last they arrived at the kitchen, and Bonnie stood in the doorway amazed. The Bartholomews had installed a bright red Aga cooker and a fairly modern sink with a teak counter. Other than that, the kitchen was as it must have been for hundreds of years. A stone fireplace, big enough to stand in, housed the Aga. The fireplace was still fitted with the old iron rails and rods formerly used to hang whole oxen and sheep over the open fire. Set into the wall was a bread oven.

Bonnie was enchanted as she examined the kitchen and then the pantry. Whole Cheddars and Stiltons sat under nets. Earthenware dishes of butter cooled in pans of water; running the length of the room paraded row upon row of jams and jellies, all neatly labelled and dated. "You must put a lot of love into your work," she said to Winnie.

"I do. When my husband Dan died, I had to leave our small farm and make a choice between looking after a rich old lady in London or taking a housekeeper's job in the country. I'm glad I chose this. I can feel the history of it in my bones, and imagine the Elizabethan courtiers staying here on their way to France or Holland. You know, the family that owned this place originally were Catholics. They were dreadfully persecuted for their faith. You see that row of oaks at the end of the lawn? Well, that's where the Roundheads hanged the whole family, including the three children. Only one child survived. The gardener found him hanging, but by some miracle he wasn't dead. So the gardener took him home and hid him. They called him Simon Crookneck."

Bonnie shivered. "How awful."

Winnie smiled. "Yes, but the house's history was not always so blood-stained. In the eighteenth century it was famous for its music and for the great parties which were held here." They were interrupted by a bellowing noise from the court-yard. "Ah, the rest of the family have arrived," said Winnie. "We'd better go and welcome them. His Lordship is always in a foul mood when he's been travelling."

The noise increased as Simon Bartholomew entered the house. Margaret took Simon's arm and led him off to the study. "Come on, my dear. You're tired. Winnie has laid a nice fire for us, and she'll bring us a cup of tea and your favourite walnut cake."

Simon lowered himself into a comfortable leather armchair by the fire. The study was lined with books, mostly Victorian, many first editions. On the walls hung a couple of magnificent Stubbses. "Only man who could paint a horse decently," Simon said, as indeed he unfailingly remarked every time he entered the study.

"Yes dear," Margaret agreed.

"Only things worth painting—horses or ships. All the rest of it is muck. Just muck."

Margaret sighed. She had a treasured collection of English landscapes in London. Every so often Simon would notice them and demand that they be sold. "Why do we have pictures of cows shitting in fields?" he would say.

"They're not sh . . . I mean, you are being unfair," Margaret would remonstrate.

Now, in the study, she was occupied with keeping her husband quiet. Winnie rolled the tea-trolley into the room. "I made the raspberry jam sandwiches especially for you, my Lord," she said.

Simon grunted. He poked a thick finger into the cake. "Plenty of walnuts?" he asked, looking up at Winnie.

"As many as I could fit in," Winnie said cheerfully. She smiled at Margaret. How she puts up with him I'll never know, she thought.

Everyone was tired after the drive from London. Simon and Margaret had their dinner served in the study. The rest of the family ate in the kitchen. Jugged hare was on the menu. "I shot it myself," Mark said cheerfully.

Bonnie loved the rich dark smell coming from the cooking pot. She decided to forget any squeamishness. "Umm," she said. "This really is delicious." The meat was tender, and she could taste the wine in the sauce. "There's another taste in there that I can't identify," she said.

Teresa laughed. "We didn't tell you. The hare is always cooked in its own blood."

"Oh," Bonnie was nonplussed.

John smiled. "We're a very visceral nation behind our proper manners, you know. We eat tripe, liver, kidneys, tongue, and brains. In Scotland of course, they go too far with haggis."

Bonnie grimaced. "We certainly don't eat like that in

America. But," she smiled at Winnie, "I really do like jugged hare. Will you teach me how to make it?"

"Of course I will, dear. After the shooting's all over."

"Do we all go shooting?" Bonnie asked.

"The men shoot by themselves," Pauline explained in between her efforts to subdue her four children. "Daddy won't allow women to shoot. He says their smell puts off the animals. It's our job to hang and skin and clean everything that comes in."

"Well," said Bonnie, "I guess it's all part of my English education."

"My dear," Winnie said to Bonnie, "English cooking is at its finest when we do game. Everyone thinks there is only one dish in England."

"Roast beef and Yorkshire pudding?" Bonnie said.

Winnie nodded. "But don't worry, dear. I'm cooking that for you tomorrow. The men will be away, and I'll pack hampers for them. But I asked cook in London what I could make for you, and she told me you'd mentioned our national dish." She smiled. "I'm afraid his Lordship likes his food on the well-done side. But, tomorrow, you can have your roast beef, with the men away."

"Well, I'm not going shooting," Cyril said hurriedly. "I'm afraid your father is quite likely to shoot me accidentally on purpose."

"Francis is going," Pauline said. "And he's taking Ezra with him. Aren't you, Francis?"

Francis protested. "I don't want my son witnessing indiscriminate slaughtering at the tender age of five."

"I want to go," Ezra whined. "Grandpa says he'll give me a gun when I'm nine."

"All right, all right," Francis gave in. "You bloodthirsty little ghoul. I'll take you as long as I don't have to shoot anything."

* * *

Bonnie felt warm and content. Her bedroom was in the far-thest corner of the upstairs wing. She loved the small cosy rooms and their tiny leaded windows. Most of the chairs and sofas in the pretty little manor house were upholstered in chintz. Swags of flowers in all sorts of herbaceous-border shades gaily covered the curtains and the bedspreads. Bonnie was delighted to find that her bathroom, under the eaves with a sloping roof, was warm and the water ran hot. I really am changing, she thought, as she lay in the bath looking at the highly polished brass taps. I now have time for myself. Teresa's right. I must learn to let go. It's okay to laugh.

Bonnie was wakened in the morning by the unison crowing of several roosters. Dawn was just breaking. She leaned out of her window and smelled the sharp October air. The cold bit into her face, but she was mesmerized by the pink clouds riding high above the flat Suffolk countryside. The pigeons grumbled in their loft across the courtyard.

"Rapunzel, Rapunzel, let down your fair hair." Bonnie craned out and saw John's eager face. He wore a hairy tweed Norfolk jacket, and had a game bag over his shoulder.

"What have you got on your feet?" Bonnie asked curiously.

"Gum boots. Don't you know what gum boots are?"

"No. We don't have gum boots in America."

John looked up at her. "You look so beautiful," he said.

Bonnie smiled a deep, warm smile. "And you look magnif-icent. Wait for me in the kitchen. I'll be dressed in a minute." She threw on her jeans and a thick heavy sweater. Gumboots, she thought. I never believed there were so many differences between England and America. We don't really speak the same language, she thought, as she brushed her hair and tied it into two bunches. She was still confused by the English habit of saying a very few words to make a point. She was used to long, detailed explanations. The Bartholomews, she thought, use a sort of shorthand. Then again, they all seemed to minimize any real communication. I'll get the hang of it eventually, she comforted herself.

John was waiting for her with a hot cup of tea in his hand. "Just poured. Fresh from the pot."

Bonnie laughed. "I could get addicted to this stuff," she said.

They were all sitting round the table eating breakfast. Porridge came first, with sugar and cream. "That really tastes good," Bonnie said.

Winnie smiled. "You cook it all night on the back of the Aga." Then Winnie produced huge pans of fried sausages, tomatoes and bacon. Bonnie had never tasted an English sausage before.

"We don't have anything like this in America. They're wonderful."

Simon looked up. "Imagine a country that doesn't have a good English sausage in its larders. No sausages, no guts, I say. Look at the Eyeties. Disgusting sausages they have. Full of donkey's blood. No wonder you never see their faces, only their behinds, always running away from something. And as for the Germans. . . ."

Margaret put her hand on his shoulder. "Don't upset yourself before you shoot, dear. Remember it ruins your aim."

Simon looked sheepishly at his wife. "You're quite right." He patted her hand which rested on his shoulder. "Thank you." Cyril looked startled. Simon smiled at Cyril. "I can, when I feel like it, be perfectly charming. That's why Margaret married me. But some men don't have enough charm to get a gel to marry them. Do they?"

"It's not like that, daddy," Mary interrupted.

Simon would not be interrupted. He had Cyril on a hook and he was not about to let him off. "Shooting with us, lad?"

Cyril looked tortured. "Well, actually, I . . . uh . . ."

"If you can't shoot, at least you can help the beaters. Can't have you sitting in my house eating all that food without you earning your keep, can we?"

Cyril knew he was defeated. "All right."

The beaters by now had gathered outside the kitchen door. They were local men and their sons, men who had been shooting with the family all their lives, like their grandfathers and their great-grandfathers. Each generation of Bartholomew boys would have grown up with the sons of local farmers and traders. Those links forged in the early years remained strong to maturity.

Luke had already joined the beaters and was busy catching up on the various births and deaths among his friends. The last drop of tea tipped from the teapot, and the last thick slab of toast consumed, everyone went outside.

John invited Bonnie to walk to the end of the first field. "This isn't a formal shoot at all. We carry our own game, and at the end we share what we bag with the beaters. Lovely day for it, don't you think?"

Bonnie nodded. "Well, I suppose so."

The beaters moved rapidly ahead of the guns. "They'll all fan out ahead of us," John explained, "and to the side. We wait for the hares and rabbits to break cover, or for the birds to go over. We'll all move in the direction of the Percies' land, and join up with them there."

Bonnie was suddenly very conscious of the maleness of this world. The other women were back in the kitchen. The men were entirely at home among themselves. Even Lord Bartholomew seemed less like a spoiled child in the company of his fellows. He was joking and laughing with Matthew. The beaters were silent, but the others were relaxed and happy in the pale morning air. "I must go back now," Bonnie said as they reached the gate at the end of the field.

"I'll miss spending the day with you."

Bonnie blushed. "You'll be home for dinner. I'm going to help Winnie cook it."

"That'll be lovely. Tell Winnie we must have game soup. Goodbye, Bonnie." John opened the gate and walked into the next field. He turned to wave. Bonnie watched him walk off to join the other men with his gun over his shoulder. Gumboots, she thought. He does look nice in them.

The day seemed to pass in a flash as Bonnie became totally immersed in Winnie's preparations for the evening. Then, suddenly, they were back, Mark and his father first, and then the rest of the shooting party.

Bonnie stood by the Aga and watched as they deposited the rabbits and the birds in a heap on the kitchen table. The men were red with exertion, and their fingers numb from the cold. They stamped their feet to bring the blood back into their frozen legs. They were all laughing and talking.

Suddenly, much as the sight of the bleeding animals revolted her, Bonnie had a flash of understanding. John was right. For this single moment they were doing something useful for women. Displaying their skill as hunters, they had brought meat for the table. Once, that would have meant the difference between life and death for a family. Even now it meant full bellies for the manor and the village for the next month. At least they had not been reduced to cardboard figures working in offices.

Lord Bartholomew was in a mellow mood. "What's for pudding?" he bellowed at Winnie, his large face purple from the wind.

"Bread and butter pudding," she said.

"I knew it!" he said, delighted. "I knew it all along. I smelled it on the wind. Where's Margaret?"

"I'm here, dear," she said. "Come. Let's get those boots off." They left the room arm in arm.

Winnie laughed. She looked at Bonnie. "I don't know. Sometimes I think he's impossible, and other times he's a darling. Men!"

Bonnie was amused. John was looking at her intently from across the room. "Did you miss me?" he said in the general hubbub.

Bonnie was too shy to answer his question in front of everyone else. The truth was she hadn't thought about him all day. She just smiled at him and busied herself with the plates.

Dinner was a protracted affair. Most of the conversation centered on shooting. Cyril, who had managed to sit himself next to Bonnie, was most upset. "Bloody disgusting way to spend a weekend, upended in a gorse bush. The old fool would have blown my head off. I caught the look in his mean red eyes when he sent me off with the beaters. 'Thought he was a rabbit,' he'd tell the magistrate. Then they'd go off and have a drink together while I lay starkers in the morgue. I tell you I don't trust him an inch."

"He's not that bad, Cyril," Bonnie defended. "He just lives in a different world from us."

"There's too many like him."

"Don't, Cyril." Bonnie had suddenly caught Teresa's eye. Teresa put her fingers to her lips and pushed them into an exaggerated smile. "I know the world isn't perfect, but can't you just enjoy tonight? The food is lovely, and look at those marvellous candles in the candelabra. I could sit here among the plates and the paintings with that fire in the grate and thank God. Don't." She put her hand up to forestall Cyril, who was about to mention all those who weren't so lucky. "Just don't. Be happy for now. I'm trying very hard to remember that rule at all times, and you should too."

Cyril, frustrated, turned his back on her and began a conversation with Ann. He was currently worried that lower air fares were a government plot to seduce the masses to enjoy hot beaches and cheap wine in Spain and Italy, thereby taking their minds off the serious business of the coming social revolution.

Everyone was talking. Bonnie looked around the table. Everyone but John. He stared at her so intensely that she blushed. "John," she said. "Why are you staring?"

John blinked at her from the far end of the table. "Because you're so beautiful," he said loudly. There was an immediate silence. Everyone stared at Bonnie.

"That's my boy," Simon boomed. "Straight and to the point. You've got yourself a love-sick swain, Bonnie."

Bonnie panicked. "I'll go and help Winnie," she said, hurriedly rising from the table. She ignored John as she headed for the kitchen.

"What's the matter?" Winnie looked at Bonnie's flushed face. "You look upset. Here, take a tea towel. There's nothing like drying plates to calm you down. But don't throw them around like Teresa."

Bonnie sniffed. "I just don't want the complication of a man at the moment. At least in college I could lock myself away with my books. But, in a family like this, there's no hiding."

"It's John you're talking about, isn't it?" Winnie asked. "I've noticed the way he looks at you. He's a wonderful man, Bonnie. You could do worse."

Bonnie frowned. "Winnie, all my life I've listened to women who said exactly that. 'I could do worse. At least he's not this or at least he's not that.' Honestly, you know, that's not good enough."

Winnie stopped washing the plate and rested her soapy hand on the rim of the sink. "I felt like that about Dan in the beginning. He was kind and he loved me. He was very shy. He'd been through the First World War, and there were very few men around. I didn't honestly love him then. Not that sort of throbbing ecstasy sort of love. All that came later. Maybe that is how it should be. Love at first sight is probably an illusion and downright dangerous. You see only the things you want to see."

Bonnie looked at Winnie. "But I do want to feel . . . I have never allowed myself to feel anything much at all. I want to feel alive. I want passion in my life. I want to be totally committed to a man and to love him like I loved my father. For better or for worse." She sighed. "He left me, you know."

Winnie put her hand on Bonnie's shoulder. "I'm sorry, my dear."

"I would never have left him. Never." Her voice was strained.

Winnie nodded. "I don't suppose you would have," she said. "But, with John, you would never have to worry. He would always love you."

Bonnie suddenly looked seriously at Winnie. "I know. I can feel that. But John doesn't need me. I mean not the way I need to be needed."

"Needing doesn't make for loving," Winnie began. Then she stopped herself. She decided not to argue. She had no idea that an important part of Bonnie's character had been formed by her father's need for his daughter to fill his lonely heart. To be needed, for Bonnie, was to be loved. "I tell you what. Why don't you let me have a word with John? I can explain to him that you need time to settle down. He'll understand."

Bonnie nodded. "Thank you, Winnie. Thanks a lot." She finished drying the pile of plates, and she helped Winnie slop massive chunks of bread and butter pudding into bowls.

"Please tell Margaret I'm sorry, but I'm really too tired, and I'm off to bed."

Winnie smiled. "You don't have to worry. When you're in the country, it's all much more relaxed. She'll understand."

Bonnie climbed the stairs to her room. She took out her cheque-book and wrote out a cheque for one thousand pounds. That should help mom out, she thought. She wrote a note to her mother to send along with the cheque. "I can send you the same amount monthly. My allowance is far bigger than I need. So we can split it in half." She lay awake for a while feeling guilty because she knew Augustine would not approve. Well, she *is* my mom, Bonnie thought.

The cars all left for London after breakfast on Monday. "Doesn't everybody have to be at work?" Bonnie was puzzled.

"I do," Cyril said bitterly. "I'm supposed to clock in at nine o'clock. Now I'll have to take a day of my holidays."

"Oh, I say. Bad luck, old chap." Luke was the most sympathetic of the four boys. "But one can't really expect to be in town much before noon on a Monday, not if a chap is shooting or sailing. After all, which comes first?"

Cyril shot him a furious look. "Most people don't get a choice."

Luke beamed. Leaning over Cyril, he said very slowly, as if talking to a child, "Exactly. We are not most people."

Cyril flushed. Mary pulled his arm. "Don't even try to argue with Luke, Cyril," said Mary. "You'll end up bursting a blood vessel. He believes God lives at Lord's, and when He's not there, He's at the Royal Yacht Club. Come on. Let's get daddy settled in the car."

Bonnie was packed and ready to leave when she remembered to say goodbye to Winnie. "Thank you for my first weekend in England."

Winnie was touched by the child in the woman. "Bonnie, do try and be less romantic about everything."

Bonnie nodded. "I will, Winnie." She kissed her on the cheek. "Can I come down any time I want?"

"Yes, dear. Just ask Margaret and give me a ring."

"Thank you." Bonnie ran to the car.

John had already started the engine. On the way back to London he placed his left hand on Bonnie's. "Look. I don't want to push you. Win did have a word with me." Bonnie hung her head. John continued. "Let's just take it easy and be friends. Maybe something will come of it, maybe not. Even if it doesn't, either way, I will always be your friend."

Bonnie smiled. "Thank you, John."

"That's all right," he said with a catch in his throat.

Chapter 12

Augustine missed her granddaughter dreadfully. She relied very much on Morag for the girl's high spirits and Morag's will to learn brought out the teacher in Augustine. But she often thought she heard Bonnie's step or caught the sight of her blonde hair flash by the window. Sometimes she imagined that she saw her in the rocking chair by the fire, where they would both read or talk together.

In Merrill, Laura was thrilled with the money Bonnie had sent her. Now she could really contribute to the church funds in a way that would make Father John a lot more aware of her. She watched the look on his face when she told him her daughter was living with an English noble family. It was a curious look, a flash of envy followed by a greedy stare. "Are they very rich?" he asked.

"Yes," Laura nodded. "All the English aristocrats are loaded," she said with sublime ignorance.

He nodded. "Well, Mrs Fraser, I hope your daughter will be very happy."

Father John digested this bit of news in his rectory on Terminus Road. Well, well, he thought. Little Bonnie Fraser with her bright eyes and long legs might make it into the big time. Maybe, it'll be worth my while to put up with her dreadful mother. He wandered into the bleak little dining-room and looked at the brown-stained walls. If she does marry well, she'll probably support her mother. The thought welled up, but did not pass his lips. Her mother will probably keep me, and then, if I can get her to contribute enough money to the church, the Bishop will send me to Rome. I can work at the Vatican and make myself indispensable to some Cardinal. His future suddenly looked less bleak.

His aunt Eileen who had survived his mother and now kept house for him, barged into the room carrying a large bowl of stew. She was a fat Irish woman with a mop of grey hair. She exuded an overpowering smell of sweat mingled with grease. "And what might you be smiling about?" she said, slamming the soup down on the table so hard that it slopped over the sides.

Father John refrained from wrinkling his nose in disgust. The soup, supposedly "Irish stew," had lumps of unidentified matter swimming about in a thin gruel covered with a film of fat. "Things are looking up at last," he said, smiling at her.

"Thanks be to God." She piously clasped her hands.

"No, not God," he murmured as she left the room. "Thanks be to Mrs. Laura Fraser and her hideous confessions." He spent the rest of the meal imagining the little room decorated in Italian gold and marble. In his mind, he sat on an elegant Louis XIV dining chair. The table before him was onyx inlaid with mother of pearl. The bowl was fashioned from translucent jade from China. The spoon, heavily carved, was part of the set brought from France at the time of the French Revolution. He could see it all now. Perspiration formed on his upper lip. Never a priest by choice, he now made his choice, his vocation, which he would pursue under the guise of his clean black robes. He too, like so many other priests before him, chose wealth and political power above God.

* * *

Laura was quite surprised to find Father John so attentive during her next confession. "And what happened then?" he said. "Oh . . ." Laura was confused. She hadn't expected him to be quite so interested. Usually he cut her off at this point, absolved her, and gave her a penance. "Well, he beat me."

"How did he beat you?"

"With a cane with split ends," she rapidly improvised. "Blood seeped down my back. I could feel it soaking my clothes. I begged him to stop. He refused."

"Yes. Go on, my child."

"Then he . . ." Laura sank deeply into her fantasy. "Then he pulled down my pants and he took me so hard that I fainted. When I came to, I was on the floor covered in blood. He'd left by the window. I could tell because it was open."

Father John felt tired. Where she gets all this stuff from I don't know, he thought. He absolved her and waited for her to leave.

"Father," Laura said quietly. "This money has come from my daughter, and I want you to have it. I have enough money for my humble needs." She slid the envelope under the grille.

Father John took the envelope into his hands. He lifted the flap. He saw the thick load of dollar bills. He could hear Laura fidgeting on the other side of the confessional. He hesitated for a moment. Then, without any trace of emotion, he said, "Thank you, my child. Your virtue will be rewarded in heaven."

Oh no it won't, Laura thought. My virtue will be rewarded much sooner than that. She walked out into the bright sunlight a very happy woman.

Father John counted out the money. It amounted to over two thousand dollars in cash. Well, he thought, this is going to be easier than I thought. After mass the next day he went to a bank across town, dressed in the grey business suit he had bought for the occasion. He opened an account in the name of James O'Mally.

He had enjoyed his little excursion into evil. He was alive. The world around him busied itself with the doings of the day, but Father John felt omnipotent. His hold over Laura gave him her money which, in turn, would give him power. He stopped at a restaurant for lunch. He chose the best in the neighbourhood. He ordered a steak and a bottle of their most expensive red wine. He would begin to learn how to live like a Roman Cardinal.

Chapter 13

Bonnie found life at Hamilton Terrace hard to bear. Simon's irascible temper kept the family in a constant state of tension. John, sensing the difficulty Bonnie had in coping with the atmosphere in the house, offered to take her out to dinner. The idea of eating out was still a thrill for Bonnie, for she had previously had such limited exposure to restaurants. Augustine very rarely went out to dine. She preferred not to spend her money at a restaurant when the food tasted better at home. Bonnie's friends at Brown had little money to spend on eating out. Her experience had been largely in hamburger joints.

Le Cadeau quickly became Bonnie's favourite place in London. Here the little tables were laid with pink check cloths. Each table had blue cornflowers in a cut-glass vase. The fresh innocence of the pink and the blue belied the sophistication of the food. The head waiter, seeing Bonnie's excitement on her first visit, resolved to make her evening an unforgettable experience. Besides, John was a special favourite of his. "But," he shook his head, "'ow beautiful. She is like a swan." He remembered the river at Avignon, his home town. He pulled himself together. "Do you order now?" he asked John in English seasoned with a soft French accent.

John smiled. "What do you recommend today, Pierre?"

Pierre tore his eyes away from Bonnie's slender form in its pale grey satin dress. The small emerald earrings caused a sea-change in the blue of her eyes. "I 'ave sea urchins in a champagne sauce," he suggested, "and today the salmon is perfect."

John smiled at Bonnie. "Want to try sea urchins?"

Bonnie nodded. "And I like the sound of the salmon."

"From Scotland," Pierre added. "Flown in this morning. 'Ow would you like it cooked?"

John thought for a moment. "Poached in white wine, please." John looked at Bonnie. "Would you like to try a *sauce verte?*"

"I'd love that," Bonnie said. John nodded to Pierre.

"Bon," he said. "I will 'ave the wine waiter come to your table." He went off into the kitchen with their order.

"Oh John," Bonnie said, grinning impishly. "I can't tell you what a relief this is after cook's efforts."

"I can't tell you what a relief it is to find a woman who is prepared to eat. I'm used to taking women out who order salad and a glass of mineral water."

Bonnie laughed. "I don't have to worry about weight, but even if I did I'd rather be fat than do without food. My grandmother says good food outlasts all other pleasures." She reached for the bread.

"What about wine?"

Bonnie wrinkled her nose. "I'm not much of an expert on wine. My mother drank so much, I decided never to touch the stuff. But recently my grandmother has been introducing me to different bottles. I do like a fairly fruity wine."

"All right then." John caught the wine waiter's eye. "This

looks like a nice Hermitage Blanc," he said, pointing to the wine list.

"Mais oui. Certainement," the wine waiter said as he took the wine list from John's hand. "I will chill a bottle for you immediately."

Bonnie relaxed and looked around her. The other diners in the room were deep in conversation. Bonnie watched one couple gazing fixedly into each other's eyes. They murmured to each other. So entranced were they that their food lay untouched on their plates. She could see that a bubble of golden happiness held them suspended in the middle of the crowded restaurant. An invisible band of joy kept their table aloof from the clatter of plates and the clinking of glasses. "Bonnie?" John's voice broke her reverie. "What's the matter? You look so wistful, like a child who's lost something."

Bonnie sighed. "No, I haven't lost anything, John. I've just never found anything. Not what I'm looking for, anyway."

"And what are you looking for, Bonnie?" He took her hand.

"I can't explain, but I'll know when I find it. All my life, I've been waiting for this feeling to come over me. I looked for it everywhere, in everyone. But the feeling never came. I always felt I was in a glass bubble that needed the vibration of this feeling to shatter my prison, and then I could leap out and dance for joy." Bonnie spoke with great intensity. Her voice rose and the other diners stopped talking. "People don't live life at all," she went on. "They walk around with their eyes shut, just bumping into each other." She shook her head. "I want to live with my eyes open. I want to live every electric, exciting moment. I want to live so intensely that I might die of it. I won't be satisfied with anything less."

John, sucked for a moment into her reality, forgot his normal reticence. "Moths, attracted to the fierce flames, die."

Bonnie nodded. "But at least, for one short moment, they lived gloriously." She stopped. She was suddenly aware that everyone was watching her. "I don't know what is happening to me. I seem to be a different person these days." The rest of the room reverted to its individual conversations.

A pale woman in the far corner, dining with a handsome man with narrow eyes and a small clipped black moustache, shook her head. Under her expensive jersey-dress, she had three broken ribs. She looked across the table at her husband. "A moth to a flame," she said.

He smiled thinly. "You have only yourself to blame. You married me. You should have listened to your mother."

The woman looked down at her plate. I remember when I looked like that girl, she thought, when I looked for a love that would consume me. She winced as she shifted in her chair.

"Shall we go, my dear?" her husband said. He courteously offered her his arm. Bonnie didn't see the sad look the woman gave her as she left the restaurant.

Pierre arrived with Bonnie and John's first course. "I'm sorry, we 'ave been a little be'ind with the sea urchins. We keep them alive until they are cooked, and it takes time to extract them from their shells. One must eat them absolutely fresh, or they taste of nothing. I 'ope you will enjoy them."

Bonnie looked down at the pink fleshy morsels in their pale sauce. She had recovered herself. She was now calm and practical. She and John both ate in silence. The dish was extraordinary. The champagne and the sea urchins created a taste which Bonnie found impossible to compare to anything she had eaten before. "Sort of like catching the sea in your mouth, with a sunbeam running through it," she said to John.

John nodded. "I'm afraid I'm a bit prosaic," he said, "but I love coming here. And I love being with you. But don't let that make you look so anxious," he reassured her. "I promise I'm not making a pass. I'm beginning to recognize that I'm not the man for you. I can't live all the time with the amount of intensity that you were talking about. Only occasionally,

I'm afraid. But," he looked at Bonnie very seriously, "I'll always be there for you. Never forget that, will you?"

Bonnie nodded. "Thank you, John. It's nice to know that."

Pierre cleared away their plates. "The salmon," he said. He lifted the silver lid and there, on a bed of parsley, outlined by thin slices of cucumber, lay the most perfect fish Bonnie had ever seen. It looked as if it had spent its whole life waiting for this one moment. Pierre cut two steaks from the middle of the fish and then two smaller steaks from the tail. Noticing Bonnie's surprise, he smiled. "Most people think the middle of the fish is the best. And in some ways it is. But the tail section is where the fat lies. Too much, and it can taste 'eavy and oily, so we give our customers some of each. The best of both worlds."

"You see, Bonnie," John said as he watched Pierre slice the fish, "between Winnie and Pierre, I have become something of a gourmet."

"Thank God for that," Bonnie laughed. "Without you, I would have to endure nothing but those meals at your parents' house. Was your father always so bad-tempered?"

John wrinkled his brow. "Well, that's how English gentlemen are trained to behave. Sort of 'threaten to huff and puff and blow the house down,' if he doesn't get what he wants. But, actually, mummy really rules the roost." Bonnie looked surprised. "It's true," John continued. "All of us, at one time or another, have rebelled against daddy. But I don't remember anyone ever really having a fight with mummy, not even Teresa. I know Teresa will argue occasionally, but if mummy puts her foot down in earnest, then that's it. She wins. You watch closely next time daddy's ranting. He gets himself worked up into a dreadful state, but he always has one eye on mummy. If she stares at him in a certain way, he stops immediately. He doesn't stop for anything else, not even German tanks during the war, but he worships mummy. He treasures the ground she walks on. Mind you, he'd die rather than admit it. I once caught him holding her hand in the garden at Suffolk. When he saw me, he went bright red, and screamed at me for a week."

Bonnie smiled. "I'm so glad you told me all that. I remember such awful scenes between my mother and my father, that I get frightened when people shout."

"Don't be frightened of daddy. He really has a heart of gold. His childhood was horribly bleak, and I think that made it difficult for him to show his feelings. He likes to be like his friends. They all sit in their clubs and pretend they are crusty bad-tempered old gentlemen. But just remember, in spite of the act, most of them are heads of great business empires, or professional. Daddy got a good degree from Oxford, so he's not nearly as thick as he pretends he is."

"Wednesday is deliberately avoiding me." Teresa stood on a chair while Bonnie pinned the hem of her new dress.

"Don't be silly," said Bonnie. "Only three more days, and he'll be there."

Teresa looked down at Bonnie's up-turned face. "Angus is thirty-two, you know I don't think he's ever been serious about a woman in his life."

"Maybe he doesn't like women all that much," Bonnie said through lips which were tightly holding on to the pins. "My grandmother doesn't like men. She says the only two men worth talking to were her father and her son."

"There's supposed to be something wrong with Angus's father. He's locked away in the family place in Scotland. Angela says the old man has two male nurses with him all the time. He's supposed to be quite gaga."

Bonnie shivered. "God, how awful. I always heard that the aristocracy locked its family problems away in dungeons, but I never really believed it."

"Oh yes," Teresa said airily. "And not only in dungeons. We used to stick them away where they couldn't be seen or heard, but now we mostly put them away in National Health wards. This way it doesn't cost us anything." Bonnie thought she was joking. "No, I'm serious," Teresa said. "You look at my friend Martha. She's from a fabulously rich family, but she's anorexic. That makes her a nuisance to her whole family. So they all had a family conference and decided to incarcerate her. They bribed the pyschiatrist, and bingo, she's in St. Pat's and they're free of the problem."

"That's horribly cruel."

Teresa nodded. "Yes, it is, but you must remember that, if you belong to a family like ours, you are expected to conform. If you break the rules, they'll never forgive you. Never. If you marry, and if that marriage is rotten, you won't hear anyone complain. It's just not done. You make your bed and you lie on it. That's how it works here."

"Well, it means that, when you choose a man, you know that it will be a life-time commitment," Bonnie said.

"I know. When Jane Stornaway tried to get a legal separation from her husband, not only did she end up losing her children, but no one would invite her to their house. Not because of the separation, but because she broke the rules. The major rule is that everything in the garden is perfect, and nobody admits that in a perfect garden a slug can exist. You should have seen Rodney Stornaway. He was a huge fat slimy slug of the first water. Ugh."

"Stand still," Bonnie commanded. "There." She put the last pin into the hem. "Get down and take a look."

Teresa took a flying leap off the chair and crashed in a heap on the carpet. The floor shook under her fall. Seconds later Simon Bartholomew stood panting in the doorway. "Teresa!" he roared. "What the . . ." he stopped. "Teresa?" he said uncertainly.

She smiled at him. "Do you like my dress, daddy?" She turned slowly so that the full skirt caught the breeze from the open door and lifted slightly. Bonnie had combed Teresa's hair high on her head. She had captured the thick black mane in a net of gold mesh. The dress left Teresa's shoulders bare. Her creamy white skin contrasted with the heat of the red and gold silk. The dress was caught in at Teresa's waist, which was surprisingly slim, and then fell in graceful folds to her feet.

"Good heavens." Simon cleared his throat and walked towards his daughter. "For a moment, I thought you were mummy all those years ago." He took her hand. His eyes were full of tears. "She was so lovely when she was a young gel . . ." He suddenly pulled himself together.

"Bonnie made the dress for me," Teresa said.

"Well," Simon snorted, "that probably saved a bob or two." He looked at them both. "Don't crash about like elephants when I'm trying to sleep in the library."

"We won't, daddy." Teresa kissed him on the cheek.

Alarmed, Simon started for the door. "Good heavens, child. Don't start all that." He escaped back to his sanctuary.

Bonnie shook her head. "He is soft underneath," she said. She smiled.

Bonnie was putting the final touches to her brocade dress two hours before they were due to leave for the Seabornes' party. "Do I have to go?" she asked Teresa.

"Yes, you do. I need you to hold my hand and to kick me if I start to get too noisy." Teresa was adamant.

"Well, if you're doing okay, could I get John to take me home early? Otherwise, I'll fall flat on my face and ruin your chances. Your Angus will think I'm a genetic disaster from America, and you've probably picked up some horrible recessive gene from me. That kind of mutant damage will ruin his hopes of having a son, and then where will you be, huh?"

Teresa laughed. "A couple of weeks in London, and you're fun to be with. Not like the stick in the mud you were when you came."

Bonnie looked at herself in the cheval mirror in Teresa's

bedroom. Despite the dark lines of fatigue under her eyes, she did seem somehow less detached from the flow of life. She wore the simple white dress that she had made, with a small baguette diamond at her throat. She looked at the high arch of her foot encased in gold high-heeled sandals. "I'm losing my tan," she remarked.

Teresa looked at her. "You'll always look lovely, whatever you do. You were just born that way."

Bonnie hugged her. "Everyone's born beautiful. It's all inside you. Some just start with more luck than others. Anyway," Bonnie reminded Teresa as they went downstairs, "tonight is your big night."

"Oh God, I hope so," said Teresa as she flung herself into her car. "Do I really look nice, Bonnie? Honestly."

"You do, Teresa," Bonnie reassured her. "Really. Just remember to walk slowly, and don't shout. If he asks you to dance, let him lead. Don't shove him around."

Teresa nodded. "I promise."

"Okay. I'll be watching you. And, if I tap you on the shoulder, that means you're talking too loud."

"All right. God! I am so nervous I could die."

The house in Cadogan Square took Bonnie by surprise. Maids in black dresses and mob-caps were taking coats from the guests. Footmen stood formally in two lines up the great marbled hall, with its gigantic pillars and painted ceiling decorated with gold leaf. On the first landing two ornate doors opened into a massive ballroom.

"I didn't realize the Seabornes would be giving such a sumptuous party," Bonnie whispered.

"Oh yes," Teresa said. "It's the party of the year. I forgot to tell you, Angela's mother isn't English, you know. Lady Seaborne's father was a rag merchant worth millions. Awful scandal. She's Jewish. Lord Seaborne let everybody down by marrying her, you know."

Bonnie frowned. "Well, how do you think *her* father must have felt, with his daughter marrying a Gentile."

Teresa looked at her. "It's funny you should mention that. It was quite amazing. Her people made the most awful fuss. Here she was marrying practically into the Royal Family, and this little nobody of a father called the Seabornes rude names."

Bonnie was delighted. She threw back her head and laughed. "They probably called them *goyim.*" She remembered Mitzi's mother.

As their names were called, Bonnie just had time to see a tall man with thick curly black hair standing talking to an elderly lady by the fireplace. A jolt of electricity shot through her. Her hands tingled and her legs went numb. Oh, my God! I've seen him, she thought. He's here.

"Miss Teresa Bartholomew and Miss Bonnie Fraser," the major-domo bellowed across the room.

"Come on, Bonnie," Teresa muttered impatiently, as Bonnie stood immobilized, staring from the doorway. "Come on. We've got to shake hands."

Bonnie nodded dumbly. She shook hands with Lady Seaborne.

"Teresa," Bonnie whispered, "I've seen him."

"Who?"

"The man I've been waiting for all my life. He's here. I can't believe it." Bonnie was shaking.

"Hey, are you all right? You look as if you're going to faint. Hang on. Let's go and sit down." Teresa led Bonnie slowly through the throng. Bonnie was looking for the man. Suddenly Teresa squeezed her arm. "Look." Teresa nodded her head to the right. "That's Angus." He was the man she had seen from the doorway. Teresa's face was alight with joy. "Angus!" she called. Bonnie stayed back as Teresa surged forward into the crowd. She returned with Angus by her side.

"Angus, I want you to meet my cousin Bonnie Fraser from Boston."

Angus held out his hand. Bonnie looked down and hesitated. Then she held out her own. Bonnie stared into his eyes. They reminded her of two cigarette burns set in his white face. She looked deep into his black eyes, and was lost. She had never felt like this about any man in her life. Angus's hot gaze immediately reminded her of her father. The ache in her heart for the loss all those years ago was now replaced by the pain at the knowledge that Angus belonged to Teresa. Bonnie knew she could not betray her friend.

Angus stared at Bonnie. Apart from treasuring a vision of his mother, he had never felt the wish to possess forever any of the women in his life. For the first time ever, he felt a need not only to possess a woman, but also to absorb her into his dark and troubled soul, the soul of a man "past any human redemption." He remembered those words now. They had been spoken by the madam of a whore-house in Rome. There had been a fight, a man had died. She had cursed Angus as he left.

"Aren't you two going to say hello?" Teresa was puzzled. Both of them stood silently gazing into each other's souls.

"Well, well. What have we here?" John had joined the little group with his sister Ann. He was less than pleased to see Angus staring at Bonnie. He put his arm protectively around her shoulders. Bonnie, distracted by John's manner, turned and gave him a lost, bemused smile. She felt she had been on a long journey in that split second. She had lost her soul forever to another human being. She felt an empty hollowness that could only be filled by her possessor. Unseen to the people about them both, a thin cord connected them invisibly. John was impatient to get Bonnie away. He tugged at her arm, "I want you to meet Sacheverell. He's a good friend of mine and an excellent designer. Come on. Don't day-dream!"

Bonnie turned to go. She could not betray Teresa. She

knew that, if she stayed, Angus would ask her to dance, and then, she felt with a strange shudder of pleasure, all would be lost. She thought, my life as Bonnie Fraser from Merrill, Pennsylvania, would be over. As she walked away from her happiness, she glanced over her shoulder. Teresa had moved in front of Angus, but Bonnie could see his face. He was smiling directly at Bonnie. Her last memory was of his radiant smile disfigured by one chipped front tooth. She saw again the utter despair in his bleak black eyes. She had to discipline herself not to run back and to cradle his head in her arms.

"John," she said, as they walked away, "do you mind if I ask you to take me home?"

"No, not at all. I'll dump Ann on Sacheverell and we'll go."

Sacheverell was tiny and sandy-haired. "John, darling," he squealed. "How lovely to see you. Let's get plastered." He waved frantically at a passing waiter. "Bring champagne!" he ordered imperiously.

"No, I've got to take Bonnie home. She's not feeling well."

Sacheverell's gaze rested on Bonnie's face. "Ah, a woman crossed in love. What an illness," he said, taking Bonnie's hand. "You stick to John and you won't come to any harm."
Bonnie blushed. Ann, who had been following them, laughed. "Mark my words," Sacheverell continued portentously, "you have the look of a woman who has sold her soul to the devil."

"Hey," John put his hand up. "She's only just met Angus for the first time."

"Angus Macpherson? Well, this is more serious than I had anticipated. Bonnie, my dear, that man *is* the very devil. Believe you me." He shook his head. "Many is the time I've comforted a woman dying of love for that man." His gaze was sombre. "Take the advice of a morally corrupt degenerate like myself: stay away from him."

Bonnie smiled. "You don't have to worry. Teresa's after him."

John snorted. "She's not his type. He goes for the young

and innocent. Anyway, let's get you home. Take care of Ann for me, will you, Sacheverell? Thanks a lot."

On the drive home, John was very serious. "Look, Bonnie. I don't mind Teresa chasing Angus, because he's not going to be interested in her. But you're just the sort of woman he loves. I'm two years younger than him, but he was at St. Gregory's at the same time as me. He was dreadfully wild. Most of us fought back if we had to defend ourselves. But it was different with Angus." John shook his head. "He didn't seem to feel pain. And it wasn't just that. He was with the local girls from the time he was thirteen. I think there was some rumour that his father had done something so horrific that the rest of the MacPhersons took Angus away from Drummossie Castle. After that, Angus lived with his aunt and uncle in London."

Bonnie felt suspended in time, incapable of sensation, except that, even though the car was now miles away from the brightly lit house in Cadogan Square and from the man whose black burning eyes had seen and taken her soul, she could feel the tightness of the invisible cord pulling gently but insistently at her heart. "Maybe he just needs love," she said seriously. "Teresa said that Angus didn't have a mother."

John nodded. "No, he didn't. She's supposed to have died in a hunting accident, but then again some people think she was murdered by old MacPherson. I believe it, too. Apparently he's capable of doing something like that. I saw him once at the Braemar Games." And John shuddered.

Bonnie looked at him. "I wonder if Angus is afraid he'll end up like his father."

"Well, the way he's going, there's every chance that he will." He laughed a short nervous laugh. "No, I mustn't make Angus out to be too bad, or you'll start feeling sorry for him."

"I already do," Bonnie said. "I really do feel sorry for someone like that." What he needs, she thought, is a woman who can take away the pain in his eyes. She didn't consider it possible that she could be that woman. "Let's hope Teresa can help him," she said.

John laughed again. "Just let Teresa try throwing a punch at him. He'll hit her straight back." He shook his head. "Angus is not above hitting women, you know."

Bonnie was shocked. "I can't imagine he'd ever hit a woman unless she provoked him. I mean I never saw my father hit my mother, but she really knew how to push him. And, if she had been married to a man with less self-control, then she would have been hit, and she'd have deserved it too."

John parked outside the house in Hamilton Terrace. "No, Bonnie. That's not right. No man should ever hit a woman under any circumstance. A man always has a choice. You can lash out or you can get out."

Bonnie shook her head. "You don't know my mother."

"No I don't. And from what you've told me your father must have put up with an amazing amount from her, but it still would never have been right if he had hit her. Anyway," John took her by the shoulders and kissed her gently on her forehead, "here you are home. You get to sleep and forget all about the Angus MacPhersons of this world."

"Thank you for bringing me back." Bonnie patted John's arm. "I am grateful."

"Good night. I'll see you on Friday. I've promised Winnie we'll be in Suffolk by eight in time for dinner." John smiled. "I'm really looking forward to that—a weekend on our own without the family."

"That'll be lovely." Bonnie smiled and went upstairs to her room. She shut the door behind her and then she took a deep breath. If I breathe slowly and evenly, she said to herself, maybe the trembling will go away. She put her hand on her chest and gently massaged herself. For a moment the gesture soothed her, but then the fluttering was back again. She felt as if a small bird were trapped in her throat. She walked over to her bed and lay down. But her restlessness refused to go.

She got off the bed, she paced up and down. She sat at her dressing table. She began to remember Angus as he had smiled at her over Teresa's shoulder. First she remembered the chip on his front tooth. I bet that was from playing football, she thought. Then she remembered his eyes. I could make them gentle, she thought, imagining herself kissing each eyelid. Then there was his mouth, full, with the corners that tilted down. Just like a small boy when he can't get what he wants. I could give him everything he needs, and then those corners would curl upwards. She imagined kissing those corners until they lifted.

She remembered how his thick black hair sat on his head, and how the blackness was abruptly broken by the whiteness of his skin. She could see herself stroking his impatient head until he lay calm in her arms. Then she remembered his long slim fingers as they had taken her hand. She had glanced down at his strong fingers and had noticed the fine black hair that lay on the back of the hand. She thought of his slim body lying beside her on the bed. His body would be alabaster white, and the hair under his arms and across his belly would be thick and black.

Bonnie had never felt such a surge of longing, such a need to be held by a man. "No other man has existed or ever will exist again for me," she whispered. "Only him. Only Angus. Dear God," she prayed, "let me have this man. Let me marry Angus MacPherson. I promise you I'll love him forever. He'll never know an unhappy day in his life with me. I know I can make him happy, dear God. Please let me marry him."

She was praying so intensely that she jumped as a roll of thunder shook the house. She leapt to her feet and ran to the window. She threw open the shutters and leaned out as far as she could. The rain was rushing down in large fat bullets. The drops exploded on the street below her. She stretched out her arms and cried, "I hope that this means 'Yes.'" A jagged fork of lightning seemed to bounce on the roof of the house opposite.

Chapter 14

After breakfast the next morning, a messenger delivered a long cardboard box. "For you, Miss Fraser," Johnson said. Wonderingly, she opened it. Inside was one long-stemmed white rose. No message was enclosed. Her heart rollercoasted up and down in her rib-cage. "Angus," she said to herself.

Each day, at the same time, the messenger would bring yet another rose. Soon the flowers were a family joke. Bonnie never minded. She just smiled and said, "If whoever is sending the flowers wishes to keep himself anonymous, then that's fine with me." And then one day a small package arrived. Inside, glinting on the black velvet lining, lay a heavy gold signet ring. Engraved on it were two eagles.

Weeks passed by from November to December, and everyone began to make plans for Christmas. Bonnie spent most of her waking time lost in her dream of Angus. Teresa thought he had gone to Hong Kong, or was it New Zealand? Wherever he was, Bonnie felt his absence like a deep physical pain. Everyone noticed the change in her. It was as if a light had suddenly switched off. Instead of the warm friendly girl who had arrived from America, there was now a thin, anxious-looking woman.

"I don't know what the matter is with the child," Margaret said one day in the country.

Winnie looked up from the dried flowers she was arranging.

"Oh I expect she's just going through a stage of calf-love. Remember, she's had virtually no experience with men. Maybe she's homesick. I think a trip home will do her the world of good."

"You're probably right," Margaret smiled. "I'm so fond of her, you know. I'd like to see her marry well and be happy."

"I know," Winnie nodded. "There's nothing like a truly happy marriage," she said, remembering her years with Dan.

Margaret could hear Simon's footsteps in the hall. She put her hand on Winnie's shoulder. "Your husband must have been a lovely man," she said comfortingly. "Coming dear," she called to Simon.

Winnie continued to arrange the flowers. Funny, she thought, after all these years. Her eyes were full of tears. She watched Margaret and Simon as they walked across the lawn. He really does love her, Winnie thought, as she saw Simon shyly take his wife's hand.

Bonnie was very excited the day before she was due to fly back to Boston for Christmas. Her suitcase bulged with presents for her grandmother, and for Morag she had bought a soft fair-isle tam o'shanter with a warm matching shawl.

She had also occupied her last two weeks organizing Christmas presents for the Bartholomew family. Finding something suitable for Cyril proved to be somewhat taxing. "Get him a little china piggy bank, and say it's an anticapitalist statement," Teresa had suggested. "Go on. He'd like that."

"I don't think all that stuff about politics has much to do with the real Cyril," Bonnie had said. "I think he's angry because his mom was so poor. He must have been very bright, but he never had much of a chance."

On her last day in London, Bonnie delivered her present to the house shared by the Bartholomew daughters. Cyril refused to wait to open it. "I don't like Christmas," he said. "My Christmasses were all terrible."

"Really?" Bonnie said. "That's awfully sad."

Cyril was surprised to find anyone listening sincerely to him. "We couldn't even afford turkey." He paused to see if Bonnie was still interested. He decided to continue. "We had chicken. The only toys I had were from a patronizing Christmas party given by a local bigwig, where the poor children like me mixed with the sons and daughters of the local landed gentry." He grimaced. "I was always so ashamed of my threadbare clothes and then I was so guilty of being ashamed when my mother tried so hard." He tore open the parcel. "A jersey, for me?"

Bonnie smiled. "Well, I thought the soft brown of the sweater would match your eyes. You have lovely eyes, you know."

Cyril was embarrassed. He flushed and looked at his feet. "Do you really think so?" he said gruffly.

"I do," Bonnie said. "Your eyes were the first thing I noticed about you." Cyril looked at Bonnie, then he charged out of the room. "Did I upset him?" Bonnie was worried.

Mary smiled. "Well, you did in a way, I suppose. Cyril isn't used to anybody liking him or even noticing him."

A moment later, Cyril marched back into the room wearing the sweater. His eyes were shining. "You're right. It does match my eyes," he beamed. "I'll wear it on Christmas day." He smiled at Mary. "What do you think, Mary? Shall we tell Bonnie?" Mary nodded. "We are going to get married," Cyril said.

"Fantastic!" Bonnie was pleased. "When did you decide?"

Mary blushed. "I proposed to Cyril in the end. He wouldn't propose to me in case I thought he was only after my money."

Cyril looked lovingly at Mary. "Not even your money would make up for having to eat the food at your parents' house." He smiled at Bonnie. "My mother is delighted, but we still have to tackle Mary's parents."

Mary shrugged. "Oh, daddy will scream and froth at the mouth, but mummy will be pleased. Anyway, she doesn't like us living in sin."

"I'm hardly the son-in-law she prayed for," Cyril said.

"No, but you are the man I prayed for," said Mary, "and that's what's important. If we have any children, they won't be brought up in an ivory tower like we were. No nannies, no boarding schools."

Bonnie looked at Mary with sympathy. "It must have been awfully hard to go away to school at seven or eight."

"It was," Mary said, "but things are getting better. I hope we can all keep the good things of English social life, and drop all the prejudice and bigotry. I don't want to end up like Ann, pretending to speak Cockney just to hide."

Bonnie nodded. "You know, I'm going to have so much to tell my grandmother about England. She sent me over to be her eyes and her ears. I'm stuffed with information." She kissed Mary and Cyril goodbye.

Good Lord, Bonnie thought as she packed her last blouse into her suitcase. She climbed into bed and let Morgan settle his huge frame beside her. "I'm going to miss you, you know," she said, patting his great head. Morgan wagged his tail. "I'll be back before you know it," she promised.

"Dear God," she said, "when I come back, please can I find Angus waiting for me?" I'll miss the roses, she thought as she fell asleep.

PART THREE

In Holy Wedlock

Chapter 15

Once the plane had completed its ascent, Bonnie handed her tweed coat to the stewardess and went to the lavatory to change from her neat grey suit into her jeans. The flight back to Boston was going to be very pleasant. Bonnie ate lobster and sipped a glass of champagne. She glanced at her neighbour. The woman looked tired and harassed.

In due course, they fell into general conversation. Marion was an English doctor. "I'm going to pick up my sister in Hartford, Connecticut," she said. She threw a worried look at Bonnie. "She's in trouble again with that husband of hers. He's a maniac, but," she shook her head, "every time anyone in the family helps her out and sets her up with a new life, she goes back to him. Thank God there aren't any children."

"Maybe she loves him," Bonnie said.

"You can't love someone who ill-treats and abuses you like that."

"I remember saying something like that once," Bonnie said, "but now I'm not so sure. I knew I could never let a man abuse me, but then, I'd never been in love." She looked seriously at Marion. "I couldn't imagine life without Angus."

Marion smiled at her. "Well, I assume he wouldn't hurt

you, or you wouldn't be in love with him. But it's different with my sister. Sally knew her man was dangerous even before she married him. He beat her up when they were engaged. And she still went ahead, even though everybody warned her about him. 'Sonny will change. You'll see,' she'd say to my mother." Marion put her chair back. "This is the last time I'm going to her rescue. She has just spent seven weeks in hospital. Next time, she'll be dead."

"How awful." Bonnie was appalled.

"I don't know." Marion's eyes were closed. "Sometimes I think she likes it, you know. When she's away from Sonny, she spends all her time talking about the beatings. It's funny. I treat heroin addicts at my surgery. They have the same ecstatic look on their faces when they talk about their needles. I don't know. Any normal person would want to get away and forget all about that kind of life."

Bonnie nodded her head. "I didn't realize people got beaten so badly. I mean, my mother got herself beaten up on several occasions, but nothing like that."

Marion sat up. She fixed Bonnie with an impassioned stare. "Bonnie, thank God you're too young to know about such things. But every day I sit in my surgery in Oxford, and I dread the visits of those women who live with men who beat them. If he ill-treats his children, I can at least have them taken into safety, but then that means the woman is deprived of her own children. Sometimes, after I see a particularly horrific beating, when a woman is crying hopelessly in my office with a broken nose and huge marks all over her body, and the man who claims to love her has kicked her black and blue . . . it's all I can do not to cry. I know it's not professional. We doctors have been trained not to ask too many questions. After all, we are not supposed to be social workers. But I feel so helpless.

"I suppose there was a time when the poor woman had a large family to go back to. But now that's all fallen apart, and the women are left with no place to go. Families have no room for their daughters or their grandchildren any more. And as for the rich women," she sighed, "why just look at Sally. She's beaten by Sonny. Rich, elegant, charming Sonny. No one would believe her. We all like to think that sort of thing only happens in the lower classes. We say it because they're socially deprived. What a load of rubbish. I suppose it lets us off the hook. If we can blame it all on 'society,' then no one really has to take any responsibility, do they?"

"I think I know what you mean. My mother always blamed everything on her own father, but my dad kept telling her that the way she behaved was her own responsibility. She never really listened."

Marion shook her head. "Exactly. Well, the political argument falls down when you see women with everything going for them. A big house, lots of money, good social life, everything. But they are still battered by their men. After all my years of listening to all walks of life, I can tell you that one day all the excuses have to stop. We'll all have to face up to the fact that violence is a learned pattern of behaviour."

Bonnie put back her seat. Marion smiled. "I'm sorry. I didn't mean to deliver a lecture. I'd better have some sleep. I'll need all my strength tomorrow to deal with Sally." Marion lay back and closed her eyes.

Bonnie took Angus's ring out of her pocket. How horrible for those poor women, she thought. Angus would never lift his hand to me. She clutched the ring tightly in her palm and drifted off to sleep.

The lurch of the plane woke Bonnie as it started its descent towards Boston. Bonnie wondered whether she should change back into her suit. On second thoughts, she decided to stay in her jeans. After all, she told herself, this is America.

The Great House looked exactly as she remembered it, except that she had forgotten just how big everything in America was. She ran into the drawing-room, where the chauffeur had told her Augustine would be waiting. Her grandmother rose to greet her. Only three months had elapsed since she had seen Bonnie, but she had been greatly worried by a letter from Margaret referring to Bonnie's sudden lack of high spirits. Bonnie ran to Augustine and enveloped her in a warm hug. "Oh grandma, it's so good to be back." The room smelled, as it always did, of a mixture of lemon-scented polish and rich pine from the logs that crackled in the grate. Bonnie put her hand under her grandmother's elbow as she sat stiffly back in her winged armchair. "I brought you a Christmas pudding from Margaret," Bonnie said, and she didn't stop talking until it was time to change for dinner.

Up in her own bedroom, Bonnie stood and surveyed the room with joy. Nothing had changed. Then she noticed a long grey box with gold lettering lying on her bed. "I don't believe it," she said. Inside there lay a single blue cornflower. Bonnie drew her breath. There was a small note attached to the flower. "For the blue of your eyes," it read. Bonnie studied the handwriting with surprise. It seemed very small and cramped. The message was not signed, but she knew that Angus had written it himself. Funny, she thought, I would have expected a much firmer hand from someone as confident as Angus. But then, he was a very hurt child, she reminded herself. She felt a wave of compassion.

She put the blue flower in a glass and took it to the bathroom so that she could lie in the bath, gaze at it and think of Angus. Maybe, she wondered, maybe if I think of him hard enough, he'll think about me. She was so engrossed in her thoughts that Morag had to pound hard on her bedroom door. "Augustine says to hurry up. Dinner is waiting," Morag called.

Bonnie leapt out of the bath, grabbed a towel, and opened the door. "Morag!" she said. "How lovely to be home. Quick. See that suitcase? Your present is on the top."

Morag was delighted. "That's a really lovely hat, you know." She put on the hat and the shawl, and she looked at herself in the mirror. "Thanks, Bonnie. I've missed you."

"And I've missed you. How has grandma been?"

"Well, I've grown very close to Augustine while you've been away. I love her very much. She won't let me be a servant any longer, so I am a sort of companion to her now. I can't tell you how much we have all been looking forward to having you back."

Bonnie grinned. "My God. I can't tell you how great it is to be back in a good, luxurious, American household. England is so backward when it comes to comfort."

"Well, Augustine says it's all because of their Puritanical outlook on life."

"I suppose so. It takes a lot of getting used to." Bonnie quickly pulled a rust-coloured dress over her head. She twisted her hair up on top of her head, and skewered it with a white comb.

"You've lost weight," Morag said.

"I know. I'm in love, Morag."

Morag grinned. "I wish love would make me thin. All I ever do when I'm in love is raid the fridge and eat my way through boxes and boxes of chocolates. By the way, I get to have dinner with you now."

"Oh lovely." Bonnie slipped her arm around Morag's waist, and they went chattering and laughing down the grand staircase.

Augustine was waiting for them at the table. She smiled at Bonnie. "Well, tell me all about the Bartholomew family," she said.

"Oh dear. First I've got to tell you about their food. Apart from Winnie, their housekeeper in Suffolk, and one party I went to where the wife wasn't English, the food was terrible."

Bonnie went on to describe the various puddings and their differing degrees of leadenness. Augustine was highly amused, and Morag shook with laughter. "It's all such a shame," Augustine was quiet for a moment. "Right up until Victorian times, English cooking and entertaining was the best in the world." She wiped her mouth with the corner of her linen napkin. "I think that when England lost her empire, she lost her heart. They are an odd people, the English. They live on a tiny island, yet they have such a need to rule the world. Not like the rest of Europe, who do a bit of colonizing in their spare time. No, the English actually need to reach out and to live away from their island. Then they remember their home-land with affection. Odd. I always feel that English men need something to die for, while American men need something to live for."

Bonnie remembered how wise her grandmother was. "You're right. Matthew wants to go abroad and save heathen African souls, but the others are all rather trapped. I can't see them working in other countries. John says he feels terribly trapped. I couldn't get used to fifty-six million people cramped together in such a confined space. There isn't room in London to have any time to yourself."

After dinner, Morag left Bonnie and her grandmother alone in the drawing-room. Bonnie sat in her rocking chair, gazing into the fire. "You do look very tired, my child," Augustine began, "and you are thinner."

"I know," Bonnie beamed. "I'm in love, grandma." She looked at Augustine. "Don't tell anybody, will you? I mean, don't tell the Bartholomews."

Augustine looked surprised. "Why not, darling? You have nothing to hide, have you?"

"No, it's not that. I just want to wait until I'm sure of him." Bonnie felt guilty. She never had prevaricated before. She hadn't yet worked out exactly what she would tell the family. She knew they would be horrified. Carefully she explained Angus's sad past. ". . . So you see, grandma, he needs me to love him."

Despite her worldly wisdom, Augustine knew very little about affairs of the heart. "Well," she said cautiously, "of course we are shaped by our past, but people can transcend their backgrounds. You certainly did, but are you sure that Angus has?"

"Yes, I'm very sure," said Bonnie. "No one who isn't kind and sensitive would think of sending flowers every day. And," she said, "he sent me his signet ring. Hang on, and I'll get it for you." Bonnie ran upstairs to her room.

Augustine stared into the fire. A sudden sense of dread filled her heart. She remembered her own son James's face all those years ago filled with concern for a young girl who was using him for her own ends. Well, Augustine thought, at least it's not her money he's after, and it sounds like he can have any woman he wants. Maybe the fact that he has the good sense to choose Bonnie weighs in his favour. She smiled as Bonnie came back. "Let me see, child," she said as she took the ring. "Good heavens," she said looking closely at it. "Bonnie, bring my genealogy book."

Bonnie went to the bookcase and pulled the heavy book from the shelf. "Do you know the family then?"

"Well, yes. I think I do. What a remarkable coincidence." She began to turn the pages of the book. "Here we are." She stopped at a colour plate. Holding the ring next to the illustration, she saw that the ring matched exactly. "The crest shows the MacPherson eagles," Augustine said. She turned the page and began to read.

"At the battle of Culloden in 1745, Stuart Macpherson, chieftain of the Clan MacPherson, saved the life of his friend James Fraser by throwing his body in front of Fraser . . ."

"My word," said Augustine.

Bonnie's eyes were shining. "So someone in Angus's family all those years ago saved someone in our family, which is how Malcolm Fraser got to Boston . . ." Bonnie stood up and walked to the weather-beaten portrait of James Fraser. "My

God," she said. "It really is amazing." She walked back to her chair. "You see, we both knew when we first met that we were meant for each other."

Augustine sighed. "I don't doubt that, child, if that is how you feel. But the MacPhersons have a terribly blood-stained history." She shut the book. "However, I am prepared to trust your judgement."

Bonnie smiled. "Thank you, grandma. Let's go to bed. You look tired. I must have worn you out with all my talking. Can I borrow the book, please?"

"Yes, indeed, dear." Bonnie helped her grandmother to her feet and walked the old woman up the stairs and to her room. "Good night, darling," Augustine said. She kissed her granddaughter on the cheek. "We'll soon fatten you up and bring the roses back into your cheeks. You just need a week of some good Lexington air."

Bonnie took her grandmother's hand. "I know you'll like him, grandma. I promise."

"I know I will, darling. Off you go to bed."

Bonnie sat bolt upright in her bed, reading the Macpherson family history. Poor Angus, she thought. With a history of murder and mayhem, it's no wonder people gossip all the time. Poor Angus. She lay in her bed and looked across at the cornflower. Dear Angus, she thought.

Chapter 16

Bonnie was determined to make the best of her week away from London. But, much as she complained about its discomforts, she realized, as she lay in bed on her first morning home, that England, like the old ivy that clung to the walls of its buildings, had a way of burrowing deep into the cracks of the soul of an unwary traveller. Then, slowly, it grew, putting out little tendrils of history. She basked in the memory of the Thames, of pheasants rising in the sunlight, of the Persil-white coats of the sheep with their lambs. She smiled as she remembered the little villages with their neat stone faces sitting primly along the road to Suffolk. Bonnie stretched. She decided to get up and telephone her mother.

"Well, it's sure good to hear from you." Laura's voice was cold. "Are you coming over?"

"I'll fly down on the 26th for two days. I'm only here for a week, and then I'm going to Scotland for the New Year."

Laura was relieved. She did not need any interruption in her little house. Her indulgence in fantasy had become so ritualized that she had no time for anyone. Her day began with prayers and confessions of any lewd thoughts or actions during the night. As Laura constantly fantasized about sex, she always had plenty to confess. Then came the penance. Laura by now had fully internalized Father John's mannerisms. She would play both parts. Crouching on her knees she would humbly confess her sins. Then, leaping to her feet, she would take her place on the other side of her bedroom. Mimicking Father John's voice, she would sternly order herself six or twelve lashes, depending on the length of her confession.

During the day, Laura kept a tally of her misdeeds. By ten

o'clock at night, she would be ready to confess her sins again. Bruised and bleeding from the morning, she would lash herself in a frenzy of remorse. Then she would fall asleep and dream.

So intense was her private world that she cut herself off from any social contacts. When she was not at home, she was in church. Father John was now certain of her monthly cash. With three months' money in his bank account, he calculated that he would need to humour Laura's obsession for only a few more years before he could leave for Rome with a large sum at his disposal. A few more years were nothing compared to the lifetime of service in that church, a lifetime that had stretched endlessly ahead of him until the arrival of Laura.

"Bonnie," Laura's voice was hesitant. "I'm refurnishing your room. I'm afraid it's in an awful mess. Any chance . . ."

"Don't worry, mom. I can stay with Mitzi. I want to see her anyway."

Both mother and daughter were relieved.

Bonnie spent a marvellous Christmas with Augustine and Morag. Augustine had come to find large gatherings of people tiring, so the holiday was celebrated privately and quietly at the Great House. At midnight on Christmas Eve, Bonnie walked slowly through the snow with her grandmother and Morag to the family chapel. The rest of the House staff had already found their places in the small rows of pews, waiting for their employer to arrive. After Father Gregory had said the sacred mass in Latin, the three women walked again in the clear night under a sky full of sharp and radiant stars.

Next morning, the Great House was filled with an air of gentle festivity. The butler had overseen the decoration of the twenty-foot Christmas tree in the main hall. Beneath the tree, Bonnie found her grandmother's present for her. "How lovely," she said as she opened the box of Joy perfume. "Now open my presents to you."

Bonnie handed her grandmother three gaily wrapped parcels. The first contained a duck pâté, the second a small Stilton cheese from Fortnum's. Augustine sat in expectation as the third and largest parcel lay across her lap. Her eyes shone with delight. "Oh Bonnie. The gifts are lovely. But what's in this one? I can't imagine what could be this size. How on earth did you fit it in your suitcase?"

"Open it," Bonnie laughed. Augustine tore through the paper and revealed a shiny pair of gum boots. "They're from Harrods," Bonnie said. "I thought you could use them when you walk through the gardens."

"How thoughtful. You know, I've always seen pictures of English people wearing these, and I secretly wanted a pair for myself. Thank you, dear," She held out her arms, and Bonnie leaned forward to hug her grandmother.

The table was laid in all its finery for the Christmas dinner. At the end of the meal, following Bonnie's instructions, the cook carried in the flaming Christmas pudding. Bonnie suddenly felt something hard against her teeth as she ate her slice. She looked at her fork, and on it lay a threepenny piece. "Oh, I nearly forgot!" she exclaimed. "Winnie said that whoever found the coin in their Christmas pudding was sure to have good luck."

Mitzi was delighted to see Bonnie. "You really do look like a lady of fashion," Mitzi said, wiping her hands on her striped maternity smock.

Bonnie put her suitcase down in the middle of the small, tidy living-room. Two bright-eyed children scampered in and out of the kitchen. Bonnie looked at Mitzi. "You're pregnant again. You didn't tell me."

Mitzi laughed self-consciously. "I thought you'd give me a lecture."

Bonnie smiled. "I promise I won't, Mitzi. Not now. I've changed."

"Yes, I can see that you've changed." Mitzi plonked herself down in a fat squashy velour armchair. "I guess you must be in love."

"How did you know?"

"Remember, I used to be an expert on the subject. And here I see a young woman, fashionably dressed, perfectly groomed, but looking as if only part of her is here. You have all the symptoms. The diagnosis is easy."

"Oh Mitzi," Bonnie said, "it's so good to talk to you. Other people don't understand me like you do."

Mitzi sighed. "Well, you always were totally dedicated to anything you set your mind to. It used to be your studies. So now it's a man. So tell me. What's he like?" Mitzi listened patiently while Bonnie went into a rapturous and lengthy description of Angus. They were interrupted by a shriek and a crash from the kitchen. "Oy," said Mitzi. "Excuse me while I yell at my beloved children. Max! Rebecca!" she lifted her head to scream. "You two are driving me meshuggie! Now stop before I give you both a potch on the tukhis!"

Two giggles could be heard from the kitchen. "Okay, mommy," the children said in unison.

"You were saying," Mitzi said to Bonnie who sat slumped in the other armchair. "So. Am I to understand that you have only *seen* this wonderful boychikul?"

Bonnie frowned. "We're not like other people. After one look we both knew we were destined for each other. Look. Here's the ring he sent me. Did you know that his ancestor saved my ancestor, James Fraser, from being killed? He shielded him from a bullet. That is how James survived all those years ago. And then his son Malcolm came to Boston and built the Great House."

"Incredible," said Mitzi. "It all sounds so romantic. You are lucky, Bonnie. Of course," she said quickly, "I love Ray, but two children with another on the way doesn't do a hell of a lot to add romance to life." She made a face. "Come into the kitchen. I've made some corned beef sandwiches for the kids' lunch. You have some too."

"You know, it's funny," Bonnie said, sitting at the kitchen table with Max on her knee. "I never saw myself married or with children. Now I think of having children as a very necessary part of my life." She nuzzled her cheek against Max's hair. "I wonder if Mother Nature sets off a biological trigger when you fall in love, and then suddenly even the most austere women get all clucky and fussy."

Mitzi smiled. "Yeah, it is something like that, I suppose. I know I just love having kids, and I love just being home. I know it's not fashionable, but, every evening when Ray gets home, I like to kiss him hello and then surprise him with a nice meal. He says I cook so well that he skips lunch to make sure he has room for dinner." Mitzi laughed. She had put on weight, but she looked happy and content. That's how I want to be, Bonnie thought. Home for Angus, home for my kids.

After the children had finished eating their lunch, Mitzi sent them out to play in the backyard. "This is my adult time," she told Bonnie. "Now I either read or write letters."

Bonnie smiled. "You're the first person I know who hasn't said horrid things about Angus."

Mitzi shrugged. "What's to say? You tell me he had a rotten childhood, but then so did you. I remember when your mom hit you and she used to be drunk all the time." Mitzi's face was soft and gentle. "Honestly, Bonnie, you deserve all the love in the world. Not many people are as lucky as Ray and me. We have our happiness, and I wish that for you also."

Bonnie looked across the shining kitchen. "I know everything will be all right. I know I sound crazy to other people, when Angus and I have never even spoken, but our love doesn't need words. I think Angus is really very shy and quiet underneath. I know he goes to lots of parties and things, but he does that because he's expected to go. When we're married, we won't have to bother. We can sit side by side and watch the fire. I can read poems to him." She laughed. "There. See? I've got it all mapped out."

"Boy oh boy, Bonnie. It all sounds marvellous."

"Ooh. I must run. I promised mom I'd meet her in town. She wants to see a movie called *Seeds of Satan*. She has awful taste in movies. Anyway, it'll make her happy. We really don't have much to say to each other."

"Okay," Mitzi said, getting to her feet. "If you come in late tonight, use the back door. We'll leave it unlocked for you."

"I won't be late. I'll just stay up all night after the movie has scared me out of my wits." Giving her friend a quick kiss, Bonnie grabbed her handbag and ran for the bus into town.

The movie was long, boring, and bad. Laura discussed the plot all through dinner, which they ate in a nearby restaurant. "Mom," Bonnie interrupted. "Listen. I want to tell you something." Laura stopped for a moment. "I'm going to get married."

Laura's eyebrows shot up. "Married, Bonnie? Who's the lucky man?"

Bonnie took the gold signet ring from her handbag. "Here. Angus sent me this. He wouldn't do a thing like that unless he was really serious."

Laura looked at Bonnie. "Who is this man? I mean, what does he do for a living?"

"Well, he kind of . . . well, he has a huge estate in Scotland and a house in London. Teresa knows more about it than I do. He sort of runs all that, but then I guess he's so rich he doesn't have to do anything."

Laura gazed at her daughter with growing interest. "Is he a lord or anything like that?"

Bonnie nodded. "Well, almost. As a matter of fact, he'll inherit everything when his father dies, and then he'll be Lord

MacPherson, and I," she grinned, "will be Lady Macpherson. How about that, mom?" Laura looked impressed.

Laura *was* impressed. "My goodness, Bonnie. Who would have thought that my little baby would go to England and marry a lord. Is he a good Catholic?"

Bonnie nodded. "I know he's a Catholic."

Laura put her hand out to touch Bonnie's cheek. Bonnie blushed. She wasn't used to gestures of affection from her mother. "Listen, honey," Laura said, "whatever happens, you see that he settles his money on you before you get married. Remember what happened to me." An uncomfortable silence lay between them.

Bonnie picked up her glass of wine. "Honestly, mom, my marriage won't be like that. I trust Angus absolutely. He would never leave me."

Laura looked down at her plate. "I thought that once too. But your daddy did leave us."

"I know," Bonnie sighed. "I guess I still feel guilty when I think of him going off and dying all on his own. I should have tried harder. I always feel it was my fault."

"Well, you were his little girl, and you did grow away from him in those last years. You were at school, and you had your friends, I suppose."

Bonnie was horrified. "Did I abandon him?"

Laura recognized that it would not be wise to upset Bonnie. Her eyes were already full of tears. "No, not really," she said. "He abandoned us, and now I don't know what I would do if I didn't have an allowance from you." She allowed tears to form in her own eyes.

Bonnie was immediately defensive. "That's not an allowance. I'll always send you as much as I can. I'm sure when we're married Angus will let me give you more money."

"That would be nice, darling. I would appreciate it very much. But don't worry about me. I'll get by." She looked at her watch. "Oh, I must go to church now and make my confession."

"Mom," Bonnie was amused, "you can't have all that much to confess. You don't do anything except serve God and Father John."

Laura smiled. Suddenly she looked years younger. Her face shone, her eyes gleamed. She looked as if she were suffering from a high fever. "Yes," she said. "I serve God, and where there is God, there is always the Devil." She looked distracted for a moment. "I really must go, Bonnie. Give my love to Mitzi."

"Okay." Bonnie rose from the table. "I'll pick up the bill," she said to her mother.

"That's kind of you. Thanks a lot. I'll see you next time."

"Next time," Bonnie said with a laugh in her voice, "I hope we will meet in church at my wedding."

"And then he took a long chain and bound me to the wall in his basement. He was wearing a black . . ."

. . . a black leather mask, and carrying a whip, Father John completed the sentence in his mind before Laura had even finished speaking. He knew most of Laura's lines by heart. Oh well, he thought. At least it's a whip this week. Makes for a change, I suppose. We've just had two weeks of hanging off the ceiling and leather thongs.

After saying her assigned Hail Marys and Our Fathers, Laura waited, sitting quietly in the shadow of the altar. She watched as Father John extinguished the lights in the church. Only the red glow of the lamp dimly illuminated the altar. As he walked towards the door, he felt a presence beside him. "Oh goodness, Laura," he said, squinting to see her in the gloom. "You made me jump."

"Did I, Father?" she said. Her lips drew back into a knowing smile. "Did I really? I didn't mean to, you know." Father John shifted uneasily. "I have news for you, Father." She smiled. "My daughter is going to marry an English lord, and live in a castle in England."

"Really?" Father John was suddenly interested. "And is this young man a Catholic?"

Laura nodded triumphantly. "Of course. My daughter would never consider marrying out of the Church. One day I will bring them both here."

Father John looked impressed. "Well," he said, "you must be delighted. I tell you what. I'll finish locking up, and we can go back to my house and have a cup of coffee. Would you like that?"

Laura was ecstatic. "Very much indeed," she said demurely.

Later, in her own home, she flogged herself until the last lewd fantasy of coupling with Father John had left her mind.

Back at the Great House, Bonnie was pleased to see that two more flowers had arrived during her absence. Augustine smiled as Bonnie carried them into the drawing-room. "You look so happy, Bonnie," she said.

"Yes, I am. I'm much happier than I was when I arrived. I was so confused by my feelings for Angus and by all those people who kept warning me against him. But now," she paused and looked tenderly at the flowers, "now I know that I love him. I want to marry him, and no one will discourage me. I don't care if the first few years are difficult. I know he will find it hard to accept my love and to learn to really trust me, but I'm prepared for that. I can cope with the bad times. After all, unlike most of the girls in London, I know what it's like to live through a time that is very unhappy. Look at mom. She's pulled through, and now she's devoted to the Church and to Father John."

More likely only to the priest, Augustine thought, but she said nothing to Bonnie. If Laura was playing another of her games, provided she left Bonnie alone, Augustine didn't care.

Besides, Augustine reasoned, it probably comforts Bonnie to believe that her mother is involved with the Church instead of with some drunken lunatic in Merrill. "I'm so glad to hear that," she said. "Oh, by the way, I rang Margaret to thank her for the presents. She said to tell you John will pick you up at the airport in Inverness."

Bonnie and Morag went into Boston to shop for several very formal dresses for the various balls that were to take place in Scotland. "The MacGregors are giving theirs on New Year's Eve," Bonnie told Morag. "And Teresa says that at midnight the men go first-footing. That means a man with dark hair and a lump of coal in his hand has to come over the doorstep to bring the house good luck for the next year." They browsed among the racks of clothes at Bonwit Teller's. "I think I'll buy that ivory satin dress over there. Grandma says I can take back her silver fox. If it's cold in English homes, I hate to think how freezing it'll be in Scottish castles." She shivered. "I can always wear the coat in bed, I suppose."

Morag pulled out a black chiffon dress. "Try this one, Bonnie. You look lovely in black."

"We can't show it to grandma, though."

Morag smiled. "Listen, if you're old enough to get married, you're old enough to wear black. Whoops." She put her hand to her mouth. "I didn't mean for it to sound like a funeral."

Bonnie laughed. "That does it. We definitely won't buy the black dress. I've become totally superstitious."

The few remaining days in Boston flew by. "I'll be back in the summer," Bonnie said to Augustine. "Even if I do get engaged, I won't get married for a while. If it all works out, we could get married in October."

"Bonnie, I've been meaning to ask you," a tone of worry edged Augustine's voice. "Are you going to apply to the Brown graduate school? I think it would be wise, dear. After all, everything may fall through, and you'll need to complete your education."

Bonnie was adamant. "It won't fall through, grandma. I've never been so sure of anything in my life. I don't even want to think about the possibility of not being with Angus. I only feel alive when I'm thinking of him. He *is* my life. He makes me feel everything so vividly that the rest of the world falls away. There's just the two of us in the whole universe."

Augustine kissed her granddaughter goodbye. "Just remember, in case your universe ever explodes, there is always a small piece of it right here in Lexington."

"I will, and it won't," Bonnie laughed.

Morag accompanied Bonnie to Logan airport. "Goodbye," she said as Bonnie's flight was announced. "Good luck, and be sure to send me a photograph of Angus."

Bonnie nodded and hugged Morag. "Goodbye, Boston," she said as the plane rose steeply over the harbour islands. "Goodbye." She lay back and dreamed of returning someday with Angus on her arm.

Chapter 17

John was there to meet Bonnie at Dalcross airport. The silver tips of her fox fur coat framed her face. "Oh, Bonnie," John said, giving her a tight hug. "You get more beautiful every time I see you."

Bonnie hugged him back and she laughed. "That was all grandma's good food. I put on five pounds." Bonnie was greatly excited as they moved off into the snowy Scottish countryside. As John drove, Bonnie prised news out of him. "Who's up here for the parties?" she asked.

"Everybody. All the Inverness families have opened their houses, and the English contingent arrived after the hunting on Boxing Day. Tonight is the biggest ball of the lot. I hope you're not too tired."

"No, I had a lovely flight over. I slept all the way. By the way, is Angus back?" she said casually.

John looked across at Bonnie as she played nonchalantly with her gloves. "I don't know, but even if he was, he's not welcome round here. Everybody knows too much about him."

Bonnie's heart contracted at the thought of Angus being boycotted by all the local lairds. "Really," she said crossly. "It's such a shame that the poor man is so persecuted."

"No more than he deserves," John said sternly. "I say, Bonnie, you're not still carrying a torch for him, are you? Even Teresa had the good sense to get out, and she'd take on Attila the Hun if given half a chance."

"I don't know, John. I'll see what happens, and then I'll let you know." She was imagining dancing in Angus's arms.

Teresa was at the MacGregors' house waiting to greet Bonnie. The MacGregors looked like large English sheepdogs. They all had the same amount of hair and the same pale blue eyes. There were seven brothers and sisters, and Sir Ian MacGregor was stone deaf. He carried an old brass trumpet, which he frequently jammed into his ear, but he rarely listened long enough to hear a reply. He shrieked at Bonnie. "Bonnie? You can't be Bonnie! That's not a name; it's a word!"

His wife Charlotte had hair which stood up in a wild crown on her head. "She's American, dear!" she shouted down the trumpet. "Americans have funny names!"

"Ah!" said Sir Ian, the light of comprehension illuminating his face. "Do you chew gum?" Bonnie nodded. The old man was delighted.

Teresa rescued her from the noisy enthusiastic family that surrounded her. "I'll show you our room," Teresa said as she took Bonnie by the arm.

"That sounds a good idea," Bonnie said with relief. She had never stayed in a castle before, and very quickly promised herself that she would never repeat the experience. It was one thing to walk through Windsor Castle, and to feel the history and to look at the magnificent furniture and tapestries, but it was quite another matter when, after puffing up narrow winding stairs with Teresa, she found herself in a stone chamber with narrow slits for windows. Bonnie sat on one of the two white hospital beds. "This is a bit bare," she said.

Teresa bounced on the bed. "With any luck, I shan't be sleeping here tonight." She lay back. "I'm in love with Patrick Fitzgibbon. I plan to seduce him tonight. You know, they should really make tartan diaphragms. English girls could have Union Jacks. They're such boring things. Such a drag, having to carry it about in my handbag. It's all a bit obvious when you reach in to get a handkerchief, and the bloody tin rolls out onto the floor. Besides, the loos are a million miles away in these draughty castles. Why is life so complicated?" she moaned.

There was a knock on the door. A young boy in a kilt stood holding a huge bunch of flowers. They looked expectantly at him. "For Miss Bonnie Fraser," the boy said.

"Oh how lovely!" Bonnie exclaimed. She tore off the cellophane. "Spring flowers. Aren't they gorgeous? Just imagine, spring flowers in the depth of winter." She picked up the note. It was written in the same familiar crippled handwriting: "I will be with you tonight." Bonnie gazed wildly at Teresa.

"John says they won't let him into the house."

Teresa snorted. "Probably come down the chimney, seize you in his great talons, and flap slowly off into the night."

"No, really. Don't be silly."

Teresa laughed. "I wouldn't worry about Angus. If he wants to see you, no one will try to stop him."

"Oh good." Bonnie was melting with happiness.

"I suppose we'd better make the best of our little room. After all, we are here for the next few weeks."

Bonnie chose and discarded and chose again the dress she would wear for Angus. One minute, she thought she should wear a pale red silk dress. The next minute, she decided it should be her cream satin. "I suggest you hurry and make up your mind, or he'll have been and gone," Teresa said. "By the way, if you are thinking of having a bath, don't. The water is stone cold."

Bonnie sighed. "You go ahead. I'll be down soon." She wanted very much to be alone. Once Teresa had stamped off down the stone corridor, Bonnie stopped fluttering about. Pull yourself together, she said firmly. I will wear my cream satin dress with the matching shoes. There. That's decided. She picked out her baguette diamond. She smiled at her reflection in the mirror. "He's coming," she said. Her eyes were a brilliant blue. "Angus will soon be here."

When Bonnie was finally dressed, she took the bottle of Joy which her grandmother had given her, and dabbed the perfume behind her ears. Running lightly down the staircase, she stopped when she reached the gallery. Down below she could see the guests milling about in the Great Hall. Suits of armour lined the walls, and old standards hung down. Bonnie stood for a while, drinking it all in. She could not see Angus.

The men, in full Highland dress, looked magnificent. Bonnie had seen the occasional kilt, but never before a huge gathering of men all dressed in the vivid blues, greens, and reds of their clans. The other men in their formal tails looked as if they were cut out of cardboard. "Love it. *Love* it!" Sacheverell was at her side. "Darling," he said, "you're so beautiful." His designer eyes took in the cross cut on the satin dress. "Wonderful fall," he said. "Suits you exactly." He glanced at the diamond at her neck. "A little on the small side," he said, cocking his head to one side. "Shouldn't really wear anything on the neck under two carats. But," he bowed from the waist, "you are still the belle of the ball."

"Stop trying to look up John's kilt!" Teresa yelled.

"Rude girl." Sacheverell stood up.

John smiled at Bonnie. "You look marvellous."

"Must stop trying to look at men's bare botties." Teresa whacked Sacheverell with her ornate fan.

Sacheverell winced. "Teresa dearest, that hurts." He turned to Bonnie. "But you must admit, all those big hairy knees . . . I don't know how I'm going to restrain myself."

John pulled her away. "Don't listen to Sacheverell. He'd corrupt a deer-hound if he could. Stay away, Sacheverell."

Sacheverell put his hand on his hip and minced off. "One day you'll need me, Bonnie. People like me tend to understand people like you," were his parting words.

Bonnie was puzzled. "Just what did he mean by that?" she asked.

"Pay no attention," John said. "Sacheverell's a nice enough man when he isn't camping it up, which is not often."

Bonnie watched him disappear into the crowd, and suddenly realized that she missed his company. There was something multi-layered and complicated about the man. The people who stood around her all seemed to live on one plane of life. Bonnie was acutely aware that everything was far more complex than that. For a long time, she had wanted to explore those other levels. Sacheverell was the only person she had met in England who at least seemed to acknowledge the otherness of life. Winnie, for all her affection, saw only the light side of the coin. But Bonnie knew that there was a dark side. In choosing Angus, Bonnie had chosen that side. "I like Sacheverell. He makes me laugh," she said to John.

Teresa, with John behind her, was pushing slowly through the crowd to reach their table. Mary and Cyril were already ensconced. "Mummy and daddy are sitting with the MacGregors." Mary was in an organizing mood. "Bonnie, you sit next to Cyril, and John, you sit over here. Otherwise you'll hog Bonnie all evening."

The servants were carrying in massive silver dishes of venison and pheasant. The hall was lit by the candelabra placed on each table. Women in silks and satins floated by Bonnie's table. Some wore white dresses with tartan sashes pinned at the right shoulder. "I can't believe I'm here," Bonnie said to Cyril.

"Neither can I." Cyril's eyes twinkled. "You have to be born into this kind of thing, otherwise it all seems like a film set. That's where I learned about life. The local cinema."

Bonnie nodded. "I certainly wasn't born into all this, but it's all very beautiful."

There was one extraordinary moment during the meal when most of the guests rose to their feet. Bonnie knew that it was usual to stand for the Royal Toast, but many people remained in their seats. "Sit," Cyril said. "This is not for us."

"The king over the water!" A very old man stood with a small bowl of water pressed to his chest. He waved his wine glass over the water, then brought the wine to his lips and drained the glass. All those standing followed suit. Suddenly Bonnie could hear the skirl of the pipes. It came closer and closer, then a huge door opened at the far end. The lament gathered momentum as the solitary piper walked slowly and purposefully around the Great Hall.

Bonnie could hear the sob in the escaping air of the pipes. The sobbing grew louder—"Will ye no come back again? No come back?"—as the music dipped and whirled in the sadness of the country, once a fierce and proud people, who had lost their king. With the Stuarts had gone their pride and their independent spirit; now they were all slaves to London and to England. Some of the older men were crying openly as the music encircled the room. Bonnie thought of Malcolm Fraser and his father. Her heart grew heavy with sorrow for them both.

Slowly the music was coming to an end. The piper departed. The guests began to eat and drink again. The noise of many people talking filled the Great Hall so that the last notes of the sobbing pipes rose up to the rafters and waited unheard.

Matthew arrived after the meal, just as the dance band started to play. He put his hands over his ears. "Oh God, I hate this music." Bonnie danced with Francis. Over Francis's shoulder she saw Teresa with Patrick Fitzgibbon. He looks nice enough, Bonnie thought.

She found it almost impossible to eat throughout the meal. Her stomach was in knots as she waited for the moment when Angus would find her. She dutifully danced every number, until John finally pulled her on to the floor. They had just started when the music stopped. An expectant hush fell upon the guests. Even the servants stood still. John looked at his watch. "Midnight," he whispered to Bonnie. "Everyone is waiting for the first-footing, for someone to come over the . . ."

Even as he spoke there was a great knocking on the huge wooden doors that led from the Great Hall to the front courtyard of the castle. Sir Ian strode forward and threw them open. There, standing beneath the iron chandelier which hung in the archway, was Angus. He wore the MacPherson dress tartan. The silver buttons on his velvet jacket gleamed, as did the silver buckles on his shoes. The white lace at his throat accentuated the black thickness of his hair. In his hand he held a large lump of coal.

Sir Ian was shaken. Like many others, he had sworn never to allow Angus MacPherson into his house. But Angus was the first-footer, and Sir Ian knew that to turn him away would be to call bad luck upon his family, his house, and his land. "Welcome," he said frostily.

"I'll not stay long. I have business here," Angus replied.

There was a nervous ripple of excitement through the crowd. As Angus walked forward, people fell away. His stern dark eyes searched the dance floor, and then he saw Bonnie. She slowly moved forward to greet him. There was a hush as they walked towards each other, Bonnie so fair and so guileless, and Angus so full of wild darkness. When they met in the middle of the Great Hall, Angus put his arms around her. "I have come to take you away," he said.

Bonnie smiled. "I know." Her clear young voice rang out without hesitation. I know, I know, I know. The words echoed up into the rafters, where they joined the silent music that had waited.

Bonnie and Angus walked out of the Great Hall, past Lord and Lady Bartholomew, past the MacGregors, and out into the night. "My coat . . ." Bonnie said.

Angus took her hand. "You don't need a coat. I have brought a thick fur rug." He took the rug from his driver and put it over her shoulders. They descended the great stone steps. Angus handed her into the silver Rolls Royce. The car drove away.

"Where are we going?" Bonnie asked.

Angus threw back his head and laughed. Bonnie noticed again the animal excitement held in Angus's chipped front tooth. "We are going to Drummossie Castle, and tomorrow we will formally announce our engagement.

"Truly, Angus?"

"Truly, my Bonnie." He lowered his mouth to hers.

Chapter 18

When the great front door slammed behind Bonnie and Angus, there was an explosion among the guests. "Damn cheek!" said Sir Ian to his wife. Other guests talked among themselves and shook their heads in horror.

Sacheverell, who had been dancing with Teresa, sighed. "Poor sweet fool," he said. "She has no idea what she's let herself in for."

Teresa looked at him. "I think that is the most romantic thing I have ever seen in my whole life."

"That's the problem with Angus. He likes to live as if the world were his stage. He's always staging events of great drama. He probably spent hours thinking this particular scene out. Bonnie doesn't realize that she's just part of his cast of characters, as I am whenever he wants me to decorate a house for him or to amuse a dinner party. You watch. He'll take a great delight in marrying Bonnie just because everyone loves her and doesn't want him to have her. If your parents have any sense, they will ignore him. Then his game would be spoiled. Angus would tire of the whole thing quite quickly and give her back."

Teresa looked shocked. "You mean he doesn't love her?"

Sacheverell frowned. "Men like Angus don't love anybody but themselves. He'll have convinced himself that Bonnie is what he needs for a wife. He's always been obsessionally attached to the idea of marrying a virgin. He's murderously jealous. That's why he beat up Sonia so badly. I redid her kitchen a few months ago, and she told me he'd forced her to confess all her affairs. A few days later, he got drunk and threw it all back at her."

Margaret interrupted them. "Teresa," she said, "don't you

think we'd better warn Bonnie? I mean, she doesn't really know much about Angus. Maybe if you give them half an hour to get back to Drummossie, then 'phone her and tell her not to do anything rash," Margaret flushed, "if you know what I mean."

Teresa grinned. "You mean not to get ravished. No, I don't think that would be wise, mummy. I think Sacheverell might be right. If we leave her alone, and if this is only one of Angus's dramas, he may well get bored. After all, he's used to exciting women of the world, not twenty-three-year-old American virgins."

"Shoot him!" Simon bellowed right behind Sacheverell's ear. Sacheverell jumped. "I don't mean you, you fool. Angus. Let's get a hunting party together and shoot him."

"Damned fine idea!" Sir Ian delighted. "String him up!"

Mary sighed. "I don't know. I think there's more to Bonnie and Angus than just one of Angus's whims. Did you see the way they looked at each other?"

Pauline nodded. "Yes, it was like an electric current. I almost thought I could see sparks flying between them." She drew a deep breath. "Even if I was offered everything that Bonnie will be offered by Angus, I would say no. He tried once with me, you know."

"No, I didn't realize." Mary was interested.

"Yes. Oh, it was years ago. He staged a huge fight at a party. After it was all over, I felt so sorry for him I went too when he stormed out into the night." She paused, remembering the anguish in his eyes. " 'Come home with me,' he said." Pauline looked at Mary. "I said no. That's the difference between Bonnie and me. We had all that teaching from both mummy and daddy. We watched them care for each other. I know instinctively that he just needed me for that moment to cram down into that deep dark hole inside him. It would only have been a matter of time before he spat me out. Poor Bonnie." She shivered. Mary looked surprised. Pauline very rarely talked about herself. Pauline laughed defensively. "I know I do make it all sound rather dramatic, but men like Angus are exciting. They're dangerous, and that can be a challenge. But I made a choice in my life to live with a man like Francis who will love me and our children, even if he's dull at times. But then, so am I."

"But we knew we had a choice," Mary said. "I don't know if Bonnie knows. She walked away with him as if she was going to meet her destiny."

Cyril joined in. "She had been waiting for Angus all her life," he said. "She told me that she took the responsibility for her father's sorrow and pain, and she felt betrayed by him when he left. She had waited all her life to find someone with a similar depth of sorrow. And now she's found Angus. No doubt she believes she can cure him." Cyril's face was sad. "My aunt in the East End did just the same thing. Her father used to beat her mother. You'd think she would marry exactly the opposite type of man. My mother did. But Aunt Florrie. . . ."

John was distraught. "We must do something," he said to Luke and Matthew.

Teresa interrupted. "Leave her alone. If we interfere, it'll just make her more obstinate. Let's just hope he throws one of his tantrums, and then she'll come home. If we nag her, she'll feel disloyal to Angus. I'm going to wait and just continue to be her friend."

John looked at his sister with new respect. "You're right, you know."

Somehow the vibrant air of excitement that always surrounded Angus had permeated the Great Hall. Now that he was gone, the room seemed dark and gloomy. The women wanted to go home to dream of that marvellous moment. They wanted to believe that someone would love them enough to break into a castle to rescue them from lives which were largely boring and meaningless. The men wanted to dream of a beautiful woman waiting for them forever. There were many dreamers that night as guests slept in unfamiliar bedrooms.

"Good night, Simon." Margaret was in tears.

"Don't cry." Simon's voice was gruff. He sat up and put his arms round his wife. "Silly little fool will come to her senses."

"I do hope so. I'll ring her grandmother in the morning. I feel such a failure."

"Don't be silly. You're a wonderful woman." His voice was gruffer. "I love you."

"I know you do." Margaret suddenly smiled. "Would you do for me what Angus did for Bonnie?"

Simon nodded. "Of course, my dear." Margaret sighed a small contented sigh. Simon pulled her close to him.

Chapter 19

Bonnie opened her eyes. For a moment she thought she was back in the Great House in Lexington. Then she remembered the events of the night before. She sat up and looked around her. She lay in a large four-poster bed with red and gold damask hangings. The curtains matched the bed. The walls were panelled in a light-coloured wood. The remains of a fire smouldered in the fireplace. Beside the fire were two comfortable Victorian velvet nursing chairs, and against the wall by the door there was a large mahogany armoire. Bonnie immediately felt at home in this warm sunny room. She noticed the radiator and smiled. I've got nothing to wear but my ball gown, she remembered.

She got out of bed and went to the window. The moat around the castle was deeply filled with water. She could see snow-covered fields stretching over the horizon. Huge trees with their bare branches stood sentinel, guarding the ancient walls of Drummossie.

There was a knock at the door. "Who is it?" It's Angus, she thought.

"I'm Ginny, your maid. The master gave me a robe for you."

"Oh." Bonnie opened the door.

The maid looked startled. She was expecting the usual kind of woman her master brought home. Instead, here was a sensible-looking young woman of her own age, with eager innocent face and a warm smile.

"The master says he wants you to have breakfast with him in the morning-room. I'm to show you the way."

Bonnie's face lit up. "Give me five minutes, and I'll be with you." She took the black silk robe from Ginny and closed the door. She had tried very hard so far not to think of Angus.

Their drive back to the castle the previous night had been almost silent. "What did you think of my performance?" Angus asked at one point.

"Performance?" she said.

"Yes," he said with a hint of impatience.

"Oh." Bonnie was hurt. "Do you often do things like that?"

"As often as I can," he laughed. "I love the look on their silly vacuous faces. I knew old MacGregor couldn't refuse to let me in. It would have been bad luck. It took me hours to find out where you were staying, you know."

Bonnie was mollified by the fact that Angus had gone through all that trouble just to find her. She smiled. "What's going to happen now?" Angus did not answer. Bonnie suddenly realized that all her fantasies of making love with Angus were about to come true. She didn't know whether she wanted fantasy to materialize into fact while she still felt so confused. "I thought you were wonderful. When I saw you in the doorway, I knew you had come to take me away," she said.

Angus looked pleased. "That was the one bit in the plot that I couldn't be sure of."

"Is this all a play?"

"Yes and no." Angus pulled Bonnie to him. "Yes. All my life is a play. But no. I do love you, Bonnie. From the first moment I saw your face I knew we were destined to be together for all time. So that part of me isn't playing." He paused. "All those people who know me will expect me to get bored with you. I'll never be bored by you." He looked down at her lying with her head on his chest. Even at this late hour she had a freshness and a radiance which he wanted to preserve, and then, he realized, he wanted to destroy. He shifted. Why must I always look for happiness and then cause pain? he asked himself. This time, he silently promised, it will be different.

Bonnie was nearly asleep. "I could lie like this forever," she murmured as he gently woke her.

"We're here," he said. She allowed him to lead her into the dark shadows surrounding the castle. He took her up many stairs, and then opened the door of the bedroom. "Sleep well, my darling," he said, and he kissed her forehead. She looked surprised. He smiled. "I'm no raper of virgins," he said, "despite what you may have heard to the contrary." He kissed her mouth tenderly. "Tomorrow we will make our plans." He gently pushed her into the room and closed the door.

In his own bedroom with its immense chandelier hanging from the oak beams, Angus opened a plain velvet box. There sparkled three perfect diamonds. The last time he had seen that ring, it had been on his dead mother's hand.

He remembered standing at the foot of the stone staircase leading from the bedroom which he now called his own down to the central hall below. He was nearly four, and he held his teddybear in one hand and a red wooden fire engine in the other. He looked at his mother. She lay sprawled on her back, her neck twisted so that her face was turned in his direction. Her eyes were blank, and her mouth was open. There was a thin trickle of blood running down the side of her face.

The little boy dropped his toys and took a step towards his mother. He heard a muffled sound. The huge looming bulk of his father stood at the top of the stairs, staring down at the dead woman's body. "Get out!" his father shrieked at him. "Get out!"

Angus turned and ran for his life. He heard his father descend the stairs and begin to follow him through the rooms of the castle. "I'll kill you!" his father shrieked. "I'll kill you just as I killed your whore of a mother!"

Angus made for the back staircase and the servants' quarters. If he could get to John, one of the gillies, he knew he would be safe. John wasn't afraid of his father. Angus shot into the kitchen and into John's arms. "Wist now." John patted the trembling child. "No harm will come, lad. Is your father after you?"

Angus nodded. "He killed my mother," he said.

Just then the servants' bell sounded furiously. "That'll be your father," John said. "Wait by the fire. I'll calm him."

"He killed my mother!" Angus's voice began to rise.

"No, no, lad. He'd not do a thing like that. He . . ." But the fury of the bell interrupted him. "Stay until I return," John said. Angus nodded. He stayed by the fire for a very long time. He knew his mother was dead because her eyes looked like the eyes of a young doe he had once found in the forest. They too had been rolled back, and blood had lain on the ground. He also knew his father had killed his mother, who had loved Angus so passionately that the boy had rarely been out of her sight. He loved her for her love of him. He hated her because she loved his father who beat them both. He hated his father because he beat his mother and made her cry and he hated himself because he could not defend his mother. Now I'm alone, he thought. Even at the age of three, Angus realized he had lost what little protection he had had. An awful searing loneliness enveloped him.

John came back into the kitchen. "It's a bad business," he said. "Your mother slipped and fell down the stairs." He took Angus in his arms. "Your mother is dead, little man, but your father didn't kill her. She slipped." The man and the child looked at each other. John recognized the truth in the boy's eyes. Tears ran down Angus's face. John fought to control his own sorrow, for he too had loved the gentle, quiet, Spanish lady who had lived like a shadow in the vastness of the castle.

"I've told the master I'll be taking you home with me," John said. "You'll stay with Sheila and the bairns for the next few days." Later that night, with Angus asleep, John talked to his wife before falling asleep himself. "The old bastard'll be drunk as a hog by now. The boy's telling the truth. He pushed her. But they'll have the wine-soaked jack-ass of a doctor declare it death by misadventure. The boy will know the truth. It's a heavy burden for a man to bear."

Angus put the jewel box on his night-table. Usually, he was driven to the whisky bottle by the awful memory of that and many other moments. But tonight he fought the urge to get drunk and to destroy things in order to rid himself of the pain. Ever since he had seen Bonnie's face, his heart had held a temporary peace. She had the same gentle luminous glow about her which his mother had possessed. His memories of his mother were fragmented and blurred, lost in the mists of terror and violence. His mother's hair had been black, and Bonnie's was blonde, yet Bonnie still had the same smile about her lips, and he felt the same serenity in her company, a serenity he had not felt for twenty-nine years. He knew he would have to tell Bonnie about his father, but he trusted her even without knowing her. She would understand.

Chapter 20

After she had laid the black silk robe on the bed, Bonnie washed her face in the pretty little bathroom attached to her bedroom. She felt almost as if she were in a dream, and that if she took charge of the situation with her brain she might wake up and everything would evaporate and she would be back in the little stone room of the MacGregor castle. She wiped her face on a thick yellow towel. That feels real, she said to herself.

She walked over to the bed and picked up the heavy silk dressing-gown. On its lapel there was the MacPherson crest embroidered in gold and red. She slipped the gown over her shoulders. It hung in folds down to the floor. The smooth silk felt very real. I think I'll pinch myself, she thought, just to make sure. She did, and the resulting pain made her laugh. She was laughing when she opened the door and joined Ginny. Ginny smiled. "What's so funny?"

"I've decided this is really happening. This is not a dream. This is real."

Ginny nodded. "This is real, all right. The house has been in an uproar ever since the master told us you were coming. He's never made such a fuss over anyone else before. I mean any guests, of course."

Bonnie didn't hear her. She was looking at the walls hung with paintings, some by English masters, but many by Dutch, Italian, and French painters. Ginny led her through room after room furnished so ornately that they could have been in an Italian palace. Much of the furniture came from Spain, Bonnie realized, and then she remembered that Angus's mother had been Spanish.

Crossing the great ballroom, she saw an enormous portrait

of a woman who looked very like Angus. "That," Ginny nodded, "was the last mistress of this house. Wasn't she beautiful?"

Bonnie gazed up at the quiet composed face. "How sad she looks."

Ginny was about to say something, but she changed her mind. She'll find out soon enough if she stays, Ginny thought. When the master was home, he would often take his bottle of whisky and stand in front of his mother's portrait. Some nights he was quiet. Other nights, the servants learned to dread his screams and his cries. The windows and the furniture in the grand room had been repaired so many times, even Ginny had lost count. Only old John could calm him. Poor John, Ginny thought. He has the old master locked away upstairs in his suite, and the male nurses try, but John still has to do much of the tending himself, and then he has the young master down here to look after. "We had better hurry," Ginny said, "or the master will be getting impatient for his breakfast."

Bonnie smiled. "Does he often become impatient?" Ginny only rolled her eyes.

Angus showed no sign of impatience when he rose to greet Bonnie as she entered the morning-room. Bonnie ran forward into his outstretched arms. She tripped on the ends of the robe just as she reached Angus, and she tumbled into his arms and lay giggling with delight. "Did I keep you waiting, darling?" she said.

"No. I've waited for this moment for so long, I wouldn't spoil it with impatience."

She smiled at him. "Well, what plans do you have for us today?"

Angus looked thoughtful. "I expect we will be hearing from the Bartholomews. No doubt, Margaret will be on the telephone to your grandmother."

Bonnie was surprised. "How do you know all this?"

"I know everything." he said, childishly pleased that he had surprised her. "For instance, I know that your grandmother has a companion called Morag." Bonnie nodded as he continued, "and that you have a four-poster double bed with flowers on the covers."

Bonnie was amazed. "But how do you know?"

"I call it 'my magic.' When I was a little boy, I was alone a lot of the time and I used to find out everything I could about everybody who worked for us. Every little minute detail, and then . . ." He stopped. A strange look stole over his face. His normally gentle mild voice changed. It became harsh and metallic. "And then," he continued, "when I knew absolutely everything there was to know about a person, I controlled them. I could climb up into their skull and I could *be* them. I could think like them. I could act like them." His eyes glittered. Suddenly he saw the look of concern on Bonnie's face.

"You don't still do that, do you?" she asked uncertainly.

Angus's face changed. He kissed her softly on the lips. "No, my darling. Not any more. I just wanted to know how you lived and what you liked so that I could please you."

"Oh, that's all right then," she said. "By the way, what are we going to do about my clothes?"

Angus rang the bell for breakfast. "Well, we can't shop today, because everywhere will be closed for New Year's day. But we can telephone your cousin Teresa, and get her to drive your things over. Before she comes, I intend to propose to you."

"Do you really?" Bonnie was thrilled. "I've always wanted a proper proposal. You know, red roses and everything."

Angus nodded. She's like a soft downy duckling, he thought. "Then you can show the ring to Teresa, and she can go and broadcast the fact that we are officially engaged far and wide." The telephone rang by his elbow. "Good morning, Teresa," he said without waiting to hear who it was.

"How did you know it was me?" Teresa was flustered. She had a room full of people hanging on her every word.

"Would you like to speak to Bonnie?" Angus asked courteously.

"Yes, I would. Thank you." Teresa nodded at Margaret who was twisting her hands. "Bonnie? Are you all right?"

Bonnie laughed. "Oh honestly, Teresa. Of course I'm all right. Listen, can you pack my clothes and bring them over this morning?"

"Aren't you coming back?" Teresa asked.

Bonnie looked at Angus. "Am I going back?" she asked with her hand over the mouthpiece. He shook his head. "No," Bonnie said. "Not for the moment. But I have a wonderful surprise for you."

Teresa's voice was sharp. "Surprise? What sort of surprise?"

"Just wait and see. Oh, here comes breakfast. I'll see you later."

"All right." Teresa put down the telephone. She turned to John. "Well, she wants me to pack her things and take them over."

Margaret began to cry. "Oh dear," she said. "If only we'd known that she was so intent on marrying Angus."

Teresa sighed. "She was always so suspicious of men, I didn't think she was the sort who would go off the deep end. On the other hand, I do remember saying once that she was just the type to lose her head when she did finally decide to give herself to a man. But I didn't expect it would be Angus. And I certainly didn't expect her to get herself *this* involved so quickly."

John looked at his mother. "I did, you know. I knew her better than anyone. Underneath that cool exterior, she was extraordinarily intense. After an evening with Bonnie, I was exhausted. Every moment she was with me had to be lived to the full."

Cyril nodded. "I know what you mean. Well, she'll have her hands full with Angus. All we can do is wait and hope she'll see sense."

Margaret dried her eyes. "I'm going to ring Augustine, and see if she can do anything with Bonnie. Leave me alone, everyone. I need to concentrate."

Much to Margaret's surprise, Augustine took the news very calmly. "Ah yes," Augustine said. "The MacPherson boy, is it? Bonnie told me when she was here. She made me promise not to tell until she was more sure of him. She's a very impetuous girl in some ways." Augustine remembered how Bonnie had packed her bags four years ago and left Merrill and her mother without so much as a backward glance. "Don't worry, Margaret. I trust Bonnie absolutely. I'll get her to bring the boy home, and then I'll talk to her."

"Would you?" Margaret was immediately relieved and grateful. "All we can do at our end, I suppose, is wait for her to contact us, and then behave as if we are delighted. I really don't want to give Angus an excuse to cut her off from us." Margaret put the telephone down and, for the first time since Bonnie had gone, she felt a ray of hope. Maybe he will change, she thought. The love of a good woman. . . . She remembered the old proverb. She left the room and searched for her husband.

After Bonnie and Angus had eaten a huge breakfast, Bonnie sank back in her chair and sighed. "I don't always eat this much, but my stomach was in knots last night wondering when you would show up. I could hardly eat."

Angus stretched. He smiled at Bonnie. "Let's get the plates cleared away, and I'll show you the ring."

Bonnie's eyes widened. "You have it here?"

"I do." He patted his pocket. "Garrett!" he shouted.

A young man wandered into the morning-room. "Yes?" he said, staring insolently at Bonnie.

"Damn you Garrett, you're a servant here." Garrett went white. Angus's face was cold and hard. "Take the breakfast things."

"Yes," said Garrett. Just wait, he thought, as he cleared the table. Just wait until you're drunk next time. I'll leave you in your own vomit. He looked at Bonnie from under his long curling lashes. And you, he thought, just you wait until your face is a bleeding lump of meat, you cow.

Garrett was, in effect, Angus's drinking and whoring companion. He had travelled all over the world with the man. He had seen Angus attack a prostitute in Singapore one night. It had taken all Garrett's strength to knock Angus out before Angus kicked the girl's head in. Now, walking with the breakfast tray down the long corridor, Garrett remembered a number of scenes from the past.

Once Garrett had gone, Angus took Bonnie by the arm. "Come," he said. "Follow me."

She obediently accompanied Angus through the French windows of the morning-room into a large solarium filled with different species of palm trees. Part of the battlements had been roofed in with glass to make a spacious and airy room. The view across the wintry Scottish moorland made Bonnie pause for breath. "What a beautiful sight," she said.

"Here," Angus said softly. She turned and saw that he held a large bouquet of white roses. "I chose white roses," he explained very seriously. "Red roses always remind me of blood."

"Oh Angus," she laughed. "Don't be so morbid."

He looked at her from the empty holes of his eyes. She doesn't understand, he thought. She didn't see her lying there. He felt a surge of anger but before it could turn to rage, he calmed himself. He went down on one knee and put the flowers in her right hand. "Bonnie. Will you marry me, Bonnie?" he said simply.

"Oh yes, Angus." Bonnie's eyes were full of tears. "Of course I'll marry you."

Angus pulled the little leather jewel box out of his pocket. He opened it and took out the ring. "Then now with this ring I plight thee my troth." He slipped the ring on to Bonnie's finger. He stood up. He took Bonnie into his arms and kissed her with such passion that Bonnie forgot who she was and where she was.

When he let go of her, she was breathless. She looked at the ring. The three diamonds glittered on her finger. "What a beautiful ring," she said.

"It belonged to my mother."

"Oh." Bonnie looked seriously at him. "Do you think of her often?"

"All the time." There was such a look of anguish on his face that Bonnie put her arms around him.

"Poor Angus," she said. "Tell me what happened."

She sat curled up beside him in the solarium and listened for the first time to the awful story of his mother's death. Before he could finish, they were interrupted abruptly by Teresa's bouncing arrival. "I say," she said. "What a gloomy atmosphere for two love-birds." She stopped. "Oh, Angus, you're not in a mood again, are you?"

Angus forced himself to smile. He had spent weeks being nice to Teresa in order to extract information about Bonnie. He wasn't going to let her irritate him into an explosion. "We were talking about something you wouldn't understand." His rebuke fell on deaf ears.

Teresa gave a loud shriek and grabbed Bonnie's hand. "You're engaged!" she shouted.

"Please." Angus put his hand to his head. "Please, Teresa. You'll frighten all the cows in the fields."

"Good heavens," Teresa continued. "We've got diamonds, but nothing like this."

Bonnie smiled at Angus. "It isn't diamonds that count, Teresa."

"Oh yes. I know all about the sloppy side of getting engaged. I say, Angus. You didn't get down on one knee and do all that old-fashioned garbage, did you?"

Angus stiffened. Bonnie, seeing his face, spoke for him. "It isn't old-fashioned garbage, and it's none of your business."

Teresa threw back her head and guffawed. "Wait until I tell everybody that the terrible Angus MacPherson bent his knee to a woman!"

Bonnie realized that Teresa had gone too far. Angus's face was flushed, and his fists were clenched. "Where's my suitcase, Teresa?"

"Oh, I gave it to the parlour maid. She said her name was Ginny."

"Thank you. I think you'd better go now."

"Really? I've only just arrived. Anyway, I haven't forgotten you yet for ruining my night with Patrick. After your little display, he simply said that it was an impossible act to follow. And off he went to bed. But don't feel too bad. There will be other chances with Patrick. And it was well worth watching you two. God, I've never seen anything so romantic. Oh well, if you two want to be alone, I'll hop off, I suppose." Teresa was plainly disappointed. "Mummy says you should phone her some time today."

"Oh yes. I will. I must apologize to her. I must have seemed dreadfully ungrateful." Bonnie suddenly felt very guilty at turning her friend and cousin away. "Angus, we do owe a lot of our happiness to Teresa. If she hadn't taken me to the Seabornes' party, we might never have met each other." She saw Angus relax.

"That's true," he said. "I suppose you're right."

Teresa grinned. "Can I be bridesmaid?"

Bonnie nodded. "Of course," she said.

Chapter 21

"Bonnie?" Augustine had been waiting anxiously for her call. It was five o'clock in the evening in Lexington, and the snow lay deep outside the Great House. Augustine was in her favourite chair, and Morag sat close beside her. "Is everything all right, child?" She wanted the news to come directly from her granddaughter.

"Oh grandma, you'll never guess what has happened?" Bonnie's voice was singing with happiness. "I'm here with Angus, and we're engaged to be married." Bonnie looked lovingly at her engagement ring. "I've never been so happy in my life. Everything is wonderful. I apologized to Margaret for running off, but she's been fine. She says as long as I'm happy, she's happy." She paused to catch her breath. "Teresa will be my bridesmaid. I want Morag to be a bridesmaid as well. Will you come for the wedding?"

"Wait, child, wait." Augustine smiled. "You're going too fast for an old woman. When do you plan to get married?"

"Angus said April would be a good time to marry. We have a small chapel here on the estate and Father MacBride will marry us. I'd much rather have a small wedding up here than a big one in London."

"It all sounds lovely, dear, but I would like to meet your young man first." Augustine's voice was stern. "I have every faith in your choice, but I do feel I should meet Angus before you make an irrevocable decision to get married."

Bonnie glanced at Angus, who stared back at her intently. "Grandma wants to meet you," she said, with the receiver pressed to her shoulder.

Angus smiled. Old women always loved him. "Wonderful," he said. "Tell your grandmother that we will be back in

London in a few days, and we should be ready to travel in two weeks' time."

Bonnie relayed the information to Augustine. "Fine," Augustine said. "We look forward to seeing you both. Bonnie, I hope you are not planning to live with Angus before you are married."

Bonnie laughed. "You are old-fashioned, grandma. But don't worry, we've talked that through. Angus will move into his club until we are married, and I'll live at Heath House. That's his London home."

"Very good." Augustine was relieved. Fashions may come and go, but a girl with a tarnished reputation will always find it hard to marry a decent man. Angus sounds like a very decent and honourable man, she thought. "Well, I am pleased for you, my dear. I've always hoped you would marry well and be happy. I love you, my child, very much."

"I know." Bonnie felt a lump in her throat. "I know that, grandma. I'm so looking forward to being with the two people I love most in this world. Can I bring you anything?"

Augustine thought for a moment. "Yes. Please bring me some of those English sausages. I understand they're delicious."

"Done," Bonnie said happily. "Good night, grandma," she said. "God bless, and sleep well." She had a vision of the firelight in the drawing-room gleaming on her grandmother's white hair.

Angus looked at Bonnie as she put the telephone down. "The two people you love most in the world?" he asked.

"Yes." Bonnie threw herself into his lap and wound her arms around his neck. "Grandma and you."

"I come first, don't I?"

Bonnie was struck by the cold tone in his voice. She felt confused. "Well, my love for my grandmother and my love for you are two totally different things."

Angus's fingers tightened around her wrist. "No, they're

not. Love is love. And I want you to love me before anything else in the world." His black eyes glittered. "I mean that, Bonnie. I won't accept anything less than that."

Bonnie frowned. "Angus, you're hurting my wrist. Let go." But he did not let go.

His mouth was set in a thin line. "I'm serious, Bonnie." His voice took on the metallic tone she had heard before.

"Of course I love you best in all the world," she said, kissing him gently on the cheek.

"More than your grandmother?"

"More than my grandmother." Bonnie felt guilty, but she reasoned that Angus had lost his own mother so young that he needed her reassurance. "I'll love you for ever and ever," she promised him.

Angus relaxed. The tension left his face and his eyes softened. He stroked her hair and brushed his lips against her cheek. Bonnie had never known such physical tension in her life. Slowly he moved his lips to her mouth. Bonnie moaned with pleasure. "We'll have to stop," Angus said. He picked her up and deposited her on the chair opposite the sofa.

Bonnie marvelled at his self-control. One minute, he was a man full of passion. A split second later, he was cool and calm. She was still aroused, however. Her heart pounded, and she doubted whether her legs would support her.

"Tomorrow," Angus announced, "we will go racing, and then I want to show you Loch Ness." He drew up a list of engagements that would fill the rest of the week.

Time passed so swiftly that Bonnie was amazed to find herself packed and on the train to London. Angus had given Sacheverell instructions to be at the house the morning they arrived. "I hear on the grapevine that you're going to marry her," Sacheverell said on the telephone.

"Yes."

"She's not your type, you know, Angus."

"What does a pansy designer like you know about my tastes?" Angus's voice was hostile.

"Come on, Angus. Don't treat me like that. We've been in lots of scrapes together."

Angus's voice softened. "Well, I know what you mean. Bonnie is different. That's why I want to marry her."

"Don't hurt her, will you?"

"I'll try not to." Angus was sincere.

The night before he and Bonnie left for London, Angus paid a visit to his father's quarters. The old man lay in his bed in the stark white square room. There was no furniture apart from the hospital bed. His male nurses had long ago become tired of the old man's rages, so they had removed the chairs and the tables. Angus stood looking down at the old man's haggard face. He was too drugged to recognize Angus. His vacant blue eyes stared into space.

"You fucking bastard," Angus said. "I'm getting married to a girl who's as beautiful as my mother was until you got your rotten filthy hands on her." He could feel a terrible black rage welling inside his soul. "I hate you. You destroyed my mother. You tried to destroy me. You filthy lewd monster." He spat in his father's face. The saliva ran down the old man's cheek. He blinked like a surprised child.

The door opened behind Angus, and old John walked in. He put his hand on Angus's shoulder. "Leave him be. He's too far gone to hear what you say. Leave him."

Angus turned on his heel. "Aye, he's too far gone even to remember what he did to my mother and then to me."

John nodded. "Go to your bed. It's late, and you have a train to catch in the morning."

Angus nodded. He always felt comforted by old John.

John wiped the spittle from Lord MacPherson's face. He was lucky this time, old John thought. With a wedding on his mind, Angus had not physically assaulted his father. Many was the time the male nurses had had to haul Angus off. "You'll kill your father and spend the rest of your life in gaol," John had warned him.

Now he sighed deeply and shook his head. "The lad has good reason to hate you," he said to Lord MacPherson. The old man's eyes held fast in their empty stare. John remembered the day he was summoned to the foot of the steps to see the poor mistress of the house lying dead in a pool of blood. Even more vividly he remembered an incident four years later. John had been sitting in the kitchen when suddenly he heard a high-pitched scream coming from the drawing-room. John ran through the corridors, following the screams as they bounced off the walls. He burst into the sitting-room. On the floor, Angus laying sobbing hysterically. "Put him to bed," Alexander MacPherson ordered. "I've chastised him. Put him to bed." John took Angus in his arms. Although he was eight years old, the boy was as thin and as weightless as a feather. John carried the boy to his room.

"Tell me," John said when he had put Angus down, "tell me. Exactly what did your father do to you?" Blood seeped out from under the boy's kilt. The child was in such pain he howled as he threw himself about the bed.

There was a knock on the door. Philip MacTaggart, Alexander's cousin, came into the room. "I was passing," he said. "Is the lad all right?"

"No," said John. "He'll need the doctor." Philip, seeing the blood, went immediately to the telephone.

Old Dr. Rogers was less drunk than usual when he arrived. After examining Angus, he was stone-cold sober. "The boy's been sodomized," he said to Philip. "Perhaps one of the servants . . ." He looked at John. John looked at the floor. The howling had subsided and Angus was mercifully asleep. "He'll have to go to hospital," the doctor continued. "There's too much stitching for me to do here." He paused. "This is a very serious offence. We can press charges."

That drunken old madman, Philip MacTaggart thought. Can't even keep his hands off his own son. "No thank you, doctor," he said. All three men in the hall knew who had so cruelly abused the child. Philip cleared his throat. "I, um . . . I'm leaving for London in a week. I'll take the boy home with me. Joan is very fond of children, and we have none of our own." The doctor looked relieved. First Lady MacPherson dead, now this. He wanted the responsibility off his shoulders. "I'll speak to Alexander now," said Philip, and he strode off.

The doctor picked up his bag. "I'll send the ambulance to collect the lad. I'd like him stitched before the sedative I've given him wears off. I'll have a word with Matron at the hospital. None of this must get out." A week later, still in dreadful pain and full of morphine, Angus was transferred to a hospital in Hampstead.

Old John remembered the rage in the boy's eyes the last time he saw his white face before Angus left for London. Now, a quarter of a century later, the same rage drove Angus hither and thither all over the world. "Maybe," old John muttered as he stood over Lord MacPherson, "just maybe the love of a sweet young bride will heal the wounds." He sighed.

Angus enjoyed the expression on Bonnie's face when she walked into the house that faced Hampstead Heath. Though Bonnie had imagined it would be very like the Bartholomews' home, she was amazed to find herself surrounded by comfort, even luxury. "Yes," Angus said, when he saw her surprise, "I even have showers in all the bathrooms."

Bonnie immediately loved the house and its garden. Heath House had been built in Victorian times by Philip MacTaggart's grandfather with the vast amount of money he had made in the Far East. Philip had modernized the interior when he inherited the house, removing the grotesque elephants' feet used to hold dripping umbrellas and walking sticks, banishing the leather pouffes brought from the Middle East, and throwing out much of the huge old Victorian furniture because his wife said it depressed her. Much to her displeasure, Philip was unable to do anything about the exterior crenellations and turrets that could put even Drummossie Castle to shame.

Bonnie laughed. "My goodness, it's a cross between a Bavarian monstrosity and a wedding cake." She was in the back garden within minutes of arriving. She looked approvingly at the lawns and the flower beds. "Do you have a kitchen garden?" she asked the old man who was busy weeding.

"Yes, ma'am."

Angus joined her on the lawn. "Bonnie, this is Ben. He's been here since he was a boy, and his father was gardener before him."

Ben bowed his head. "How d'you do."

"This is Miss Fraser. We will be married in the spring."

Ben nodded. "Word travels fast," he said.

"Come on, Bonnie. I want to show you the inside of the house."

Bonnie turned to look over her shoulder as she walked off arm-in-arm with Angus. "As soon as I'm settled, I'd love to see the vegetable garden."

Ben nodded his old tortoise head. "That'll be a pleasure, Miss Fraser."

Bonnie looked at Angus and smiled. "I love gardens," she said. She described the greenhouses at Lexington as they walked back to the house.

"You see," Angus said as they came to a light airy room. "You can have this room until we are married." He frowned. "Some nights I like to be alone." Bonnie looked surprised. "I get these awful headaches," he explained, "and I can't bear anyone near me. I just have to lie by myself until it's over."

"Poor Angus," Bonnie said with tender sympathy. "Can't anything be done?"

"No. I've been everywhere and I've tried everything." Fortunately, he thought, I've had my room sound proofed. He didn't want Bonnie to hear his raging.

Sacheverell had carried out the sound proofing. He was the only person to know that the room was sound proofed, just as he was the only one of Angus's friends apart from old John to know that Angus had been molested as a boy. Sacheverell had had a brief affair with him. He knew more about Angus than did anyone else. "You hate women, Angus," Sacheverell once said to Angus. "Why don't you give up, and just live with a man?"

Angus remembered that conversation now as he heard Sacheverell come shrieking up the stairs. "Bonnie, darling!" Sacheverell kissed her cheek. "I'll be the only person allowed to so much as kiss your hand, now that you're going to marry your demon prince. And it's only because he knows I'm safe."

Bonnie giggled. She had noticed that Angus very rarely let her out of his sight, even though they had only been together for a week. Bonnie remembered an incident from their trip to London. Coming down on the train, a young man had tried to engage Bonnie in conversation. "Mind your own bloody business," Angus had said. Later, when Angus came into her sleeper to wish her good-night, he was sulking. "You encouraged him," he said.

"I didn't." Bonnie was indignant. "Of course I didn't. I didn't even notice he was there."

Bonnie now felt a queer sense of power and security when Sacheverell acknowledged Angus's jealousy. He loves me so much, she thought, he's terrified of losing me. I guess Angus must be used to women who cheat on their husbands. "You never have to worry about me betraying you, Angus. I wouldn't ever do that," she said. "Never. You know that, don't you, Angus?"

He smiled at her. "They say, never trust a woman. Don't they?" His eyes glittered.

"Well, you can certainly trust me," Sacheverell butted in. "Now do concentrate, Bonnie. Let's see what we have here . . . Angus, Bonnie and I must attend to the business of putting this room into some form of order. Isn't there something you can find to do?"

Angus laughed. "I suppose I'll have to trust you with my best-beloved. All right then, Sacheverell. I have some telephone calls to make. I'll leave her in your hands. But you're wasting your breath if you plan to corrupt her against me. She won't hear a word of it. Will you, darling?"

"Of course not," Bonnie said with a smile. Angus kissed her on the cheek.

"Now what shall we do with this room?" Sacheverell said in his most professional tone.

It had been used as a bedroom by the housekeeper, but Angus had moved her from the main house to a small flat over the stables. "No doubt so I shan't hear his wife scream," the housekeeper had said to the cook. She had heard plenty of screaming in her time, and she knew when to leave well alone. Those servants who tried to interfere were promptly dismissed with no references, and now, with a flood of immigrants prepared to work for little money, good jobs with decent salaries were hard to find. Angus paid well for silence, but the housekeeper disliked him, as did most of the women on the staff. The men felt that most of the women-friends who chose to stay in Angus's house deserved what they got. Word had come from the castle, however, that Angus's future bride was a young thing from abroad who had no idea of what she was taking on. The housekeeper, Mrs. Turner, was a good woman, and she worried for Bonnie as she set up her own little flat above the stables.

Sacheverell also held his tongue. He too wished that Bonnie might be distracted from a headlong path to destruction. Understanding Angus as he did, he knew he could guarantee

Angus's inability to change his ways. "How would you like this room to look, Bonnie?" he asked again.

She bit her lip. "Well, maybe a sort of sitting-room with a bed in it. I don't expect I'll need to stay here much. It's Angus's headaches, you know. He can't bear anybody to be near him when he has them. But," she looked trustingly at Sacheverell, "I'm sure the headaches will go away once we're married. He needs someone like me who is prepared to devote her life to him and to his children."

Sacheverell was incredulous. "Angus hates children."

"Oh, he just says that. He'll love his own kids. Lots of men think they hate children, but when they hold their babies in their arms, they fall in love with them."

"Bonnie, is there any room in your gossamer dreams for a black thread?"

Bonnie looked squarely at Sacheverell. "No," she said firmly. "I don't think about negative things. If you do, you just encourage them to go wrong." She smiled sweetly. "I know Angus has a quick temper, but. . . ."

"That's putting it very mildly." Sacheverell was getting impatient.

"I know, I know. But Angus has never had a settled home with someone to love him."

"Bonnie, Angus has had a trail of women, most of whom have tried to give him a settled home and to love him."

"Yes, but they can't have been the sort of women that could have made him happy. Otherwise, he would have married one of them, wouldn't he?"

Sacheverell groaned. "Never argue with a woman," he said. "All right, Bonnie. I'll keep my mouth shut. Now, let's go off tomorrow and choose some furniture, assuming that Angus will let you off the chain."

Angus was perfectly happy for Sacheverell to take Bonnie anywhere. Unlike Garrett, who had shared Angus's bed on several occasions, Sacheverell would be discreet about Angus's forays into homosexuality. Garrett, Angus knew, must stay at Drummossie. "Of course you can go, darling," he said to Bonnie as he said goodnight to her in one of the guest rooms. "Spend whatever you want, and we'll enjoy ourselves for a week, and then fly to see your grandmother." Bonnie fell asleep dreaming of Angus. Angus fell asleeping dreaming that an old lady was chasing him with a riding whip.

Bonnie bought a pretty little mahogany carved bed with a white linen canopy. Sacheverell found two small spoon-back Victorian chairs upholstered in salmon-pink velvet. He matched the pink with the heavy cotton curtains, and together they found a thick white carpet for the floor. "I'll turn the little room on the left of the sewing-room into a matching bathroom, and you'll need a dressing table," Sacheverell said.

Bonnie thought for a moment. "I've always wanted one of those dressing tables that have a mirror surrounded by electric light bulbs. You know, the kind that has all the shelves hidden by a curtain that you can pull back, and it has a bench seat? Lana Turner had one in an old movie I saw at Brown."

Sacheverell nodded. "You shall have your wish, my fairy princess." He took Bonnie's hand. "We'd better get you back to the ogre, or he'll bite my head off and spit it out at a passing bus."

"Why do you call Angus such awful names?"

"Because, in my own sensitive, subtle way, I am trying to warn you, Bonnie Fraser."

She tilted her chin. "Okay. Consider me warned. Now please don't warn me again if we are to remain friends."

Sacheverell nodded. "Speaking of friends," he said, to change the subject, "I hear Teresa and her mob are back in town. Why don't you give her a ring."

"I will," Bonnie said, "but we'll be flying off to Boston on Saturday, and we have an awful lot to do."

Sacheverell saw Bonnie into the Rolls, and the chauffeur headed for home. "I'll have your little nest ready by the time you get home from the States." Sacheverell promised her as the car pulled up in front of his little house in Eaton Mews West.

Angus was not pleased to learn that Bonnie wanted an early night. "Whither thou goest, I go," he said very firmly. "I go gambling most nights."

Bonnie was sitting in the dining-room at Heath House. She was wearing a black silk dress with her baguette diamond gleaming at her throat. They sat across from each other at a small Regency table. Bonnie had insisted that all the table's flaps be removed. She didn't want to isolate herself from Angus. Now, sitting within an arm's reach of him, she could feel his irritation. "Please, Angus. I've got an awful headache and I'm tired," she pleaded.

"Damn it, Bonnie, don't ever argue with me. Take some aspirins and we'll go." They were drinking coffee. Angus had a large glass of brandy in his hand. His foot tapped with impatience.

"I really don't want to go, Angus." She caught sight of his flushed face. "I don't see why you should force me. You'll have a much better time without . . ."

Angus threw his brandy glass against the wall. He reached out and grabbed at her neck. Bonnie flinched backwards; he missed her throat. His hand, however, caught the diamond and the chain snapped. Full of the energy of anger, Angus leapt to his feet and ran across to the window. He forced it up and then threw the necklace as far as he could. Bonnie had been too shocked to move. She burst into tears.

Angus left the room. A moment later, Bonnie heard him slam the front door. Ginny scurried nervously into the room carrying a dustpan and brush. "Shall I clear the table?" she said tactfully.

Bonnie nodded. "I'm tired, Ginny. I think I'll go to bed." She lay there looking at the ceiling. Well, mom used to throw things, she thought, and look how she's changed. She cried herself to sleep.

Angus returned in the early hours of the morning. He had lost a lot of money at the tables and got very drunk. Eventually, he had insulted a wealthy Arab and the bouncer had thrown him out of the club. Angus lost money so regularly that he was never barred despite his bad behaviour. The bouncers knew that, at a certain point on many an evening, they would have to throw him out. After a good fight with the bouncers, Angus usually felt at peace with the world.

This time, however, he experienced a sense of discomfort. He had left Bonnie crying. He cursed his foul temper. He loved the woman. He didn't want to hurt her. "Bruton Street," Angus had said to the cab-driver after he had picked himself up off the pavement outside the club. He stuffed a five pound note into the driver's hand. Within three minutes they had stopped outside a jeweller's shop. "Wait," Angus told the taxi. "I won't be long." He gave the driver another five pound note.

"Happy to oblige," the cab-driver said. Queer one, he thought as he watched Angus yelling and banging against the door.

A light appeared in the window above the shop. A face peered out. "I want the best diamond necklace you've got!" Angus shouted up at the owner.

"Oh. It's you, Angus. I might have known. Hang on. I'll be down in a minute."

Angus disappeared into the shop. A few minutes later he returned in triumph to the taxi. "Take me to Heath House in Hampstead," he commanded, "and wait for me outside."

"Whatever you say, sir." The driver had never seen anything quite like this before.

Angus let himself in to Heath House and tiptoed up the stairs. He slipped into Bonnie's bedroom and put a blue velvet box on her bedside table. He looked down at her tear-stained face. It's a funny feeling to make a woman cry, he thought. Almost powerful. Odd. He turned, quietly let himself out and told the taxi-driver to take him to his club. She'll have to forgive me, Angus thought. That damned necklace just cost me forty grand.

Bonnie opened her eyes and sat up. We've had our first quarrel, she thought. She saw the jewel box on the little table beside her. She opened it and stared at the stunning baguette diamond. The jewel was three times the size of the diamond given to her by her grandmother. It's not the same, she thought, but it is Angus's way of saying he's sorry. She smiled. I'll have to learn not to argue with him. She was still smiling when she went downstairs for breakfast.

When Angus arrived at midday, she was waiting for him. She wore a plain grey dress with a vee-neck. The diamond hung at her throat. "Thank you, Angus," she said, throwing herself into his arms. "What a lovely present." She kissed him fervently. "I'm sorry I argued with you. I won't do it again."

"That's all right, darling. Lovers have to have quarrels. After all, we get to kiss and make up, don't we?"

Bonnie clung to him. "I don't like quarrelling."

Angus laughed. "Don't be a goose. That's half the fun of it." Bonnie said nothing. She was learning.

Twenty yards from the house, Bonnie's other diamond lay unnoticed until a Saturday weeks later when a small child picked it up and took it to his mother. Must be from a Christmas cracker, she thought. Very pretty, though. She put it away in a drawer.

Chapter 22

The visit to Boston passed entirely harmoniously. Angus loved the Great House. He floated on his back in the large white marble pool and gazed at the ceiling. "Let's build a pool like this," he said to Bonnie who was perched on the pool's edge.

"Oh, Angus. That'd be great. I really miss swimming."

Laughing suddenly, Angus lunged at Bonnie, grabbed hold of her ankles, and dragged her kicking and screaming into the water. Augustine came into the room and watched the two of them for a moment. What a perfectly attractive couple, she thought. He's so caring of her. He never leaves her side. "Time for lunch," Augustine called out with a smile on her face.

Angus stood up and shook the water out of his hair. "We'll be with you in a minute." He helped Bonnie out of the pool. "What's for lunch?" he asked, smiling at Augustine.

"Roast lamb."

"Ah, wonderful. You run a magnificent establishment." Angus bowed with a flourish to Augustine.

Augustine's eyes twinkled. "And you," she said, "mustn't waste your charm on an old woman."

"Augustine, your beauty will never age. Like wine, women only improve with years."

Augustine was delightfully flustered. She shook her head. "Off with both of you," she said. Augustine watched them wistfully. Such a passionate man, she thought. So electric. Lucky Bonnie. The old lady made her way slowly to the dining-room.

Laura was thrilled with Angus. She had booked them into the Post House Hotel, the same hotel where she and James had stayed upon their arrival at Merrill. It remained a mean, derelict hotel, but it was the best Merrill had to offer. She had explained to Angus and Bonnie that her own simple little home was not comfortable enough for Angus. "We should get your mother a decent place, you know, Bonnie," Angus said. He imagined that she lived in a hovel.

Bonnie looked at him. "Really, it's quite a sweet little house, you know."

Angus soon recognized a kindred soul in Laura. "We'll see," he said.

Angus was charming to Laura, and very civil to the priest. He was amused at the obsequious manner Father John employed when Angus attended mass. Angus watched Laura with Father John and smiled thinly. So, he thought, she's lusting after the priest. She hasn't changed at all, for all Bonnie says. Then again, women never do. Angus did not concentrate at all on the service. He looked sideways at Bonnie who was singing a hymn, oblivious to the world about her. She sang with joy. Here she was in Merrill, the town that had been the setting of so much sadness in her life, now with the man she loved at her side.

Angus observed that Laura, too, sang with joy. Her daughter had just delivered a prize catch into her hands. Now she would not only go up in the world, she would also engineer sufficient funds to keep Father John attached to his church through her largesse. Father John, in turn, would be so grateful that he would be bound to obey her deepest need. Laura looked up at Angus. Bonnie stood between them, singing sweetly. Laura smiled at Angus. Angus looked down at her, and for an instant they shared a moment of communion as the gates of hell opened before them. Laura shivered. Poor Bonnie, she thought. Laura had seen the same eyes in other men. Violent men. She lowered her own eyes to her missal and began to pray furiously.

* * *

Mitzi was equally thrilled to meet Angus. She bustled about her little sitting-room, which smelled of furniture polish and good food, shoving the children out of the way. She looked as if she would give birth at any minute. "Here, Angus," Mitzi said. "Have some tsimis. It's the kids' favourite." Angus shot Bonnie a desperate look as Mitzi thrust a plate of pudding before him. "What's the matter? Don't they have tsimis in Scotland?" Mitzi said.

Bonnie could see that Angus was getting nervous. "You'll get used to Mitzi," Bonnie said with a laugh.

"That's right," Mitzi joined in. "Don't pay any attention to me. Forcing food down people's throats is just the way we show affection." Angus smiled. Mitzi stared at Angus. "You didn't tell me he was so good-looking," she said to Bonnie.

"Mom says Jane Ashly got married last week."

Mitzi nodded. "And you remember Mike Edwards? Well, he got married too. To that mousey little Caroline."

"Oh yes," Bonnie wrinkled her brow in an attempt to remember Caroline.

Max chose that moment to grab at Angus's food with his sticky little hand. "Get off," Angus snapped. He looked up and saw the surprise on Bonnie's face. He put down his fork and picked Max up onto his lap. He tried to play with him but Max, upset by the anger in Angus's voice, began to howl uncontrollably. "Children don't like me," Angus said helplessly.

Bonnie took Max and comforted him. "Wait until we have our own children," she said.

"I don't want children." Angus glared at Bonnie. "I don't ever want to have children."

Mitzi smiled at Angus. "Don't worry. You're not the first man to say that. But everybody loves their own kids." She smiled benevolently at Angus. "Who couldn't love kids?"

Angus stared back. His face was white and his eyes were bitter. "You never knew my father," he said. Into his mind flashed a memory of his father's groping fingers and fleshy mouth.

Bonnie took his hand gently. "Darling," she said, "we must be going. We've got to get the plane for Boston." Angus nodded. He was fighting to control himself.

"We won't have children, will we?" he said anxiously in the cab on the way to the hotel.

Bonnie sighed. "Oh, Angus. I would love to have kids. Lots of them." She smiled. "Imagine a little boy who looked just like you."

"No." Angus was tense. "No, Bonnie. I shouldn't have children."

"Why not?" Bonnie was puzzled. "You'd be a wonderful father."

Angus shuddered. "I'm the last of the MacPhersons." He looked down at the floor. He frowned. "We're a bad lot. There's a terrible history in our family. It's better that the history dies with me." He looked earnestly at Bonnie. "Anyway, I don't want to have to share you with anyone, not even children."

Bonnie smiled uncertainly. "I suppose if you feel that passionately about not having kids, I'll have to accept it."

Angus nodded. "I do feel that passionately. I don't want children. Ever."

"Okay," Bonnie said. "That's settled then." In her heart of hearts she knew she could bide her time. A loving warm marriage would soon change Angus into a different person. She could wait until then.

Bonnie and Angus returned to Boston, but he was clearly bored. "What do Bostonians do for sport?" he asked as he sat with Bonnie in her favourite spot in the entire city, the court-yard of the Boston Public Library, now grey with winter.

"Well, in the summer we have the Red Sox. And, in the winter, we do have the Celtics playing basketball at the Boston Garden. And there's the Bruins playing ice-hockey. I tell you what," Bonnie said with sudden enthusiasm. "If you really want to see a hockey game, we could go down to Brown, my old university, and watch the Brown team play. That way I can also show you where I went to school."

Angus could not have been less interested in visiting a university, but he did like the idea of the hockey game. "If it will make you happy," he said to Bonnie, kissing her lightly on the cheek.

Providence, Rhode Island, was only an hour from Boston by either train or car. Angus, however, insisted upon flying, believing it would be quicker and more comfortable. The plane was small and uncomfortable, tightly packed with businessmen. It landed in a very grey Providence. The taxi ride from the airport to the centre of town was long and tedious. The small city sat burdened down by a heavy icy fog that had lumbered in from Narragansett Bay. Angus despised Providence.

They put their cases in their suite at the Biltmore Hotel, hired a car from the front desk, and drove up College Hill to Brown University. Angus was appalled by the hockey game and by the crowd of onlookers. Bonnie, on the other hand, loved every minute of it. As the third period was approaching its end, the Brown forward slapped the puck into the Harvard goal, putting Brown in the lead. "Wow!" Bonnie shrieked. "Look at that! Way to go!" she screamed to the rink.

"Hey." A hand descended on her shoulder. Angus looked up sharply. Bonnie turned round. It was Mike Edwards with his wife Caroline. "Hey," Mike said. "Bonnie! Great to see you again."

Bonnie smiled. "Mike! We were just talking about you the other day. Here. Meet Angus. We're engaged to be married."

Mike passed his beer bottle from his right to his left hand, and shook Angus's hand vigorously. "Nice to meet you," he said good-naturedly. Turning to his wife he said, "Honey, this is Bonnie and, ah, Angus, was it?"

Caroline nodded. "I used to take classes with you, Bonnie."

Angus had stopped listening. He sat glowering at Mike. "So," Mike said to Bonnie. "Somebody at last has woken the princess from her sleep and claimed her for his own?" There was such a note of yearning in his voice that Bonnie was embarrassed.

"Let's go." Angus stood up. "I'm very bored."

"Oh, I'm sorry." Bonnie jumped up quickly.

Angus strode out of the auditorium. The yells and chants of the audience faded away as he walked through the door into the cold night. He marched in complete silence to the hired car in the parking lot. Bonnie, breathless, tried to keep up. Once in the car, Angus drove recklessly down the hill to the hotel. "You'll kill us!" Bonnie said, holding tightly to her seat as Angus drove through a red light on North Main Street.

"No, I won't," Angus said calmly. "But I will kill that bastard Mike."

"Why?" Bonnie was astonished. "What on earth did Mike do to make you so angry."

"He fancies you." He turned his head and glared at Bonnie. "Do you fancy him?"

"Oh, don't be ridiculous, Angus. I've known Mike since I was a child. We grew up in Merrill together. Besides, he's married."

"That's never stopped a man."

"Look, if I had really wanted to be with Mike, I could have done so in high school or at Brown. But I didn't. I chose you."

"Don't tell me about your years before you met me. I really don't want to hear the sordid details."

"Angus . . ." Bonnie recognized that arguing was futile. "Angus, please don't be cross," she wheedled. "Please. We've been having such a good time together. I'm sorry you didn't like the hockey game. I promise I won't drag you through that ever again. Okay?"

Angus was not to be mollified. He slammed the car to a halt in front of the hotel. He stormed into the lobby with Bonnie running behind him. "You have dinner in your room," he said. "I'm going out."

Bonnie knew by now that any further discussion would only lead to a fight. She very much did not want to fight with Angus. "All right," she said quietly. "You have a night out. I can do with a good sleep." She smiled at him. "Good night, darling." She put her hand on his shoulder to draw his face closer.

He pushed her hand away and strode off. "I'll see you at breakfast," he said over his shoulder.

Bonnie shrugged.

After Angus had left the hotel, he walked briskly through the icy night for nearly an hour. He was restless. He knew he needed to get drunk, or to get into a fight with someone. He walked with his hands clenched in his coat pockets. He watched passers-by, waiting for someone to brush past him or to stare for a moment too long at his face. He felt electric. He needed to explode. His problem was solved as he walked a block past the bus station. He looked up and saw a large neon sign. "ALL-NIGHT BOXING," it read.

Angus paid for a ticket and went inside the brightly-lit arena. Here are real men, Angus thought. He took his place in the third row among the packed bodies that lined the ring. He could smell the sweat of the audience. Soon two men climbed between the ropes into the ring. The first was a two-hundred-and-fifty-pound black man with gleaming ebony skin. He danced around the ring with his hands in the air. The crowd loved him. The second man had a thick-set body with pasty white skin covered in ginger hair. He scowled at the audience. Pleased to have someone to hate, they jeered back.

The bell sounded and the match began. Angus was thrilled. He roared with the crowd. He watched, alight with pleasure, as the blood flowed from a cut above the black man's eye in the sixth round. "Hit him again!" Angus shouted. As if following Angus's instructions, the white man laid into the black man with renewed vigour. Blinded by a curtain of blood which poured down his face, the black man was unable to dodge a powerful left hook to his belly. He fell with a thud.

"Foul!" screamed the crowd. "Too low! Too low!" Suddenly Angus was furious. His chosen boxer was a cheat. He had thrown a low blow. He jumped from his seat and ran to the ringside. He yelled at the referee. The referee was busy trying, with the help of both trainers, to pull the white man off the slumped figure on the mats. The referee had little time to be insulted by a spectator. "Fuck off," he snarled at Angus.

Angus started to climb into the ring. Hands pulled at him from behind. Turning, Angus saw a large determined man with his hand planted firmly on Angus's collar. "Sit down, ya bastard!" the man said. "Sit down or I'll make ya sit down."

Angus grinned. "Let's see you then," he said coldly and with menace.

Angus felt as if he had been hit by an express train. And then he went wild. He threw himself at the man. They kicked and bit and punched each other until they were torn apart by a gang of onlookers. "Knock it off!" the referee said sternly, leaning over the ropes, after the two men had been pinned by the hired bouncers.

Angus smiled. He felt better inside, much much better. Shaking off the bouncers, he shook hands with his opponent. "Come on," he said. "Show me somewhere where a man can get a drink."

"Sure thing. I know just the place." The two men left the

arena and walked out into the frozen slush of a Providence winter's night.

"What happened to your face?" Bonnie asked him at breakfast.

"Oh, nothing," Angus lied. "I had a collision with a fire hydrant. I'm not used to the beastly little things. I fell over and hit my face on the pavement."

Bonnie was relieved that Angus was in such a good mood. "Let's go to Boston today," she said. "I'll say goodbye to grandma, and we'll go back to London."

Angus was delighted. Apart from the lobster bars on the wharves, he didn't much like Boston. He looked at her. "Get packed and we can be there by lunchtime. Only let's take the train this time. I couldn't bear to be stuck on that ghastly plane again."

Bonnie smiled. "Okay, I'll ring for the car to meet us at South Station."

Angus continued to charm Augustine back in Lexington. On Bonnie and Angus's last night in the Great House, Augustine promised that she would make her first trip to England with Morag as her companion. "Come a week before the wedding so that I can fix Morag's dress," Bonnie said. "We'll leave London for Drummossie on the Thursday. That will give us Friday to relax, and then Saturday will be my magic day."

Angus smiled across the table at her. "Who else do you want to invite?"

"Well, mom of course." She made a face. "I'll bet she'll want to invite Father John. You know I would like Mitzi and her family to come. Her mother was awfully good to me."

Angus was in a magnanimous mood. Bored as he was by the virtue of Augustine's life, he did enjoy the luxury of the Great House. "I think that's a lovely idea, Bonnie. Do have as many people as you like. Just tell Mrs. Turner, and she can arrange the whole thing with my travel agent."

"Thank you, Angus," Bonnie said with joy. "You're so generous."

Angus nodded. I think I'll buy a bigger house, he thought. He smiled. "I'm going to buy you a house for a wedding present."

Bonnie was astounded. "But you've just spent a fortune on my room."

"True, but I'd like to live along the Embankment."

Bonnie was delighted. "Oh, how lovely. The river is so gorgeous at night."

Angus frowned. "How do you know?" he asked suspiciously.

"Oh, Teresa drove me down there one night." Good, she thought. I'm learning not to upset him.

"Shall we play a hand of bridge?" Augustine asked suddenly.

"What a good idea," Morag said. "I'll go ahead and set up the table."

Just as Bonnie had finished saying goodbye to the butterflies in the greenhouse the next day, Morag followed her into the corridor which ran between the greenhouses and the pool. "Bonnie," Morag said uncertainly, "I don't want you to get me wrong, but it's your last day here." She hesitated.

"Go on, Morag," Bonnie said encouragingly. "What's bothering you?"

"I like Angus," Morag said. "But I feel that he's dangerous. I was watching his face at dinner last night, and he changes moods like the wind. One moment his face is happy, and then something happens and he's sad or he gets angry. He doesn't show it, but, boy, I wouldn't like to upset him."

Bonnie was silent for a moment. She put her arm round Morag, and they walked back to the house through the pool room. "You're right, Morag. He is very changeable and very possessive. But that's because he's insecure. He had such a dreadful childhood. He told me all about his father. I must say, I've seen Lord MacPherson a couple of times walking in the grounds of the castle with his nurses, but quite honestly I'm terrified of him. I know Angus will change. Once he really trusts me and believes that I won't betray him."

Morag was still unsure. "Bonnie, people don't change that much unless they really want to change. I'm sorry about Angus's father, but a person can't use a bad childhood as an excuse. Most people have awful childhoods. What makes you think that Angus will change?"

"My mother did."

Morag could see that she was wasting her breath. "Okay, okay. I'm sure you're right, Bonnie. But just be careful."

They walked into the main hall with their arms around each other. Angus waited impatiently for Bonnie in the main hall. "You're ten minutes late," he said when she walked in with Morag.

Bonnie smiled. "I'll just run and kiss grandma goodbye."

"We haven't got the time." Angus was angry.

"I'll only be a minute." She ran off upstairs. "Goodbye, grandma," she said kissing Augustine, who had been reading her missal. "See you in April."

Augustine smiled. "You have chosen a lovely husband for yourself." Augustine had been completely taken in by Angus. "He has wonderful manners and he obviously adores you."

Bonnie nodded. "I must run. He hates to be kept waiting." She flew down the stairs, kissed Morag, and jumped into the car. Angus sulked all the way to the airport. When he sulked he looked just like a small boy. His lower lip stuck out, and his long dark lashes rested on his cheeks. Bonnie, instead of being irritated, always felt protective. "I'm sorry I kept you waiting, Angus. Really. I know you don't like me to be late. I won't do it again."

"It's not just that," he said, pleased with her apology. "I don't want you to have that little lesbian as your bridesmaid."

"Angus." Bonnie was suddenly angry. "You take that back. Morag is not a lesbian. She is my friend. And anyway, even if she were, I would still want her to be my bridesmaid."

Angus had never seen Bonnie angry before. He knew he had gone too far. He gave a short bark of a laugh. "All right, if you insist. Have her, but don't expect me to like her."

Bonnie was still angry. "And don't you expect Morag to like you."

"I know. I'm not very likeable."

Bonnie immediately felt guilty. "Oh no, Angus. You're adorable, really." She was glad the glass partition was closed so that the chauffeur did not have to hear her sweet-talk Angus back into a good mood.

Chapter 23

Bonnie was delighted with her new bedroom. Sacheverell hopped about like an animated chicken. "Aren't I clever?" he crowed.

Bonnie hugged him. "You are indeed," she said. "Did Angus tell you? We're buying another house."

"Oh. That again."

"What do you mean?"

"Well," Sacheverell said, "he's always buying houses. But don't worry. You won't be moving. Men like Angus are extremely territorial. They never leave their lairs. He gets easily bored, and if he isn't travelling, he'll buy houses or horses. Then he sells them, or gives them away if he's in a good mood. But never mind, my dear. Tell me all about your visit."

Bonnie filled Sacheverell in on the details of their stay in America. "You're learning, Bonnie," Sacheverell said when Bonnie mentioned how bored Angus had been at the Brown hockey game. He looked at her seriously. "Living with Angus is going to be like managing a very unpredictable animal. If you don't watch what you're doing, you'll be in great danger."

Bonnie paused and let her honest blue eyes rest on Sacheverell's concerned face. "I know," she said. "And, after spending a few weeks with Angus, I can see why people have been trying to warn me. I can see all that. But what *they* can't see is that he's soft as butter inside." She raised her eyebrows. "How many brides go to the altar a virgin at the *groom's* insistence?"

"How very noble of him." Sacheverell was on the spot. I can't really tell her that he hates making love to women, can I? he asked himself.

"Gossiping again?" Angus strode into the room. "Sacheverell, I want to buy a big house on the Embankment. I want a huge greenhouse with a marble pool."

Sacheverell was delighted. "I know just the house, Angus. You'll love it." Angus smiled broadly. "Oh, Angus," said Sacheverell. "You still haven't had that beastly chipped tooth of yours fixed."

Angus smiled again. "And I never will. I like to think of myself as being *slightly* flawed."

Sacheverell threw Bonnie a quick, concerned look. But she chose to smile lovingly at Angus. "Well, I like the way it looks," she said. "It makes you special, Angus." She kissed him on the cheek. "How did you chip your tooth anyway?"

"Oh, an accident in my wilder years. But that's all over now." He smiled at Bonnie. Only Sacheverell did not smile. "Anyway," Angus said to Sacheverell, "let's get this new house bought right away."

The three of them returned to making plans.

* * *

Bonnie contacted Teresa as soon as she had recovered from the flight. "Do you think I could ask your father to give me away?" she asked.

Teresa sounded doubtful. "I don't know about that," she said. "Daddy's awfully rude about Angus. I'll ask mummy. Hang on." She charged up the corridor. A moment later, she picked up the phone. "Mummy says daddy would be delighted, and will you come over and she'll help you with the wedding arrangements?"

"Thanks so much, Teresa. I was really worried about the arangements. I haven't got a clue how to get the whole thing together."

Teresa snorted. "Mummy will love it. She said it would be good practice for my wedding. What with Cyril and Mary getting married and in a synagogue, and daddy says wild hogs wouldn't drag him into a temple. He'll give in, though. He usually bellows for a day or two, but he loves Mary."

Bonnie laughed. "Are they having a traditional Jewish wedding?"

"Yes. Mary is taking Jewish lessons and everything. She's going to be converted." Teresa was giggling. "Anyway, I have your invitation. They will be married just before you. Have you set an exact date yet?"

Bonnie thought for a moment. "I think I'd like to get married on the last Saturday in April. Winnie told me that's when spring in England is at its best. I'll ask Angus and let you know."

"You'll have to organize your list for presents, you know." Teresa was enjoying herself. "Otherwise you'll end up with thousands of silver toast racks."

"I don't think we need anything very much." Bonnie pictured the well-stocked cupboards in each of Angus's houses.

"That doesn't make a difference. Ask for it anyway, and give it to charity."

"Okay," Bonnie was amused. "I'll inundate the N.S.P.C.C. with silver toast racks."

"No, not the N.S.P.C.C., idiot. In England you always give to an animal charity first, then whatever's left over goes to humans."

"Oh dear. I forgot."

"By the way, I'm not supposed to tell you, but John has decided to give you Morgan as a wedding present."

"Oh Teresa, he'll be furious that you told me."

"I know," Teresa said matter-of-factly. "John's been train-ing Morgan to growl every time he says 'Angus.'"

"You're making that up," Bonnie laughed.

"Yes, well maybe I am, but John is very fond of you."

"I know, and I am very fond of him. Anyway, I'm delighted to have Morgan as a present. I know Angus will love him. Listen, I must go now. Can I come for tea next week?"

"Okay. Make it Wednesday week at four o'clock. We can organize a committee meeting with Mary and Pauline and mummy. Ann'll be at work."

"Lovely. Looking forward to seeing you all again. And Morgan." Bonnie put down the phone. So much to do, she thought.

Next Wednesday was the first of many meetings. Mary and Cyril sat next to each other like two love-birds. Cyril attended any meeting that occurred in the evenings or whenever he could get the time off work, but Angus refused to go to a single one. "As long as that fellow John isn't hanging about the house, I don't mind you being there," he said to Bonnie the day before a family session had been scheduled to convene. "Even that great black brute of a dog of yours is bad enough, but John always was a perfect wet."

"Don't be horrid about my family. They're my friends."

"Your friends? Why do you need all those people around you? And why the Bartholomews in particular? They're a boring bunch at the best of times." He saw the look on Bonnie's face. "All right," he said through clenched teeth. "If you insist on putting those people before me, I'll leave. You have dinner by yourself."

"I'm not putting anybody before you, Angus," Bonnie protested.

"Yes, you fucking well are."

Bonnie was dismayed. She had heard Angus swear before, but never with such venom. "Angus, why do you use such an awful word?"

" 'Fuck,' you mean?" he sneered. "Have you never heard the word before, my little princess?"

Bonnie stared at his distorted face. "Yes. Lots of times. That's a word my mother used all the time until she changed. That word and lots of others." She could hear her mother's voice swearing at her. She could see her ten-year-old self scrubbing the shabby linoleum floor. "Really, Angus, you don't shock me. You just remind me of parts of my life I'd rather forget."

Angus yet again realized that he must not take Bonnie for granted. For herself she had very little care, but for those she loved she was fiercely loyal and protective. "I didn't mean to upset you, darling," he said, taking her into his arms. "I just love you so much I can't bear for you ever to care about anyone else." Skilfully, expertly, he began to kiss her. Gently he caressed her breasts. "Just think," he breathed softly against her neck. "Once we're married we can make love all day and all night."

Bonnie was imagining just that—both of them locked in an impassioned embrace in front of a huge roaring fire. "Our wedding night," she murmured.

Angus drew back and gazed at her. "Where do you want to go for your honeymoon?" he asked.

"I don't know," she said. "Where are you happiest?"

Angus smiled. He thought of a certain brothel in Cairo. No,

maybe the little transvestite bar in Casablanca. More recently he had come to frequent a bar in Berlin. "Berlin," he said. Taking Bonnie to Berlin would be like introducing a pure white baked Alaska to the fires of hell. Very interesting, he thought. "You'll love Berlin. It's a fabulous city."

Bonnie smiled. "Darling Angus. You're so good to me. I'm sorry if I made you cross. You know I love you more than anything else in the world."

"More than Morgan?"

"Yes, of course."

"All right. I'll forgive you. I'll even take you out to dinner tonight."

Bonnie was very busy during the months preceding her marriage. She was amazed at the amount of work involved in the simple words "I do." Margaret was a great help, and after much trumpeting Simon agreed to give her away. "I'll never like the fellow, Bonnie. They say he cheats at cards," Simon said.

Bonnie tossed her head. "They say he does lots of things, but I know him better than anyone else. I *know* Angus would never cheat at anything. Anyway," she smiled at Simon, "you'll get to like him once you know him."

Simon grunted. Teresa linked arms with her father. "He's not that bad, daddy. I'm sure Bonnie'll work wonders. Look at Patrick. Ever since we've been going out together, he's given up wearing those old hairy tweeds and his tatty shooting jacket. He looks quite dashing now in his cavalry twill trousers. We women have a way of changing the men in our lives almost beyond recognition."

Simon hurrumphed. He remembered how shy and speechless he had been before he had met Margaret. He patted his daughter's hand. "Well, your mother performed a miracle. That young man of yours, Teresa, is a nice boy. Knew his father. Went shooting on his estate in Ireland. Good shot, his father. Boy takes after him. Good eye, steady hand, make a good husband."

Teresa laughed. "I make Patrick's hands shake and his eyes cross." She winked at Bonnie. Simon left the room in search of Margaret.

"Well," said Bonnie, "you seem pretty well settled with Patrick."

Teresa made a face. "Yes. He's nothing like Angus. I mean I miss the Heathcliff Syndrome. You know, all that dark despair and anguish. I don't have to wait by the phone or cry myself to sleep because Patrick failed to show up. No, not Patrick. He always phones when he says he will, and he is good and kind. I wonder why I miss all the pain I've had from other men."

"I really don't know." Bonnie was serious. "Angus is often late, and he rarely remembers to phone me. I think it's because he isn't used to having someone to love him. He forgets I'm there waiting for him."

"And Patrick," Teresa interrupted, "will never run out into the stormy night calling 'Teresa, Teresa' across some wind-swept moor. I've talked to lots of my friends, you know. They say the same thing. Women seem to need the Heathcliffs of this world. Have you read *Wuthering Heights?*"

"Yeah. I read that book when I was fourteen. I always thought Heathcliff was an absolute fool. Cathy reminded me of bits of my mother in the bad old days. God, I couldn't love anybody who was as cruel as she was."

Teresa raised her eyebrows. "Don't you find Angus cruel?"

Bonnie shook her head. "No," she said vehemently. "He can be thoughtless and sometimes he is domineering, but that's all stuff that can be changed."

"I hope you're right. But anyway," Teresa grinned, "life with Patrick can be dull at times, but you can't say that for life with Angus."

"You can say that again." Bonnie picked up her clipboard. "Come on. Let's get on with the guest list."

The weeks fled by. Angus took little interest in the arrangements for the wedding. Instead he busied himself with his everyday life. He was heavily occupied with the new house on the Embankment. It had been empty for some time, and Angus had bought the huge mansion for cash and completed the purchase within forty-eight hours. He was tearing out the interior and building a huge marble swimming pool. "This will be even grander than the Great House in Lexington," he said to Sacheverell.

"You are a competitive bastard," Sacheverell said affectionately. "All this so that Bonnie may live in greater luxury than she'd have if she stayed at home."

Angus showed his teeth in the familiar shark-like smile. "I want her to have the best."

Sacheverell didn't answer. "Here. Look at this mosaic. Shall we use it in the hall?"

Angus was bored. "Do what you want. I'll get Bonnie. We'll go racing this afternoon."

Sacheverell looked at him. "Don't you think she gets *bored* sitting about while you bet on horses during the day and gamble all night?"

"No. She's used to it now. She even knows how to interpret a racing form. Besides, she never gets bored with me." He laughed. "I'm terribly exciting, you see."

"Oh yes," Sacheverell grinned. "And you've been a good boy all this time. How long will you last?"

"Bonnie will keep me on the straight and narrow. She's just what I need."

Sacheverell looked keenly at Angus. "Well, I must say, you haven't picked fights at any parties I've attended. All of London agrees you're a reformed rake."

Angus's eyes stared bleakly back at his friend. "I do hope

I have reformed. I do feel that, once I'm safely married, maybe I'll feel less angry. I don't know though. Somehow I hope I won't feel trapped."

Sacheverell put his hand on Angus's shoulder. "I don't see why you should feel trapped. Bonnie isn't the sort of woman who would keep you on a tight leash, you know." More likely the other way round, he thought. He kept his last thought to himself. After all, for Angus to express any feelings of doubt or anxiety was so unusual that Sacheverell felt protective of this confession. "Well, I'll stay and have a look at the ball-room. Do you still want to keep all that glass on the walls?"

"You decide. I'm off. Don't want to keep Bonnie waiting."

Bonnie had indeed become something of an expert in the racing world. She realized that gambling and racing were an integral part of Angus's life. Angus knew that an important pleasure for Bonnie was going off for an unexpected trip or "an adventure," as Angus called it. They spent a week in Paris, because Angus wanted to track down a Marcel painting owned by an old French prostitute. Bonnie was intrigued by that adventure. Apart from her years with her mother, she had never experienced the seamy side of life as they found it in Paris.

Angus pursued every lead with an almost religious zeal. Finally, after nights in brothels questioning the older whores, they were given an address. Even though it was three in the morning, Angus insisted on waking up the old woman who indeed did have the painting. Bonnie was amazed when she looked at the canvas. There, sprawled on a brown background, lay the figure of a nude girl with a thick black bush of hair between her legs. Bonnie looked at the old lady, who was plainly mesmerized by Angus's charm. "Was that you?" Bonnie asked.

The old lady nodded her head. "Oui. Many years ago, mademoiselle."

Angus was impatient. "How much do you want for the painting?" The old lady hesitated. "Here," said Angus. "I will give you nine hundred thousand francs." He handed her the money in cash.

The old lady was speechless. Finally she spluttered, "Monsieur is too generous."

Angus picked up the painting and indicated to Bonnie that they should leave. "Au revoir!" the old lady shouted down the stairs. She heard a car door slam, and she sat down on her little lumpy brown sofa. The room smelled of garlic and herbs. How odd, the old lady thought. All that way, and all that money . . . he didn't even look at my painting. But that girl he had with him, what a beauty. The old lady suddenly felt alone. She began to cry as she sat by her empty grate. On the wall, a large pale square where her painting had hung stared blankly back at her.

The Marcel hung in the new house over the sideboard in the dining-room. Angus laughed when Bonnie complained that she didn't like the idea of eating her meals facing a naked woman. He shot a conspiratorial smile at Sacheverell who was lunching with them. "Wait 'til you see my collection."

"Your collection?" Bonnie was intrigued. "Of what?"

Angus looked again at Sacheverell. "I'll tell you some other time. Maybe when you're a little older. Finest in Europe. Isn't it, Sacheverell?"

Sacheverell looked uneasy. There was such an innocence about Bonnie that he didn't feel she would appreciate Angus's perverse collection of erotic art. Angus changed the subject back to the design of the greenhouse. "I want an orchid house and a house for camellias."

"How about putting in some parrots?" Sacheverell suggested.

"That's a good idea." Angus was pleased. "After lunch,

Bonnie, let's go to Harrods' pet department and buy half a dozen birds."

"Don't you think we'd better wait until we've moved in?"

"No. Let's do it today. Never put off 'til tomorrow what can be done today."

"Patience is a virtue," Bonnie countered.

"Life's too short to exercise patience," Angus replied. "Hurry up, Bonnie. You eat too slowly."

"Don't bully her," Sacheverell said. "Don't pay any attention to him, Bonnie. If you let him bully you, he'll walk all over you."

"I'm sorry, Bonnie. I don't mean to bully you."

Bonnie was thrown. She was getting used to Angus's domineering ways, but every so often he would admit to a fault, and she would immediately feel real anguish for him. "Don't apologize, darling. I know I'm slow at times. My mother was always yelling at me because I took so long to do anything. Come on. Let's go." She pushed away her unfinished plate.

Sacheverell sat in the silence that they left behind them. Surprising, he thought. Angus really is trying. Maybe he really does love her. God, he thought, I hope he can control himself with Bonnie. He pottered off to the ballroom. "A little more red," he said to the artist who was painting a woodland scene on one of the walls. "A little more red." The artist obediently dipped his brush into a pool of crimson paint.

Later that night, Bonnie listened to the sound of the lone parrot lamenting the loss of his pet department friends. Angus was furious that Harrods had only one parrot for sale. "God," he said, "I thought you were supposed to be able to supply me with anything I wanted. I want six parrots now."

The manager of the department was polite but firm. "We can supply you with the other five by the end of the week."

"That's no good. I want them today."

"I'm sorry. That's not possible."

"Do you know who I am?" Angus was in a rage.

"Yes, sir. I read the newspapers, and," he smiled at Bonnie, "I remember your engagement photograph. I must say . . ."

"Don't say anything, you miserable bastard." Angus's voice began to rise. The parrot, sensing the upset, began to screech. Bonnie quickly signed her name to the £200 bill, and dragged Angus, still yelling insults, out of the department. She cast an apologetic look at the manager. She carried the cage and the squawking parrot behind Angus who tore through the shop and threw himself into the waiting car. He complained all the way home.

Bonnie smiled now into her pillow. She was getting used to his tantrums. He'll be sorry tomorrow, she thought. Thank God the parrot's fallen asleep. We'll have to try and find him a mirror tomorrow.

At breakfast the next morning, Mrs. Turner came in, very upset. "I'm sorry to tell you that your parrot was found dead in its cage. Ben went to give the bird a drink this morning, and he says its neck had been broken. I can't think how that could have happened."

"Neither can I." Bonnie looked at Angus. "I heard him squawking last night, but then he went to sleep."

"He was squawking away when I was reading in the library, but then I went off to the club about two in the morning." Angus remembered the moment of ecstasy when the parrot, which had made it impossible for him to concentrate, lay dead in his hand. He felt that familiar feeling of omnipotence when something weak and vulnerable was helpless in his power. The bird deserved to die. When he took the cloth off the cage, it refused to respond to his command. He put his hand in and quite calmly squeezed the bird's neck until the life faded from its eyes. He always enjoyed that moment of death. He felt included in some great mystery. The bird was dead, but here he was eating an early breakfast with Bonnie.

Nobody in the house would know what really happened except him.

Mrs. Turner was puzzled. "We haven't had anything like this happen since those baby rabbits of yours were strangled one by one. Do you remember that?"

Angus nodded. "I buried them all in shoe-boxes," he said.

"How you cried!" Mrs. Turner said to Bonnie, "We thought he'd never stop."

"How awful." Bonnie was appalled.

"I'll show you where I buried them." Angus was cheerful again.

Angus had a large old farmhouse in Spain. It had been willed to his mother, and he loved to go there and look from the topmost window, down on to the great plain that lay spread out at the back of the house. Legend had it that Hannibal had passed that way across Spain and over the Alps.

Bonnie was enchanted by the idea of a quick dash to Spain. She had read all Hemingway's books, and felt she already knew the proud fierce people of that country. Two weeks before the wedding, they flew to Gerona, and Paulo the chauffeur was there to meet them. "How's everything going?" Angus asked.

"Well. Very well. The harvest was good last year. The barn is full of vegetables. We all took our share and the families ate well all winter." Angus was pleased.

Bonnie looked at the countryside. "I must say, it's very beautiful. Just as I imagined it would be. Look at those lovely shades of green." The road from Gerona to the little village of San Martin sparkled in the bright hot April sunlight. The trees lining the road were pale green. Donkeys ambled along, pursued by small boys with long switches in their hands. The air was filled with a sweet smell from the pine trees, and wild flowers carpeted the hillsides. "Gee," Bonnie said, looking up at Angus. "It's absolutely gorgeous. Isn't it?"

Angus was in a good mood. "Yes," he said. "But just wait until you see La Massa. I think it's my favourite house." Soon they arrived at the foot of the road that led to the village of San Martin.

"Good lord." Bonnie was surprised. "The whole village looks as if it was built inside a wall."

Angus nodded. "Yes. You see, it was a fortified Greek village originally. Then the Romans came along and built a town over there." He pointed to a large building set a little way back from the village. "That's a museum. They're still excavating the old Roman town. Paulo, let's take the back route to the farmhouse. I want Miss Fraser to see the plain behind it."

When the car stopped by the back gate, Bonnie got out and gazed across the plain. She stood with Angus on a promontory that jutted out like the prow of a ship, several hundred feet high above the land below. The sun was just setting over the flat land below her. Long rays of sunlight tipped the green plants and grass now lush from the spring rains. Later in the year, the plain would become dry as a desert, but now the view was colourfully magic. Bonnie took Angus's hand. They stood in silence. Bonnie could imagine the heavy line of Hannibal's elephants swaying across the fields. She could almost see the swarthy soldiers hurrying along beside the great animals, some on horseback, some on foot. "Listen," she said to Angus. "I can hear the chink of their armour and the sound of their trumpets. Can't you, Angus?"

Angus laughed. "Don't be a goose, darling. You have too much imagination." Bonnie turned from the view. "Let's send Paulo on with the car," Angus said, "and we'll walk up to the house."

Paulo opened the big gates. He drove on ahead. Slowly Bonnie and Angus walked up the drive. Angus led Bonnie through a belt of trees; suddenly there appeared an enormous house. It was a vast stone fortress with tiny square windows.

Quickly, Angus led the way to a small door in an otherwise impenetrable wall. Bonnie stepped through the door into a huge square-tiled corridor. Angus took her through the hall and into yet another vast room that was full of old Spanish furniture. Bonnie was impressed. "Goodness," she said. "I feel like a midget."

Angus smiled. "Well, it used to be that all the village would take refuge in this house if there was danger about. Remember, this would have been a central hall where the cows and the sheep would be quartered. In those days, your animals were too valuable to leave outside for bandits to take them off and sell them. I'll show you your room," he said. He led her upstairs. "Here," he said, opening a door.

Bonnie was pleased. She had been expecting another bleak room full of austere furniture. Instead, she found herself in a small cheerful room with every available inch covered in dolls. There were dolls from China, dolls from Japan, and even an English sailor doll with a sailor suit and a little straw boater. "Whose room was this?" Bonnie asked.

"My mother's," Angus said.

"Oh." Bonnie caught her breath. "Do you really want me to sleep here?"

"Yes," he said. "I'll call you when you've changed for dinner."

At eight o'clock, Bonnie was dressed and ready to eat. She had changed from her neat grey travelling suit to a long white dress with a blue sash around the waist. For once Angus was punctual. Together they proceeded downstairs to dinner. Maria served Bonnie a traditional paella. The saffron had coloured the rice a rich ochre, and the prawns lay pinkly beside the blue-grey of the mussel shells. Bonnie poked at the small tentacles lying in an agonized knot among the tomatoes and onions. "At least try one," Angus argued.

Bonnie put a small squid into her mouth. "Ugh," she said.

Angus was immediately angry. "Don't be so squeamish, Bonnie. Here they eat almost anything that moves. You'll get used to Spanish food."

"But do I have to eat this now?" She remembered her mother standing over her as a child. To leave so much as a crumb on her plate then was a serious crime, and her mother would hurl abuse at her. "I was starving at your age, and now you're pushing food away that I would have died for. Eat up, you little bitch," Laura would say. Bonnie winced at the memory.

"Yes, you do have to eat it." Angus looked humourlessly at her. "Maria will be very hurt if you leave anything on your plate."

Bonnie was grateful that Angus was merely irritated instead of furious. "All right," she said. "I'll learn to eat everything put in front of me." Except tapioca, she silently promised herself. Fortunately, Angus did not seem to like nursery food.

She regretted her promise the next day. After a good night's sleep, they spent Saturday walking around the Roman ruins and visiting the museum. On the way back across a field filled with fresh oregano and wild parsley, Bonnie discovered some bits of old Roman pottery and glass. "How wonderful!" she exclaimed with great joy. "I've always wanted to find things like this. Oh, look!" She bent down. "Look what I've got."

"What?" Angus was very bored by the past.

"It's half an amphora. Look." She held a small earthen oil-lamp in her hand. "Can you imagine," she said, "two thousand years ago, a Roman must have walked across this field with this little flickering lamp. He must have dropped it, and now, all this time later, the little amphora waited for me to come along and pick it up. Take it in your hand, Angus. Can you feel the history?"

Angus hadn't really been listening, but he saw the look of pleasure on Bonnie's face. He didn't like that look unless he had put it there himself. He drew back his hand and, before Bonnie could protest, he had thrown the lamp as far as he could across the field.

"Why did you do that, Angus?" Bonnie was furious.

"Because I wanted to," he said casually. "Anyway, it was only half an amphora. I'll buy you a perfect one, if you like."

"It won't be the same," Bonnie mourned. "That one was waiting for *me.*"

"Don't be stupid. How could a little piece of clay *wait* for you? Now hurry up. We're going into the village for dinner, and you're wasting time."

Bonnie struggled to keep up with Angus as he strode off to the house. Oh dear, Bonnie thought. I hope I'm not going to make him angry all evening.

Angus *was* angry, and he proceeded to get even angrier during dinner. Tapas turned out to be a grisly collection of intestines. "And," said Angus, picking up a gruesome shrivelled object on a cocktail stick, "this is part of a pig's testicle." He plonked the morsel down on Bonnie's plate. Bonnie suppressed a shudder. She knew she would have to eat it. She didn't dare risk upsetting Angus. They were sitting in the village square. All around them were families and couples having dinner. Usually the weather was not warm enough to eat outside, but this April the weather had been unseasonably hot. At the beginning of the month, the manager of the restaurant had put his tables, covered in cheerful red-checked cloths, outside. Small candles lit each one. Children darted in and out of the square. Bonnie and Angus sat under a large and ancient tree. Two lovers next to Bonnie's table were holding hands and whispering. "Mi amor, te amo," she heard the man say to the woman. If only Angus . . . she stopped the disloyal thought before it even began. He's from England, and they don't act romantic over there, she reminded herself.

"Go on." Angus was feeling vicious. "Let's see you eat the pig's testicle."

"Okay," Bonnie said pleasantly. She reverted to the old trick that she had used as a child. She thought very hard about a nice forkful of juicy rare steak. At the same time, she swallowed the tapa. "It's not too bad," she said. Indeed, if you could keep your mind off the main ingredient, the accompanying sauce was delicious.

Angus rocked back in his chair. He yelled for a waiter. A young girl came running to the table. Angus's temper was well known in the village. "Bring me the menu," he ordered. The girl stood for a moment with the menu in her hand. Angus snatched it from her and glared. He looked at the chef's choice of the day. "We'll have the prawns and then the lamb. Bring me a bottle of Sangre de Toro immediately. I mean now. No *mañana*. You understand?"

The girl nodded. "Capitalist pig," she muttered to herself, and she hurried off to get the wine.

Angus grunted with disgust. "They get worse every year. At one time there were no tourists here at all. Now, all the rich Spanish from Barcelona buy out the peasants' houses, and then the tourists flood in during the summer. The peasants are spoiled rotten. They don't bother even to grow their own crops any longer. The old way is dying out."

"Maybe the young people don't want to live all their lives in a village," Bonnie said. "Perhaps they want to save up and go away to college. Maybe being a peasant your whole life isn't really all that attractive." She thought of Maria's careworn hands.

"You Americans," Angus sneered. "You and your sloppy liberal thinking. You've no idea of history. Peasants should stay peasants. Just like the working class in England. They should stay in their factories and on the shop floor. Look what happens when they start crossing the Channel like lemmings. They drink too much, vomit everywhere, and wear those awful handkerchiefs on their heads on the beaches. They should all be obliged to take their holidays in Blackpool, where they don't embarrass the rest of us."

Bonnie let Angus rant on. As long as he was talking, she had learned from his tantrums, everything was all right. If he stopped talking when he was angry, she knew from several episodes that he was heading for a fight. So she had learned to listen respectfully and to keep him talking. "When did English people first start coming here on their holidays?" she asked, hoping to keep Angus on a topic which he could discuss peacefully.

The waitress reappeared with the wine. Angus greedily downed his glass. Oh dear, Bonnie thought, he's going to get drunk. She nervously sipped her wine. By the time the prawns arrived, Angus was ready for another bottle. Bonnie tried to fill her glass and then surreptitiously to tip some wine out under the table, but she only succeeded in doing this a few times.

A cheerful, impudent, brown-eyed waiter doubling as a musician strolled around the restaurant serenading the customers with his voice and his guitar. Bonnie laughed when he came to their table, but she fell silent when she remembered how Angus hated her to pay attention to any man. She dropped her gaze to her plate. "This lamb is lovely," she said to distract Angus, as the waiter played and sang on. She thought she had succeeded.

After coffee had been served at the end of the meal, Angus ordered himself a huge glass of brandy. So far, so good, Bonnie thought. He was drunk, but he was talking happily about the Labour party in England. He seemed to have a personal grudge against every member of the Labour government. Bonnie relaxed. The table in front of her was littered with plates. The prawn shells lay in the remains of the tomato sauce. The plates that had been full of pink moist lamb were heaped now with bones. Two empty wine bottles stood guard over the chaos on the table. Bonnie felt full and slightly drowsy.

The waiter had exchanged his guitar for a large oval tray. He put the corner of the tray on their table and piled it high with dishes and glasses. He raised the tray expertly to his shoulder. Angus lazily stretched out a foot, just in front of the waiter. The man went flying, and so did the immense pile of crockery. Bonnie was appalled. She leapt to her feet and fled to the farmhouse.

Angus caught up with her before she had reached her room. "Bonnie, I didn't mean to do it." Angus was repentant. The surge of pleasure he felt as he saw the man go flying had put him back into a more reasonable frame of mind.

"You did mean to do it. I saw. You quite deliberately put your foot in his way. Just as you quite deliberately threw my amphora away. Maybe I should have listened to all those warnings. You're cruel, Angus. You really are cruel." With that she slammed into her bedroom.

Angus was hurt. I'm not cruel, he thought. He went down the stairs to the drinks cupboard in the drawingroom. "I'm not at all cruel," he said out loud as he poured himself another brandy. He stood in front of the fireplace looking up at a portrait of his mother. She smiled gently down at him. He finished his brandy, and then he had another. The world slowly became a softer place. He gazed up at his mother. "I'm not going to be like my father," he said despairingly. All at once, he very much wanted to be held by Bonnie.

He raced up the stairs and burst into her room. "I'm not like my father, Bonnie. I don't *want* to be like him." He wrapped his arms tightly around her. She had been awake, wondering if she was making a mistake by marrying Angus. Tears streamed down his face. "Don't let me be like my father."

Bonnie held him close. "I won't," she whispered. "I promise. I won't."

"Thank you." Angus was grateful. He sighed deeply. The tears on his cheeks melted away, and he slept, fully clothed, in Bonnie's sheltering arms.

Bonnie watched his face in the moonlight. His mouth softened in sleep, and his long dark eyelashes lay like fans. He looked very lost, very alone. I'll try harder, she thought. Eventually she too fell asleep and dreamed of Angus. Angus was also dreaming. He dreamed about Garrett's small rosy bottom. He smiled in his sleep. The moon dropped from the window, and a gnarled old apricot tree outside the house sighed in the wind.

 Chapter 24

The day of Bonnie's wedding dawned bright and clear. She woke just as the sun rose above the mountains. She leaned out of the window of her little room in the turret of Drummossie Castle. The dew lay winking in the grass in the morning sunlight. Cows grazed unconcerned with the bustle and the comings and goings at Drummossie.

Bonnie thought of her grandmother. Augustine had arrived looking pale and tired, but after her first few days in Scotland she had recovered her strength. With Morag, the three women had explored the area around Culloden. Augustine's face changed. "I feel as if I am completing our history," she said as she stood by Loch Ness, where Malcolm Fraser had dreamed his faraway dreams.

Bonnie smiled. "Well, when Angus and I are married, we will unite two great families."

Augustine was radiant. "I know, my child. I'm so happy for

you. Who could have guessed that an act of friendship hundreds of years ago would reverberate through time to give us such joy."

Now, on her wedding day, Bonnie remembered the jubilant smile on her grandmother's face. I'm glad I've repaid her kindness, she thought.

Laura, as Bonnie had predicted, turned up with Father John in tow. "He can help officiate at your wedding," Laura informed Bonnie.

"No thanks, mom." Bonnie was adamant. "I'll leave my wedding up to Father MacBride." Bonnie liked Father Mac-Bride. He was a small bald man with gentle blue eyes. He had spent much time during the week before the wedding talking to Bonnie about her future life with Angus. He had been with the MacPherson family as private chaplain for nearly forty years. He did not know Angus very well, as the latter had spent so much of his youth in London and away at school. Now, Angus only rarely attended the little family chapel in the keep of the castle. He did, however, know Lord MacPherson, and he struggled daily for the soul of the demented and tortured man. "He wants to attend your wedding," Father MacBride said after Bonnie's confession.

"That's fine with me." Bonnie did not give the matter much thought.

Angus was not at all pleased. "Bloody old fool," he said when he heard about the request.

Bonnie was upset. "Really, Angus. I don't see why you are so awful about your dad."

Angus just stared at her. "You don't understand," he said.

"Yes, I do. My mom was awful for a while, but I've forgiven her."

Angus smiled his razor-sharp grin, razor-sharp except for the one chipped tooth that seemed to gape spitefully at Bonnie. "Oh, I've forgiven him, Bonnie," he said mockingly.

"Why shouldn't I forgive him? He's a vast beached hulk on an island of pain and confusion."

Bonnie could feel Angus's tension. She went over and put her arms around him. "Nothing can spoil our day. I won't let it," she promised.

Angus looked at her. He pulled her close and whispered into her hair. "I love you, Bonnie. I love you more than I've ever loved anything in my life. I love you more than my life itself."

Bonnie kissed his neck. Her lips travelled to his ear lobe. "Darling, we have the rest of our lives together. Nothing will ever separate us."

Angus's eyes were haunted. He so much wanted to love this woman until the day he died. But part of him knew, even as he confessed his love, that a dark side of the moon, his soul, was forever cut adrift from warm human relationships. His need to hurt as he had been hurt would always outlast his need to love. He sighed. "I must spend some time with Garrett," he said.

Bonnie nodded. "He doesn't like me, you know."

Angus frowned. "He doesn't like anybody, Bonnie. He's all right. But don't worry, we will be in London most of the time, and he'll stay mostly up here." Angus made a resolution to refrain from the delights offered by Garrett's shapely body. He felt very virtuous.

Bonnie was relieved at the thought of staying away from Garrett. Something in his manner always made her uneasy. Gazing out over the pink countryside, Bonnie smiled. This is the most perfect day of my life, she thought.

The perfect day progressed evenly and calmly through to the ceremony. By three o'clock, all the guests were waiting quietly in the small chapel. Angus stood in front of the altar. Sacheverell was beside him. As best man, he had the ancient wedding ring which had been taken from Angus's dead mother's finger. For once, Sacheverell was well-behaved and silent. The day was hot. The sky was an intense blue with puffs of white cloud shredded above the walls of the keep. Stately white swans floated across the water in the moat. The ducks, aware of an occasion, seemed to keep up a running commentary on the guests.

Suddenly even their gossiping voices fell silent. From the massive front door of the castle appeared the bridal procession. First came Bonnie, in a clinging white silk dress, absolutely plain with a simple round neck. The dress's train, however, was five yards long. Embroidered with pearls, it was the same train that Evangeline had worn at her wedding to Malcolm Fraser. In her hand Bonnie carried long-stemmed white roses. Behind her, there were six little children, three boys and three girls, dressed in white. Morag and Teresa, dressed in the palest pink, brought up the rear.

Slowly and silently, Bonnie descended the steep stone steps of the castle. She appeared to float across the green lawn, before stopping in front of Simon Bartholomew who waited for her outside the chapel door. Radiant with her love for Angus, she took Simon's arm and they entered the chapel. "You look very beautiful, my dear," he grumbled softly as he patted her hand.

Augustine caught her breath as she saw her granddaughter, her blue eyes bright beneath her veil, proceed up the aisle. How like Evangeline she looks, Augustine thought, remembering the portrait of Malcolm's bride which hung in the Great House.

As Bonnie walked slowly between the rows of pews, she passed the Bartholomew family. Margaret sat beside her sons. Matthew and Luke were both staring wide-eyed at Bonnie. John's eyes, however, held a special look—a look of yearning mingled with sadness.

Father MacBride greeted the bride and groom. Privately, he dreaded the ceremony. He knew Angus by reputation.

Very little of what he had heard made him anxious to join this man with his eager, innocent young bride. "Do you, Bonnie Fraser, take this man, Angus Charles Ian MacPherson, to be your lawfully wedded husband, to have and to hold . . ."

"I do." Bonnie's voice was firm and joyful. In the pews Cyril squeezed his new wife's hand as Mary let out a small sigh of happiness.

"And do you, Angus Charles Ian Macpherson, take this woman, Bonnie Fraser, to be your . . ."

"I do." Even Angus was surprised by the passion of his answer.

Way back in the dim shadows of the church, staunchly guarded by his two male nurses, Lord MacPherson let out a maniacal shrill giggle. "Like father like son!" The male nurses, obeying Angus's instructions, hurried the demented old man out of the church. Fortunately, he was so drugged that his words rose little above a whisper. Nevertheless, the shreds of his voice lingered and seemed to cling to the glow of the gold band that Angus slipped onto Bonnie's finger. But Bonnie was too caught up in her own happiness to hear him. Her thoughts rested only on Angus.

"With this ring, I thee wed," said Angus. From that moment on, Bonnie was irrevocably tied to Angus, tied to his love, tied to his hate, tied to him by the twin chains of pity and compassion. There was no going back.

As if to mark the occasion, Morgan, who had come with John, began to howl. He had resented being left in the porch of the church. Most of the guests were amused by the noise. His long wolf-like wails pierced the quiet serenity of the ceremony. Bonnie was oblivious to the noise. Turning slowly, so that the little children could gather her train, she walked back down the aisle. The memory of her first married kiss still fresh on her lips, she smiled at the congregation. The veil, now free from her face, floated behind her. The music played at her request. The soaring, lilting music, Pachelbel's Canon, danced along with the jets of light refracted from the jewels in her train. Bonnie held Angus's arm tightly. There were tears in her eyes as she stopped in front of her grandmother in the front pew. "Thank you, grandma," she said. "Thank you for making this day possible."

Augustine smiled at them both. "I know you'll both be very happy," she said.

"And thank you," Bonnie said to Margaret who sat in the row behind Augustine. "If you hadn't taken me in, I never would have met Angus. You've been such a help. Thank you." She leaned forward and kissed Margaret on the cheek.

The procession moved out of the church into the bright sunlight. "She could at least have acknowledged me." Laura was furious. "After all, I am her mother."

Father John laid a placatory hand on her shoulder. He was utterly entranced by the castle and by the wealth of Laura's new relations. "Give her time," he said. "After all, the old lady's paying for everything." Father John couldn't wait to have a man-to-man talk with Angus. "It's our turn to go," he gently reminded Laura.

They joined the tumble of guests who erupted out of the church and made for the great dining-room. The servants walked through the crowds serving Dom Pérignon, and the Pouilly Fumé that Bonnie had specially requested. Angus drank very little. He was doing a superb job of welcoming his guests.

"Mazel tov!" Mitzi came through the crowd to greet Bonnie. She carried her newborn child in her arms. Ray stood by her side smiling warmly, while Max and Rebecca wrapped themselves around their parents' legs, unbearably bored by the whole occasion. "Such a lovely bride," Mitzi said with delight, "and, mein Gott, such a groom. You know, Bonnie, you could have done a lot worse. I hope the two of you will be very happy." She kissed Bonnie on the cheek.

Ray shook Angus's hand. "Congratulations, Angus. It was

a lovely wedding. And it was extremely nice of you to fly us all out here. Thank you very much."

"Think nothing of it," Angus said. "Bonnie wouldn't have it any other way. Her friends are frightfully important to her."

"Well, we all love her very much. Thanks again. Come on, Mitzi," Ray said, taking her arm. "Let's give the newly weds a chance to talk to their other guests. Lots of luck, Bonnie." He kissed Bonnie on the cheek and bore Mitzi and the children off to get some food.

Angus was greatly relieved to see them go. What dreadful people, he thought. He said nothing. He smiled as sweetly as he could at Bonnie, and departed to find some of his own friends.

"Well, my little rosebud," Sacheverell sidled up to Bonnie. "Won't be long now and you'll be in full bloom."

"Oh, Sacheverell," Bonnie blushed. "Don't be so crude."

"I'm never crude, dearest," Sacheverell giggled. "I must say I never thought I'd see the day a woman anchored Angus MacPherson." Suddenly his face grew stern. "Promise me one thing, Bonnie." She looked at him. Sacheverell was seldom this serious. "Just promise that, if he ill-treats you, you'll leave him."

Bonnie smiled. "You're not very good at making appropriate wedding chit-chat, are you? He won't ill-treat me, Sacheverell. Anyway, I just took a vow before God that nothing will separate us. I said 'till death do us part.' That's forever, Sacheverell. I'm a Catholic, and it would be a mortal sin for either of us to part. Ever."

Sacheverell shook his head. He knew there was no point in antagonizing Bonnie.

"Talking about me?" Angus wandered into the silence after the conversation.

"Yes," Sacheverell said. "I was just telling Bonnie that if you ill-treat her, I'll come after you with a whip."

Angus looked at his friend. "I won't ill-treat her. I promise you."

Sacheverell grimaced. Their friendship was littered with Angus's broken promises. "All right then. I'm going off now to see the car's ready for your dash to the airport." Angus had arranged for them to catch the seven o'clock flight to Berlin.

"Okay." Bonnie smiled at Angus. "I'll go upstairs and change." Half an hour later she was back wearing a pale blue dress. Over her arm she carried a camelhair coat. Angus, soberly dressed in a dark suit, waited for her on the steps of the castle. The guests, lined up on both sides, waved and jostled. Bonnie threw her bouquet with great accuracy to Teresa. She caught the roses and smiled at Bonnie. Kissing her grandmother and her mother goodbye, Bonnie was unable to avoid the cold clammy hand of Father John. "Have a wonderful time," he said, his eyes full of innuendo.

"Thank you," Bonnie said coolly. She slid into the back seat of the Rolls.

"Happy, darling?" Angus asked solicitously.

"Wonderfully happy," she said.

Chapter 25

Making love with Angus was all she had dreamed it would be. Gently, with practised ease, he taught Bonnie the delights of sensual pleasure. Playing her body like a priceless violin, he drew sounds of excitement from Bonnie that surprised even her. His mouth probed her shadows, and she, in turn, passionately clasped and unclasped his slender white body. Exhausted, they fell apart. Now, Bonnie lay fully satisfied by his side. What a perfect day, she thought. She fell asleep dreaming of the small church set in a sea of white swans.

The next morning, Bonnie was up early in the Hotel Berliner on the Kurfürstendamm. She was eager to see the city. "One doesn't come to Berlin to look at the city," Angus said. "Most of Berlin was bombed out during the war. No, you come here for the nightlife." His eyes sparkled. "Tonight, I'll take you to the Flotsam Club."

Bonnie tried to look thrilled. She was fed up with Angus's nightlife. But, she consoled herself, after a few more years and a couple of kids, he'll slow down and stay home with me. She smiled. "That sounds great," she said. "Let's just go for a walk now."

Angus was still aroused from making love to Bonnie the night before. He stretched out his arms. "Let's make love first," he said.

Bonnie threw off her nightdress and flung herself into his arms.

"You *are* a wanton young thing." Angus was amused by her whole-hearted passion.

"I know," Bonnie said breathlessly. "I always knew that love was worth waiting for. I used to see all those girls running after perfectly dreadful men. But I just said no to any offers." She smiled. "I knew someday I'd be doing this with you. I knew all along."

Angus was suddenly aware that he felt claustrophobic, trapped by Bonnie's simple statement of faith. "Don't love me too much, Bonnie," he said, pushing her away. "Don't expect too much of me. I've been living a pretty lurid life all these years. I can't change all at once."

"I don't expect you to change all at once." Bonnie was contrite. "I really don't want you to change much anyway."

Angus sighed. The prospect of a walk bored him, but intense conversation with Bonnie made him nervous. "I think I'll give Frieda a ring," he said.

"Frieda?" Bonnie's eyebrows rose. "Who's Frieda?"

"Oh, she's an old girlfriend of mine. Now she's married to Gunter. They own a huge shipping firm. I sail with them from time to time." He reached for the phone. Within minutes he had arranged to have lunch with the couple at a restaurant down the road.

Bonnie was disappointed. She very rarely had Angus to herself. He was always surrounded by his friends. Even when they were home, Sacheverell was usually present. Angus could see she was hurt, but he was busy struggling hard to subdue a rapidly growing feeling of panic. Why, after a night of enjoyable love-making, did he so much want to lash out? He was puzzled. Often in his life, when faced with moments of love and trust, he would deliberately destroy those moments for himself. It was as if he stood on the other side of a thick pane of glass, looking at the world pass him by. Behind the pane of glass, he was a small defenceless child, full of love and good will, but his adult self, out in the real world, was made of steel. No emotions stirred his depths except for pain and rage. If the child felt love, the adult rejected the emotion and turned all that was good and lovable into the familiar and comforting fire of anger. Knowing as he did that Bonnie was hurt, he couldn't help deriving a perverse twinge of satisfaction from the pain on her face. "You'll like them," he said. "They're great fun."

Frieda and Gunter were both drunk when they joined Angus and Bonnie at the restaurant on the Kurfürstendamm. The day was hot, and Angus chose to order lunch outside under the red-striped awning. The restaurant was full of earnest businessmen with thick waists and impersonal blue eyes. Angus was studying the wine list when his friends swayed into view. Frieda was fat with thick yellow hair that fell down her back in large sausage-shaped curls. She wore an elaborate amount of bright red lipstick and a tight green dress that strained and clung to her ample figure. Gunter was tall, taller than Angus. He clicked his heels and bowed low over Bonnie's hand. She didn't like the way his hair flopped over his forehead. She also noticed that she didn't like the military precision of his moustache. In fact, she realized, she didn't like him at all.

After a great deal of noise, they seated themselves for lunch. Angus ordered artichokes with hollandaise sauce, followed by roast pork and sauerkraut. "You'll love the sauce," he said to Bonnie.

Bonnie tried to smile. Pork had never been a favourite dish of hers. She found it far too heavy. By now, however, she had accepted that Angus did not consult her when he ordered a meal. "I like you to eat what I eat," he explained once. "It makes things so much easier for the waiter." Privately, Bonnie understood Angus enough to realize that he only felt secure when he was in total control of his relationship with her. She saw for herself that any attempt she made to assert her independence served only to shake him badly. She never offered to drive. Her one attempt at driving the Rolls with Angus beside her had so angered him that she decided there and then not to repeat the experience.

Bonnie prepared herself to be nice to Angus's friends. Frieda ordered a double vodka and lime, and leant back in her chair. "Darling," Frieda said to Bonnie, "I saw your picture in the paper."

Bonnie was surprised. "Really? Here in Berlin?"

"Oh yes. Angus is always news everywhere. At least this time, he was good news. Weren't you, darling?"

Angus frowned. "That's enough, Frieda. I've reformed."

"Yes?" Frieda arched her thick corn-coloured eyebrows. "Never," she breathed. "As long as there's breath in your body. You'll always be Angus. Don't reform, darling. We'll all be so bored without your mischief. Won't we, Gunter?"

Gunter, whose nose was deep in a beer mug, said, "Yes. Of

course." He wiped his moustache with the back of his hand and looked slyly at Angus. "There's a new act tonight at the Flim Flam Club. Shall we celebrate your wedding by attending?"

Angus stared at Gunter. The last time they had been at the Flim Flam Club, they had both picked up a German boy of sixteen, and had shared him. Frieda had lain in the room next door snoring loudly. A familiar twinge of excitement and lust made Angus's eyes glitter. "We'd love to," he said, and he ordered himself another whisky.

Oh dear, Bonnie worried, if he starts drinking whisky now, he'll be unpredictable for the rest of the evening. But she need not have worried. Angus was charming all day. After lunch, Angus agreed with Frieda and Gunter to meet at the same restaurant for dinner. Saying goodbye to his friends, Angus walked Bonnie round the shops. "Berlin is a very rich city," Bonnie remarked.

"Yes." Angus was bored. He missed his malicious friends. Lunch with Gunter and Frieda had reminded him how dull Bonnie could be. She didn't have a malicious bone in her body. "Here." Angus decided that spending money would be the only way he could get through the afternoon. "Let's go into this shop, and I'll buy you a watch."

"Eight thousand dollars? Just for a watch?" Bonnie was horrified when she heard the price of the one she had casually admired.

Angus laughed. He enjoyed her outraged expression. He bought her the watch, and then took her on to a little shop in the centre of town where he had often bought clothes for his mistresses. The cheerful brisk woman who ran the shop was pleased to see him again. It only took a moment before Angus had the shop in an uproar as he rooted through the shelves. He stood Bonnie in the middle of the salon, and pulled out dress after dress which he handed to the owner. "I'll take that and that. Now let me see," he said, enjoying every moment.

"No, no. I don't like the neck at all." He waved away a slim jade evening gown. "Anyway, Bonnie, I don't ever want you to wear green again."

"Okay." Bonnie was enjoying herself. Green never had been her favourite colour.

After amassing some thirty different outfits, Angus told the owner to have the clothes delivered to the hotel by five o'clock. "Now," he said to Bonnie, as he strode into the busy street, "we'll find a shoe shop." There he bought Bonnie ten pairs with stiletto heels in assorted colours. He also bought her five pairs of evening shoes.

"Please, Angus," Bonnie was getting a little flustered, "I really don't need any more clothes. Let's go back to the hotel."

"Just one more shop." Angus hailed a taxi. "Take us to the Body Shop," he ordered in fluent German.

The Body Shop sold what is normally called intimate underwear. Angus was in heaven. He sat Bonnie down on a spindly gilt chair, and chose several exotic satin gowns. "I'm really not too crazy about revealing nightdresses," Bonnie said nervously. She remembered that Angus had been drinking, and tried to express her reluctance in as gentle a way as possible for fear of upsetting him.

"You'll wear what I buy for you." Angus was irritated. "Here I am spending the whole afternoon buying you beautiful clothes, and now you're complaining."

"No, I'm not. Honestly, Angus. I am grateful. It's just that I've never really bothered much about clothes."

"I've noticed." Angus's voice was still sharp. "Now you're my wife, you'll have to be a credit to me. I can't have you looking like a country bumpkin."

"Is that how I've looked?" Bonnie was hurt.

"Yes, but never mind. I'll change all that." He held up a black négligée with a plunging neck-line and a slit up to the top of the thigh. He looked at Bonnie. His eyes were shining.

"This'll suit you." He imagined the combination of the innocence of his wife and the decadence of the gown. It was irresistible. "I'll take that pile there," he said. He pointed to a pile of brassières and briefs. "Throw in a dozen pairs of stockings," he said. "The ones with the seams down the back. And send it all to my hotel." The manager nodded.

Bonnie felt miserable. Oh well, she thought, leaning back in the taxi, I'll get used to wearing more fashionable clothes, but God knows if I'll ever be able to walk in those stilettoes.

"I want you to wear that yellow dress that you tried on for me," Angus said.

Bonnie nodded. The dress was deceptively simple; it was cut in such a way as to highlight Bonnie's slim figure and to flatter her long legs. Still lightly tanned from their trip to Spain, she looked like a daffodil in the dress. The thought of her innocent face among the crowd at the Flim Flam Club further excited Angus. When he had paid the taxi, he put his arm around Bonnie's waist. "I can't wait to make love to you," he murmured in her ear. Bonnie smiled.

He rushed her into the empty lift and pressed her up against the wall. He was impatiently passionate. His mouth closed on hers, and she gave a little whimper of pain as he bruised her lips with his kiss. Once in the bedroom, he tore off Bonnie's clothes. Without removing his own, he threw her onto the bed, and then lunged into her.

Bonnie was so surprised, she lay quite still until he finished. Angus saw the look on her face, and he grinned. "Don't you like real sex?" he asked.

"I don't know what you mean." Bonnie was tearful. "That hurt, and I don't like being hurt."

Angus grinned. "There's a lot I will have to teach you," he said. "Sometimes there is pleasure to be found in pain."

"Not for me." Bonnie was adamant. "I don't like being hurt at all."

Angus rolled over onto his stomach. He had quite enjoyed that moment of urgent sex.

There was a knock on the door. Angus rearranged his clothes and sauntered into the palatial sitting-room. A procession of hotel porters and maids poured in, bearing a mountain of boxes and packages, the result of Angus's spree that afternoon. "Put them all here," he said. "Then I want you to take all the clothes from the left-hand side of the wardrobe. Do you understand? All the clothes, all the shoes, everything."

The servants looked at each other. Then they looked at Angus. "What do you want us to do with the clothes?" one of them asked.

Angus shrugged. "Throw them away if you want to. Just get rid of them fast, and you," he pointed to a maid, "you hang all this new stuff up in their place."

Angus retreated to the bedroom. He wanted to see Bonnie's face when she realized that the clothes she had so carefully chosen for her honeymoon were now all gone. Anyway, he thought, she has such dull taste. She needs to be taught how to dress. From now on, I'll choose her clothes and tell her what to wear.

Angus had always ordered his women to wear tight clothes and thin high-heeled shoes. He was excited by the cruel sharp spike of the shoe, and by the way the black seam of the stockings stretched up the leg and into the dark hollows of the body. He didn't like those new-fangled nylon tights. He lusted after the severity of the restraining suspenders. Bonnie will have to get used to my ways, he thought.

After the door had slammed shut and all the porters had left, Angus smiled. They were alone in the suite. He asked Bonnie if she would like to have a shower. Hot and sticky as she was, she immediately agreed. She was feeling very bruised. The thought of pleasing Angus, however, filled her with delight. She got out of bed and walked naked into the huge bathroom. The floor had a thick white carpet, and the walls were lined with cupboards. She opened the door to the wardrobe to pull out her favourite old blue bathrobe. There, hanging neatly from the bar, were the new clothes. On the racks, her new shoes stood in gleaming rows. She frowned and pulled open another door. That wardrobe was empty. "Angus," she said. "There's been a mistake. Someone has taken my clothes away."

Angus came into the room. "There's no mistake," he said. He was amused. "No mistake at all. I had the porters take all that old junk away."

Bonnie was startled. "But that was all brand new, except for my bathrobe. And that bathrobe is my security blanket."

"From now on, I'm your security blanket," Angus said firmly. He drew Bonnie's naked body into his arms. "I love you, darling," he said. Looking over her shoulder, he noticed how flat her bottom was, and it pleased him greatly. He didn't like women with heavy buttocks. Bonnie buried herself in his chest. She held back her emotion until she was in the shower with Angus. He couldn't see the tears for the water running down her face.

I suppose he needs to feel he owns me, she thought as she sat at the dressing-table in the bathroom applying her make-up. "What shall I wear with the yellow dress?" she called out to Angus as he fixed his tie.

"Wear your gold earrings. Then we'll shop for more jewellery in Italy."

"Italy?"

"Yes. I've just decided that I'd like to pick up a new Lamborghini. Anyway, I love Rome. Such a decadent city. Full of whores and priests."

Bonnie thought of Father John. "That's where Father John wants to go."

"Yes," Angus nodded. "I know. He cornered me at the wedding. He's a sharp bugger." I wonder what he does to

Laura, he thought. Whatever it is, it gives the woman one hell of a kick.

"I promised grandma I'd be back for a visit at the end of the summer."

"All right." Angus was in a good temper. He handed her a lipstick. "Try this."

She took it obediently. "Do you want to come?" she said.

"No. I'll trust you at your grandmother's house," he laughed.

Bonnie looked up at his face in the mirror. "You can trust me anywhere," she said. "I know you don't believe me now, but you will."

Angus kissed the top of her head. "Let's get going or we'll be late."

They dined inside the restaurant. Frieda and Gunter were late. When they did arrive, they were slightly tipsy. Angus ordered lobster for himself and for Bonnie, and a salad of oranges and kiwis. During dinner, Frieda and Angus talked about mutual friends. Gunter tried to engage Bonnie in a light flirtatious conversation, but he soon gave up. Bonnie had no talent at all for small talk. She felt uncomfortable in her new underwear. She was not used to wearing a boned and padded bra, nor was she accustomed to black elastic suspender belts. They made her feel cheap. Still, she thought, Angus must really love me a lot to take so much care about what I wear and how I look.

She wished she could entertain Angus as Frieda was doing. Angus smiled and chuckled as Frieda filled him with the gossip of Berlin. "The in-place for Berliners these days is Dakar," she said. "The French hate us still. Such fun going to all the embassy parties. They have to talk to us there."

Angus was interested. "Anything to shoot in Dakar?" he asked.

"No, not really, but the water-skiing is excellent."

Angus smiled at Bonnie. "That'll be a good adventure," he said.

They finished dinner and climbed into Gunter's Mercedes. Outside the Flim Flam Club, Bonnie shot Angus a worried look. The pavement outside was crowded with men and women wearing heavily-studded leather jackets. One woman, Bonnie realized with shock, was actually a man. Angus led her deep down into the basement of the club. Through the haze of smoke, she saw ghostly figures suddenly stopping their shrill chatter and gazing at Bonnie's young face. She was horrified, as she realized it was a club for transvestites. For the second time that day, she burst into tears. "Don't be silly, Bonnie," Angus said. "It's about time you grew up."

Half an hour later, she noticed that Angus had vanished. She asked Frieda where Gunter was. Frieda shrugged. "He'll be off somewhere with Angus. Don't worry. We'll call a taxi, and I'll drop you off at your hotel."

Bonnie felt a stab of pain. Frieda yawned and said, "Come on. It's late. Gunter and I leave for Istanbul tomorrow."

Just before the taxi reached the hotel, Bonnie timidly asked Frieda if she knew where Gunter and Angus were. "Never ask those sorts of men questions. Gunter would beat me up if I ever interfered."

Bonnie was incredulous. "Beat you up?"

Frieda nodded. Obviously Angus hasn't laid a finger on her yet, she thought. "Take my advice," Frieda liked the girl. "Don't ever cross Angus if you can help it."

"I won't," Bonnie said. "I try not to make him angry. It's very difficult."

"I know. Let him out if he wants to go out. Men like that are, as you say in America, tomcats. They need their freedom."

"Okay," Bonnie nodded. "I hope we meet again."

"Oh, we will." Frieda smiled. "With men like ours, we need to be friends. I'll probably see you around Christmas.

We'll be in London. I like to buy my presents there. I always think a London postmark has such style." She kissed Bonnie goodbye. "Sleep well, and don't worry. He'll be back with the dawn."

In their suite, Bonnie lay in the big wide bed waiting for Angus, but she was asleep when he slipped in. Angus felt totally refreshed after a night of debauchery with Gunter.

The very next morning Angus said they should leave for Italy. "Just throw a few things into a suitcase," he said to Bonnie. "We'll have the rest of our stuff sent back to London." Bonnie sat listlessly on the bed. She was very tired. "Don't sulk, Bonnie." Angus's voice rose. "I can't bear anyone who sulks."

"You could at least have told me you were going off with Gunter."

"Well, I didn't. And I don't want to live with a woman who has to know my every move. Anyway, I knew Frieda would take you home. You were having a good time and I didn't want to disturb you, so I just slipped off. You'd have been very bored with Gunter's new gun collection." Bonnie looked flatly at him. He could see she didn't believe him. He began to pace up and down the room. "You don't believe me, do you? You think I was out chasing women.

"Well, I wasn't. All right. If you don't believe me, I'll ring Gunter and you can ask him yourself."

"No," Bonnie protested. "I don't want to talk to Gunter. I believe you."

It was too late. Angus's whole body was awash with adrenaline. His rage was pushing him to the point of explosion. He grabbed Bonnie by the back of the neck, holding her as one would hold a cat. He propelled her to the phone by his side of the bed. "Dial!" he said.

She dialled the numbers he dictated. The phone rang for what seemed like minutes. "Yes?" It was Gunter's polite, humourless voice.

"Say something!" Angus hissed as he shook her.

"Gunter," Bonnie said in a small tearful voice, "Gunter, can you tell me what you did last night?"

"But of course." Gunter grinned into the telephone. "We were examining my new rifle collection. We are off to Istanbul, and I needed to oil the guns and put them away."

"Oh. I see. Thank you."

"A pleasure, my dear. And I heard you had a pleasant evening with Frieda. We both felt you would have been very bored. . . ."

Bonnie put the phone down. "Look at me." Angus let his hand fall to his side.

Bonnie looked at him. She didn't believe either of them. "I'm sorry, Angus," she said, but Angus could see that her eyes did not glow with that familiar trusting love. He drew back his hand and slapped her face. She went very white. Only the ugly crimson imprint of his fingers glowed on her cheek.

"You bitch!" he spat at her. "I do everything I can for you, and you still don't trust me!"

"I do," Bonnie said, "but I can't lie to you. I love you too much."

"Get dressed. We'll leave for Rome immediately. I've had enough of this hotel." He stalked out of the room.

The flight to Rome passed mostly in silence. Angus stared out of the window and drank whisky. Bonnie read a novel and tried to forget the blow she had so recently endured. Her face, under the heavy coat of make-up, was bruised and her left eye was puffy. He's just very tense, she reasoned. Gunter brings out the worst in him. By the time they landed, she had decided that she would forget the incident and concentrate on enjoying Rome. Seeing a smile on her face as the plane touched down, Angus forgave her.

The taxi drew up in front of the Hotel Spinoza near the

Coliseum. Only in Italy could a hotel be so grand and so ornate. Acres of marble halls, and lines of porters with little red caps, awaited their arrival. Angus was clearly well-known. Many a drunken evening he had smashed his way through the bar with his friends. The hotel never minded. The reports in the daily papers subsequent to one of Angus's sprees meant free publicity for the hotel. The publicity was good, for everyone wanted to drink where the rich and famous played their dangerous games. Alfonso, the hotel's manager, saw to it that no furniture of real value ever stayed in a suite with Angus. "Welcome," he said, coming personally to the door to greet them. Ah, he thought, looking at a barely visible finger-mark on Bonnie's face, so he's started already. "Welcome to my hotel." He bent to kiss Bonnie's fingers. Bonnie smiled. The old man's susceptible heart was touched. She's not for a man like him, he thought.

She's not for him. Alfonso repeated the remark to himself as he walked back to his office. But that's the sort of innocent fool they all pick to marry. I wonder how long it will take her to find out?

PART FOUR

Refuge

Chapter 26

It took nine years for Bonnie to recognize fully that Angus would probably kill her. For nine years, however, she lived on trusts and promises. When she first discovered she was pregnant, she was terrified. She knew that Angus was deadly serious about not wanting children. Angus, in fact, did not want anyone to share Bonnie's attentions. Not even Morgan. When they arrived back from their honeymoon, Bonnie opened the door to Heath House to find herself pounced upon by the dog. She was delighted. John had obviously brought Morgan to the house during their absence. Angus stood in the doorway and watched coldly as Bonnie put her arms around the dog's neck and squeezed him tightly. "He'll live in the garage," Angus said. "I'll not have that horrible beast slobbering all over my house."

They had been back in London for two months when Bonnie discovered she was pregnant. She went to Angus's doctor in July. Dr. Simpson was a beefy, red-faced man. Bonnie did not care for him. A few days later he telephoned to confirm that she was pregnant. "Baby's due in January," he said.

"Oh. Thank you." Bonnie had taken the call in the morning-room. It was just eleven o'clock.

Angus came up behind her as she put the phone down. "Who was that?" he asked.

"Um. . . ." Bonnie was nonplussed. She hadn't worked out how she was going to tell Angus. By now, he regularly slapped her whenever he was angry. Despite his early promises to control his temper, he allowed it free rein. Why not? She was married to him now. She was his. He knew she would never leave him. Bonnie had developed various ways of keeping the peace. Now, she knew, she would have no defence. The fact that she took the Pill would be no excuse at all. "That was Dr. Simpson. You know, Angus, I really don't like him. Can't I go to another doctor?"

"No." Angus was not to be distracted. "What does he want?"

"Well," she took a deep breath. Then, in a small voice she whispered, "I'm afraid I'm pregnant."

Angus lashed out without a moment's hesitation. She caught the full force of his blow in her stomach. "You bitch!" he shrieked. "You whore! You did this on purpose!" Bonnie was rolling on the floor trying to catch her breath. "I'll kick the fucking thing out of you!" Angus drew back his leg.

He was interrupted by Mrs. Turner. Hearing his voice, she had rushed out of the kitchen and up the stairs. She stood now, out of breath, desperately trying to think of a way to distract him. "Mr. Angus!" Mrs. Turner said. Angus stopped and glared at her. "Your tailor telephoned to say your new suits are ready for a fitting," she said calmly.

The veins on Angus's forehead bulged. His eyes glittered. Struggling for breath, Bonnie lay curled up in a ball. Angus's rage slowly subsided. He nodded his head. "Thank you," he said. He turned and slammed out of the house.

Mrs. Turner went over to Bonnie. "Here," she said, "let me help you up." Bonnie took her hand. Mrs. Turner pulled Bonnie to her feet and helped her to a chair. "Wait here," she said. "I'll get you a cup of tea."

Bonnie nodded weakly. "I fell," Bonnie said. "I'm afraid I'm very clumsy." Tears rolled down her cheeks.

"Poor woman," Mrs. Turner muttered for the hundredth time. She took up a cup of tea from the kitchen and suggested that Bonnie go to bed for the rest of the day.

"I think I will," Bonnie said, her hands lying protectively over her stomach. "I'm pregnant, you see."

"How wonderful!" But Mrs. Turner was horrified. Everyone knew that the master hated children. She had been wondering how long Morgan would last. Living creatures tended to die around Angus.

Bonnie, surprised by the warmth of Mrs. Turner's response, burst into tears. She cried now, not so much for the pain but for herself and for her unborn child.

Late that night, as she lay in bed, Angus came home. Bonnie had learned to dread his late-night arrivals. Sometimes he would be angry. Then he would shout at her. Sometimes he would slap her even if she agreed with everything he said. Bonnie soon realized that he was waiting for any faint pretext to hit her. It was wiser to disagree earlier, when he was still rousing himself into a rage, than to prolong the moment when he would be fully aroused and his blows would be more frequent. Life for Bonnie was one long exhaustion. She lived in his shadow.

Sometimes he would come home in a good mood. Then he would bring her flowers and expensive gifts. He would woo her as he had done before their wedding. He would make love to her and promise to reform. She would believe him on and off for nine years.

That night Bonnie listened anxiously to the sound of Angus's footsteps in Heath House. She listened as the front door closed. She listened as Angus climbed the stairs. She listened as he walked past their bedroom. She listened as the door to one of the guest rooms closed behind him. Bonnie sighed. She fell asleep in deep relief.

When Bonnie gave birth to a daughter in the January of 1969, Angus was not seen for three days. Rosemary was born with her father's mop of black hair. She had inherited his white skin and his huge staring black eyes. By the time she was three months, Rosemary was, spasmodically, the apple of her father's eye. When he was home, an increasingly infrequent occurrence, he would take her from her cot and play with her. If she cried, he had her instantly banned from the house. "Take her, Mrs. Turner!" he would yell into the house phone. "Take her over to your place. I can't stand the noise."

Bonnie would retrieve the baby at night, and pray that in the nursery up the hall she would heed the soft-spoken nanny who knew she was paid to allow Angus his undisturbed sleep. If Angus did wake up, he would rant and rave at Bonnie for bringing the child into the world.

Bonnie's life was full of responsibility. In between her efforts to placate her husband, she tried to squeeze in the time and the attention to give to her baby. Morgan, too, made demands upon Bonnie. He grew recalcitrant and irritable in the confines of his garage. He came to life only when Bonnie could find the time to sneak and pet him. One of the additional requirements of her life with Angus was to play hostess whenever he had the whim to give a dinner party. As far as being the wife of a socially prominent man, Bonnie learned fast and she learned well. Sacheverell proved to be a constant guide and companion, coaching her in the fine art of preparing an evening for guests and conducting a civilized conversation, regardless of what might transpire in one's more private moments.

When the baby was four months, Angus arrived home one evening to find John and Teresa dining with Bonnie. They both sensed that he was angry. He was glacially polite and they left as soon as they decently could. "My God," John said, as he got into the car, "she never comes to see us now. We only see her at formal dinner parties. She looks awful."

Teresa agreed. "She told me that Angus is very possessive. He doesn't like visitors, but she did say she thought he wouldn't be in tonight. He was supposed to have gone over to France for a wine-tasting." Teresa shivered. It was late April now, but the night air still held the trace of a chill from the dying winter. Teresa didn't know if she shivered from the crisp air or from fear. "I hope he's not angry with Bonnie," she said.

Inside the house, Angus was beside himself. "You fucking cunt." He began his familiar litany. He looked at the table strewn with the remains of an excellent dinner. "You cow." He seized the edge of the table. Bonnie winced. She knew everything would go flying. "You just had Teresa here as a decoy, so that you could fuck that cunt John. You've always wanted him, haven't you?" Angus overturned the table. "I said, *haven't you?*" He advanced towards her through the crushed glass and china. "Well, let me tell you, *nobody* fucks you. You're *my* wife. I'll kill anybody that lays a hand on you!"

Bonnie was backing towards the door. Angus ran after her. "Don't hide, you little coward. Take your punishment like the whore you are," he said. He punched her twice in the face. Slow, hard, deliberate blows. Blood gushed down her cheeks. Then he hit her so hard that the back of her head cracked against the wall. She passed out. He picked her up like a ragdoll and threw her over his shoulder.

She came to with a terrible headache. Angus was raping her. "I'll show you, you whore!" he was shouting. She pretended to be still unconscious. "I'll kill you, you bitch!" His hands were around her neck. He was squeezing with such force that she could feel her eyes bulging out of her head.

Angus came. Then he flopped over to his side of the bed and fell into an immediate sleep.

This was the first time, in the nine years she would remain with Angus, that she knew she was living with a pathologically dangerous man. I'll go back to grandma, she promised herself that night. I'll take the baby back on a visit, and then I'll tell him I'm not coming back. She felt jubilant. She had found a solution.

The next morning Angus got up and dressed without any reference to the night before; nor did he seem to notice Bonnie's bruised face. Bonnie went into the bathroom. She was appalled by the damage he had inflicted. She gazed in the mirror at her swollen eyelids. Both eyes were so engorged that she found it difficult to see through them. She thanked God that her nose wasn't broken. She stood, gripping the basin with her hands. Tears painfully forced their way through her eyelids and poured down her face. She had a fleeting flash of memory of her mother swaying down the little hall, her eyes as black and as bruised as Bonnie's now looked. She'll understand, Bonnie thought. I'll go and talk to her. Maybe she can help me.

Bonnie ran the cold water and gingerly dabbed at her eyes, trying to reduce the swelling. Her face, however, was too badly damaged. She stayed alone in the house for two weeks while the bruises faded. She saw no one and telephoned no one. Teresa rang, but Bonnie told her she was ill. Bonnie knew that living with a violent man like Angus meant that he would not tolerate his wife to have friends of her own, however gregarious *he* might be.

When Angus was at home, even if Bonnie played with Rosemary in his presence, his face would redden and his brow would crease. Bonnie learned for the sake of Rosemary's safety to stay away from the child, and allow Angus to play with her on his own. In that way jealous confrontations could be avoided.

Two months later, Bonnie was back in circulation. Then she discovered she was pregnant again; she knew instinctively that she had conceived on the night of the rape. This time she decided to press Angus to let her take Rosemary to see Augustine. So far he had refused to allow her to go. He was busy buying and selling houses. As Sacheverell had predicted, he never made any attempt to move into the new house on the Embankment. He was now planning to get rid of the house. First, however, he would throw a great party in the marble pool-room so that he could show it off to all his friends. After the party, the house would immediately be put on the market.

Bonnie approached the subject of her visit to Lexington the night before the party. Angus was in an excellent mood. "I don't see why not," he said.

Bonnie was persuasive. "Augustine is old now," she explained, "and she would love to see her only great-grandchild."

Angus nodded absently. "You can go on Monday," he said. It was Friday evening. Angus was occupied checking the guest list. "You'll have to be back a week later. We're going to Drummossie for a couple of weeks. I want to sort out the wine-cellar."

"All right." Bonnie looked down at the list in her hand. "I'll get Mrs. Turner to book the tickets." She kept her voice calm. Angus could pick up even the slightest change in her behaviour. It was as if he could read her mind. Now Bonnie knew much more about Angus. She studied his ways and his habits, and she guarded herself as much as she could. "What do you want me to wear at the party?" she asked.

He considered for a moment. "Wear the cornflower silk dress I bought you two weeks ago."

It had been a present after he had raped her again.

* * *

For all that Bonnie had learned to predict his actions and his moods, Angus still had the power to hurt and to confuse her. The night of the party was no exception. All Saturday he had been cheerful. When Angus was happy, the world around Bonnie lit up like a Christmas tree. She smiled and sang to herself all day. While Angus was attending to the last-minute details, she took Rosemary to the park and then went upstairs to get ready. She had just changed when Angus returned from his preparations. "You look lovely, darling," he said as he handed her a long velvet box. On the white silk lining lay a double row of black pearls with a gold and diamond clasp.

"It's beautiful!" Bonnie said. "It's absolutely gorgeous."

Angus smiled. Bonnie hadn't looked at him with such love for a long time. He pulled her to him. "I know I've been a beast at times, Bonnie, but you know I really do love you. You're the one person who's never betrayed me. You always stand by me. I couldn't live without you."

These were the old familiar lines. By now, Bonnie had heard them so often she could repeat them in her sleep. Yet somehow they still had the power to move her. She felt guilty that she was planning to leave him. I'll just go to Boston for a visit, she told herself. I'll try one more time.

They left for the party. We look just like any other rich, successful couple, she thought. She put her hand to her neck, and hoped that nobody would notice the finger-marks that were yellowing now upon her throat. Bonnie had become an expert with make-up.

The guests were already arriving. Sacheverell stood watching Bonnie very closely. He had seen very little of her since the birth of the baby. She looks thin, he thought. Gone was the warm bubbly girl. Instead she was polished and elegant, quite at home among the glittering crowd. She shook hands with the guests and finally went to talk to Margaret Bartholomew.

Bonnie knew this would annoy Angus. He had hit her when she had insisted on inviting the Bartholomews. After so many beatings, however, her tolerance for pain had become higher. It was only the following day, when she was calm, that she could feel the bruises. Then she would take large doses of aspirin, and ask for buckets of ice to be brought up to her. "I've been clumsy again," she would say on the house telephone.

Bonnie badly needed to see Margaret, even if she risked a beating. She wanted reassurance that a marriage, though at times problematical, could endure between two people who loved each other. Bonnie knew that, if she could stay near good sensible people, she would regain her own sense of reality. Living with Angus, who totally dominated her thoughts, words, and deeds, she was beginning to lose touch with herself. Angus insisted that she was ill, mad, that she didn't know what she was doing. At times, Bonnie was so confused that she really did think she was mad. She found herself almost believing that he had the right to beat her. She somehow deserved the dreadful physical attacks because she had failed him. "Say it, whore," he would slap her face. "Say you're mad. Go on. Say it." He would spit at her. Grudgingly she learned to say that she was a whore, a cunt, a dirty prostitute. All the while he would hit her until she passed out or he became exhausted. Angus was very rarely exhausted. The violence excited him. It made him feel alive and in control.

All these secrets Bonnie carried on her thin shoulders. "You do look weary," Margaret said, taking Bonnie's arm. "Winnie's been asking after you. Will you promise to visit her before Christmas?"

Bonnie nodded. "I'd love to see Winnie again." She tried not to let the tears slide down her face. She so much wanted to tell Margaret what was happening, but she felt too ashamed to admit that she had been terribly wrong about Angus. She looked across the room at his handsome profile. He was in his element tonight. Guests were all around him as he led them from the pool-room out into the great greenhouses filled with tropical plants and gaily-coloured parrots. Bonnie winced at the memory of the first parrot. Thank God, she thought, Morgan had the good sense to keep out of his way. Bonnie found herself unable to say anything important to Margaret. Instead she merely chatted casually about the house, and asked Margaret about the family. Margaret felt an uneasy sensation that something was terribly wrong in Bonnie's life. She found no way, however, of broaching the subject. It was as if Bonnie stood encased in an impervious crystal tomb of polite smiles.

"Why is my petal so pensive?" Sacheverell stood in front of her.

She smiled. "I was just thinking how much work went into this house."

"No, you weren't. You're not very happy, Bonnie. I'm an old friend. You can tell me what lies in those sad shadows of your eyes."

Bonnie looked at the kind face of her husband's best friend. I couldn't do that to Angus, she thought. "I've had a real dose of homesickness," she said lightly, "so I'm taking Rosemary across to the States to see my grandmother and to eat a decent hamburger."

"By yourself?"

"Yes," Bonnie nodded. "Angus is sailing all next week, so I'd be home on my own even if I stayed here."

Things can't be as bad as I thought, Sacheverell told himself. He felt great relief.

The band broke into an energetic rhythm. Bonnie slipped away, knowing how Angus hated anyone else to dance with her. She hurried upstairs to the bedroom. As she opened the door, she saw Angus on the bed astride a woman whom Bonnie had never seen before. They were too occupied even to notice her. Trembling with rage, Bonnie ran down the stairs and staggered into a little-used room off the main dining-room. She sat on the brown-tiled floor and sobbed her heart out.

Gradually her sobs receded. More than the beatings, the pain of his betrayal strengthened her decision to leave him. Then the confusion started. She sat on the floor, puzzled. Why should she mind so terribly that he was in bed with another woman when he had half-killed her on so many occasions? I suppose I'm getting used to the beatings, she thought, but not to the idea of sharing him. She wondered if the other woman was a permanent fixture in his life. Maybe he had agreed to let Bonnie go to her grandmother's house so that he could have the time to be with his mistress? This thought lingered in her mind as she dried her face before returning to the party.

Angus was back by now, surprisingly dancing with Teresa. He saw Bonnie and gestured for her to come and join them. Bonnie walked over. Teresa promptly announced that she was engaged to be married. Bonnie was delighted. "Patrick and I decided to get married just before Christmas. You will come, won't you?" Teresa said.

Angus could hardly refuse the invitation, and Bonnie was thrilled for Teresa. "We'd love to come. Wouldn't we, Angus?" For a moment she forgot her intention of leaving Angus for good. . . .

The music stopped and Angus drew Bonnie off into the dining-room. "You look so lovely tonight," he said. "I've never seen you lovelier." Bonnie glanced at him. Had she imagined seeing him on the bed upstairs? Was that only another illusion? Maybe she really was going mad. How could this man gazing at her in adoration be the same man who had blacked her eyes and bloodied her nose? "Darling," Angus said with a smile. "We have such a wonderful future together." His voice was choked with emotion. "I've just been offered three-quarters of a million for this house. As soon as you get back from visiting your grandmother, let's go to

Africa. Remember, Frieda says Dakar is lovely. Let's have an adventure. Okay?"

Bonnie nodded. Angus stayed by her side all night.

The plane took off for Boston. Bonnie felt at peace. She looked down at the child sleeping in her arms. We're getting further apart, she thought as she remembered all the times she had rejected Rosemary's efforts to be loved. "I can't tell you now," she whispered, "but one day I'll explain it all. Anyway, you are going to have a little playmate for a Christmas present." At least I don't face having to tell Angus about the baby, she thought. I can just apply for a separation order, and I know Augustine will take care of us. The plane carried her on to Boston and to what Bonnie expected would be her new life.

 Chapter 27

Augustine was shocked to see how frail Bonnie had become. "I'm pregnant again," Bonnie said defensively.

"How marvellous!" Augustine had fallen immediately in love with Rosemary. She smiled. "She's her father's daughter, all right. Exact same colouring . . . and look at those lovely eyelashes. . . ."

Morag was thrilled to see Bonnie. She put her arms round her, then drew back. "I can feel the bones of your back, Bonnie."

Bonnie frowned. "I know. I can't tell you how hard I have to work. Being Angus's wife means one long round of dinner parties. I have to be back next week to open Drummossie for the shooting season."

Morag smiled. "Well, I can always come over and help."

"I'll remember that." Bonnie decided not to say anything about leaving Angus. She would talk to her mother first.

Rosemary pined for her father after the first two days. As she crawled in and out of the large rooms of the Great House she looked everywhere for Angus. Bonnie couldn't bear to hear her calling for her father. She, on the other hand, felt a huge, exultant surge of relief. She lay in bed knowing that Angus would not walk through the door and attack her. And yet, much to her surprise, she still shook whenever the front door of the Great House slammed. She still jumped when someone entered a room silently behind her.

One evening Morag came into the library where Bonnie sat reading a book. Hearing a footstep, Bonnie cowered against the chair. She raised her arm over her face. "Hey, Bonnie," Morag was puzzled. "What on earth is the matter with you? You look as if I'm going to hit you. Bonnie?" Morag dropped to one knee. "You've been so jumpy these last two days. What's the matter?"

Bonnie put her arm down and sighed. "Well, I'm pregnant again, and I'm frightened of telling Angus. He loves Rosemary, but he doesn't want any more children."

Morag was sympathetic. "Gee, that's awful. But I wouldn't worry about it too much. He'll be a bit upset at first, but he'll get over it. My mom had to tell my dad that she was pregnant with my sister. And that was after my dad had retired. Boy, was he angry! He threw a plate at the wall. But now my sister's his favourite. Really. Don't worry too much." Morag looked into Bonnie's face. Bonnie didn't say anything. "What time are you leaving to see your mother?"

Bonnie looked distracted. "Um, I'm staying with Mitzi again. I'll take Rosemary without Nanny because Mitzi only has one spare room." She brightened. "Mitzi says she's having a little high school reunion dinner for me. Caroline will be there with Mike, and Jack Smith, and Alice Lucas. It'll be such fun to see all the old faces again. I feel I've been away for years and years. It really hasn't even been eighteen months since I got married."

Morag nodded. "It seems like ages because you're so far away."

Laura was pleased to see Bonnie. She was even mildly interested in the baby. What she was not prepared for was Bonnie bursting into tears and telling the whole ghastly story.

Laura was appalled. Bonnie couldn't leave Angus now, not just as she had decided to extract more money out of her. "There, there." Laura put a bony arm around Bonnie's shoulder. "Don't cry. There must be something we can do. Let me see." She reflected for a moment. "This is the first time you've left him, is it?" Bonnie nodded. "Well, that'll probably bring him to his senses, Bonnie. I daresay he needs to be taught a good lesson, that he can't treat you like that. He does love you, you know."

Bonnie nodded again. "I know he loves me, but I can't cope with that kind of loving. He blacks my eyes, and he kicks me, mom. Sometimes I'm afraid he'll kill me."

Laura wasn't really listening. She was busy planning. "Most men beat their wives," she said.

"Dad didn't beat you," Bonnie retorted.

"No," Laura said sharply. "He wasn't man enough." A familiar silence fell between mother and daughter.

Rosemary began to cry. "I'll take her back to Mitzi's," Bonnie said. "She's a little upset, being in a new place." She scooped the child into her arms. "Come on, darling. Let's catch a cab and go back to Mitzi's." Bonnie realized she couldn't wait to get out of her mother's house. Laura didn't understand, but at least she had agreed that staying away from Angus for a while might bring him to his senses.

As soon as Bonnie had left, Laura was on the telephone to Father John. "Bonnie tells me she wants to leave Angus."

"Why?" The priest sounded perturbed. He liked Angus. "A man after my own heart," he had said to Laura on the plane back from the wedding.

"Oh," Laura was vexed, "lovers' quarrels, that sort of thing. Bonnie always was headstrong. Maybe he had to get firm with her from time to time. What shall I do?" Laura had a glint in her eye. She knew exactly what she was going to do. That spoiled little bitch wasn't going to louse up her life again.

Father John considered the question gravely. "As a Catholic and as her mother, it's your duty, I believe, to warn Angus. After all, marriage is a holy sacrament."

"Thank you, Father. I'll take your advice." She was already rehearsing her speech. "I'll see you at confession on Friday."

Father John nodded. "Okay," he said. He fingered his cassock. It was made of the finest silk. He had ordered it from Rome. I do need a new house, he thought as he hurried from his office into the dining-room. Suddenly, Father John relaxed. He felt a lot closer to Rome. He had money in the bank and a fierce hold on Laura.

"The girl's gone completely off her head." Laura was nervous. Angus always made her feel uncomfortable.

Angus stood at the other end of the telephone in the little white morning-room. Garrett was sprawled in an armchair beside him. "I see." Angus's tone was guarded.

"I thought I ought to warn you. Maybe it's because she's pregnant again so soon after her first baby. That can make a woman do silly things, you know."

"Thank you." Angus's voice was quite unemotional. "I'm very grateful to you for telling me. By the way, we must get you a new house. I have some spare money, and I could do with a tax break. I want you to go looking for just the right place, and then I'll telephone you in a few days and you can give me the details. Please try to find something worth at least half a million, or else it won't be worthwhile for my tax purposes. All right?"

"That's very kind of you," Laura said as calmly as she could. "Thank you."

"My pleasure. I'll speak to you after you've found something then. Goodbye."

Angus put the telephone down and turned to Garrett. "You'll have to go. I've got business to attend to."

Garrett groaned. He had only just left Angus's bed, and was in no fit state to move. "Oh, Angus," he said, pouting, "I feel just as if a bus had rolled over my head. Give a man a break."

"No. Get going. I'm off to pack."

Garrett looked at him blearily. "Who is it this time?"

Angus inspected Garrett. His face was working and his eyes were glittering in a way that Garrett knew spelled trouble. "Fuck off," Angus said.

"Okay, okay. I'm going. Don't worry." Garrett walked rapidly out of the room. I'll get back to Drummossie, he thought. I'd better lie low. Angus is going on one of his benders.

Down in the morning-room, Angus was in despair. How could she? he thought. How dare the bitch leave me like that? He realized Bonnie had probably planned the whole event. Suddenly he felt a huge aching hole. He picked up the telephone and smashed it against the wall. It didn't help. The pain got worse. "You left me!" he screamed at a portrait on the wall. The portrait changed into Bonnie's face. It smiled mockingly at him. "You took my child!" Angus shrieked. He wrenched it from the wall and hurled it at the window. The heavy frame shattered the glass. He was in a frenzy. He picked up an armchair and threw it across the room. Still, despite the physical exertion, his pain and rage persisted.

"Damn you, woman," he gritted his teeth, "I'll make you pay for this."

He paused. Then a smile came to his lips. He had a just punishment. "You took away my child," he said out loud. The rage was gone. He knew how to get rid of the pain. He walked to his study across the hall, and he took a double-barrelled shotgun from the rack on the wall. From the drawer of his desk he took two cartridges. He loaded the gun and left the house.

Morgan heard footsteps. He rose to his feet as Angus entered the garage. The dog was puzzled. Angus never came to see him. He wagged his tail. Angus put the gun to his shoulder and shot Morgan at point-blank range. The huge dog toppled over, most of his head blown away. Angus's pain was gone. Retribution had been made.

He put the gun casually over his shoulder and returned to the house, whistling. He went upstairs to the bedroom to pack. The bed was still rumpled from the night spent with Garrett. Two glasses lay on the floor beside an empty whisky bottle.

"Mrs. Turner," he said down the house telephone, "I have to leave for Boston immediately. Arrange for a ticket on the first flight out, please. See that Sacheverell sorts out the morning-room by the time I'm back. I'll only be away 'til Monday. Arrange flowers, champagne, and let me see . . . ah yes, some caviar. I want Mrs. Fraser to feel welcome when we return." Then, as an afterthought, he said, "Tell Ben to see to the garage. I had to shoot the dog. He was miserable cooped up all day."

"Yes, sir." Mrs. Turner's voice showed no feeling. Inwardly she grieved for Morgan. She had heard the shot and guessed what had happened. "Well, the dog lived longer than most animals, I suppose," she said to the parlour maid.

*　*　*

Bonnie had planned to spend the day luxuriating in the company of Mitzi and her children. She was looking forward to being an ordinary mother, living in an ordinary street, taking care of her own baby. When she returned to Mitzi's house, Jack Smith had already arrived. He was leaning against the sink, clutching a can of beer in one hand, and holding Max on his shoulder. The sun was still bright on the kitchen wall, and Mitzi was talking a blue streak. "Come on, Bonnie," Mitzi said. "Say hello to Jack."

Bonnie smiled at him. Jack had always been one of the crowd. He had been a quiet, studious boy, and obviously had grown into a kind and gentle man. Bonnie suddenly felt confused.

Alice Lucas, as bumptious as ever, came through the door like an express train. "Bonnie!" she exclaimed. "I've heard all about you from Mitzi." She flung her arms round Bonnie. "What's it like to marry a lord and live in a castle?"

Bonnie laughed ruefully. "I think it's harder than living in a nice house on a quiet street." The words were so bitter that Bonnie collected herself. "I mean, I spend all my time trying to run several houses at once. I hardly ever have time to myself."

"I should have such problems," said Mitzi. "Darling." Her face lit up as Ray came into the room. Bonnie felt a pang of envy. I once felt like that, she thought. Ray hugged Bonnie and greeted his guests. "Come on," he said. "Let's get out into the garden while we still have the sun."

Six o'clock shadows lay on the small green lawn outside Mitzi's kitchen. The barbecue was already alight. A neat white picket fence and yew hedges intertwined with a trail of convolvulus provided privacy from the neighbours.

Alice laughed. "Well, I guess a barbecue in a backyard isn't quite the same as a meal in your house."

"You have no idea how much I've missed this way of life." Bonnie was serious. "Although my mother never liked guests,

I have wonderful memories of other people's homes, and my dad loved to barbecue." She felt simultaneously a pang of regret and a wave of nostalgia. She could have been in her father's carefully-tended backyard on just such an evening all those years ago. The backyard was now as derelict as the front of Laura's house. Bonnie had a moment of panic. Would her life end like a derelict deserted backyard? She was a deserter.

"Don't look so solemn." Mitzi put a plate in Bonnie's hand. "Come on. Eat."

Halfway through the meal there was a ring at the door. "That should be Caroline and Mike," Mitzi said to Bonnie. "We've become real friendly." Ray went to let them in. "Mike's having trouble with Caroline," Mitzi confided. "Caroline's having an affair with her boss."

Bonnie was sympathetic. "How awful for him."

"Thank God my Ray would never do a thing like that. Anyway, I'd break his neck if he tried," Mitzi laughed.

"You're lucky, Mitzi."

Mitzi shot a look at Bonnie. "Bonnie, you seem just a bit too serious. What's wrong? Has Angus been having an affair?"

Bonnie made a face. "I don't know if it was an affair. Probably a one-night stand." She felt she owed Mitzi some explanation for her long silences.

Mitzi was relieved to hear Bonnie opening up. "I knew something was wrong," she said. "We'll talk tomorrow."

"That'd be very nice." Bonnie was grateful. Even if she kept the violence to herself, it would be a relief to be able to talk to someone about Angus's fling with that woman the night of their last party.

"Come on, Ray," Mitzi yelled. "Don't keep them in the kitchen. The food'll get cold."

Ray came through to the garden with Mike behind him. Both men looked grim. Mike had black circles under his eyes. "Caroline left for good two days ago," he said to Mitzi. The little group in the backyard fell silent. Then Mike smiled at Bonnie. "I'm not in too good a shape right now," he said, "but I did want to come and see you. How are you, Bonnie?" Bonnie patted the seat beside her. Rosemary sat on her mother's knee. "Gee," Mike looked at the baby. "She really does look like your husband."

"I know." Bonnie tried to smile at Mike.

"Hey, why are you looking so glum? You're not having problems too, are you?" Bonnie lowered her head. "You too?" Mike said. "I don't believe it."

Bonnie nodded. Suddenly she very much wanted to talk to Mike. There was very little opportunity during the meal. Everybody was busy swapping high school stories. Before long, Bonnie forgot her own personal nightmare and joined in.

Soon it was ten o'clock. The children were all tucked up asleep in their beds, and Alice was saying goodbye. Jack stood up. "Time for me to hit the hay," he said. "Got to get up early tomorrow. Goodbye, Bonnie. See you soon I hope."

Alice hugged Bonnie again. "One day, I'll bang on the door of your castle," she teased.

Bonnie smiled. "Any time, Alice," she said. "Feel free."

Mike was still sitting at the table. Bonnie had moved into the kitchen to say her farewells. She looked back through the door to the backyard. There Mike sat, with his head in his hands. Bonnie felt deeply sorry for him. She went back into the garden and put her hand on his shoulder. "Is there anything I can do?" she said, sitting down beside him.

"Not really," Mike said.

"Talk to me. I always find that talking helps. The emptiness of the big house drives me crazy. Please, Mike. Tell me. What went wrong?"

"I don't know. I guess I was working too hard. I'm in a big law office, and it keeps me busy. It won't be long before they'll ask me to be a partner. You know how pressured all that is.

Anyway, Caroline didn't want kids. I did. Maybe that was the problem. No, but it wasn't just that. She said I wasn't intellectual enough for her. I think that bothered her a lot. I don't know."

Bonnie snorted. "You've got to be pretty bright to have graduated from Brown," she said.

Mike looked grateful. "I guess so. But she meant intellectual like the *New York Times* kind of intellectual."

"As Mitzi would say, 'Feh,'" Bonnie laughed. "I know what you mean. But that's not intellectual at all. Those people just read the book reviews, never the books," she said. "Silly woman."

"I feel I've failed," he said miserably.

"That makes two of us," she said. "I'm leaving Angus."

Mike stared at her. His mouth fell open. "But you both looked so happy."

"We're not," Bonnie said simply. "At least I'm not."

"What's the matter?" Mike took her hand. "Anything I can do?"

"No." Bonnie stared into the darkness of the night. "I'm pregnant again, and tomorrow night I'll be back in Boston. I'll probably live with Augustine. I'll grow old and potter about the garden." She smiled. "At least I'll have my children and they will be surrounded with love."

Mike sighed. "Oh, Bonnie. I remember the way you looked one day when I saw you on the green at Brown. Everybody predicted a wonderful marriage for you. You were so beautiful. You still are," he corrected himself. "But back then you were full of life. You always ran everywhere with your hair streaming over your shoulders. I can still picture your long legs running across the green."

Bonnie grinned. "Well, maybe that part of me will all come back." She looked at Mike's dependable, kind face. "I can't imagine why Caroline left you," she said gently.

Mike frowned. "She said I'm a jock."

Bonnie thought for a moment. She thought of Angus and of his concern with her dress and her make-up. She thought of Sacheverell with his tip-toe walk. She looked at Mike. "At least you're a man, Mike. And there's precious few of those around."

Mike shook his head. "I'll never know what a woman wants." He gazed at Bonnie with his warm hazel eyes.

"You look just like Morgan, my Great Dane," she giggled. "He looks all woeful and sad when I say goodbye to him."

Mitzi and Ray came to the kitchen door with their arms round each other. "Hey," said Ray, "what's keeping you two? It's late."

"We're consoling each other," Mike replied. "But you're right. It is late." Mike and Bonnie walked inside, and Mike prepared to leave. "Hey, Bonnie," he said just before he left, "I'll take you to the airport. All right?"

"Thanks, Mike. I'd like that. My plane leaves at six o'clock tomorrow evening, so I'll have to leave here about five. Okay?"

"I'll be here," Mike said. He kissed Mitzi on the cheek and hugged Bonnie very hard. "I'm glad to see you again," he said.

"So am I," Bonnie said with a smile.

 # Chapter 28

Angus was tired, dishevelled, and cross. He telephoned Augustine from Logan Airport. "Hello," he said. "I'm in Boston on business. I thought I'd join Bonnie and we could all spend some time together. What do you think of your first great-granddaughter?"

"I think she is gorgeous, Angus. She looks a lot like you." The old lady was pleased. How sweet of him to want to spend time with me, she thought.

"Well, I've got a few things to do," he said. "Then I'll come out for tea."

"Do that. Shall I send the car for you?"

"How thoughtful of you, my dear Augustine. That would be lovely. Oh," said Angus, "by the way. I know Bonnie is visiting her mother with the baby. When do you expect her back?"

"Quite late, really," Augustine replied. "About ten o'clock. She's catching the six o'clock plane. She wanted to spend the day with her friend Mitzi."

"Oh, I see. I tell you what. Let's keep my surprise a secret. You go to bed as usual, and I'll wait up for her. All right?"

Augustine was thrilled. How romantic, she thought. "All right, dear boy." The old lady was enjoying herself. Not much happens in life these days, she thought.

Angus busied himself about Boston. By the time Augustine's chauffeur collected him from Locke-Ober's, where he was lunching with some friends, he had purchased a pile of presents. On the way to the Great House, he made the chauffeur stop at a florist's. He filled the car with an assortment of sweet-smelling flowers. The chauffeur was amused. At least the arrogant bastard loves someone as much as he loves himself, he thought.

Angus was having a wonderful time. Recapturing Bonnie reminded him of stalking game in Africa. That's it, he thought. I'll take off for Dakar as I promised. We'll have a week or two at Drummossie, then we'll have an adventure. That should knock some sense into her silly head. Angus, full of presents and plans, did not believe that Bonnie really meant to leave him. After all, he thought, she obviously hasn't said anything to Augustine. Still, no harm in putting a squeeze on

Laura. Give her enough money, and she'll betray anybody, even her daughter. I'll buy Laura the house I promised her, but I'll keep it in my name, of course.

Bonnie spent all day talking to Mitzi. "I might leave Angus," she said.

Mitzi nodded fiercely. "I wouldn't stay for one minute with a man who was unfaithful."

"It's not just that." Bonnie was struggling to explain something to herself which she had never really thought about before. "I'm just a very ordinary woman," she said. "I think you have to be born into Angus's type of life. You have to love parties, enjoy huge events where hundreds of people are packed together and do nothing but stare at each other. In the beginning, I quite liked adventuring with Angus. He can't stay in one place for very long. We're always dashing out to San Martin, to our house in Spain, or we go off to Europe for a few days here and a few days there. We're very rarely alone. That's not my idea of marriage, you know. Really not." She looked at Mitzi. "I long to be like you and Ray. I love gardening, and we have huge gardens, but the gardeners get embarrassed if I do anything to help." She sighed. "I can't even arrange the flowers. My housekeeper in London gets hurt. In Scotland we have a girl who does nothing else but tend to the flowers from the grounds. I can't take her job away."

Mitzi was quiet. "Well, I know bringing up three kids is not always easy, and Ray is often terribly tired. But when I was there at your wedding, although you looked lovely, I said to Ray that I wondered how long it would take before the glamour wore off. I guess if each night a person gets to lie in the arms of the person they love, then money becomes irrelevant."

Bonnie nodded. "You can have all the money in the world, and it's meaningless if you're unhappy. Especially for someone like me, who doesn't get a kick out of spending the stuff."

Just then, Max, Rebecca, and Alan came charging into the room, with Rosemary crawling along behind. Rosemary was ecstatic to have found three new friends. Mitzi smiled. "I'll get the kids something to eat, Bonnie. You go and pack." Mitzi picked Rosemary up in her arms. "Such a shayna punim," she said as she kissed the baby on her fat cheek.

Mike was prompt. He looked much better than he had the night before. "I slept like a log," he said to Bonnie as he drove to the airport. "Probably because we're in the same boat. Everybody I know is married. No one understands what we're going through." He carried her suitcase while they walked to her gate. "Let's keep in touch," he said.

"I'd like that." Bonnie was grateful. "Here," she said. "Here's my phone number in Lexington. Give me a ring, if you're in Boston. Maybe we could get together."

"I'll make a point of coming up to see you." Mike was firm. He kissed her gently on the lips. "Goodbye, Bonnie," he said. He stroked Rosemary's cheek. "Goodbye, little girl," he said.

"Dad-dad, dad-dad," the child burbled.

Bonnie winced, Mike grinned. "You'll get over it. Lots of people do."

"I know," she said.

"Passengers for the six o'clock flight to Boston," the loud-speaker overhead boomed, "please board now."

"That's us," Bonnie said to Rosemary. "Goodbye, Mike."

Mike stood and waved until she was out of sight.

Bonnie was met at Logan Airport by Augustine's chauffeur. She was tired after her flight, and mother and child snoozed as the car glided through the brightly-lit streets of Boston and Cambridge, then out onto the highway through Arlington and Lexington. Bonnie awoke at the sound of the engine switching off in front of the Great House.

Bonnie gently carried her sleeping daughter into the main

hall. Nanny was there to take the baby. "She should sleep through the night," Bonnie said. "She must be very tired after our trip."

Bonnie looked around her. How beautiful and peaceful everything is, she thought, as she gazed at the lovely hibiscus tree which stood in the corner of the hall. Five perfect pale-pink flowers had all bloomed while she had been away. She ran lightly up to her grandmother's room to say goodnight. Augustine was propped up in bed. "Did you have a good time, dear?" she enquired.

"Yeah," she grinned. "I really enjoy staying with Mitzi. I saw some old friends. Mitzi got a group of the old high school crowd together and. . . . Grandma, what's put roses in your cheeks?"

Augustine laughed. She had spent a happy evening with Angus. He had made her laugh until tears came to her eyes. "Oh, I had dinner with an old friend."

"Good." Bonnie was pleased.

Augustine smiled. "Off you go to bed now. You must be tired after all that flying. Morag put a late-night snack in your room."

"Oh, bless her. I am a bit hungry." She leaned over and kissed her grandmother good-night.

All the way down the long, thickly-carpeted hall, Bonnie thought about Mitzi and Ray. One day, she thought, I'll find a man who will love me and the children. She paused by her bedroom door, preparing herself for the familiar rush of plea-sure that would envelop her when she put on the light. She opened the door. To her amazement, the light by her bed was already on and the room was full of flowers. She paused. Angus, she thought. She crossed the room to a large camellia plant. There was no note. On her bed lay several parcels. She sat down and picked up the largest. She didn't really want to open it. How often had she been fooled by Angus and his presents?

"Aren't you going to open it?"

Bonnie leapt to her feet. She felt the muscles tighten in the back of her neck. Angus, dressed in a black silk kimono, strode out of the bathroom. In one hand he carried a bottle of champagne, and in the other two glasses. The colour drained from Bonnie's face. She began to shake.

Angus was immediately solicitous. "Darling," he said, depositing the glasses on her bedside table, "here." He put his arms around her. "You're all upset. I'm sorry if I frightened you. I had business in Boston, and I missed you so much I decided to join you for a long weekend. Then we can fly back together."

Bonnie's heart was thumping. Then he doesn't suspect, she thought. If he did, he'd be in a rage. She looked at him. "That's very nice of you, Angus." She kept her voice steady. "Uh, let's have a drink. I'm really very tired after the flight."

Angus smiled. "Of course, darling." He went back into the bathroom. "We can have a midnight feast," he called. "Look at what I've bought for you." He returned to the bedroom carrying a large plate filled with delicacies: hard-boiled eggs stuffed with caviar, artichoke hearts, smoked salmon, strips of radish, carrots and celery with an avocado dip in a bowl in the centre of the plate. He expertly worked the champagne cork and then sat with his legs crossed in the middle of her bed. "Come on," he said. "You undo your presents." He was as excited as a small boy. His eyes were shining. "Open the flat one first."

The flat parcel contained a nightdress in creamy satin. The bodice was appliquéed with wheeling butterflies and languid flowers. The large square parcel contained a baby-crocodile handbag, its clasp fashioned from eighteen-carat gold. Bonnie tried to look happy. Inside, she was totally confused. All that had happened in the last two days receded into the past. Here she was, yet again, mesmerized by her husband.

"Hey, dreamer," he said, "get on with it. Open the last

one." Bonnie opened the box and took out the ring. She sat on her bed and stared at it. Angus laughed. He took the ring from her hand and slipped it onto her wedding ring finger. "An eternity ring," he said, as he pulled her back into his arms and kissed her.

He loved her that night as he had loved her on their wedding night. Bonnie fell asleep thanking her lucky stars that she had said nothing to her grandmother. She smiled. Grandma must have known all along that Angus was here, she thought fondly. She felt her new ring on her finger. For all eternity, she thought. She snuggled up to Angus as he slept. I'll make it work, she promised herself.

Rosemary was excited to see her father. She threw her plump little body into his arms. "Dad-dad!" she gurgled. She patted his face. "Dad-dad!"

Angus smiled. "Augustine tells me we are about to have another child." Bonnie blanched. They were alone with Rosemary at the dining table. Augustine had not yet come down for breakfast. Bonnie was frightened. "Let's hope it's another girl," Angus said. He continued to read the *Boston Globe* and mention news items.

Bonnie let him go on talking. Maybe she had been premature in planning to leave Angus. Maybe this time he really meant to change. I'll give him one more chance, she thought. They began to discuss next week's shooting party in Scotland.

The rest of the weekend in Lexington passed pleasantly. Angus was charming to everyone. He was even pleasant to Morag. He drove Bonnie into Boston for an evening at the theatre. For once he made no plans to contact any of his friends. They dined alone at Maison Robert under the old City Hall. Bonnie's smile returned and once again her eyes shone. They planned to make their trip to Africa before the next baby was due in December. "I'd like to go before October," she said.

"That's fine," said Angus. "Let's try for September." They continued to make plans all the way back to the Great House. Angus continued to be gentle and tender.

The family returned to London on the Monday. Angus told Bonnie, when they reached Heath House, that Morgan had pined for her and had escaped from the garage to look for her; he had been run over by a car on East Heath Road. "Darling," Angus said, "I didn't tell you earlier because I didn't want to ruin your holiday. Ben buried him in the orchard. I'll have a marble gravestone made for him." Bonnie sobbed and Angus held her tightly. He wiped her eyes with his handkerchief.

Bonnie decided to make her confession to Father MacBride. When she had finished, the old man sat back on his chair in the confessional. "I know that many Catholics would disagree with me," he began with hesitation, "but I've always believed that a man who practises violence against his wife is breaking the marriage vows." He paused. "Also, it is very clearly written in the Bible that, if a man commits adultery, then he annuls his marriage vows."

Bonnie listened intently. "Yes but, Father, I committed a sin. I meant to run away from Angus for good."

"I know, my child, but your reasons were not frivolous. He harmed you physically, and he was unfaithful to his marriage vows."

"I know." Bonnie was silent. "I do so much want our marriage to work. I'm having another baby, and I really do want to work hard at being a good wife to Angus."

The priest sighed. "Well, child, I'm here when you need me."

"You won't tell Angus, will you?"

"You know a confession is a sacred trust."

"I know." Bonnie felt much better. Tomorrow she could take communion with a clear conscience. In running away from her marriage, she had committed a mortal sin. Now she was absolved. She left the chapel and whistled for Morgan. For a moment she had forgotten that he was no longer alive. I miss him, she thought, as she walked alone to the castle.

Augustine was reading in her study when the telephone rang. "Hello?" she said.

"Hello, my name is Mike Edwards. I'm an old friend of Bonnie's from Merrill. I'm in Boston now, and I was wondering if it would be possible for me to speak with her, please?"

"I'm sorry, Mr. Edwards," Augustine said. "She's not here. She flew back to England on Monday."

"Back to England?" Mike's voice dropped with disappointment.

"Yes. Her husband was here on business, and they flew back together."

"Oh. I see."

"Would you like me to give you her number in England?"

Mike was silent. She's back with Angus, he thought. Well, she probably won't want to hear from me. "No, that's all right. Thank you very much anyway."

"All right. Goodbye, then," Augustine said politely, and she went back to her reading.

Chapter 29

It did not take long for Angus to return to his usual ways. Dakar was a disaster of course with all the old rages and some new nightmares. And, when he and Bonnie returned to London, he took Bonnie's passport. "For safe-keeping," he said. He also restricted her spending money. "After all," he explained, "you have so many credit accounts, you don't need much cash. If there's anything you particularly want to buy, just ask me."

By October, Bonnie was beginning to feel her second pregnancy. The weather in London was hot and sticky with a late Indian summer. Her back ached and a vein in her left leg throbbed continually. Angus was seldom home and, when he was, he was impatient and quick to anger. Bonnie's increasingly pregnant state disgusted him. He did not want to share his bed with her. He avoided looking at her belly. He brushed her away when she tried to show him affection.

Slowly Bonnie withdrew into herself. Rosemary seemed oblivious to her parents' behaviour. She still adored her father. By now, she had learned to attract his attention. One evening she toddled into the drawing-room to say goodnight. She passed Angus and climbed on to Bonnie's knee. "Mama," she said, gazing coyly at her father.

Angus frowned. "Come here," he said. Rosemary shook her head and grinned. She buried her face in Bonnie's breast. "Come here," Angus repeated. He was angry. Rosemary clung to her mother. Angus strode over and grabbed Rosemary, who proceeded to howl. Nanny, hovering outside the door, came in and took the little girl from Angus's arms.

"She's tired," Nanny said, as she carried the screaming child away.

"You spoil her," Angus said to Bonnie. "You deliberately encourage her to spite me. What do you do? Bribe her?" Bonnie was appalled. Angus's face was ashen. The old glitter in his eyes had returned. His fists clenched and unclenched.

"No, I don't," she said quickly. "I promise you I don't."

Angus was sullen throughout dinner. He drank heavily and, when they moved back into the drawing-room, poured himself a large whisky. Bonnie was shaking. Angus watched her through his lashes. He said nothing. Bonnie sat crouched waiting for a reasonable excuse to go to bed. The telephone rang. "Miss Bartholomew for you, Madam," Mrs. Turner put her head around the door.

"All right." Bonnie was relieved. She decided to take the call in the morning-room. At least she would have a break from Angus's menacing silence.

She chatted away with Teresa about plans for her wedding, about the weather, and about her own pregnancy. In a much more cheerful frame of mind, she rejoined Angus in the drawing-room. In her absence, Angus had had several more drinks. He was swaying on his feet in front of the empty marble fireplace. "What did you have to say to that fat cow that I couldn't hear?" he demanded.

Bonnie tried to calm him down. "Nothing," she said. "We were just making plans for her wedding."

"Don't lie to me, Bonnie. Which one of those fucking brothers of hers were you talking to?"

"I wasn't talking to anyone but Teresa." She realized that Angus was going out of control. His mouth had become the thin line that she dreaded. The veins on his white temples stood out like thick ropes. He was panting with suppressed rage.

"It was John, wasn't it?" He walked across the floor to

where Bonnie stood. "I'll kill you," he said, grasping her neck. He began to squeeze her throat.

"No, Angus. Don't," she whispered. "The baby."

That was all Angus needed to justify his violence. "You whore!" he shouted. "You fucking prostitute. I'll kill you and that bastard you're carrying! That's not my child. Is it? That's some other man's stinking offspring!" He increased the pressure on her throat. Bonnie was nearly unconscious. She fell to the floor. "Get up, you cunt!" Angus demanded.

Bonnie slowly struggled to her feet. The moment she was up, he knocked her down again. "Get up!" he yelled. He pulled her to her feet and then he punched her hard in the stomach. As she fell, he began to kick her.

She rolled up in a ball to protect herself, but it was too late. Even Angus was shocked at the torrent of blood that poured out from between her legs. He rang the bell. "Get Dr. Simpson," he said.

Mrs. Turner shook her head. "She needs an ambulance," she said.

"All right. Call the hospital. I'm going out."

Mrs. Turner knelt beside Bonnie. "What on earth happened?" she said.

Bonnie was barely conscious. "I fell . . ." she whispered, "I fell against . . ." she burst into tears.

"There, there," Mrs. Turner said as she stroked Bonnie's forehead. "The ambulance will be here in a minute."

Bonnie winced. "The baby," she muttered through her bruised and swollen lips. "The baby. It's coming."

The surgeon was quick and efficient. Alisdair Alexander Stuart MacPherson was born at 10:30 pm on the 12th of October, 1969. He was more than two months premature, and he weighed just over five pounds. "She's a lucky woman," the surgeon said to one of the nurses. "A few more minutes and we would have lost them both."

The nurse nodded. She had seen many bruised and broken women in her years at the hospital. She thought of the last woman who had miscarried after a beating. "I don't know," she said to the surgeon. "Why on earth do they stay with those men?" She remembered the rings on Bonnie's fingers. "She's not short of money. I can tell you that," she said, patting the envelope containing the rings. "She could leave any time she wants."

The surgeon shook his head. "That sort of woman usually deserves it. She's probably been playing around." He made a row of neat stitiches. "There," he said. "Take her up."

When at last Bonnie awoke, she found herself in a strange bed in a strange room and in great pain. She lay, looking at the ceiling. Slowly she remembered the events from the night before. She put her hand on her stomach. I must have had the baby, she thought. She rang the bell. Presently a young nurse with thick red hair bounced into the room. "My baby," Bonnie said. "Is it all right?"

"Certainly." The nurse was cheerful. "You have a lovely baby boy."

Bonnie smiled and then winced. The smile had cracked open her swollen lips. "Can I see him?" she asked.

"Let me clean you up a bit first," the nurse said, and she busied herself with Bonnie's bedclothes. "My goodness," she remarked. "You certainly have made a mess of your face."

Bonnie realized she had lost two of her top teeth. "I know," she said, "I wasn't looking where I was going. I bumped into a lamp-post."

They all say that, the nurse thought, filling a bowl with hot water. Bonnie lay humiliated. Again, she had been forced to lie. The nurse chatted on. Bonnie felt desolate. So nothing has really changed, she thought. Angus was just the same underneath. She would have to get away.

* * *

Angus did not turn up for three days. When he did arrive at the hospital, he ignored the baby.

"Get a dentist in and do something about your teeth," he said. "You look awful."

Slowly over the years, Bonnie took increasing refuge in the solace of alcohol and tranquillizers. Rosemary grew into a pretty, vivacious little girl. She often heard her parents quarrelling. She knew that her father hit her mother, but was not unduly disturbed by Bonnie's bruises nor by her tears. "I'd hit you if I was daddy," she said spitefully one day as Bonnie combed her hair. "You're always drunk and you slur your words because you take so many pills."

Bonnie nodded. "I know I do," she said humbly. "I'm sorry, but . . ." Rosemary ran out of the room.

Alisdair, who was now six, put his arms around his mother. "Don't cry, mummy," he said. "I hate daddy, and I love you. Why can't we run away?"

Bonnie looked at the handsome little boy. "He'd find us."

"No, he wouldn't. We'll find somewhere to hide." He hugged his mother. Bonnie held him in her arms.

Rosemary was her father's princess. He hated Alisdair, teasing the boy mercilessly, accusing him of being wet and unmanly. Whenever the MacPherson family paid one of their infrequent visits to Augustine, Angus was a perfect husband and a loving father. In his own home, however, he ruled the house with a rod of iron, and even Rosemary toed the line.

Bonnie looked at herself in the mirror. She sighed. She was still beautiful, but she was horribly gaunt. I'm thirty, she thought, I'm thirty and my life is melting away.

That night, she attended a dinner party given by Lady Angela de Skalle, a long-time drinking companion of Angus's. Bonnie was sitting next to a very famous actor, who was attempting to charm her with his bright blue eyes and his blond boyish hair. His wife, also well-known in her field, sat opposite Bonnie. Bonnie, far away in her own private hell, smiled and laughed with the man.

"I say," Angela was in top form, "d' you see all those women on the television last night? All complaining about their husbands beating them?" She laughed. "I must say, the way things are going," she shot a look at Clive, her portly husband, "they'll soon have to open a house for battered men," she said. Clive winced.

A thin, nervous woman cleared her throat. "Well, I think it's disgusting talking about things like that in public. I don't think it should be allowed. That woman running that awful dirty place is just doing it for the publicity. I hope she does go to gaol. The law is the law, after all. She shouldn't be overcrowding the house, taking in any woman with a bad luck story."

The man on Bonnie's left butted in. "Come on, you'd have to be pretty desperate to go to a place like that. They all sleep on the floor, you know. I'm sending a cheque."

The thin woman snorted. "They'll probably spend it on drink. That's what they do, you know, that sort of person."

Bonnie stopped paying attention. She caught the woman across the table staring at her. Bonnie held her gaze. I know that look, Bonnie thought. He beats her. Before the evening was over, Bonnie made a point of talking to the woman. "Do you think that refuge is necessary?" Bonnie asked.

"I *know* it is," the woman said. "I've been there." Her husband pulled her away before Bonnie had a chance to ask more questions.

A tiny flame of hope lit in Bonnie's heart. I'll go there, she thought. All night long she lay in her bed and made plans.

The refuge was dirty, even though the women worked hard to keep it clean. They did have to sleep on the floor, but for the first time in years Bonnie did not need to drink. Rosemary hated the place. "Ugh," she said. "Everything stinks, mummy. I don't want to stay here."

Bonnie stroked the child's thick black hair. "Only for a while, darling," she said.

Alisdair made a friend within the first few minutes. The house was very small, but there were nine families packed into its four rooms. Outside, there was a lavatory in the tiny backyard. The women washed themselves as well as they could in the kitchen sink or, as it was now summer, they bathed in an old zinc tub.

The refuge on Styx Street in North London was run by a fat woman who wore a large cross around her neck. She introduced herself to Bonnie as Valerie. She loved her mothers and her children. She fiercely protected them both from uncaring social workers and from the indifference of the law. She also refused to turn anyone away. She was constantly harassed with law suits against her determined insistence that no woman should be forced to return to a violent partner.

Not all of the women in the refuge were battered women terrified of their violent, drunken husbands; many were violent themselves. Many beat their children. Val loved them all, but she had a soft spot for the worst of them.

She welcomed Bonnie on her arrival with a warm hug and a steaming mug of tea. Other mothers took the two children to the park to play. Valerie listened to Bonnie's story.

Bonnie's words tumbled and somersaulted out of her mouth. "I haven't been able to tell anyone about this," she said. "I'm so ashamed."

Valerie nodded. "I know. Thousands of women are battered every year, and most of them never tell anyone."

A bright cheerful woman with fuzzy blonde hair chipped in. "I stayed with my old man for six years before I got out. I didn't tell anyone. Not even me mum. But now I'm getting a flat from the council next week, and I'm taking me kids and starting again."

"How long have you been here?" Bonnie asked.

"Almost a year."

Bonnie was aghast. "A year?" she said.

"Well, I needed to be here that long."

Valerie nodded. "Those women who come in and then go straight off to relatives or get themselves somewhere to live usually go back," she said. "Leaving a violent man is not just a question of walking out of his life." She took Bonnie's hand. "If things were that simple, you'd have left Angus a long time ago."

Bonnie's voice faltered. "I thought I could change him," she said.

Sally, a big broad-shouldered East Ender, came in and looked at Bonnie. "You can't change anyone, luv. Especially not your old man."

Valerie smiled at Sally. "Sal's the most amazing woman," Valerie said. "You and Viv are the only two we have at the moment who walked out and neither of you has ever looked back."

Sally laughed. "I'd be in a box by now if I went back. Besides, it wasn't what he done to me I minded. It was what he done to the kids. He used to make my Bob eat neat mustard, and then he'd laugh at him. Call him a faggot," she frowned. "At one time, I was at the hospital getting my head stitched. Bob was in a special school unit for disturbed children, and my Mary was seeing a psychiatrist for bedwetting and migraines. Everybody knew it was 'im, but nobody would say anything."

Valerie put her arm around Bonnie. "This is your first day today. Tomorow, I'll organize your social security. We'll change your name and your children can go to the local school under their new name. That way, he won't be able to trace them."

Bonnie nodded. "He's very clever, Val. He'll hunt us down."

"You're quite right. They all do. He will eventually find you, but hopefully by then, you'll have enough strength to stay away."

"I know I will this time," Bonnie was resolute. "I promise I will." She looked at Sal.

Sally nodded. "I'll help you," she said.

The first week passed quickly. In the cheerful warm atmosphere of the refuge, Bonnie found a kind of peace. Val came in every day, and the mothers all sat in the tiny sitting-room, passing babies from knee to knee while they talked.

"I dunno," Gina said one morning. "Harry called up last night, and he begged me. Said he'll kill himself if I didn't go back."

Val looked at her. "Well, he wouldn't have phoned if you hadn't given him the number."

Bonnie was sitting on the floor with Gina's fat six-month-old baby in her arms. "How can you possibly go back after he broke little Simon's arm?" Bonnie said.

Gina shifted in her chair. "I love him," she said. "I don't know why he does awful things to me, but I just can't get him out of my head."

"That's because you're addicted to him," Sal broke into the conversation. "Seems, from what I've seen here, there are two types of woman. Those that come in and stay a few days to teach their fellow a lesson, and then there's those that really want to get away like me. I stayed with Joe for years. 'E's exactly like my dad. My dad beat the shit out of us all." Sal looked at Valerie. "Val and I wrote out a family tree for me and Joe. And there's violence I can trace back to five generations."

Bonnie nodded. "Yes," she said. "Angus's family history is full of awful violence. My mom was violent, but she changed." Bonnie sat there lost in thought. Then she said, "Val, remember yesterday when you asked me what keeps me with Angus and I told you I felt sometimes if I left him I'd be leaving a little child in the middle of a crowded highway? Well, perhaps I can learn not to feel that Angus is a hurt child."

Val agreed. "My friend Sammy says that maybe that little boy you need to nourish is actually dead. All you end up doing is carrying the corpse."

Bonnie sighed with relief. "Yes. Maybe that's it."

A pale, anorexic woman looked mournfully at Bonnie. "What happens when you never have any bruises to show? Who would believe me? My husband is a High Court Judge. What chance have I got? He never lays a finger on me. He just sees that I have no money, and when he's angry, he locks me in the bedroom for days at a time. I have no food; I can't even go to the lavatory." Her thin miserable shoulders were hunched.

Sal hugged her. "You're right, luv. Bruises and bones mend, but the words . . . they break your heart."

"He says I'm mad." She screwed up her face and looked at Sal. "Am I mad?"

"No," Sal laughed. "You're perfectly sane."

"You chose to leave him," Valerie said. "That shows you're not mad."

"Yes." The little woman's face relaxed. "But I'm sixty now. I thought I'd stay for the children's sake. They were all at public schools. Nicholas was at Eton, and the twins went to St. Mary's, Ascot." She shrugged. "I needn't have bothered. They don't want to know either of us."

Bonnie felt her heart shrink. She could be that woman in thirty years' time.

Val turned her attention across the room and looked at Pamela, a pretty pert little girl. "You're quite a different story, aren't you?"

Pam giggled. "My Mick gets ever so angry," she said. "'E's going to take me to the Palais tonight."

Val sighed. "Oh, Pam. You know you'll end up having a fight, and then go home to make it up in bed."

"I know." Pam wrinkled her nose. "Exciting, isn't it?"

Val shook her head. "No, it isn't. And your three kids are all badly disturbed, between all the games you played with Mick. Don't," she said, waving her finger at Pam, "don't you dare stand him up tonight like you did last time, only to have him chasing round here on a rampage. I want my windows intact tomorrow." Pam giggled. Val turned to Bonnie, "You see, Bonnie. Women—and men too—get into violent relationships for very different reasons. The way I see it, you are a genuine battered wife. You're the victim of someone else's violence. You stay with Angus with the hope of changing him. The trick for you is to recognize that he would destroy you and your kids before he ever got round to changing himself. I can see you're well on the way to truly believing that. Pam, on the other hand, is violence-prone. She's the victim of her own violence, aren't you, Pamela my petal?" Pam smiled innocently. "We've had Pam in and out of here more times than you've had hot dinners. But she had a very rough time as a child, and she learned to re-create all that danger in her relationships."

"I don't mean to, you know," Pam interjected.

"I know you don't, my love," Valerie continued, "and no one's trying to blame you. It's just that you have to recognize that you keep getting yourself mixed up with violent men because you're addicted to their violence. I'm here to help you go back to figuring out where that addiction came from in the first place. Once you can unravel that, that's when you can start to think about making relationships because you love a person, not his violence."

After a furious search and interrogation among Bonnie's friends, Angus had drawn a blank. He telephoned Augustine on the off-chance that Bonnie had left the country by illicit means. Augustine was surprised. "No, dear. She's not here. Are you worried?"

"Oh, no." Angus made light of his query. "I knew she'd gone visiting, I just lost track of her movements. She'll call in the next few days, I'm sure."

"All right," Augustine said. "Do come over soon. I miss you all."

Morag listened to Augustine's end of the conversation as she sat by the old woman's side. For a long time, Morag had known that something was badly wrong. Augustine was by now nearly blind and very deaf. She had not seen Bonnie swaying during her last visit, nor did she hear her slurring her words. I must go and see her, Morag promised herself. I must find out what is making her so desperate.

Angus telephoned Mitzi next. "No." Mitzi was alert. "Why? What's happened?"

"Nothing's happened. I've just lost track of Bonnie. Happens all the time. She flits hither and thither. I thought maybe she might have dropped in on you."

"No, actually I haven't heard from Bonnie for years."

"Oh, all right." Angus was furious. Where is the fucking bitch? he wondered. I have her passport, and she doesn't have any money.

As a last effort he called Laura. He tried to speak to Laura as seldom as possible. There was something in her voice that always made him uncomfortable—something smug and conspiratorial and evil.

Laura was delighted to hear Angus's voice as she picked up the telephone. True to his word, Angus had provided her with the palatial home of her choice after she had helped him track down Bonnie on her first attempt to leave him five years before. Laura was now a lady of circumstance, one of Merrill's wealthiest residents.

When Angus asked if she knew of Bonnie's whereabouts, a fear seized Laura's heart. That little bitch will ruin everything for me, she thought. "No, Angus," she said, "I haven't seen her. She hasn't run off again, has she?" She tried to mask the panic in her voice.

"No, Laura," Angus said with some irritation. "I'm sure it's not that. Never mind. She'll probably come home in a few days. If she does get in touch with you, though, will you contact me?"

"Oh, I will right away." Laura put down the telephone. She was deeply agitated. If Bonnie left Angus, then what was there to ensure that Angus would not take back the house along with everything Laura owned? "Damn that girl," Laura swore to herself.

Angus was getting desperate. He telephoned his solicitor for advice. "I suggest you report her absence to the police as a missing person. That stupid woman, the one who's always on television making all that fuss about her battered wives, has encouraged the police to refuse to tell husbands where their wives are if the wife claims she's in danger. But you will know that she's in the country, and then we can go to court and get custody of the children. We can't force her back if she refuses to come, but usually a woman goes back if you take her children."

"Thanks, Rupert." Angus was grateful. "I love my children."

Rupert made a face. Lying bastard, he thought. "One thing, Angus. She hasn't any evidence, has she? I mean she hasn't got a witness to any actions on your part which a judge might deem somewhat less than uxorious?"

Angus thought of the servants. They wouldn't dare. "No," he said. "Nothing at all. I'm a model husband."

"Okay then." Rupert's voice was brisk. "As soon as we find out if she's still in England, I'll give Dan Fletcher a call, and he can get his super-sleuths on the trail."

"Thanks, Rupert." Angus put down the telephone. Where

is that scheming bitch? he thought. Suddenly he missed her dreadfully.

Bonnie spent her days talking to other women in the refuge. She suffered when new families came in covered in bruises. She helped wash away the blood and comfort the tears with cups of tea. She held small bruised children, and she shed tears over their broken emaciated bodies. She also suffered along with other mothers whenever a woman decided to go home to her man. So far, she had resisted the urge to return. "I'm horrified with myself," she said to Val as they sat in an upstairs bedroom. "I lie on my mattress and I miss Angus. I miss his voice. I miss his warmth from the good times, and I write these plays in my head about how I can change him. Worst of all," she said, "I feel guilty. Deeply, deeply guilty."

Val put her hand on Bonnie's shoulder. "I know," she said. "You took all the weight of your father's desertion on your eight-year-old shoulders. The guilt you're feeling doesn't just rest with Angus. It goes back many years earlier. You have never resolved your father's desertion or his death. But don't make Angus an atonement, luv."

Bonnie looked at Val with surprise. "Really, Val. You're right, you know. How do you know these things?"

Val smiled. "I've listened to hundreds of women. My father was violent. I always defended my mother. In fact, I tried to kill my father when I was a child." She laughed. "I wasn't successful. Anyway, for years I blamed my father until I started this little refuge with my colleague. Actually, I didn't intend to run a refuge. I just opened a place for lonely women to drop by with their children. You see, when the Women's Movement started, I believed that women should certainly demand equal rights, but I never could belong to a movement that was dedicated to hating men. So I had a fight with them, and they threw me out. Just as well, really. If I'd stayed and listened to all that jabbering, there would never have been a refuge."

"How did it become a refuge?" Bonnie asked.

"Well, one day a woman came in bruised, and I let her stay. Then women poured in from all over the country. I think I realized I was in the refuge-business when I went to the door one day and a young girl stood there with a baby in her arms and two children clinging to her skirt. We had absolutely no room, but I took her in. We squeezed some room in the corridor, and she slept well that night. Refuge-work is now my total commitment." She smiled at Bonnie. "By the way, Rosemary is sure to improve. Sarah, the senior play-group leader, is very gifted with children, and is working a lot with Rosemary."

"Oh good," Bonnie heaved a sigh of relief. "I'll go off and do the shopping for lunch. It's my turn on the rota."

"Thank you," said Valerie. "You're a lovely woman, Bonnie, and I'm glad you're here."

Bonnie blushed. "Thanks, Val," she said. "I feel quite at home now." They hugged each other.

There was a knock at the door. Val went downstairs to see who it was. A policeman from the local station stood in the entrance. "Come in, Ian." Val led the way to the kitchen. "Have a cup of tea."

The women crowded around him. He was very popular with the mothers and the children. He had restored their faith in the police force. So many of the children had seen the police only as frightened or irritable when they were called in to deal with the fighting parents. "Thanks, luv. I'm looking for a Mrs. Bonnie MacPherson. I don't think you'll have anyone here by that name."

A fat woman with ferocious teeth grinned unpleasantly. She had just been assigned to the refuge as a volunteer worker. "That must be Bonnie Turner, so-called," she said. "I knew there was something different about her. Bonnie

MacPherson!" she trilled up the stairs. "Someone here to see you!"

Bonnie was paralyzed by fright. "Shut up, Patsy." Val was furious. "Come down, Bonnie. Don't worry. It's just Ian, our friendly local copper. He won't hurt you." She put her arm around Bonnie who was shaking when she arrived at the bottom of the stairs. "Come on, luv," she said, and she drew Bonnie into the kitchen.

Ian smiled at Bonnie. "Don't worry," he said. "I don't have to tell anybody where you are. If you like, I can even see to it that a station in Cornwall gives your husband the message that you're no longer a missing person." Bonnie nodded. Ian shook his head. "I dunno," he said. "I used to think it was just bums who beat their wives. But yesterday I was called to the house of a famous comedian. I'm sure you've heard of him, but it's confidential, you know. God," he took a mouthful of tea, "I've never seen anything like it. He'd smashed up the house, and as for his lady . . . I've seen a lot of things in my life, but she was a real mess."

The women listened, nodding their heads as they remembered what they had left behind them. The talk soon got round, as it usually did, to the children. "Can you tell my Patrick he's got to stop nicking?" one woman asked Ian.

"I can, but it'll take a long time for us to retrain him. After all, he used to go nicking with his dad, didn't he? And his dad used to reward him for it. Now all of a sudden we're telling your Patrick it's wrong. It's going to take some undoing, luv."

Bonnie looked at Val. "I'm worried about Rosemary. She always was rude and difficult, but now she's impossible."

Val smiled. "Well, give her time. Lots of the kids that come in despise their mothers. They really only ever saw them as punch bags." The other mothers nodded. "But look at you now," Val smiled at Bonnie. "You've stopped drinking. You've put on weight, and you don't take more than one valium a day. You'll see. Rosemary will come to see you as you really are." Bonnie was happy. She promised herself she'd read to her children every night. She regretted the lost years.

That night she held Rosemary in her arms. "I promise darling, that things will be better between us," Bonnie said.

Rosemary looked at her mother. Her eyes were less hard. "I know, mummy. I used to hate it here, but now I have friends, and Val talked to me. She told me that lots of other mummys drink and take pills when they live with men like daddy. Somehow, it helps knowing there are other children like me."

Bonnie hugged her. "Never again," she promised. "Whatever happens to us, I won't drink or take tranquillizers. I promise."

Rosemary kissed her mother. Alisdair was already asleep. Rosemary lay in Bonnie's warm embrace. For once in her little life she felt truly happy.

Laura's unrest grew with each passing day. She had promised herself that she wouldn't ring Angus to find out if he had found Bonnie. After a week had gone by, however, she could contain herself no longer. "Angus," she said shyly into the telephone, "I'm just calling to check that everything's okay with Bonnie again."

Angus sighed. He decided there was no point in keeping the truth from Laura. "Actually, Laura, Bonnie has run away with the children. The police phoned yesterday. They say they've seen her. She's alive and well, but they won't tell me where she is."

"Oh." There was a very long pause. Laura was thinking furiously. "What are you going to do?"

"Well," Angus said, "I've contacted a private detective. I use him a lot. And he's combing the countryside. I've telephoned everyone I can telephone, and I'm desperate. I know things haven't been too good between us. She's been drinking over the last few years, and she's pretty well hooked on valium. God knows it's been difficult, but I love her and she is my wife." Angus was full of self-pity. He hated being in the house alone. "I want her back."

"Don't worry," Laura advised him. "When you hear from her, remind her that her dad deserted her. Ask her if she wants to make her kids suffer the same fate. She'll come back. Bonnie's totally incapable of coping on her own. She needs you." And I need your money, Laura thought as she looked around her beautiful home. "As soon as you find her, I'll fly over with Father John. He'll talk some sense into her."

While Bonnie was in the refuge, Lord MacPherson had a heart attack and died within a few hours. Angus's features were all over the newspapers. The heir to the MacPherson title was fabulously wealthy and extremely photogenic. His white face and haunted eyes stared out at Bonnie from the newspapers and the television screen. "Oh, Sal," she said, "staying away is harder than going back."

Sally gave her a hug. "I'll sit on you if you try to go back. Come on. Remember, 'Wedlock is a padlock when you're married to a no-good man.' "

Bonnie laughed. "Okay, okay. I'll warn you if I ever really feel the urge." She did not admit that she often longed to leave. Conditions were hard. The other women would quarrel, and the children fought with each other. There was no privacy in the refuge and no money.

Several months went by before one of Angus's private detectives noticed a little girl and a little boy holding hands on their way to school. The two children looked exactly like the ones they had been searching for all those months. He reported his find to head office. Within half an hour, Angus was down at the school. He asked politely to see the headmaster, a frightened mouse of a man. "Oh dear," the headmaster said. "Oh dear. We keep having trouble with these families."

Often the fathers of the refuge children would arrive drunk and abusive.

Angus, however, was charming. "I just want to ask the children if they would like to come home with me."

"All right," the headmaster said, entirely won over by the grace of Angus's manner. "I'll have them sent up."

Rosemary was wary of her father, and a bit frightened. "Daddy," she said, "I do want to go back to my nice bedroom, but mummy is so much better now. I like her." She hesitated. "I love her now, and I don't want her to change again."

Alisdair stood uncertainly by the door. "I think I'll stay with mummy, if you don't mind," he said quietly.

Angus held out his hand. "Please, Alisdair," he pleaded. "Come home for a little while. I promise I'll take you back to Mummy if you still feel like that by tomorrow. Anyway, I'm going to ask her to come home. I promise you I'll be a better daddy."

"You promise you'll never hit her again?" Alisdair was serious.

"I promise."

"And you promise never to make mummy unhappy again?" Rosemary asked. "She looks so much better now."

"She'll look even better when we all have a holiday together."

"A holiday?" Rosemary became more comfortable. "Where shall we go?"

"Let's ask mummy to choose," Angus said. He took the children out of the school. He saw Alisdair pause just before he got into the car. "And, on the way home, we can stop at Hamley's toy shop." Angus cheerfully announced.

"Oh boy!" Alisdair hopped into the car. "Can I buy a pogo stick?"

* * *

Bonnie was in the kitchen when the children swarmed through the door after school. "Where's Rosemary and Alisdair?" she asked after they'd come in.

"Dunno," one of the children shrugged.

Bonnie ran to the telephone. The headmaster's voice was cold. "Lord MacPherson collected his children," he said.

Bonnie burst into tears. "Why didn't he stop him?" she asked Sally.

"Few people are sorry for us," Sally said. "Most people like to think we deserved what happened to us. I suppose, if you don't know what a violent relationship is all about, you just assume that we are complaining about the odd slap or a kick . . . The headmaster's no different. He doesn't want to know that my Larry's been beaten within an inch of his life. He just resents the fact that Larry beats up his other pupils, and thinks we're all lazy sluts because our kids wear shabby clothes and occasionally have nits. God, he probably believes that we have time to pack our suitcases carefully before we leave." Bonnie was shaking and crying. Sal hugged her. "What are you going to do?"

"I don't know." Bonnie sat down at the scarred pine table. "I've been happier here than I have ever been while I've been married. Rosemary and I got to know each other. Alisdair played with the other boys and learned to laugh. I'll have to talk to Valerie. She should be back from court soon."

Angus was also in court that afternoon. Rupert had instructed a top barrister. "My client is asking for full custody of his children. As you can see from the doctor's report, his wife has a drink problem so severe that she is virtually an alcoholic, and she is hopelessly addicted to valium. I have no doubt that the court will agree that she is entirely an unfit mother." Dr. Simpson had done his job well.

The judge stared at Angus. Good heavens, he thought. Old Alexander's boy. What a hell-raiser his father used to be. "All right," the judge said. "I do not like ex parte applications, but your wife is free to come before the court at a later date if she feels I've been unfair. The court finds in favour of the petitioner." The court stood while the old man tottered out. "Can't believe any son of Alexander's would marry a drunkard," he said to his clerk as he removed his robes.

"Dunno what's happening these days," his clerk said. "All these women running away from their 'usbands. It's not right."

The old judge shook his head. "In my day, you made your bed . . ." The two men continued to lament the loss of a safe and settled generation.

Patsy, the volunteer with the fearsome teeth, was pleased that Bonnie was crying. Serves her right, she thought. Rich bitch in her gilded cage deserves whatever comes to her. Bonnie had totally disrupted a speech she had organized a few days earlier. All the mothers had been listening attentively while Patsy explained that their problems were not due to their husbands' violence, but really to the evils of a capitalist society. "Joe beat you," she said, pointing at Sally, "because he had a boring pointless job. He felt alienated in his work. He owed money to the council, and he drank to drown his misery."

She elongated the word "misery" as she spoke. Bonnie disliked the volunteer and her self-righteous politics. By their *teeth* ye shall know them, Bonnie thought as she watched Patsy expound.

Sal looked impressed. "Well," she said cautiously, "you could be right."

Bonnie lost her patience with all this meaningless rhetoric. She broke abruptly into the conversation. "But Angus doesn't owe money," she said. "He's a multi-millionaire. He doesn't beat me because he doesn't like his job, and he drinks because he likes the excuse it gives him to beat me. No," she looked at the volunteer, "your explanation is much too simple. Angus is violent because he modelled himself on his father. Still, that's no excuse. He's responsible for his anger, just as Joe is responsible for beating Sally. You can't say that a boring job or owing money is a reason for being violent to your wife. If that were true, then anyone who was homeless or jobless would batter his wife and children."

The roomful of women agreed. The volunteer flushed. She shot a furious look at Bonnie. "Rich women like you have no business in a place like this. You're taking a place that should belong to a woman with nowhere else to go."

Bonnie stared at her. Before coming to the refuge, a remark like that would have devastated her. In the few months she had been living there, however, she had changed. "Well, you don't realize this," she said pleasantly, "but *any* woman married to a violent man needs a refuge. Violent men don't let you have any control over your life. I have no more money than Sal or anybody else in this refuge. We're all in the same boat. Angus is no different from Joe. What *is* different in a refuge like this is that you get back your self-respect. Now, for the first time in my life, I know who *I* am." She laughed. "And the wonderful thing is that I like me. Thanks to Val and Sally and Pam and everyone else, I've learned an awful lot about myself and my children."

Now Patsy was delighted that Bonnie was getting her comeuppance. The volunteer watched as Bonnie cried, her long fair hair falling over her hunched shoulders.

Val, back from court, walked into the room. Her face was strained, for the trial had been difficult. She had been summoned in yet another attempt to gaol her, this time for hiding a mother and three children in Eire against a judge's orders, in spite of the fact that the man had a conviction for murder.

"Guilty," Val said to the room at large. "I'll have to find about five thousand pounds for barristers and other expenses, and another thousand pounds for the fine." She sighed. "Fortunately, I've good friends who are collecting for me. Otherwise it's nine months in gaol." She frowned. "I feel the verdict is an awful injustice. The people who should have been in the dock were the probation officers and the social worker who did nothing to help the family. Poor man," she said softly. "He had such an awful childhood. No wonder he's violent."

Valerie suddenly saw Bonnie standing in the background. She went over and put a sympathetic hand on her shoulder. "Well, Bonnie," Val said, "Angus has probably already gone for custody so that he can legally hold the children, and you won't be able to take them away again."

Bonnie nodded. "Yeah. I expect he has. I'll have to leave England with them. There's no way I can stay in this country. He'll always find me. Val, could I phone my friend Mitzi? I know it's expensive, but maybe she'll have some ideas. America is huge."

Val smiled. "There are many refuges now all over America. Maybe you could get into one."

Bonnie wiped her eyes. "I'll have to go back and lie low for a while. Then maybe Mitzi can find a refuge that'll take me until I get on my feet."

Val patted Bonnie's arm. "You really have done well, you know, Bonnie. I never thought you'd stick this refuge. What made you give up on Angus?"

Bonnie thought for a moment. "Well I think it was when you said I didn't have to blame myself for my father's desertion. That sort of opened a door for me. I don't have to punish myself anymore. Also, seeing so many other women all going through the same thing again and again. Lying about the bruises, feeling guilty about the children, excusing their husbands, blaming themselves. It's like having a mirror stuck up in front of you."

"Phone for you, Bonnie." Sally was at the kitchen door. "I think it's Rosemary."

"Okay." Bonnie got to her feet. She looked at Val. "I will get away. I'm determined."

"Good." Val nodded approvingly.

"She'll never leave." The volunteer was preparing to go home. She spoke after Bonnie had left the room. "Her bourgeois life's too cushy."

Val glared at the girl. "Wipe your arse with all your left-wing rubbish, and don't come back tomorrow. You can't play politics with other people's lives."

Patsy glared back. "Other refuges are run by organizers who understand the need for working class solidarity."

"I know," Val said. "They spend most of their money on expensive conferences dedicated to hating men. Oh, I know how much you try to cover up your hatred with all your political jargon, but underneath it all you're in this business for the hate, not for the love. No wonder the refuge movement is dying on its feet."

The volunteer wound a long, dingy scarf around her neck. "I'll report you to my superiors," she said.

"Do." Val was tired. "There's many more women like me, who don't hate all men, than there are of you."

The door slammed.

Bonnie came back into the kitchen. "I told Rosemary I'd be back tomorrow. Tonight I'm having for myself." She grimaced. "Angus is planning yet another holiday. This time he wants us to take the children."

Val smiled. "It's the honeymoon phase."

"I know. Angus is at his best when he's travelling to new places. But don't worry, Val. I know his honeymoon phases. In a way," she looked thoughtful, "only a battered woman would understand this . . . I almost prefer it when the honeymoon time is over, and Angus is back to screaming and raging. While he's being nice to me and loving, I get so confused. It's somehow worse to wait for the first blow to fall after a period of calm . . . it's all very odd."

"No, it isn't," Val said. "The only thing you can trust about Angus is his violence."

Bonnie nodded. "Rosemary says he's flying my mom in."

"Huh." Val was amused. "Well, use the time with her to really look at what her violent behaviour did to you." Bonnie looked surprised. "I know we haven't talked much about your mum," Valerie continued, "but I want you to have a really good look at her. Just think, everyone else you knew backed off from Angus, but your mother accepted stuff from him that no one else would take."

"That's true, I suppose, but my mom has become very involved in the Church, and I've always wanted to believe that she's changed. Hasn't she? I guess I always hoped that if she changed, Angus could too."

Val laughed. "Bonnie, lots of violent people disguise their violence in religion. I've known some truly dangerous men suddenly swear they've found God or Jesus, or they join a cult, but if you watch closely, they're just as brutal. They become fanatics and preach hell-fire and damnation. I don't think your mother has changed. Just changed tack. That's all." Val looked down at her watch. "I must run now and catch the bus. You ring your friend and I'll see you tomorrow before you go."

They kissed each other good-night. "Thanks, Val." Bonnie's eyes filled with tears again.

Val smiled. "I don't need thanks. All I need to know is that you're free from Angus."

Bonnie smiled. "Know it," she said.

Mitzi was amazed to hear Bonnie's voice. She sat up in her plump quilted bed. "Bonnie!" she shrieked. "I haven't heard from you for ages. Where are you? Angus phoned weeks ago. He said you'd gone off for a trip with the kids."

"Listen, Mitzi. I need your help." Bonnie quickly explained her problem.

Mitzi was appalled. "It was that bad?"

"Yeah." Bonnie was matter of fact.

"How can you go back to him? He might kill you."

"Well, I can't leave the kids with him. Going back's a risk I have to take until I get out of the country with the kids. I need you to see if you can find a refuge."

"A shelter, you mean. That's what they're called here." Mitzi was thinking. "There's a shelter here in Merrill. It opened up a couple of years ago."

"That would be the first place Angus would look. Are there any other shelters around?"

"Actually, there's one in Axelton, the next town over. I'll go and see the place this week. When do you think you can get away?"

"I don't know. First I've got to get my passport. It will take a lot of planning."

"Well, I told Mike, you remember Mike Edwards? Anyway, I told him all about Angus beating you. Please don't think I betrayed you." Mitzi was hesitant.

"No, I don't mind. Mike has always been good to me." Bonnie smiled at the memory of their last evening together at the barbecue. "I'm not ashamed anymore. I know I'm not responsible for Angus's rage. That's his problem."

"Okay." Mitzi was planning. "I'll talk to Mike. He's doing very well in his law firm. Maybe he can help out."

"Ask him if he can lend me enough money to pay my flight over with the kids. I hate asking, but I don't know anyone else to ask. Grandma would be shattered if she knew I was this unhappy. It would be great if Mike could help." Mitzi was pleased with the note of confidence in Bonnie's voice. "I'll ring again when I can," Bonnie said. "Good-bye, Mitzi, and thanks."

"Take care of yourself," Mitzi said. "Love to the kids. And be careful."

Bonnie hung up. She spent the rest of the evening talking furiously with Sally and the other mothers.

Dawn was breaking when she finally lay down on her mattress. She watched as the first pale slivers of sunlight gently touched the sleeping children. Much as she dreaded going back, she realized that she could never abandon Rosemary and Alisdair. Instead, she silently promised them that she would rescue them from a life that offered only violence and degradation. She fell asleep dreaming of her new life in America.

Chapter 30

Getting away was going to be more difficult than Bonnie had anticipated. Angus was in the house when she returned. He hugged her fiercely and promised her yet again that things would be different. She looked into his bleak eyes and she did not believe him.

Rosemary and Alisdair were delighted to see her. "I miss the refuge," Alisdair whispered as he kissed her good-night.

Rosemary also kissed her mother. "You won't drink and take pills again, will you?" she asked anxiously.

"No, I promise I won't," Bonnie said gently.

Angus sat watching his wife with his children. He was surprised at how much they had changed. Bonnie exuded a calm confidence. He could feel his rage gathering. "I want you to know that I'm going to give you much more freedom," he said.

Bonnie smiled. "That's nice. I miss all my friends."

"Well, if you've given up drinking, we can go out together again."

"Yes, I'd like that," she said.

They were like two strange suspicious dogs sniffing each other. "You'd better be careful," Rupert had warned him. "Those refuges teach women a trick or two. You only have to mark her and she'll be in court like a flash. With the right judge, she could take you for a packet, and your London house." The thought of losing his home put Angus into a panic. Only here at Heath House did he ever feel totally secure.

He looked thoughtfully at Bonnie during dinner. He would have to bide his time.

Laura flew in with Father John. "Darling," she said, putting her expensively perfumed cheek next to Bonnie's. "What ever have you been doing?"

Bonnie looked at her mother. "Trying to save my life," she snapped and walked out of the room.

Angus was not there at the time, but Father John had witnessed the scene. "You'll have to watch yourself, Laura," the priest said. "That girl has changed."

"Yes." Laura looked at him. "We'll both have to watch out. Otherwise, you won't get a roof on your new house."

Father John flushed. "And you, my dear," he said with a note of menace in his voice, "might suddenly find yourself homeless."

"I know," Laura frowned. "You'd better have a talk with her."

"Oh, I will." Father John was firm. There was too much at stake to let the little fool run off again. He left the room to find Angus.

Angus did indeed give Bonnie more freedom. He put up with Laura for a week before she decided to return to America. Laura missed her private rituals. She did have Father John's continual presence to excite her, but that did not compensate for having to abstain from fantasizing and flogging herself in the privacy of her own home. In London, in one of Heath House's luxurious guest rooms, Laura had to restrain herself. After a week she could bear it no more and she grew impatient to return. She told Bonnie of her intention to leave the following Sunday.

During the remaining days of her mother's visit, Bonnie was polite but distant. Father John berated Bonnie for leaving Angus. "You have failed in your duty to your husband," he said. "You have made a solemn vow before God that nothing, *nothing*," he said, striking the table in the library where he had chosen to admonish Bonnie, "must come between a man and his wife. You are in mortal sin," he said. "Should you die, you are doomed to a life of eternal damnation."

Bonnie looked calmly at Father John. "But, if I'd stayed with Angus, he'd have killed me."

"Bonnie," Father John frowned, "what is the death of the body? If you died by your husband's hand, you would go straight to God. But, by running away, you put your eternal soul in jeopardy." He leaned forward and fixed her with his piercing gaze. "What do a few bruises mean compared to all eternity in the Lake of Fire?" Father John had used the argument many times on women in his congregation who had asked for his advice.

I'll talk to Father MacBride, Bonnie thought. She smiled at Father John. "Well, Angus has promised to reform," she said sweetly.

Father John interrupted. "Bonnie, it was your drinking and your pills that made Angus so desperate. He was just trying to knock some sense into you."

Bonnie didn't bother to argue. She was too busy thinking about Teresa. She'll help me, she thought.

* * *

"I'd like to take mom down to meet Winnie," Bonnie announced at the breakfast table. "I haven't seen Winnie for years."

Angus looked surprised. "All right," he said pleasantly. "You go off, and I'll keep the children amused." He knew she would never try to leave without them.

The children were delighted. "Take us to the zoo!" Alisdair demanded.

Bonnie looked at her mother. "We can leave on Friday and get back Sunday morning in time for you to pack for the plane. You'll love the house."

Laura smiled. "I'd like that, Bonnie," she said. Maybe I can get her to see sense, Laura thought. She did not approve of the new confident Bonnie at all.

Margaret was pleased to hear Bonnie's voice; she had picked up rumours of Bonnie's drinking problem. She was also delighted to offer Bonnie a weekend in the country. "Winnie often talks about you," she reminded Bonnie.

"I'll give her a ring. Could you please ask Teresa to be there?" Bonnie's voice was urgent.

"Well, I don't know if she can make it at such short notice, you know she's pregnant with her second child."

"Please, Margaret. Tell Teresa I need her. She has to help me. Please."

"All right, dear," said Margaret, impressed by Bonnie's vehemence. "I'll see that she's there."

Bonnie put the telephone down. She felt someone standing behind her. She turned.

"Who were you speaking to?" Angus stared at her.

"Only Margaret. I very much want to see Teresa." She hoped he hadn't heard too much. She tried hard to keep her voice steady. "After all, we missed her wedding, and she's expecting another baby." Bonnie babbled on until the mist of suspicion left Angus's face.

"Well," he said, "you can't get into much trouble, I suppose. Stay off the booze."

"I will," Bonnie was grateful that Angus had been successfully distracted. "I will."

By the time Laura and Bonnie arrived at the farm house, they were both tired. Bonnie had kept the conversation light all the way down. The chauffeur dropped them at the front entrance to the manor. Winnie waited eagerly to greet Bonnie. "Darling," she said, giving Bonnie a big hug. "I've been so worried about you."

Bonnie gazed at Winnie's cheerful loving face. "I know," she said. "I should have listened."

Laura came up behind Bonnie. She was impressed by the antiquity of the house and by the beauty of its grounds. She shook Winnie's hand. "I'd like a cup of tea," she said.

"Help yourself," Winnie said politely. "The water's boiling."

Huh, Laura thought. How rude. The English have no sense of service. She walked into the kitchen and poured a cup of tea from the kettle on the Aga.

"Come on." Winnie took Bonnie's suitcase. "Let's go upstairs." To Laura she said, "I'll be down in a minute and I'll show you your room."

"Okay." Laura sat at the kitchen table.

Once they were in Bonnie's room, Winnie put the suitcase down and looked at Bonnie. "I can't tell you how pleased we all are to see you again. Teresa will be here soon, and John is coming a bit later."

Bonnie bit her lip. "Oh Winnie, John can't come."

Winnie frowned. "Why ever not? He's always cared about you. He's bringing his fiancée. You'll love her. She's a sweet thing, and she'll make him an excellent wife."

Bonnie stared bleakly out of the window. "Winnie, every

time Angus got angry, he'd use John as an excuse to beat me."

Winnie fell very silent. "Angus hits you?"

Bonnie's voice dropped to a whisper. "He doesn't just hit me. He beats me. He kicks me. He tries to strangle me. Winnie, you have no idea how difficult it is for me to admit to being a battered wife." She drew a deep breath. "I am a battered wife," she said firmly. "I don't want to be, and I don't deserve it. That much I learned from the refuge. I also learned that it wasn't just poor women whose husbands can't express their feelings. No, there were women who came from all walks of life. In fact, there was a very famous comedian's wife who came to see Val. I was shocked. The man always gives the impression on television and films of being a family man. Some family man. You know, it was the wife of a famous film star who told me about the refuge in the first place." She gazed at Winnie. "Now that I've told you, I feel better. I've been so ashamed all these years. I was too proud to admit I was wrong. Too proud, I suppose, to accept that I couldn't change him."

Winnie put her arms around Bonnie. "Oh, Bonnie. We all knew something was dreadfully wrong, but no one could reach out to you. It was as if Angus held you prisoner."

"Yes," Bonnie agreed. "Only no one could help me because my prison had no bars. On the surface, it looked as if I could leave anytime I wanted to, but underneath there were invisible bars all around me." She gave a bitter laugh. "Those bars were made by fear, and then by the pills and the alcohol." She sighed. "I'll never let myself get into such a state again."

"What are you going to do now?" Winnie said. "You can't stay with him."

"No, I know. But I'll have to play it carefully if I want to get away. He has custody of the kids, he tells me. So if I run away I'll be breaking the law. Anyway, I can't hide here in

England. He's too well-known. Too many people are on his side. I'll have to get away to America."

"Will your grandmother help?"

Bonnie shook her head. "I'd rather die than tell her. She feels such a failure over dad, I couldn't tell her I've made the same mistake. No, I'll get away with the kids, and eventually I'll surface and just tell her that it didn't work out."

Winnie nodded. "She is getting on, I suppose. A shock like that could kill her. Anyway, my dear, I must run downstairs and see to your mother." She gave Bonnie another hug. "Well, at least I have you for the weekend. Get cleaned up and we'll all have supper."

Teresa, when she arrived, greeted Laura cautiously, and then after supper hauled Bonnie into the library. "Tell," she commanded. "Mummy says you're in trouble."

Bonnie sat by the fireplace in Simon's old chair and told her cousin everything. Teresa listened intently. "The bastard," Teresa said when Bonnie had finished. "Oh, Bonnie, why didn't you tell us before? Why have you waited all this time?"

Bonnie shook her head. "I suppose it's almost impossible for other people to understand what it's like to be beaten by the person you love. After a while, the beatings don't even matter. You're just a zombie. I lived the past six years in a dream."

"I know. I watched you at parties."

Bonnie blushed. "I was drunk a lot of the time, and I became addicted to valium. I know everybody felt sorry for Angus because it did look as though he was married to an alcoholic drug-addict. But that was the only way I could cope with the fear of him."

Teresa took Bonnie's face in her hands. "How can I help?" she said.

"Well, I think I need to phone Mitzi. I don't have any

money because Angus keeps me short of cash. Can I phone from here?"

Teresa nodded. "Of course you can, you idiot."

"Mitzi's asking an old friend of mine named Mike if he can send me the plane fare for me and the kids. If I can get Mike to lend me the money, I can wait. I can slip away with the children when the time is right. Valerie, that's the woman who runs the refuge, tells me that even if Angus's solicitor puts a stop on all the airports, he may very well not remember to notify the Scottish courts as well. In which case I may be able to slip away and fly from Scotland while we're at Drummossie."

"Good." Teresa's eyes were shining.

"Also," Bonnie continued, "if I can meet you at Harrods every Friday, I can give Mike your address, and he can write to me through you. I'm sorry to have to ask you to involve yourself like this. I know it all sounds very melodramatic, but Angus checks my every move."

"Don't be sorry. I'll do everything I can to help you, Bonnie. God, if only I hadn't introduced you to Angus that night."

Bonnie shook her head. "It wouldn't have made any difference. I would have found another Angus. I now know I was looking for a man to rescue, and most men who need rescuing are violent. I guess I've learned the hard way that I'm not a fairy with a problem-solving wand. I'm Bonnie, and I want to live in peace with my children. Is it all right if I ring Mitzi tomorrow?"

"That's fine," said Teresa, and the two women walked back to the kitchen arm in arm.

"What have you been talking about?" Laura's voice was peevish.

"Oh, a little gossip," Teresa laughed.

Laura sensed that she was being excluded from important conversations. I must warn Angus, she thought.

Just then, John walked in with his fiancée. She was a

sweet-faced, plump woman. Bonnie smiled at John. "I'm pleased to see you."

John kissed her cheek. "And I'm so pleased to see you."

Laura's eyes picked up the affection between them. I'll definitely have to warn Angus, she thought.

The next day, Bonnie telephoned Mitzi from the library. Mitzi was excited. "Mike says he wants to talk to you," she said. "He says he'll give you the money and he . . ."

"It's not just money," Bonnie interrupted. "I'll be a fugitive. I didn't know, when I last spoke to you, that Angus had already been to court and got full custody of the kids." Her voice was bitter. "There's not much I can do about that. He had his doctor and his lawyer behind him."

"Never mind," Mitzi said. "You can sort all that out with Mike. He wants to speak with you. Have you got a pen?"

"Hang on." Bonnie went to the writing desk. "Yeah, okay," she said. "I've got a pen." She took down Mike's number. "I'll ring him now."

Mike's voice was reassuring. "Mitzi's told me all about Angus," he said. "We'll just have to wait until you can slip away."

The fact that Mike said "we" made Bonnie infinitely happy. "Oh, Mike, you've no idea how alone I've been."

"I do," he said. Something in his voice alerted Bonnie.

"Oh dear. I'm sorry. I'm so immersed in my own problems, I forgot to ask. I didn't mean to be selfish. What happened to your wife?"

Mike laughed a short unhappy laugh. "Well, she yo-yos back and forth. We've just split up for the fourth time. I don't know, I just feel so responsible for her."

"Huh," Bonnie snorted. "Mike, I know the feeling, but at some point you'll recognize how stupid it is to feel that way."

"I know, but then relationships aren't rational, are they?"

There was silence. "No," Bonnie said, "but from now on,

mine are going to be. Mike, can you lend me the money for the plane tickets?"

"No problem. I'm glad to help."

"Oh, Mike, that's very kind of you. I'll never be able to thank you enough. God! I'm so relieved. Could you please send the money via my cousin Teresa. I'll give you her address." Through the library window Bonnie could see Teresa deep in conversation with Laura. "Don't worry," she had told Bonnie, "I'll keep your mother busy for as long as you need to talk on the phone."

"Fine," Mike said. "I'll send the money right away. Aside from that, I suppose all I can do for the moment is to wait for you to contact me. How long do you think that will be?"

"Well, at the moment, Angus gives me a fair amount of freedom, but that may not last long. I am going to meet Teresa regularly at Harrods, so you can write to me as often as you want through her."

"I'll do that. And, Bonnie, please call me collect any time you can either at my home or at the office. I don't go out much."

Bonnie was pleased and touched. "I will whenever I can." Mike was so reassuring.

"Take care of yourself, Bonnie."

"I will. And you too, okay?"

"Okay, Bonnie," Mike said with real tenderness.

"Mike, before you hang up, you do realize that I'll be on the run with my kids, don't you? Angus has legal custody of them."

"No, I hadn't realized. But it doesn't make any difference. I'll just have to make plans to keep you out of the way while we have time to think. Bye-bye, Bonnie. And good luck."

Chapter 31

"You'd better keep a very close eye on Bonnie," Laura warned Angus just before she left for America. "I don't trust those friends of hers at all. That Teresa is trouble, and as for John," Laura sniffed, "I don't like the way he looks at Bonnie."

Angus went white. "I didn't know John was going to be there."

"Neither did I, but Bonnie didn't seem at all surprised to see him."

"Remember your marriage vows," Father John said to Bonnie. "Be a good wife to Angus. I shall pray for you."

Bonnie said nothing.

Angus could barely control his anger. "Did you enjoy your weekend?" he asked.

"Yes," Bonnie said absently. "I did. John's engaged to be married."

"I didn't know he was going to be there."

"Neither did I." Bonnie's eyes rested on Angus's face.

He clenched his fists. Take it easy, he reminded himself. Remember what Rupert said.

"We'll all go to New Zealand," Angus informed the family at breakfast the next morning.

The children were jubilant. "Great!" Alisdair was thrilled. He loved flying. "Is it a long way away?" he asked his father.

"Yes," Angus laughed. "New Zealand is on the other side of the world." He looked at Bonnie. "When we get back, I've organized two good boarding schools for the children. Yours has horses," he informed Rosemary.

"I don't want to go to boarding school." Alisdair was indignant. "I don't want to leave mummy."

"You *will* go to boarding school. It'll make a man of you."

Bonnie's heart sank. Getting away from Angus looked more and more impossible.

The trip to New Zealand was pleasant enough. Angus treated Bonnie with affection and respect. He made love to her most nights, and she found herself at times falling into her familiar state of confusion.

Once back in London, however, Angus became increasingly angry with Bonnie. "Tell Dan Fletcher to get his boys after Bonnie. I want her followed everywhere. I've an uncomfortable feeling that she's planning something," he said to Rupert.

Bonnie was busy ordering the children's clothes for their new schools. "I'm off shopping," she told Angus on Friday morning at breakfast.

"Have a good time," he said, smiling.

Bonnie tried to hide her excitement. I hope Teresa has the money from Mike, she thought. Despite all Angus's efforts at charm and kindness, Bonnie still knew that she had to get away. Now, after knowing so many other women who lived with violent men, Bonnie could see that Angus would never really change. She knew that Angus, the man she loved so passionately, was not there, even when they were making love. Instead, she realized, the Angus she adored had never existed. She had invented him from fractured bits of love for her father. Her mother's visit had confirmed the feeling that Laura was incapable of loving her daughter. Bonnie no longer needed to forgive either her mother or her father. Most of all, she no longer needed to forgive herself. She smiled at Angus. "I'll see you for lunch," she said.

"All right." Angus was waiting for Sacheverell. "By the way, Morag phoned this morning. She wants to visit us. She'll be flying over at the weekend."

"Wonderful!" Bonnie was thrilled. *I musn't tell her anything*, Bonnie promised herself.

Teresa handed Bonnie a letter from Mike. They were having a cup of coffee in the health bar in Harrods. A man watched them carefully. Bonnie put the letter in her bag. Teresa looked anxiously at Bonnie. "Are you all right?" she asked. "How was the trip to New Zealand?"

"Okay, I guess. Angus is being charming, but I know it won't last. He can usually keep himself together for about six weeks, and then he goes berserk. God, I hope I'll be away by then. He'll want to pay me out for having left him."

Teresa touched Bonnie's hand. "If he hurts you, I'll kill him."

Bonnie shook her head. "If he didn't have custody of the kids, I'd slip away now. But, if I get caught, he could go back to court, and I'll be barred from seeing them again. That happened to one of the mothers in the refuge." Bonnie shuddered. "I'll always remember her screaming and sobbing. The judge wouldn't listen to Val or our barrister. Even though the man had a criminal record as long as your arm, the judge insisted that the man had reformed. Anyway, she killed herself." Bonnie's face was grim.

"My God! How awful."

"Her husband put the kids into care. He never wanted them in the first place. The whole thing was just his way of trying to get her back."

"I don't mean to interrupt," Teresa said. She was nearing the end of her pregnancy. "But I must go to the loo."

"All right." Bonnie sat in a deep chair while she waited for Teresa. She took out the letter. Inside the envelope she found a large cheque and a note from Mike. Good, she thought, as she held the cheque in her hand. That will cover the plane tickets and then some. She began to read the note.

Mike's letter was full of reassurance. He had a safe plan. They would go down to Mexico. He would pick her up from a shelter which Mitzi had found in Axelton. The shelter would expect her at any time. No one would know she was there. Then Mike would drive her down to New Mexico, where Mike had a friend who knew how to get across the Mexican border illegally. That way, even if Angus had anyone watching the border, no one would expect them to cross illegally. They would stay in Mexico for several months. "I need a sabbatical anyway," Mike wrote. "And Mexico is lovely."

Bonnie looked up from the letter. Her eyes were shining. "Boy, he's really got it together," she said to Teresa who was combing her hair in the mirror. Teresa was pleased. Bonnie saw the telephone on the wall. "I'll call him now," she said. "I'll sign this cheque over to you, if you'll cash it for me. I can't cash anything without Angus knowing." Teresa nodded. Bonnie tore the letter to shreds and put the pieces in the wastepaper basket. She phoned Mike collect.

"Bonnie," he said. "I'm so pleased to hear from you."

Bonnie laughed. "I can't tell you how pleased I am to hear your voice. Angus doesn't seem so omnipotent now. We have a plan at last. It sounds fine to me. Why Mexico?" she asked.

"There's no extradition," he said. "Even if Angus goes to an American court, they can't order us to return."

"Oh, I see." Bonnie remembered Val's underground network for smuggling women and children away from violent men. "We often used Eire at the refuge." Suddenly she wished she was back in the warm and loving little house.

She finished her talk to Mike, and turned to Teresa. "Thank you so much for everything," she said. "I'd better be getting back now. Angus is expecting me for lunch."

Teresa hugged Bonnie. "I'll see you next week."

"Wonderful. The kids will be in school by then. I'll have to try to make a break for it at Christmas."

Morag was delighted to see Bonnie. "You look so much better," she said.

"Well, we were having a bit of trouble, but everything's all right again." Bonnie had decided not to say anything to Morag until she was safely in Mexico. The less she knew, the less Angus could bully her for information. Besides, it would be hard for Morag not to tell Augustine if she knew the truth.

Angus, Bonnie and Morag were in Scotland for the week. The children were in their new boarding schools. One day, Bonnie walked quickly to the chapel. She had a purpose for her visit to Drummossie: she wanted to talk to Father Mac-Bride.

"Father," she said after her confession. "Do you remember when I confessed my wish to leave Angus, and you gave me absolution?"

"I remember it well," the old priest said, "and I would grant you absolution again. You have to leave the man. Which is not to say that I approve of remarriage. A vow is a vow. But that does not exclude the possibility of a permanent separation. Angus is a dangerous man. He is dangerous to you and to your children." The priest smiled gently at Bonnie. "Walk in peace, my child," he said. "And my prayers will go with you."

Bonnie lowered her head. "Thank you, Father. I needed your blessing." Once out in the bright sunlight, she blinked. Angus was waiting for her.

"Confessing your secrets?" he said lightly.

Bonnie laughed. "How could I keep anything secret from you?" she said.

Angus had a meticulous report from the detective tucked away in his pocket. "You can't," he said. "Come on. Let's go for a walk."

Morag joined them. "It's lovely up here," Morag said. "I think I'll start travelling in the Highlands and then go down to Devon before I go back home. I hear Devon is gorgeous."

"You'll love it," Bonnie said. She smiled. "We'll say good-bye on Sunday. Then, if we don't see you back in London we'll catch up with you when we're next in Lexington."

The week in Scotland slipped by peacefully. But I still feel there's trouble, Morag thought.

They arrived back in Heath House to find two letters waiting. One was a cheerful note from Rosemary. The other was a tear-stained scrap of paper from Alisdair. Oh dear, Bonnie thought. Poor little boy. Angus saw Bonnie standing with Alisdair's letter in her hand. He saw the unhappiness on her face. "Don't be so sentimental," Angus said sharply. "We all went through it in our time. Do you think St. Gregory's was any easier? The boy's a sissy. That's his problem." Bonnie sighed. She couldn't wait for Friday.

Again, Teresa handed Bonnie a long and detailed letter from Mike. He was buying camping equipment. "If we stick to camp-grounds, we won't be traced," he wrote. "They don't check your name or your address." Again, Bonnie telephoned him. "Mike," she said, "we'll have to wait for the Christmas holidays. Angus has put the kids in boarding schools."

"Never mind." Mike's voice was calm and comforting. "You'll get a chance sometime. I can wait."

"Mike, you are a darling." Bonnie's voice trembled. "I don't know what I'd do without you."

"You're not going to do without me," he said. "Don't worry. We'll have a wonderful time. Just be sure to keep yourself safe until Christmas."

Angus by now had received several reports from the detective. It was apparent that Bonnie was either planning something or that she had a lover. To Angus, the idea of a lover was intolerable. He assumed that Teresa was acting as a carrier pigeon for John. The detective suggested they hire a woman to sit by the ladies' lavatory at Harrods. Angus agreed. Now we'll get to the heart of this, he thought. Now I'm back in control.

By the Sunday, however, after a weekend full of parties, Angus was unable to contain his rage and his suspicions any longer. It was seven o'clock in the evening as he rushed through the front door of Heath House after a drinking bout with Sacheverell and his friends. Angus had got into a huge argument with Christopher, Sacheverell's new lover. Angus was enraged that the boy knew that he had once had an affair with Sacheverell. "Come on, Angus, there are no secrets," Christopher had teased. "And we all know that you're cruel to your wife." Christopher smirked at Angus. "Other people may not pick up on it, but in our world, we have to be super-sensitive. Anyway, it doesn't take much knowing to see how Bonnie used to hide her bruises. I had a lover who beat me. I know where to put the rouge."

"Mind your own sodding business!" Angus roared.

"All right, ducky. Don't get upset." Christopher smiled. "One day she'll fly the coop, and then where will you be?"

Angus had a chilling vision of himself lying in his father's white room drooling helplessly.

Bonnie sat reading by the fire. It was warm and the windows were open. Angus could no longer control himself. He seized Bonnie by the hair and began to throw her around like a rag-doll. He punched her in the face and then, excited by the flow of blood from her nose, he began to strangle her.

He did not hear the doorbell. Nor did he hear Morag until she screamed. "Angus! What do you think you're doing?"

"Get out!" he roared. His face was red as he spun round to Morag. He was totally aroused by the slow ebb of Bonnie's life draining from her body. He wanted his act of violence to end in a satisfactory orgasm. This orgasmic violence was his secret, known only by him and a few perceptive and willing partners in his life. He was furious with Morag. She was interrupting him.

Morag stood her ground. Angus dropped Bonnie to the floor. He picked up a poker from beside the fireplace. "This is none of your business!" he screamed. "Get out!"

Morag ran from the house. She was alone, a stranger in London. I must get back to Lexington, she thought. I'll tell Augustine. She'll know what to do.

In the taxi on the way to the airport, she covered her eyes and wept. Poor Bonnie, if only she'd told us before, she sobbed.

"I've never seen anything like it," Morag told Augustine. "There was nothing I could do. Bonnie was unconscious." She began to cry again. "I'll never forget his face. He's a maniac. What are we going to do?" Morag was wringing her hands and walking up and down the drawing-room. "He'll kill her. I know he will."

Augustine sat very quietly. She felt a vice close around her chest. An old familiar pain crept back into her heart. It was the same unendurable agony she had suffered when her son James had left her all those years ago. "Go upstairs, child," she said quietly to Morag, "and wash your face. We will have to make a plan." Morag left the room. The frail old woman struggled to rise from her chair. "I failed her," she muttered. "I failed Bonnie." The vice tightened its hold. She just had time to call Bonnie's name before she fell back in her chair. Augustine was dead. Morag found the old lady lying in her chair clutching her beloved Bible.

Chapter 32

The funeral was arranged for a week later. Bonnie, still bruised and shattered from her appalling experience, realized that this would probably be her last chance. She grieved deeply for her grandmother. Her grief added to her absolute conviction that she must leave.

The children came home from their schools so that they could fly with their parents to the funeral. "You've hit mummy again." Rosemary was furious with her father. "You promised you wouldn't."

Angus gazed at his daughter. "She deserved it," he said.

"No one deserves to be hit," Rosemary corrected him. "We were much happier when we were away from you. Alisdair stopped wetting the bed, and my eczema cleared up. Now you're going to start losing your temper all over again."

A muscle in Angus's cheek quivered. "No, I'm not," he said. Lucky, he thought, we're going off to the funeral. She doesn't have time to get a lawyer.

Bonnie didn't leave the house all week. When they landed at Boston, she casually told Angus to take the children for an ice-cream while she went to the restroom. Once there, she telephoned Mike. Quickly she told him what had happened, that she would have to get away this time. Mike agreed. "How are you going to do it?" he asked.

"I don't know yet," she said. "But I'll find a way."

The funeral in the Great House chapel was attended by members of all the leading Boston families. Augustine lay in her simple casket at the foot of the altar. Bonnie cried for her grandmother and took a last fond look at the coffin as the grave diggers gently slid Augustine's body into the vault to lie with Malcolm Fraser her ancestor, Duncan Fraser her father, and James Fraser her son. A bright, flinty resolve settled in Bonnie's heart. Your death will give me life, she silently promised Augustine as the door to the tomb was closed.

Morag stood a short distance away with her head bowed. Bonnie's dark glasses covered her bruised eyes. I must talk to Morag, Bonnie thought. I'll need her to drive me into Boston.

"The only way I can think of shaking off Angus is if we drug him." They were in the sewing-room, as Bonnie continued to explain her plan to Morag. "After the lawyer reads the will, we're supposed to fly back to London. Angus wants to go to Newport but I've got to get the kids back to school. So I must go some time tomorrow."

"Well," Morag frowned. "Have you got any sleeping pills?"

"I've got a large box of valium, thanks to Dr. Simpson." Morag nodded. "I'll get cook to make a really hot curry. Angus likes it that way. And then I'll put a heavy dose of valium into the mixture."

Morag took up the plan. "I'll stay away from the table. I don't feel comfortable with him any more. You just be sure to avoid eating the curry yourself."

It could work. Bonnie was scared. She had no idea how much valium would be needed to knock Angus out, but she knew she could count on him to drink a fair amount with his dinner. Valium mixed with that amount of alcohol should keep him asleep while she fled with the children. "Can you ring Mike for me?" Bonnie asked Morag. "Tell him to meet me at Merrill Airport. No, make it Axelton Airport. Angus won't think to check there. Angus is usually asleep by midnight. I should be away with the kids by two in the morning, so I'll be in Axelton by six. Tell Mike I'll be there." Bonnie was vehement. I'll make it, she told herself. She clenched her hands. I've got to make it. I can't fail.

* * *

Bonnie went about the business of sorting out her grandmother's papers with particular attention to detail. Angus, bored, glanced about the house. "You'll have to get rid of Morag," he said. "I won't have her living in my house."

Bonnie sighed. It was indeed his house. With the best of intentions, Augustine had left Bonnie with no power over her vast inheritance. Angus would take it all. "All right," she said. "Augustine has left Morag quite a large sum of money. She'll probably be quite happy to get her own place." Bonnie had always imagined that Morag would continue to run the Great House, and that they would spend enjoyable holidays together. She sighed. She looked round the drawing-room. "I know, Angus," she said. "Why don't you have a look at some of the paintings. Maybe you'd like some for Heath House."

Angus smiled.

That evening, one of Angus's friends, an art dealer, stayed for dinner. With an extra guest at the table, Morag knew she would not be able to lace the curry. Seeing that her plan for escape had to be abandoned, Bonnie was desperate. Angus and Johnny spent their dinner arguing over a Spanish painter. "I tell you," Johnny said, "the man's a genius."

"Oh, bullshit." Angus was in a good mood. "The man's a charlatan. He can't paint to save his life." Both men were drinking heavily.

"I tell you what," Johnny was belligerent. "I'll bet you a grand you'll change your mind when you see his new paintings in my gallery." He stood up and put out his hand.

"Done," said Angus.

"Come on then." Johnny slapped him on the shoulder. "Let's go into town, and I'll relieve you of your money."

"Okay," Angus was too drunk to think properly. He forgot his vigil over Bonnie. "Go to bed," he ordered Bonnie. "I'll be back late."

Bonnie sat at the table, her mind racing. "Now," she said. "I must go now." She raced upstairs. Morag was in her own room. "He's gone off to Boston with Johnny," Bonnie panted. "They'll be away for hours. If you drive me to the station, I'll take the train into Boston and make my way to the airport. I can ring Mike from there . . . Oh God," Bonnie suddenly remembered, "I haven't any money."

"Don't worry," Morag said. "I drew the money for your tickets out this afternoon. Here." She took a wad of twenty-dollar bills from her bedside table.

"Thank you, Morag. Come on." Bonnie was panicking. "He could change his mind and come back."

"He could but he won't," Morag was calm and firm. "You know what he's like. He'll stay with Johnny 'til dawn. Johnny talks all night."

Both women ran along the corridor leading to the nursery. "Rosemary, wake up at once."

"What's happening, mummy?"

"We're leaving, darling." Bonnie took her daughter by the shoulders.

"For good?" Rosemary looked warily at her mother.

"Yes, for good."

"Well," the child sat in her bed and considered the matter, "I'm glad. I'll miss daddy, but we're much happier without him." She hugged Bonnie. "Where are we going?" she said.

"It's a secret. I'll tell you on the plane. Now hurry and get dressed."

Morag appeared at the door with Alisdair. He was grinning. "I'm glad we're running away. I don't have to go back to that school, do I?"

"No, darling." Bonnie gave him a hug. "Never again."

"I'll ring the housekeeper at the Great House and say I've had to attend a sick friend," Morag said as she dropped Bonnie off at Lexington station. "I'll have to lie low until Angus has gone."

"Thanks, Morag." Bonnie kissed her on the cheek. "Thanks for everything."

"You'll make it," Morag said with tears in her eyes.

"I will." Bonnie dashed off down the dark platform and onto the train, the two children hurrying to keep up.

"I'll be there," Mike said when she telephoned him from Logan Airport. "I'll ring the shelter and tell them to expect you. We'll all stay cool for a couple of days, and then we'll go off to Mexico. My office knows I'm due for a long leave."

"Phone Mitzi, Mike."

"I will, but I won't tell her any more than she needs to know. Angus is sure to check her out. I'll see you at the airport."

Bonnie sat on the plane and began to feel safe. America was such a vast country, she couldn't see how Angus could locate her. At Axelton she flew into Mike's welcoming arms. The children stared at him. "This is Mike," she introduced him to Rosemary.

Rosemary smiled sweetly at him. "We're running away from daddy," she said. "If he finds us, he'll kill us." She looked at Mike.

"No, he won't," Mike said firmly. "I'll be there. I'll see that he doesn't."

Mike drove Bonnie to the shelter. It was eight o'clock in the morning when they arrived. Bonnie was pleased to be back in the security of other women who understood her fear. "I'll leave you at the door," Mike said. "I don't mean to be rude by not taking you in, but I hear a lot of these places don't allow men in." Mike grinned. "Personally, I think it's a bit silly. I think women and kids need to know that there are also good and gentle men in the world."

Bonnie smiled. "Actually, not all refuges ban men." She kissed Mike goodbye and rang the bell.

The door opened. An old nun stood smiling at Bonnie. "Come in, my dear," she said. "We've been expecting you. Was that the man who telephoned who drove you here?"

"Yes," Bonnie said. "That's my friend Mike."

"It's a shame he didn't come in for a cup of coffee. He sounds like a lovely man." Bonnie was pleased. The house was quite large and well-furnished. "Yes, we are lucky," the nun said. "We have a very good local support group of both men and women who paint and decorate for us and donate the money to keep us going." She walked ahead of Bonnie, holding the children by the hand. "Here is the living-room," she said. Two women looked up at her from the television. "Sit down, Bonnie, and meet April and Sue."

"Jesus," Sue laughed. "Just think what black eyes do for the dark-glasses business."

Bonnie took off her glasses. The swelling had gone down, but her eyes were still bruised. Rosemary sat beside her mother. "He always hit her," she informed the two women.

Alisdair nodded his head in agreement. "We gave him another chance, and he did it again."

"And it makes Alisdair wet his bed," Rosemary chimed in.

Sue smiled at the children. "Sure thing, honey. My kids all wet their beds, and my big boy, he shakes all the time."

Bonnie relaxed in her chair. "Thank God for shelters," she said.

April, plump with bright pink cheeks, smiled at Bonnie. "Yup, and this one is particularly good. I've been to lots of them, and I know," she said. "Sister Norman knows about violence. She doesn't judge us or say we should all be lesbians." She looked at Bonnie. "Some of the shelters here are run by women who hate men. I don't hate men, I just hate one man."

"April," Sister Norman reappeared carrying a coffee pot, "as long as you hate Randy, you're still attached to him. Hate is a very powerful emotion."

Bonnie nodded. "You're right, you know. I don't feel anything for Angus," she said. "Maybe pity."

Sue interrupted. "I feel compassion for Ed. He's a loser, and I want to be a winner. This is one black woman that's going to make it. Me and my kids."

"Come on, kids! Time for school!" A group of small children charged into the living-room to kiss their mothers good-bye before being driven off by van to the shelter's own nursery. "My God," Bonnie said. "They're a handful."

"You're telling me?" Sue said, hugging and kissing them. "Okay, okay, kids. Have a good time." The children poured out of the door and followed the playgroup leader into the van. "Well," said Sue. "I'm on kitchen duty. You get the rest of the day off because you're new. Come on, I'll show you your room on my way to the stove."

Unlike the refuge in the north of London, the Axelton shelter was not only very comfortable, but also uncrowded. There were enough rooms in the pretty house for each mother to have a room of her own shared only with her children. Much to her surprise, Bonnie found herself wishing that she could sleep on a mattress on the floor packed into a crowd of other sleeping bodies. The privacy in the American shelter allowed her to sit alone with her fear. Without the constant distraction of noisy bustling mothers and children, the old familiar feeling of panic began to rise. The fear was over-powering as she lay in her clean, well-made bed. The two children slept heavily after an exhausting day with all the other children in the shelter.

Trying to ward off her terror, Bonnie went downstairs and

joined the other mothers. But even at three o'clock in the morning, when she finally did go to bed, she lay staring at the ceiling, wondering what Angus was doing.

Angus was wondering where Bonnie was. He was also getting very drunk and cursing the absent Morag.

As Morag had predicted, it was dawn when he arrived back at the Great House. He was still in a good mood and a thousand dollars richer. He burst into the bedroom to tell Bonnie the good news. She was not there. He stood still. Then he raced to the nursery. Maybe she was sleeping with one of the children. He reached for the telephone and dialled Rupert's number. Rupert was in conference with a client. "Get him out," he told the secretary, "it's urgent."

"Hello?" Rupert's voice was cheerful. "What's the problem?"

Hurriedly Angus explained. "We'll have to go back to court," he said.

"No," Rupert thought out loud. "I wouldn't do that. Court's not the right way to play this game. She's in America, and they don't hand children to their fathers that easily over there. Besides, all she has to do is hop from one state to the next, and you'll find yourself up against an entirely different system of laws. No, you could be in serious trouble. After all, there are records over here of Bonnie spending months in a refuge, aren't there? And you could end up standing before some bleeding-heart American judge."

Angus sighed impatiently. "What shall I do? She could be anywhere."

"Well, hang on a minute. There's an organization I've used before. They're called SAK. Stands for 'Save a Kid.' They're sort of mercenaries. Soldiers of fortune. Very tough. They'll get your kids back for you. Here's the number." Angus scribbled it down. "They have their headquarters in New York, but they have their private stations everywhere. They'll snatch a child for whoever pays the most money. They're expensive, and they don't ask questions. I suggest you give them a ring."

"All right, old boy. Thanks for the help." He was suddenly tired. "It's Bonnie I want," he said.

Rupert laughed. "Oh Angus, make up your mind."

"No, I'm serious. I love her, Rupert. I really do," Angus was crying. Why do I do all those dreadful things to her? he wondered as he walked over to the mirror above the mantelpiece. He looked at his face. The tears made his eyes swell. His nose was red, and a night's worth of alcohol had bloated his face. He stared at himself with horror. I'm getting to look like him, he thought. I'm getting to look just like my father. If I do get like him, I'll kill myself. Angus imagined the roar of a double-barrelled shotgun. A memory quickly flashed of Morgan's head. Angus winced. He went upstairs and had a bath while he waited for the SAK office to open.

He telephoned New York at nine o'clock on the dot. "Billy Brody," said a voice on the telephone. "How can I help you?"

"I want to talk to someone about a job I need done," Angus said.

"Yes." The voice was polite.

"Shall I explain?" Angus was flustered.

"Please do." The voice was neutral.

"My wife has run away with my two children. I have legal custody of them."

"That makes no difference to us. Can you pay two thousand dollars a day plus expenses?"

"Yes," Angus said.

"Fine then." The voice was suddenly very charming. "Now let's see. Where are you calling from?"

"I'm in Lexington, Massachusetts."

"Okay, I'll have two men at your house within a couple of hours. We have a big office in Boston."

"Thank you." Angus gave him the address.

"Don't worry about a thing," said the voice. "We're the best there is."

Angus felt strangely comforted. He ordered a pot of coffee and a newspaper.

"Mitzi," Mike looked at her urgently, "she's at the shelter, and I'm just making last-minute arrangements. I've got a house-sitter coming tomorrow to look after my cats. I'll take Pluto with us. He's a good guard dog." Mike sat with Mitzi at her kitchen table. He smiled. "I can't tell you how wonderful I feel now that Bonnie is back."

"You really do love her, don't you, Mike?" Mitzi's brown eyes sparkled.

"Yes, I do. But I'm not going to burden her with that now. She has enough on her plate already. Her kids are great," he said, helping himself to a piece of toast. "Their English accents crack me up."

"Can I speak to her?" Mitzi asked.

"I'm afraid they keep the shelter number unlisted."

That same bit of information was being relayed to Angus by a small and energetic young man. "They all keep themselves to themselves. We can't get in there. We do have a team of women with kids whom we plant sometimes in some of the shelters to get information, but many of the workers have cottoned on by now and they're very paranoid. They watch for our women, so it's difficult."

Angus groaned. "Don't worry," said the second man. "We'll find her for you. The only problem is that there are literally hundreds of shelters all over the country. She could have touched base in any one of them. But first we'll check the shelters around here, and then where did you say her friend lived?" He took a clipboard out of his briefcase. On the back was engraved the SAK logo: an elf-like man in silhouette with a large and obviously full sack over his shoulder. "I'll get some details," he said. "I'll need pictures. Did she take her passport?"

"No." Angus shook his head. "I keep that locked up."

"Okay. Well, give us forty-eight hours. Then we should be ready for the kill." He looked at Angus. "Do you want to be there when we nab them, or do you want us to bring you the kids?" Angus hesitated. "For a small additional fee, we can knock her off so she doesn't bother you again?" The man's face was impassive.

"No." Angus looked at them both. "I don't want any of them hurt." Recognizing the violence in both the men, he said, "I'll come with you."

"Okay, we'll leave tomorrow morning."

"All right." Angus suddenly and desperately wanted to sleep. He saw the men out and fell into bed. He was asleep as soon as his head touched the pillow. He dreamed of guns, and he dreamed of finding Bonnie. She smiled at him in his dreams, a big lovely warm smile. He cried in his sleep.

 Chapter 33

Just as the two mercenaries knocked on Mitzi's door, Mike was pulling away from the shelter in his large green Volvo. Bonnie sat beside him and the children were jumping up and down with excitement in the back-seat. "We're going camping! We're going camping!" they chorused. "We're going to Mexico for our holidays!"

"Oh." Mike looked at Bonnie. "You told them."

Bonnie smiled. "Don't worry, Mike. I didn't tell them about Mexico until last night."

"That should be all right then. First stop," he said with a smile, "Cherokee National Forest campground, Tennessee."

Bonnie grinned. "I haven't been camping since I was a kid." The children were busy playing with Pluto, a large and hairy dog.

"Feeling safe?"

"Yeah," she said. "They'll never find me." She smiled at Mike. "I'm just going to enjoy the trip."

"Well, it should be a nice drive," he said. "Once we're out of Pennsylvania, we'll drive down through Maryland, and then all the way across Virginia. It's a gorgeous road all along the Appalachian Mountains. We'll be camping in the mountains of Tennessee tonight." He put a protective hand on her knee. "Don't worry," he said. "I've thought of everything."

That night, sitting by a fire outside his small tent, Mike explained to Bonnie that the last part of their trip would be organized with the help of Chucky, a friend of Mike's from law school, who now lived in Santa Fe, New Mexico. "He's an expert on just about everything," Mike said. "Funny guy. Bright guy. He did really well at law school, then suddenly decided it wasn't the life for him, so he upped and went to Santa Fe. He runs a place down there doing up old cars. Seems totally happy. They say he does the best car work in the South-West. Anyway, I've called him, and he's waiting for us. He's setting up a guide for us to take us down to the Mexican border. Then the guide will drive this car back up to Chucky. We'll have to walk over the border, but he's arranged to have another car waiting for us on the other side with Mexican licence plates. All we have to do is follow the guide across some fields, and then wade across the Rio Grande. Chucky's found a part of the river that's shallow and there aren't any immigration guards along that stretch. Apparently there's a not-so-legal wet-back labour agency in California that pays the guards off to turn a blind eye to this piece of the river."

Bonnie was tired. "Sounds good to me," she said.

Mike hugged her. "Crawl into your tent and get a good night's sleep. Tomorrow we drive all the way to Arkansas, and then the day after we'll go on into Oklahoma."

Bonnie wedged herself between the two sleeping children. She kissed them both goodnight, and she smiled at the stars that twinkled at her through the open flap of her tent. An owl hooted.

Mitzi was surprised by the hostility shown by her two visitors. "No, I don't know where Bonnie is," she said indignantly.

"Shall we slap her about a bit, Tony?" the short man asked the tall ginger-haired man.

"Naw." Tony was bored. The house was tiny. There were no children about. Bonnie obviously wasn't there. Mitzi looked the sort of woman who could make a lot of trouble, and Tony didn't want to begin this hunt with a dead body. The police could be a nuisance at this stage of the game. "Naw, c'mon, Jerry. Leave her alone. I'm sorry to trouble you," he said to Mitzi, and the men left the house.

Mitzi burst into tears. She felt very afraid for Bonnie. Ray comforted her when he arrived home that night. "She'll be fine," he said. "Mike's a fine man. A real starker. No one'll mess with him."

Angus telephoned Laura. "She's gone again," he said glumly. "Listen, Laura. I'll wire a quarter of a million dollars to your bank account if you can get me a lead on Bonnie. All I need is just one break. I have men ready to find her, but they've drawn a blank at her friend Mitzi's house. She's not in any of the Boston shelters. Can you check at the ones around you?"

Laura was stunned. A quarter of a million dollars. She was thrilled. "Well, I'll try," she said calmly. "Father John can visit some shelters, and I'll visit some more. There's one in

Merrill, you know, and I think there are a few in the towns around here."

"Thank you," Angus said.

"Don't worry, dear," Laura said comfortingly. "I'll do what I can to help. We'll find her in the end."

Father John, Laura knew, had connections at the Merrill Shelter. Although he personally did not approve of the whole idea of shelter, a fellow priest whom he had met on several occasions did a lot of work with some of the shelter's Catholic mothers. Father John asked his friend to check if Bonnie was there. "I'm looking for this woman because her mother is very ill. The old woman wants to see her daughter before she dies." Moved by Father John's story, the priest asked the shelter in Merrill if Bonnie was there. Laura was disappointed when Father John relayed the news that his friend had come up with nothing. "He said maybe you should try Haddingly," Father John told Laura.

Laura collected a pile of old clothes which she had been saving for the church bazaar. She put them in the back of her little Subaru and set off for the address given to her by Father John. She arrived at the Haddingly shelter and charmed her way into the little office. She deposited some clothes with the organizer, and she played with some children on the floor. "I'd love to volunteer," she said to one of the mothers. "I have so much free time on my hands."

The mother smiled. "All the shelters could do with as much help as a body can give. The government sure as hell doesn't care if women and kids live or die."

"Could you suggest a shelter a little closer to Merrill?"

"Oh ya. Here." The mother was new. She took Laura to a map pinned to the wall. "Take your pick."

Laura was delighted. She quickly jotted down as many addresses as she could. "Thank you, dear," she said. She pressed a ten-dollar bill into the woman's hand. "Buy something for your children," Laura said.

"Hey thanks." The woman was pleased.

"I didn't like the look of that lady," the organizer said after she had shown Laura to the door.

"She only wanted to help," said the woman with the ten-dollar bill in her pocket.

"I don't feel it's us she wants to help." The telephone rang and the organizer answered it. "Uh-huh," she said as she made a note. "I see. Okay. Thanks a lot." She hung up. "Hey," she called out to the women working around the shelter. "I just got a call from the Apple County shelter. They say SAK is out looking for a woman with two children. They've been checking all the shelters in the area. So I want you all to take care with any new woman coming in. Okay?"

The mothers all knew of SAK's dreadful reputation. "God," one mother said. "I'm glad they're not after me." She went back to sorting out the pile of clothes which Laura had taken in.

Finding a lead took Laura two entire days. Finally she reached the shelter in Axelton. She had perfected a technique for probing for information. Her method involved trying clothes on the children. This way she could ask them innocently if Rosemary and Alisdair had played with them. "Did they talk kind of funny?" a little boy in the Axelton shelter asked as he struggled with the zip of the new jeans which Laura had purchased for her quest.

"Yes, they have English accents."

"That's right. I've heard people talk like that on TV. Yeah, they spent a night here."

"Oh, really? Was their mommy with them?"

"Yeah." The little boy pulled up the zipper. "And a man came and took them away. He had a big car, the kind I'm gonna get when I'm bigger."

"What kind of car was it?"

"Green."

"Green? A green what?"

"A green car," the boy said proudly. "Hey, can I have that Star Wars T-shirt?"

Laura hid her impatience. "I'll make you a deal. You tell me what kind of a green car it was, and I'll give you the T-shirt."

"I think it's called a Volvo. Now can I have the T-shirt?"

"A Volvo. Well, you've been a very good little boy. Here's your shirt. My, don't you look smart in it."

"Alisdair was my friend," the boy said.

"Do you know where they went?" Laura asked.

"No." The little boy lost interest in the conversation. "Are you older than my mom?" he asked distractedly.

"Here." Laura took out her purse. "I'll give you two whole dollars if you can remember where they were going."

"Two dollars, wow!" the boy said. "Can I buy anything I want?"

"You can if you tell me where they went," Laura said sweetly.

The little boy screwed up his face. "Um, I think he said they were taking a vacation. He said Mexico, I think. Is that where they have big hats?" Laura nodded. "Then it was Mexico. Because he promised to buy a big hat for me."

"When did they leave?" Laura asked. "Do you remember?"

"I haven't learned days yet." The boy started to pick his nose. "Hey, wait. Do you know what day *Space Bunnies* is on TV? That's when he left. We were gonna watch *Space Bunnies* together, but he left too soon."

"My, aren't you a clever young man." Laura kissed him on the forehead and left the shelter. She quickly went to a supermarket and bought a *TV Guide*. "*Space Bunnies, Space Bunnies,*" she muttered as she flipped through the pages. "Ah. Here it is. Three days ago."

Laura was pleased with herself. "They're heading for Mexico in a big green Volvo," she told Angus. "She was picked up outside the shelter three days ago."

Angus's face contracted. "Thank you, Laura," he said. "The money will be in your bank this afternoon."

"Oh, that's very kind of you, dear. Thank you," Laura said. She was ecstatic.

"Ah," said Tony when Angus telephoned him at the Boston SAK office. "So they're making for the border. This one's a piece of cake. You say you still have your wife's passport?"

"Yes." Angus was tense.

"Then they'll have to sneak across the border. There's always the chance they've crossed already in some place like Laredo if they left three days ago, but I've got a hunch they're going to cross further west. Let me see, probably somewhere in California, most likely in the country between Tijuana and Mexicali. There are some open stretches there that are relatively safe. Hang on a minute, will you?" Tony had a brief word with his colleague. "Ya," he said as he returned to the telephone. "We'll need to pull in five hundred of our men to cover the two thousand miles of border. Cost you an extra five thousand dollars a day."

"I'll pay."

"Okay. Get packed and we'll leave for California. I'll put out a call and check all green Volvos at gas stations along the Interstate 40. We'll follow my hunch."

"Right you are," said Angus. Tony turned to Jerry. "We might as well get moving. We gotta make him feel he's getting his money's worth." Tony turned to his secretary. "Call the Volvo showroom in Merrill. See who's bought a car like that in the last few years. Ring me out in Lexington before lunch."

Tony and Jerry drove to the Great House in silence. "I'm having the Volvo dealer checked out," Tony said to Angus when they arrived. "If the car's new, we can find out who the owner is and get a licence plate number. That'd make it even easier to track them."

Angus was impatient. "She could have made an arrangement with anyone from anywhere."

"No." Tony was serious. "Usually you'll find that the subject will choose a friend. Does she have any boyfriends?"

Angus looked startled. He thought of John. "No, not as far as I know. There's a family in England she's very close to. She has a friend there, her cousin actually, called Teresa. I learned that Bonnie was meeting Teresa on the sly. Teresa would give her letters . . ." His voice trailed off.

"So she probably did have a boyfriend," Jerry interjected.

"Why didn't you tell us this days ago?" Tony asked.

"I just didn't think." Angus felt as if his heart would break. It was bad enough to have Bonnie running away, but the thought of her running with another man was unbearable.

"This Teresa," Jerry asked. "What's she like?"

"Well," Angus thought for a moment. "She's not very bright. Cheerful. A horsy type of girl."

"Okay," said Tony. "I got the picture. Let's phone her and see what we can find out." Tony put his square hand on the telephone and dialled the number Angus gave him. "Mrs. Teresa Fitzgibbon, please," he said. He waited for a moment. He whistled quietly through his teeth and tapped the desk with the flat side of his ballpoint pen. "Hello," he said, sounding friendly and warm. "Is this Teresa?"

"Yes." Teresa was puzzled.

"I have a message for you from Bonnie." Tony shot Angus a conspiratorial wink.

"Oh, how wonderful!"

"Yes, she says to tell you she's left her husband and that she was picked up safely."

"Thank God Mike found her. Where is she?" Teresa asked.

"Well, they're travelling at the moment."

"Will you be speaking to Bonnie soon?

"I hope to see her very soon," Tony smiled.

"Do send her my love and say thank you to her for the message. I'm glad she's safe and away from that brute. Mike Edwards is a wonderful man," she rattled on. Tony wasn't listening.

He put down the phone before Teresa had stopped talking. "See?" he said to Angus. He shook his head. "People don't think. But now we have the man's name. Do you know a Mike Edwards?"

Angus thought hard. "Yes," he said. "He went to Brown University with Bonnie. I met him at a hockey match. In fact . . . that's right. He came from Merrill." He wanted to cry. He wanted to shriek and to roll on the floor. How could Bonnie do this to him?

Tony was already busy again on the telephone. "Brown Alumnae Magazine, please," he said. "Hello, I'm an alumnus of Brown. I'm trying to get hold of my old roommate, Michael Edwards, class of '67. We've sort of lost touch over the years. You know how it is. You wouldn't happen to know Mike's current address, would you? . . . Yes, I'll hold." He turned to Angus. "Like I said, people don't think." He turned back to the telephone. "Yes . . . right. Got it. And that's his office number, you say? . . . Great, well thanks a hell of a lot. I know Mike will be surprised to hear from me. Bye now."

He dialled Mike's office. "Mr. Edwards is away on sabbatical," Mike's secretary said. "We don't expect him back for some time."

"Do you have a forwarding address?" Tony's voice was anonymous.

"Well, yes. But if it's business . . ."

"No, it's a family matter. It's really very urgent . . . Oh, thank you." Tony took the address down. "He's heading for Santa Fe," Tony said to Angus with his hand over the mouthpiece. "That's lovely," he said to the secretary. "Oh listen,

I've always been interested in buying that Volvo from him. You know, the green one? Does he still have it?"

"Well, he still has a green Volvo, but not that nice old one you're thinking of. He traded it in for a newer model about a year ago."

"Isn't that always the way it goes?" Tony said. "Some lucky dog's driving that honey of a car, and it could have been me if I'd spoken up before. But never mind. There'll be other cars. Thank you for your time. And have a good day." Tony was charming.

He looked at Angus. "Well," he said, "she's run off with her lover. Women," he said. "Who'd trust them?" He smiled at Jerry.

"I keep the hell away from them myself," Jerry laughed. "Let's get going. I've always wanted to see Santa Fe. They say the most beautiful boys in the world hang out there."

"Your secretary's on the other phone," Angus said.

"Tell her I don't need the information. I'll phone in tomorrow." Tony was businesslike. The three men climbed into the Mercedes 300SE Sedan, the trademark of the SAK organization. "All our men drive these babies," Tony explained to Angus. "Fastest sedan on the road."

The three days passed like a dream for Bonnie. She relaxed beside Mike in the comfortable Volvo. The children sometimes played with the dog, and other times quarrelled furiously. If they weren't playing or arguing, they were sleeping or reading or playing with puzzles. Each evening Mike would set up the tents at a clean little camp-site, and Bonnie would barbecue dinner on the Hibachi and prepare a large salad. "Hm," she said on the third night when they were camped just east of Oklahoma City. "I feel alive again."

Mike grinned at her. "You look much, much better. All this clean living suits you."

"You're right, you know. I'm really a simple woman at

heart. I like a good book. I like to garden, and I like a person to share my life with." There was silence.

Mike looked at her. She had just come back from the shower. Her hair was tied in a pony-tail. She was smiling at him. Her deep blue eyes held a well-remembered sparkle. The children played in a stream that ran behind the tents. "I'll share your life with you, Bonnie," he said. He pulled her gently into his arms. "I know this is no time for romance, but I want you to know that I've always hoped that one day you'd give up that awful man, and come home to Merrill and marry me." He shook his head. "I'm not used to my dreams turning out right."

Secure in his arms, Bonnie felt content. This is what love should be like, she thought. "Mike," she said. "Let's leave all this until we're in Mexico. My feelings are so jumbled up. I don't really know what I feel!"

"Okay." Mike kissed her forehead. "What's for dinner?"

After the meal, the children were tucked into bed inside their tent. Bonnie stretched out on the rug. "Isn't this heaven?" she said. She lay back with her hands under her head. "I want you to know, Mike, that I haven't been so happy in years."

Mike lay beside her. "And I want you to know," he said with more seriousness in his voice than he had intended, "that I have *never* ever been so happy."

"I'm glad." She turned and kissed him gently on the lips. They both lay back and looked at the stars.

Mike drove all through the fourth day. They were on the Interstate 25 to Albuquerque. Bonnie was entranced by the New Mexico scenery. Much of it was flat and barren, but in an instant, an unexpectedly lush green valley would wipe away the memory of the dry desert. Huge mountain ranges sprang from nowhere. "It doesn't feel like America," she said.

"No," Mike agreed. "I think it feels like Europe without all the problems."

Tony was gathering regular information over his CB radio. "Ten-four," he said into the microphone. He turned to Angus in the back seat of the Mercedes. "A gas station reported seeing the car in Oklahoma City. And a cop phoned in to say he saw the car pass through Amarillo."

Angus was impressed. "Do the police work for you, then?" Tony grinned. "*Everybody* works for us." He turned his attention to the road ahead of him. "Remember the Pinkertons?" he said over his shoulder. "They were practically a private army a long time ago. Well, we're sort of like them. Only we're bigger. We can find just about anyone, anytime, anywhere. Do you realize," he said, "that there are about two thousand kids a year missing from their homes in the U.S.? Most of them are snatched by one parent or the other. Do you know how much dough that puts in our pockets?"

Angus was even more impressed. Now that he knew where Bonnie was, even if she had betrayed him, he was prepared to give her another chance. He made his plans as he sat in the back of the car. The CB clicked and spluttered. The two men in the front-seats listened intently and issued commands to the people all across America who served as the well-paid eyes and ears of SAK. Angus let the men get on with their job. I'll take her back to Drummossie, he thought. We'll be happier there. He slept.

Mike decided to make camp outside Albuquerque. "I know I said I'd drive those last miles into Santa Fe tonight, but to tell you the truth, I'm really tired."

Bonnie took his hand. "Let's have our last night by our campfire."

"Good idea," Mike said. "After tonight, we'll stay with Chucky in Santa Fe, and then once we're in Mexico, we'll stop at motels. I don't think the camp-grounds are too clean down there. Anyway, checking into a motel won't be a problem. Once we're over the border, we won't have to hide."

"I wonder if Angus is back in England." Bonnie looked at Mike. "You know, Rupert his lawyer will move heaven and earth."

"He can try," Mike said, "but he won't be able to touch us. They can't trace us. No one knows we're heading for Mexico."

"Can I buy my friend from the shelter a hat?" Alisdair piped in from the back seat.

"What sort of hat?" Bonnie was amused.

"You know, those big Mexican hats."

"Okay, but we won't be going back to the shelter, darling," Bonnie said.

"Oh look!" Rosemary pointed to a sign. "I've found the camp-ground!" she sang loudly.

The men did not stop. Jerry slept while Tony drove, and while Tony slept Jerry drove. "We have the address in Santa Fe," Jerry said. "Must be a friend of the boyfriend's."

"Um," Tony agreed. "Well, we'll catch up to them with no problem if they're bothering to visit a friend in Santa Fe. It's out of the way to Mexico." Tony blew a bubble from the fat wad of gum which he chewed and sucked loudly.

"Why can't we pick them up in Santa Fe?" Angus asked. He wanted this nonsense to be over. He missed Bonnie. He wanted to hold her again and to be held by her.

"Because," Tony said, speaking slowly as if to a child, "she might not want to leave her lover boy, and things might have to get unpleasant. And we don't want lover boy's friend in Santa Fe to help them out, now do we?" He blew another bubble. It popped loudly. "No, we'll police the border from El Paso. They'll probably try for El Galio. That's the most likely point for them to go across. When we get to Santa Fe,

I'll put the word out among the guides. We'll top any deal they made, and then just sit tight." He laughed. "Gee, I can imagine their faces."

"So can I," Angus said grimly. What if Bonnie really did have a lover? What if she didn't want to go back with Angus? Angus held his head in his hands.

"Do you want us to dispose of lover boy?"

"No." Angus shook his head. "No, I don't want any trouble. I just want to go home with my wife and my children. Anyway, he won't be her lover. Bonnie loves only me."

Tony looked sideways at Jerry. "They all think that," he said softly. Angus didn't hear over the roar of the engine.

Chucky turned out to be an expansive friendly man with close-cropped blond hair and grey eyes. "Come on in," he said, shaking Mike's hand and slapping him on the shoulder. He turned to Bonnie. "I've got a big Oldsmobile lined up for you in Mexico." He looked at the children. "Come on," he said. "I'll show you our latest cars."

"Oh look, mummy." Alisdair was dazzled. "Look at that beautiful white car."

"Yup," said Chucky. "That's a '51 Chevy. Belongs to a young singer here in town. They don't make 'em like that anymore."

"Look at that!" Alisdair was running around the huge garage which was stuffed with vintage cars. Cars jammed the floor. Cars were raised on hydraulic lifts. Cars even hung suspended on thick metal cables from the ceiling.

"Hey, come on," Chucky said to Mike. "Let me buy you a coke from the machine in back."

Mike followed him. "This sure is good of you, Chucky."

"Aw, Mike." Chucky was embarrassed. "I'll get a good deal for your car. Sanchez is going to guide you across the river. He says El Galio is the quickest of all the crossings."

"How much does he want?"

"He says he wants two thousand dollars before you leave . . ."

"I have that for you now," Mike said, counting from a thick wad of bills. "You warned me I'd need cash."

"And another two thousand when you cross."

Mike shook his head. "My God. That's a lot of money for a quick paddle."

"What can I tell you? It's the going rate. But, once you're over, you're safe."

"It's worth it." Mike put his hand on his friend's shoulder. "Not just safe, but with the woman I've always loved. By the way, where are they all now? Bonnie!" he called.

She didn't hear him. She was crouching by a little red MG. The mechanic was showing her his work with such pride that she was completely absorbed. The children were climbing in and out of an old derelict Cadillac.

Chucky grinned. "Here," he said. "Take the key to my place and relax. I'll be home after five. Ella my housekeeper has been dying to meet you."

"Sounds great." Mike was tired after the long drive from Merrill. "We can do with a couple of days' break."

Bonnie called the children. "Thank you, Chucky," she said. "Thanks for helping."

Chucky blushed. "Oh, forget it," he said, and he stomped off into the back office. Mike's a lucky man, he thought. He put the money Mike had given him into the safe. He frowned. Sanchez was a well-known alcoholic, but he was the best guide there was.

It took the fast Mercedes another day to reach Santa Fe. All three men were tired. They booked into a motel outside the town. "I don't want you to bump into your wife at this stage," Tony said firmly to Angus. "Santa Fe is a small place."

Angus nodded. He ached to see Bonnie again. He so much wanted to take her into his arms. "All right," he said.

"You two stay here," Tony said. "I'm going into town to see who's around. I'll find out which guides are in town. So just hang loose." He slipped out of the motel.

Angus felt too tired to eat. He ordered an omelette and a bottle of Californian wine from room service, and fell asleep before he finished the bottle.

In town, Tony was in his element. He loved a good chase. He didn't take long to find his eyes and ears in the person of Julio Castillo. Julio was hugely fat with four warts on his face. "Keeps off the evil eye," he told his women.

"Who's here?" Tony asked after shaking Julio's moist hand.

"Well, let me see. Mario Feruzzi has just moved into the north side of town. He pocketed five million after the last picture he made." Julio grinned. "Word is that he's in the market for coke and broads. So it looks like we're in business." Tony was pleased. SAK was only one of Tony's business interests. "And who else . . . ah yes. Joan Patrice arrived a week ago. Her house-boy tells me she has her diamonds with her."

"Hm. Interesting. How much does this guy want for helping lift them?"

"Well," Julio said. "He says he's willing to help out any way he can, but he wants a ten per cent cut when we sell."

"Not unreasonable," Tony said. "But I think it's more reasonable to make another arrangement for the enterprising man." He winked at Julio. "He could have an unfortunate hunting accident in the mountains, don't you think? It would take the heat off us for a while." He slapped the old Mexican on the back. "It's nice to be back in town," he said. "Lots of business, lots of deals. My kind of town. Hey, any guides in town now? I like to keep my finger on everything."

Julio nodded. "I happened to see Sanchez in the bar by the Plaza earlier today. He must have a job. He was plastered out of his head. Buying drinks for the whole house, which isn't like Sanchez."

"Interesting," Tony said again. "You know me. I like to know who's moving around on the borders. I think I'll stop by and have a word with Sanchez. Big money, border work. Maybe we should consider a little business side-line."

Julio burped. "I'm too old and too fat. Besides I have a family to keep."

Tony grinned. "Not to mention your harem of working girls."

"Yes, but they're family too." Julio smiled. "You want me to find you a little company for your first night back in our fair city?"

"Thanks, but I'll take a rain-check. I'm bushed. Anyway, you look after yourself, amigo," Tony said. "I've got some business to take care of, then I'll come by and see you in a couple of days."

Tony found Sanchez, just as Julio had predicted, very drunk and very willing to talk business. "Yes," said Sanchez, "I am to take this family across the river at El Galio. We leave early in the morning the day after tomorrow, and then cross late that afternoon."

"Describe the area to me where you leave the car to cross the river."

Sanchez was swaying. "It's just a river. Nothing you'd be interested in."

"I'm very interested," Tony said without humour.

"Okay, whatever you say. Well, it's pretty flat around there. And pretty green. We have only to walk maybe quarter of a mile before we reach the trees and then the river. You want these people?"

"We want the woman and the two kids. Not the man."

"Oh." Sanchez was interested.

"Her husband wants her back."

"She ran off with a lover?" Sanchez, a good Catholic, was disapproving.

"Yeah. Something like that. How much are they paying you?" Sanchez frowned. "Three thousand now, three thousand later. But you know how it goes. No later, no?" Sanchez said with a shrug.

"No," Tony agreed. "Okay. I'll give you three thousand now, and *five* thousand later to see there's no crossing. And with me you can count on there being a later. We'll be waiting there. Okay?"

Sanchez was pleased. The money meant he could spend the winter holed up in his little adobe house with his wife Maria.

Early the next morning, Tony woke Angus. "We got to leave," he said. "Your wife and children will be starting to drive south tomorrow morning. I want to be in a position to pick them up without any bother. The area has trees. We can wait for Sanchez. He says he'll lead them across tomorrow afternoon."

"Fine," said Angus. Jerry was refreshed from his night's sleep. He joined them. "Can you arrange transport?" Angus asked.

Jerry scratched his head. "Yeah. I'll organize a helicopter to wait out of sight, and then once we have your wife and kids, we can call it in. Where do you want to go after that?"

"To Scotland."

"Okay," Jerry said. "No problem. We'll get the pilot to take you to Albuquerque Airport, and you can catch a plane home from there."

"Good." Angus felt much better. By tomorrow evening he would have his beloved Bonnie back in his arms.

Tony smiled. "Well, now that we know where they're going to be, we don't have to patrol the whole border. The guide wants eight thou. Pretty expensive, huh?"

Angus shook his head. "I don't care."

"Maybe not, but your accountant sure does. He's been beefing back at headquarters."

"Well," said Angus, "as long as he pays, don't worry."

Tony was serious. "Oh, he'll pay all right. We always get paid."

"I can believe it." Angus looked at the two men. They were like ruthless machines. At least I have feelings, Angus thought.

The Mercedes roared off into the bright New Mexican light, out of Santa Fe, past Albuquerque, and down to the Mexican border.

Chapter 34

"Come on, darling." Mike was bending over Bonnie's bed. "You must wake up. Our guide is here and he wants us to leave today."

Bonnie yawned and stretched. She put her arms around Mike's neck and nuzzled him. "Can't we stay another day?"

"No," Mike said. "I'm anxious to get to Mexico and find a nice house and a nice school for the kids."

"Okay then." Bonnie kissed him. "I'll get up and we'll go."

After an enormous breakfast, Chucky and Ella waved them off. "Good luck," Chucky said.

"Come and visit," Bonnie smiled.

"I will." Chucky headed for his garage. He whistled in his car as he drove. He was pleased with himself.

Sanchez tapped Mike on the shoulder. "There," he said, pointing ahead to a rough track off the main road.

"Okay," Mike said. "This is it, folks. The Rio Grande and then Mexico."

The children were excited. "Do we have to take our shoes off to cross the river?" Rosemary asked.

Sanchez nodded. He wished by now that he had never agreed to betray this little group of people. He had fallen in love with Bonnie, and he liked Mike. He played games with the kids all the way down from Sante Fe, and he was even fond of the hairy mutt. He remembered Tony's eyes. He knew the SAK outfit well. If he went back on his word, he'd be found dead. Maybe not today. Maybe not tomorrow, but one day they'd find him.

Mike squinted into the sunlight. They drove along the dirt road for a quarter of an hour. Then they came to a wilderness area. "We leave the car here," Sanchez said. "Too rough for a car. We walk."

"Isn't this exciting," Bonnie said. "I feel like a real fugitive. You know, I once saw this film where this woman is being chased by a man."

She went on to describe the scene with great enthusiasm to Mike, who had Alisdair by the hand, and a suitcase in his other hand. Sanchez carried Rosemary. Pluto was dashing about in circles. They walked for a hundred yards or so towards a large clump of trees that bordered the river. Mike smiled down at Bonnie. "We're nearly there, darling," he said. Pluto shot off into the undergrowth in fast pursuit of a rabbit. "Come here, Pluto," Mike called.

Two men advanced through the trees. Mike and Bonnie stopped. The two men had pistols in their hands. "Lady MacPherson?" one of the men said.

Bonnie went white. "Yes?" she said in as firm a voice as she could manage.

"Your husband is here to take you home."

Angus stepped out from behind a tree. "Oh, my God!" Bonnie said. Angus stood gazing at her. Flies buzzed about his head. "I don't want to go back with you, Angus," Bonnie said. The children were rooted to the spot.

Angus held out his arms. "You have to come back to England," he said.

Rosemary began to cry. "I don't want to go back. I want to stay with Mike," she sobbed.

Angus's face tightened. "Well, if you're going to make this difficult . . ." He stared at Bonnie. "I can't make you come back, but if you don't come with me now, I'll take the children, and you'll never ever see them again."

Tony muttered something into a hand-held walkie-talkie. Behind the trees, the helicopter suddenly revved its engine. Mike looked at Bonnie. Then he said to Angus. "You can't blackmail her like that." He shook his head. "You damned nearly kill her."

Bonnie squeezed his hand. She knew Angus's temper, and she was frightened for Mike. "No, Mike," she said. "We're trapped. I'll have to go back."

Pluto suddenly appeared. Sensing danger, he began to growl protectively. The helicopter reared up over the trees and hovered overhead, disturbing the motionless humid air with its blades. Mike dropped to his knees and held tight to Pluto's collar. Angus walked over to the children and took their hands. "Come on," he said. "Enough of this drama." The helicopter lowered itself to the ground. Angus climbed in with the children.

Bonnie was left standing by Mike. "I have to go, Mike," she said. "I have no choice." She was crying. "I love you, Mike," she said.

"I'll wait for you," Mike said. He watched her walk to the helicopter. He watched her climb in. The two mercenaries moved away from the helicopter as it slowly rose in a cloud of dust. They walked to their Mercedes behind the trees and quickly drove off. Sanchez had already slipped away unnoticed into the Mexican countryside. Mike was alone, sobbing with grief.

After a very long time, Mike got to his feet. I'll wait for her, he promised, and then he retraced his steps to the Volvo.

PART FIVE

In the Shadow of the Castle

Chapter 35

Bonnie knew she was a prisoner at Drummossie. Throughout the autumn and early winter, Angus was remote and withdrawn, tense and silent. Both children had been sent back to their boarding schools. Bonnie was entirely alone. Angus no longer trusted anybody. Only Garrett slinked around Drummossie.

To Father MacBride, Bonnie confessed her love for Mike. The priest had grown too old to kneel in his confessional. "My child," he said, "there are many kinds of sin that God will not forgive. However, your love for Mike is a good clean love. In that pure love, you commit less of a sin now than when you clung to your need for your husband."

Bonnie's voice dropped. "I know. He was like a drug, you know. I tried to break free, but every time, except for this last time, I would get addicted all over again just by seeing his face or hearing his voice. I know now that it never really was love at all. Valerie taught me that in the refuge. I was no better than a junky with a drug habit or an alcoholic with a bottle. Angus was *my* drug." She shook her head. "I feel so disgusted with myself."

Father MacBride sighed. "No, Bonnie. Disgust is a sin of

remorse. All that pain is in the past. And it will stay in the past. I can't say for sure how violent Angus will be in the future, but I can tell you this; as a man, somehow he is broken."

Bonnie nodded. "Yes, he has actually changed. He still gets angry and he screams and he shouts, but he hasn't hit me again. But it's more than just that. Something is happening to him. He imagines that he hears things. He often says that the television speaks to him, and then he becomes very secretive. I am worried about him." The old priest was silent. "I know what you're thinking, Father," Bonnie said. "That's how his father went mad."

"Yes," the priest sighed a long sigh. "That's how all the MacPherson men go mad and die. Slowly . . ."

"Never Alisdair." Bonnie's voice was joyful. "He sincerely isn't violent."

Father MacBride smiled. "Both your children are fine, thanks to your love."

Bonnie finished her confession and knelt in front of the altar. "I'll wait until Alisdair and Rosemary have lives of their own, and then I'll join Mike," she said. "I know I can't remarry in the Catholic Church, but I don't believe it's right for a man like Angus to try to kill me and then to expect his marriage vows still to be more sacred than my love for Mike." Having made her peace with God, Bonnie felt a calm filling her soul. She would have to wait, but one day her life would be happy. "We never were married," she said as she walked towards the chapel door. "We never even knew each other."

In Merrill, Laura was pleased to receive another cheque from Angus for two hundred thousand dollars along with a small note saying that Bonnie was back in Scotland. She hurried to the telephone. Father John listened. Two hundred thousand dollars. How could he refuse? He made an appointment for Laura to meet him in the new rectory at 6:30, when his aunt would be out gossiping with the neighbours. A few weeks earlier, when Laura had offered Father John the enormous sum of money Angus had promised her for helping to find Bonnie, she had left no doubt as to her desires. "I want you to whip me," she said bluntly. "I want to bring my canes to your house, and I want you to punish me for my sins until the blood runs down my back."

Father John had no wish to whip Laura, but he did have an urgent desire for money. Into the church's bank account he had deposited a quarter of a million dollars from Angus's first cheque to Laura. Keeping his end of the agreement, he held weekly sessions with Laura during which he would beat her for her transgressions. He planned to have the church itself refurbished. He now drove a Peugeot. His house kept the finest table in Merrill. He regularly entertained his Bishop, and his Bishop, after all these years, was finally talking of Rome. The Bishop was grateful for the money Father John had brought into the Church. With his financial obligations to his own church met, Father John secured a promise from his Bishop that any additional contributions would be applied to sending him to Rome. His ultimate ambition was now only an arm's length away. This final donation of Laura's would be sufficient to ensure his future. Then he would never have to see her or Merrill again.

To each of her weekly appointments with the priest Laura carried a selection of canes. She was always decorously dressed. She knelt at his feet and bent her head. "Forgive me, Father," she began.

This particular night, Father John was irritable and tired. He had been busy with Christmas preparations, and the need to sit down and write his holiday sermons hung over him. Laura was confessing to a particularly lewd piece of fantasy. Father John felt an overwhelming wish to be anywhere but standing in his sitting-room, lashing at Laura's pale white shoulders. Her back was an obscene cross-hatching of old scars and fresh scabs.

A pernicious and powerful feeling descended with sudden force upon Father John—a feeling of being trapped. Trapped by Laura. Trapped by her revolting needs. Trapped. He frowned. He could feel the anger building within him. With great vigour, he began to lash Laura's humble and suppliant body. He whipped her to lessen his anger, to make himself feel less trapped. He whipped her until she lay beneath him struggling for breath.

Through the perspiration that burned in his eyes, he could see only *her* ecstatic bright eyes. She smiled up at him. "I never knew you had it in you," she said softly.

He began to scream at her. "You witch!" he screamed, "you demon!" She still smiled. He raised the cane in his hand and began to whip her mercilessly again and again. Still, she only smiled. Suddenly the priest stopped. A massive pain gripped his heart. He fell to the floor.

Laura rose to her feet. She bent over him. Dead, she thought. She pulled on her sweater and picked up her cheque to the priest from the table. She ran out of the house. She looked to the left and to the right down the quiet leafy lane. She walked slowly towards her car, discreetly parked a few blocks away. Shit, she thought.

"My God." The doctor was amused. You find these perverts everywhere, he thought. He comforted Father John's aunt. "It was all over for him in a minute," the doctor said.

Aunt Eileen was shaking. "I'm not crying for him, the dirty bastard," she said. "It's just the shock."

"Well, I do suggest you dispose of the brassière and the canes before too many unpleasant questions are asked," the doctor said. He packed his bag and walked out through the rectory door. "Bad business," he muttered to himself as he left. "A really bad business."

Later that night, the news of the priest's death was all over the town. The doctor, not well-known for his professional reticence, quickly became the toast of the local bar. "Yes," the doctor said in between sips of red wine, "the guy was lying there surrounded by whips and chains."

"I'm not surprised," a small quiet woman joined in the conversation. "When I was a little girl, the Archbishop used to visit the convent I was in. He used to grope all the little girls when they knelt to kiss his ring."

"Oh really?" The doctor was amused.

"I think it's a dreadful thing when a priest like Father John goes wrong," said the bartender with a sad shake of his head.

"I couldn't agree with you more," said the doctor. "But I suppose priests are human too. Then again, I never really liked the man myself." The subject of conversation in the bar soon drifted to local politics.

Father John, meanwhile, lay white and still in Merrill, Pennsylvania's city morgue. His cruel eyes were closed forever. His thin tapering fingers lay clasped across his chest, holding a crucifix for all eternity.

Chapter 36

Christmas at Drummossie found Angus even more depressed. On Christmas Eve, he went to find Father MacBride. The old man sat in his neat little Victorian parlour with his feet in a bowl of hot water and mustard. "Come in, my boy." Father MacBride was very worried about Angus.

"Father," Angus said as he sat down in a chair across from the old man, "I have made a decision."

MacBride raised his eyebrows. "Have you?" he said.

"Yes," Angus gazed into the softly glowing coals in the

fireplace. "I realize that I've lost Bonnie." He looked up at the priest. "I've lost the love of my children. And now," he lowered his head, "now I see things, and I hear things, just as my father did. I've been to my doctor, but he can't help. The pills he gave me just make the visions worse." There was a long pause. "Well, as I said, I've made a decision. No." He looked at the expectant priest. "No. I don't want to discuss it with you. I just want you to remember this conversation."

The priest nodded. "All right, Angus," he said. "I do hope you get better."

"Oh, I will." Angus stood up and smiled. " 'Give unto them rest,' " he quoted.

"Yes," said the frail old man. " 'Dona eis requiem sempiternam. Give unto them rest for evermore.' God bless you my boy."

"Thank you, Father."

On Christmas day, Angus was unusually kind and gentle with the children. He took Alisdair out for a walk on the white snowy lawns. "I know I haven't been all I should have been as a father," he began.

Alisdair looked up at him. He was seven now. He very much wanted a good father. "Will you come and watch me play rugger?" he asked.

Angus smiled. "Yes, if you'd really like that."

The little boy tentatively slipped his hand into his father's long thin fingers. Angus drew the little hand firmly into his own. "You're not going to hit mummy any more?"

"No." Angus looked down at his son's trusting blue eyes. "I won't ever hit your mother again. Just always remember, whatever happens next, in my own funny way, I do love you. All of you."

Alisdair smiled. "Okay, daddy," he said. "Let's go back. I'm freezing."

* * *

Angus knew he would become like his father. His mother's voice called to him constantly. "I'm waiting for you, Angus," the voice said. "I'm waiting for you."

Other voices filled Angus's head. He found himself cursing and swearing as if he was possessed by evil demons. He knew he would have to kill himself, or else he would take his father's place in the remote wing of Drummossie Castle. This thought was unbearable, for Angus was a proud man. To be incarcerated, to be dependent on tranquillizers that would bloat his face and thicken his figure—all this was unthinkable. No. Far better to take a bullet in the brain. Far better to embrace immediate extinction.

Angus seemed withdrawn throughout the holiday festivities. Bonnie, preoccupied with her own pain and loss, was grateful that he left her alone. They shared their bedroom in silence. The voices in Angus's head continued to menace him. The walls of the castle accused him of evil things. He felt he was being watched.

On New Year's Eve, the children came into the drawing-room to say good-night. Angus kissed them both with a passionate intensity. "I love you, daddy," Rosemary said. She looked into his ashen face, the eyes as lifeless as coals which had lost their flame. "You look tired," she said.

"I am tired, Rosemary. I'm very tired." The children left the room hand in hand.

A silence descended. Bonnie was nervous. She glanced at Angus. She feared that his silence might be the prelude to a rage. "I think I'll go to bed too," she said apprehensively.

"All right," Angus said. He walked across the room and gave her a small kiss on the top of her head. "Good-night, darling." Bonnie left the room and Angus sat alone.

Just before midnight, Angus took his favourite hunting rifle from the study. He walked through the snow to the chapel. There, he stood in front of the altar. As the bells above him in the belfry began to chime in the New Year, Angus pulled the trigger. The bell-ringers heard the shot. They left the bells and ran into the little church. Angus lay in front of the altar. Blood was spreading in a pool on the stone floor. The old priest came hobbling into the church. He too had heard the sound. "Dear God," he prayed when he saw the blood. He stood for a moment over Angus's body. He remembered, all those years ago, when he was a young priest and Angus lay in his arms at his christening. "Dear God," he said.

Father MacBride gave instructions to carry Angus's body, covered in a blanket, to a guest bedroom. He made his way slowly across to the castle. He watched as the bell-ringers carried the body across the keep. The moon shone brightly on the thick white snow. Clouds sent huge shadows scudding across the lawn. The feet of the bell-ringers crunched on the gravel. The iron tips of their boots rang against the stone steps. The great door creaked open to welcome the body of its master. Angus was gone.

Bonnie heard the news in silence. She had been watching at the window. She had been waiting for midnight, hoping that the new year would be a happier time. The old priest took her hand. "He told me he was going to kill himself," he said, "although I didn't fully understand at the time. Now I realize what he was saying." Bonnie was too stunned to respond. "I'll call the doctor," Father MacBride said. He was worried by Bonnie's sudden pallor.

She nodded weakly. "Please," she said.

Alone in her room, Bonnie stood for a long time by her window, looking out over the white cold snow. She thought in silence. She could feel the great wall of fear, which for so many years had stood before her, begin to fall away. It would take time, she knew, for the final stones of that wall to crumble. But now she had time. Angus had given her back her life. She would go to Mike, she knew, and make a life for herself with him, a life without pain. Alisdair would grow to inherit the family property but not its legacy of suffering. None of them would suffer again.

Bonnie still stared, out into the snow. She suddenly remembered Angus on the night of the MacGregors' ball when he had come for her. He had come on New Year's Eve. She could see him quite clearly. She could see the velvet of his jacket, the froth of the lace at his throat, the gleam of his silver buttons. She saw him standing out there on the snow-covered lawn. He was smiling. She remembered his smile as he crossed the MacGregors' great hall, his odd, enchanting, chipped-tooth smile. "Thank you," she said softly. She looked again. He was gone.

Bonnie lowered her eyes from the window. She wiped a tear from her cheek. "It's over," she whispered. "It really is over."

Erin Pizzey is the author of THE SNOW LEOPARD OF SHANGHAI, THE CONSUL GENERAL'S DAUGHTER, FIRST LADY, THE WATERSHED, and IN THE SHADOW OF THE CASTLE. Well known for her work with battered wives and their children, she is an accomplished journalist and has written a number of nonfiction books as well. She lives in Tuscany.

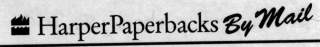

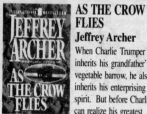
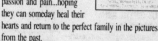

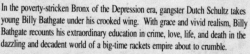

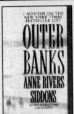

OUTER BANKS
Anne Rivers Siddons

Four sorority sisters bound by friendship spent two idyllic spring breaks at Nag's Head, North Carolina. Now, thirty years later, they are coming back to recapture the magic of those early years and confront the betrayal that shaped four young girls into women and set them all adrift on the Outer Banks.

"A wonderful saga." — *Cosmopolitan*

MAGIC HOUR
Susan Isaacs

A witty mixture of murder, satire, and romance set in the fashionable Hamptons, Long Island's beach resort of choice. Movie producer Sy Spencer has been shot dead beside his pool. Topping the list of suspects is Sy's ex-wife, Bonnie. But it isn't before long that Detective Steve Brady is ignoring all the rules and evidence to save her.

"Vintage Susan Isaacs."
— *The New York Times Book Review*

ANY WOMAN'S BLUES
Erica Jong

Leila Sand's life has left her feeling betrayed and empty. Her efforts to change result in a sensual and spiritual odyssey that takes her from Alcoholics Anonymous meetings to glittering parties to a liaison with a millionaire antiques merchant. Along the way, she learns the rules of love and the secret of happiness.

"A very timely and important book...Jong's greatest heroine." — *Elle*

For Fastest Service—Visa and MasterCard Holders Call
1-800-331-3761 refer to offer HO471

MAIL TO: **Harper Collins Publishers**
P. O. Box 588 Dunmore, PA 18512-0588
OR CALL FOR FASTEST SERVICE: (800) 331-3761

Yes, please send me the books I have checked:

☐ AS THE CROW FLIES (0-06-109934-1) $6.50
☐ FAMILY PICTURES (0-06-109925-2) $5.95
☐ PALINDROME (0-06-109936-8) $5.99
☐ THE CROWN OF COLUMBUS (0-06-109057-0) $5.99
☐ BILLY BATHGATE (0-06-100007-8) $5.95
☐ OUTER BANKS (0-06-109973-2) $5.99
☐ MAGIC HOUR (0-06-109948-1) $5.99
☐ ANY WOMAN'S BLUES (0-06-109916-3) $5.95

SUBTOTAL .... $_____
POSTAGE AND HANDLING .... $ 2.00*
SALES TAX (Add state sales tax) .... $_____
                                    TOTAL: $_____
(Remit in US funds.
Do not send cash.)

Name _____

Address _____

City _____

State _____ Zip _____   Allow up to 6 weeks delivery.
Prices subject to change.

*FREE postage & handling if you buy four or more books! Valid in U.S./CAN only.   HO471